I0760889

Destroyer of Legends

Books by Clayton Taylor Wood:

The Runic Series

Runic Awakening

Runic Revelation

Runic Vengeance

The Fate of Legends Series

Hunter of Legends

Seeker of Legends

Destroyer of Legends

The Magic of Havenwood Series

The Magic Collector

The Lost Gemini

Destroyer of Legends

Book III of the Fate of Legends series

Clayton Taylor Wood

Published by Clayton T. Wood.

ISBN: 978-1-948497-03-9

Cover designed by James T. Egan, Bookfly Design, LLC

Printed in the United States of America.

Special thanks to my wife and my brothers for their invaluable advice. And to my son Hunter, for whom this book was written.

Table of Contents

Destroyer of Legends

Prologue

The Crypt of Zagamar was a labyrinth carved into the base of a great mountain, built over six millennia ago. And within its gloomy depths was the Tomb of Zagamar, a domed chamber that held the remains of the great Legend himself. A chamber shrouded in utter darkness and silence since it had been sealed long ago.

Until now.

High Seeker Zeno's lantern cast its pale light on the black stone platform in the center of the chamber, bobbing madly as he sprinted across it. He spotted the rippling water of a shallow pool a few meters ahead.

There was a loud *thump* behind him, the sound echoing through the ancient chamber.

Zeno leapt into the pool, gasping as the frigid water enveloped his legs and belly. He bounded through the water frantically, ignoring the cold.

An agonizing moan came from the center of the chamber behind him, sending chills down his spine.

Zeno swore, moving faster. The other end of the pool was only a few meters ahead, a small tunnel through the stone wall beyond leading into the next room. The floor of the pool angled upward gradually, and he burst out of the pool, ducking through the tunnel into the room beyond. A large, dark room with countless skeletons scattered over the floor. Some of which he'd fed to the…

There was a splash from behind.

Oh god oh god…

Zeno sprinted across the room, bones crunching under his boots as he ran for the spiraling staircase he knew was ahead. He reached it, leaping up the steps four at a time. The *crunch, crunch* of footsteps came from behind, picking up speed.

Coming for *him.*

He reached the top of the stairs, seeing a narrow stone ledge leading forward into the darkness. A huge pit of long, sharp spikes was to his right, a stone wall to his left. Zeno ran forward across the ledge, his heart hammering in his chest, his skin slick with sweat. His guts cramped, hunger gripping them. A hunger beyond anything he'd ever experienced.

A ravenous compulsion he knew was only a fraction of what the *thing* hunting him must be experiencing.

The sound of feet running up the stairs behind echoed through the crypt, getting closer now.

Come on…

The ledge turned right abruptly, and he skidded to a stop, slamming into the wall ahead, then turning right and continuing down a narrow hallway. His lungs burned, his breath coming in rapid gasps.

Calm down, he commanded himself. *Remember your training!*

He focused, remembering the first axiom.

Emotion is temporary, action is forever.

But his heart continued to pound, fear overwhelming him. Fear of what he'd done. What he'd unleashed upon the world. Centuries of planning, and everything the Guild of Seekers had fought for had been a mistake.

A deception of apocalyptic proportions.

He sprinted down the corridor, turning left, then right as the hallway did. There were stairs ahead; he leapt them in a single bound, running down yet another hallway.

The footsteps behind him drew ever closer.

Zeno pushed himself to the limit, pumping his legs as hard and fast as he could, nearly slamming into the wall again as the corridor took a sharp left turn. He continued forward as the hall opened up into blackness, with a narrow stone ledge ahead, a black pit to the left, and a stone wall to his right.

He looked down at his hands as he ran, seeing the black flesh that had replaced his own. Small hard nubs grew from the tips of his fingers, what would eventually grow to become claws. His sacrifice for tending to the Ascension. For transforming the still-living head of the Ironclad, by injecting the liquified remains of the great Zagamar into its veins.

Zeno focused, pushing the awful vision of that head's transformation. The first moment its eyes moved.

Focusing on *him.*

He sprinted across the narrow ledge, turning right down a wide hallway. He was near the exit now, only a dozen meters from the outside world.

The footsteps grew ever closer, their tempo even faster now.

It's getting stronger.

Zeno glanced back, but saw only darkness.

Focus!

He saw skeletons ahead on the floor ahead, piled up against a set of huge double-doors. Zeno waded into them until he was waist deep in the long-dead corpses, struggling to reach the doors. One of them was slightly ajar; he reached the gap between them, squeezing through. Beyond was a dark tunnel…and beyond that, the night sky.

Yes!

Zeno broke into an all-out run, bursting from the entrance to the crypt into the cool night air. A stone path littered with the long-dead bodies of animals and men greeted him, leading away from the base of the mountain.

He followed the path, his breath coming in ragged gasps.

The sound of footsteps crunching on bone came from behind Zeno, and he ran even faster, pushing his body to its limit. His lungs were on fire now, his heart beating far too quickly. Sweat trickled into his eyes, stinging them. He wiped it away, focusing on the dark, twisted trees beyond the path…and the more conventional forest beyond.

The sensation of bugs falling onto his scalp came to him, and he swiped at them furiously. But more took their place, landing on his neck and shoulders, then crawling under his clothes.

It's not real, he told himself. *They're not…*

He heard the footsteps behind him closing in rapidly, and fumbled for the sword at his left hip, drawing it free from its scabbard.

Something slammed into his back, knocking his sword out of his hand and sending him flying onto his belly on the rocky path!

He slid for a few meters, rocks scraping at his belly and chest. He gasped, scrambling to his feet and rushing forward. But something grabbed his shoulder from behind, yanking him backward. Sharp black claws sank into his flesh there, sending agonizing pain shooting down his arm.

Zeno cried out, seeing another black hand reach around from behind, raking its claws down his chest and belly.

His uniform and flesh tore, his intestines spilling out of a gaping hole in his abdomen.

He stared at his innards, unable to comprehend what he was seeing. He felt numb, as if he was outside of his own body. As if this was happening to someone else.

The hand on his shoulder spun him around, then gripped him by the throat, claws piercing the flesh around his windpipe and wrapping around it.

Zeno's gaze drew upward, his eyes widening. He heard a chanting sound in the distance, thousands of long-dead voices echoing in his mind.

Za-ga-mar!

He opened his mouth to scream, but never got the chance. There was a loud *crunch* as his windpipe was torn from his neck. Blood filled his mouth rapidly, a horrible *hissing* sound coming from his throat with each desperate, gurgling breath.

He was thrown backward onto the rocky path, a shadow looming over him, blocking the light of the stars and the three moons of Varta.

And even as he drowned in his own blood, Zeno could only watch in horror as the Dark One plunged a pitch-black hand into his guts, and began to feed its insatiable hunger.

A hunger that would devour the world.

Chapter 1

At first, there was only darkness.

There was no sound, no feeling. Only a vague sense of self. When it had begun, it didn't know. Time did not exist. There was only infinite nothingness, a void with no end. A sleep without dreams.

And then came the visions.

Bursts of color at first, then fully formed images. A white house on a hill. An old, wrinkled hand holding a much smaller hand. *His* hand, he realized. And he knew then that he *was* a he. That he was human. That the wrinkled hand holding his had been his grandfather's.

He felt a profound sense of comfort, holding that hand. The air was sweet with flowers, and the pleasant hum of bees buzzing around them.

I am Dominus.

The image faded, replaced by others. Hints of a castle, then a bed of flowers. Soft lips on his, and twinkling blue eyes. His wife. Young, beautiful. Before…

An image of fire. Screams piercing the air. And a small boy holding a broken lantern, cheeks wet with tears.

Just a mistake, Conlan. It's not your fault.

Dominus smelled the smoke, the scent of flesh burning. Tasted the ash on his tongue, dry and bitter. Bitter like his memories.

Too young to remember. He'll never know.

But Dominus had remembered.

The images faded, but the smell of smoke remained, as did the ashen taste in his mouth. He realized that he *had* a mouth. That he could feel it. A tongue. Teeth. And the ash…the horrible ash.

His mouth started to burn.

The pain spread to his tongue, to his lips. Spread across his face. A horrible burning, along with a pins-and-needles sensation, as when a limb fell asleep, then woke up. He took a breath in, and then coughed immediately as dust sucked into his lungs.

Air!

He was hungry for it suddenly, desperate for air. He hacked, then pulled air into his lungs. More dust came, and he coughed again, his head swimming. He could feel his chest now, the burning spreading across it. Then down his belly, and then his limbs.

He had arms now, and legs. And they felt as if they were on fire.

Dominus screamed, or at least he tried to. Only a wheeze came out, followed by a rattling in his throat. He took a deep breath in, and this time he did not cough.

He tried to open his eyes, but nothing happened. There was only blackness.

Where am I?

Dominus knew he was lying on his back, felt something hard and irregular underneath him through the burning pain all over his body. He tried to move, but could not. If he could've killed himself then to end the torture, he would have. But he could only lay there, accepting the pain.

Time passed.

It was impossible for Dominus to know whether he was going in and out of consciousness. Impossible to know how much time had passed since he'd become aware of himself. He only knew pain and darkness. Darkness and pain. There was no relief, no reprieve from this torture.

And then there was light.

At first he saw only brightness, in his left eye first, then his right. A blinding light that made his eyeballs ache. Then he saw blue, blurry at first, then sharpening slowly. A wisp of white against the blue. A sudden pain spread across his eyes, as if acid had been poured into them. Pain so awful that he tried to scream again. He heard an inhuman screech; at first he did not realize it was he who'd made the sound. He tried to close his eyes, but nothing happened.

At length, the pain in his eyes abated. He tried to close his eyes again, and this time he found that he could.

Dominus heard an awful rasping sound, and realized it was his own breathing. He tried to lift his head up, but couldn't. Tried to lift his arms, but they did not obey him. The burning pain all over his body was starting to fade, however. Still there, but lessened. Tolerable now.

It was clear now that he was lying on his back, staring up at the sky. His arms were at his sides, his legs out straight. And he was lying on something wet and prickly.

Grass.

He attempted to move one arm again, and this time it obeyed him. But only a little, barely lifting off the ground. It was terribly heavy, as if made of lead. He couldn't see it, still couldn't move his head.

And then the hunger came.

A horrible cramp seized his belly, a sense of hunger so powerful that it overwhelmed the pain. He was suddenly ravenous, saliva pouring into his dry mouth. He swallowed, tasting more of that horrible ash, his chest burning as his saliva coursed down his esophagus.

Dominus lay there, his breath coming in short gasps, the pain in his abdomen coming and going.

After what seemed like hours, he tried to move again, tried to roll over onto his side. After a few tries, he managed to do so, rolling onto his right side. Something flopped onto the grass in front of his face; a long, charred hunk of meat. No, it was an arm. The skin was charred, with deep cracks exposing red and gray flesh underneath. A hint of pearly-white bone shone through the deepest of these, as it did on the tips of the limb's fingers.

Dominus stared at it, wondering who had dropped it there. Wondered if whoever it was was standing on his other side, ready to attack him.

He tried to push himself away from the limb, and saw it move.

A chill ran through him.

He wiggled his fingers, and saw the limb before him move again, fingers flexing just as he'd commanded his to.

They're mine, he realized. The charred arm was *his.*

A surge of panic threatened to overtake him, and he quelled it instinctively, his heart hammering in his chest.

Breathe.

He focused on his breathing, concentrated on the air coming in through his nose, then out through his mouth. In and out, in and out. His heart slowed, and he felt the panic subsiding.

The arm is mine.

It was a fact now, nothing to be frightened of. It was his, and he had to accept it. Reality could not be bargained with. There was no god to pray to. Nothing that could save him from this.

He tried to lift his head to look at his body, and found that he could. He saw his chest and belly, and his legs. All covered in soot. All charred, like his arm.

Dominus spotted water a meter beyond his feet. A small pond nearby. The sight brought on an intense thirst; he fantasized about cool water in his mouth, about it moistening his dry throat. Imagined swallowing it. He tried to move his legs, but they were still dead; he rolled onto his belly, gripping the ground with his blackened fingers. Bit-by-bit he rotated himself, his eyes glued to the water. He rotated until he was facing it, crawling forward. After what seemed like an eternity, he made it to the edge of the water.

He dipped his head into it, sucking at the cool fluid.

Or at least he tried to; the water fell right out of his mouth. He could not move his lips, he realized. He lapped at it with his tongue, treasuring every drop.

At length, his thirst sated, he pulled his head up from the water….and saw a rippling reflection there. He couldn't make sense of it at first, not with the water having been agitated by his drinking. He waited for the surface to go still; after a while, an image came into focus. He stared at it, his breath catching in his throat.

And then he screamed.

CHAPTER 2

Birds chittered overhead, gliding lazily over the treetops of the Deep forest, the small flock forming a black 'V' against the bright blue sky. The sun's rays lit upon the forest floor, casting its warmth on Hunter's shoulders as he hiked through the woods. He savored the heat, knowing that it would end soon enough. The past few nights had been chilly, the weather gradually cooler with each passing day. Fall was approaching, and autumn and winter here on Varta were mild compared to those on Earth, the temperature rarely dropping below freezing. The leaves hadn't yet fallen from the trees, but there was a definite crispness to the air after the sun set.

Hunter adjusted his metal helmet, his scalp sore from having worn it all day. It was functional but not particularly sexy, leaving his face visible from the eyebrows down. He'd gotten into the habit of wearing it after discovering it could protect his mind from absorbing the emotions and memories of everything around him. A necessary precaution in a world where a single mistake could not only cost you your life, but your very soul.

"How you holding up, bro?" he asked, glancing to his left. A huge creature walked at his side, a beast about nine feet tall, with two pairs of heavily-muscled arms and a body covered in black armored plates. It was Xerxes, the brother he'd never known he'd had, born on this strange world after his mother Neesha had been sucked into an ancient portal. A one-way ticket from Earth to Varta…with no way back.

Xerxes grunted, raising one hand and flashing a few hand signals. Hunter concentrated, trying to figure out what Xerxes was signing. His brother had been changed by this world, turned into a half-man, half-beetle. Barely able to talk, he'd been teaching Hunter sign language for the past few days.

"Good," he saw Xerxes sign. "You?"

"Tired," Hunter grumbled. "Hungry."

Xerxes grunted again, wagging one finger.

"NO TALK," he lectured. "SIGN."

"Right," Hunter grumbled. He signed slowly, struggling to remember the words. "Tired," he signed. "Hungry."

Xerxes nodded in approval. He reached down as he walked, plucking a large white mushroom from the base of a nearby tree and offering it to Hunter, who made a face. Xerxes shrugged, chowing down on the stuff. Little pieces of it stuck to the corners of his mouth.

"Nasty," Hunter muttered. He hated mushrooms, as any rational human being should. But the Ironclad – the name for creatures like Xerxes – loved the stuff. It was the beetle in them, apparently. At least that's what Vi had told him.

He sighed, wishing she were here. Not that Xerxes wasn't fine company, but it was a whole hell of a lot easier to speak with Vi. Considering she could, you know, speak. He'd told Xerxes a lot about himself in the last couple of days. About their father. About what their mother's journey to this world had done to the man. And about what Dad had done to Hunter.

And in return, Hunter had a lot he wanted to learn about his brother, but with Xerxes barely able to say more than a few words at a time…

"What's wrong?" Xerxes signed. Hunter grimaced.

"Wish you could talk," he admitted aloud. Mostly because he didn't know how to sign it. Xerxes took the opportunity to show him, signing slowly with one of his four hands. Hunter watched him, then repeated the signs a few times.

"ME…TOO," Xerxes confessed afterward. His voice was deep and gravelly, his voice box transformed by decades of exposure to the powerful wills of beetles in the cave the Ironclad lived in. Descendants of peasants who'd risen up against the kingdom of Tykus half a century ago, the Ironclad were loyal only to Xerxes…and to Neesha, their queen. Xerxes and Neesha were both immortal, possessed of the ability to heal from nearly any injury. And they never aged. It had something to do with the blue bioluminescent goo that they generated; Xerxes had a long translucent mane extending from the top of his head all the way down his spine, forming a short, broad tail. It was filled with the glowing stuff.

"I miss Vi," Hunter signed. He felt bad about telling Xerxes, afraid he might offend his brother. But he'd promised himself he'd be brutally honest with the guy, even at the risk of hurting him.

Holding things in is the exact opposite of letting them go, Vi had taught him.

"She talks a lot," Xerxes signed, smirking down at him. Hunter chuckled.

"True," he signed back. "But most of it is worth listening to."

They continued forward, settling into a comfortable silence. It'd been days since they'd started their journey from the Ironclad caves toward the Kingdom of the Deep. Days since they'd barely escaped from the Castle Wexford – the fortress owned by Duke Dominus – with their lives. Neesha and Vi were still in the Ironclad caves, preparing for a war against Tykus.

Apparently Tykus had been attacked by the Guild of Seekers, much of it set ablaze. Rumor had it the Seekers had managed to raid the Acropolis itself, the massive fortress in the center of the kingdom.

If it weren't for Zagamar, Hunter thought darkly, *I'd still be with Vi and Mom.*

His stomach growled, loud enough that Xerxes heard it. His brother offered a hunk of mushroom again, and again Hunter declined. Still, Xerxes had a point. The longer Hunter went without eating, the more likely that Zagamar would try to take over. And that wasn't something Hunter was keen on suffering through, on account of the fact that good 'ol Zaggie was a megalomaniacal asshole.

Never shoulda drank that shit, he groused silently.

It was too late, of course. He'd swallowed the liquified brains of Zagamar, a Legend who'd died over six thousand years ago. And now the Legend's will was exerting itself slowly, taking over Hunter's body and mind bit-by-bit. There was only one way to stop the bastard from transforming Hunter into Zagamar himself…and that was to go to the Deep.

According to Mom, the Deep had the power to lock in his traits, making who he was now…his mind and body…permanent. The downside, of course, was that nothing would be able to change him afterward. He wouldn't be able to absorb memories anymore, or sense other people's emotions. He'd basically end up being the guy he'd been on Earth. An outcome he hardly looked forward to…but the alternative was to lose himself.

Hunter sighed, ignoring his tired legs, keeping up with Xerxes despite the guy's much longer stride. The sooner they made it to the Deep, the sooner he'd be rid of Zagamar. Or at least the sooner he'd stop the guy from taking over. He could summon the ancient Legend if he chose, a process that temporarily gave him Zagamar's incredible intellect and remarkable ability to view the world in slow-motion. At the expense of risking the guy taking his mind over completely.

He glanced up at Xerxes, tapping his arm.

"How you doing?" he signed.

"Tired," Xerxes signed back. "Normally sleep during the day."

Hunter nodded. Vi had mentioned that the Ironclad were nocturnal. Xerxes had flipped his sleep schedule to accommodate Hunter. He was surprisingly thoughtful and considerate for a monster. Sure, they couldn't talk much…not yet, until Hunter learned more sign language…but Xerxes was loyal as hell, and had sacrificed himself on more than one occasion to save Hunter.

"Want rest?" Hunter signed. Xerxes shook his head.

"Go until *you* tired," he signed back.

Hunter nodded. Xerxes understood Hunter's greatest fear – that with every day that passed, he might be losing a little more of himself. Subtly, imperceptibly. It was the nature of this cursed world that anyone with a stronger will than you could change you. Could make you more like them. Plants, animals, people…anyone with a more powerful will could do it. On earth, you got to stay yourself. But here…

He glanced up at Xerxes, wondering how his brother felt about having become a monster.

"Hey," he ventured. "What was it like? You know, becoming…you?" Xerxes smirked.

"A monster?" he signed.

"Well yeah."

"FEAR," Xerxes answered. He paused for a moment. "WHEN STOP? IF…STOP?"

Hunter nodded, remembering what it'd been like to have Zagamar take over. The fear he'd felt each time, wondering if he'd be able to take control back from Zagamar…or whether he'd lose himself completely.

"WONDER," Xerxes continued, tapping on his chest, then his head. "HOW MUCH…LEFT."

"How much of *you* was left?" Hunter inquired.

"IS."

Hunter considered this, saying nothing more. As much as he hated to admit it, when he first realized his brother was, well, his brother, he struggled more than a little with seeing the guy as something other than a big dumb brute. A very violent big dumb brute. He hated the fact that he'd made that assumption purely based on Xerxes' appearance…especially since people in Tykus – and those back on Earth – had done the same to him because of the color of his skin.

He sighed, trekking onward, rubbing his right shoulder absently. It still hurt after being struck by an arrow during their raid on the Castle Wexford. The cut on his lower back wasn't faring much better. Not for the first time, he wished he had Xerxes' and Mom's ability to heal almost instantly. He told his brother as much.

"GIFT," Xerxes replied. "CURSE."

"Gotta think it's more of a gift than a curse," Hunter ventured. "Watching you get burned alive and heal a few minutes later is pretty awesome." He grimaced, rubbing his shoulder some more. "Gonna take me weeks to heal from that damn arrow."

"WANT…OOZE?" Xerxes inquired. Hunter glanced at Xerxes' glowing blue mane.

"Not gonna lie," he admitted. "I'm a little tempted."

"NO…TELL MOM."

"Why?" Hunter asked. "She gonna be mad?"

"IF…ZAGAMAR…TAKE OVER…"

"Ah," Hunter muttered. He hadn't thought of that. "How about we wait until the Deep," he decided. Xerxes nodded.

"DEAL."

"Hey," Hunter stated, perking up. "Since we're going to the Deep, you can lock in your traits," he realized. "So you won't have to worry about losing your voice anymore."

"Or getting it back," Xerxes signed. Hunter grimaced.

"Right," he signed back.

He sighed, feeling suddenly glum. There was no good outcome here for either of them, only a choice between the lesser of two bad ones. He suddenly wished – and not for the first time – that he'd thought things through a little more when he'd met Lady Camilla. If he hadn't been so caught up in his guilt and obsession with revenge, he would've thought twice about trusting her. And he'd never have gone into that damn crypt. A master manipulator, Lady Camilla had sensed his weakness instantly, and had taken advantage of it.

And him…in more ways than one.

He felt a tap on his shoulder, and glanced up, realizing Xerxes was trying to get his attention.

"Yeah?" he asked. Xerxes wagged one index finger.

"Sign," Xerxes signed.

"What?" Hunter signed. Xerxes gestured ahead.

"Look," he signed.

Hunter looked ahead, spotting something rising far above the treetops a quarter-mile ahead. A huge black tower piercing through the forest, tapering to a sharp point at the top. It looked to be a few hundred feet tall, with lush green vines crawling up the sides of it. He saw more towers beyond, mostly hidden by the dense foliage.

"Almost there," Xerxes signed.

Hunter nodded, feeling a powerful sense of déjà vu. He knew this place, had seen it before. Not in his own memories, but in the memories he'd absorbed from a mace back at Vi's house, after she'd been mostly killed by Traven. He'd discovered that the more memories he absorbed, the harder time he had remembering which ones were his and which weren't. Thus his helmet.

They strode toward the spires, eventually reaching a wide dirt path leading them toward it. A few minutes later, the path ended abruptly in a chasm easily a quarter-mile wide ahead. A black stone bridge some twenty feet wide spanned the gap, supported by thick stone columns rising up from the chasm. This bridge led to a massive wall made of the same black stone. Trees grew against the wall, and thick vines crawled up its surface all the way to the top…so densely that their leaves almost completely obscured the stone. Hunter and Xerxes stopped before the bridge.

"Guessing this is it," Hunter ventured, glancing up at Xerxes.

"Yes," his brother signed.

"Don't see any guards," Hunter noted. Xerxes grunted, pointing up with one hand. Hunter frowned, spotting a flock of large birds gliding near the top of the spires high above. He raised an eyebrow at his brother. "You're saying this place is guarded by birds?"

Xerxes didn't answer, stepping onto the bridge, his feet *thumping* on the black stone as he made his way toward the wall ahead. Hunter sighed, following behind. He glanced over the edge of the bridge; there was a several-hundred-foot drop to a river below…and no railing to stop people from stumbling off to their deaths.

"Not exactly kid-friendly," he grumbled.

They made their way across the bridge, reaching a huge stone archway in the wall ahead. There was no closed portcullis, no massive double-doors. Nothing to stop them from coming in. Which was odd. Why go through all the trouble of building a wall if you were going to let anyone walk through? But he didn't have time to ponder the question. They passed under the archway, coming to wide stairs leading upward a good thirty feet. This too was strange; the leftmost part of the staircase was normal, with normal-sized steps. The middle had much larger steps, while the rightmost part was a ramp leading upward, its surface roughened instead of slippery…and with a carpet of dead vines sprawled all the way up its surface.

"Huh," Hunter said, stopping at the foot of the stairs. "Weird."

If Xerxes found it weird, he certainly didn't show it; the big brute started walking up the middle portion of the stairs, the huge steps slightly too large for even him. Hunter stuck to the leftmost section – the one with sensibly-proportioned steps – making his way up to the top.

And stopped dead in his tracks.

For there, spread out before him, was a massive open space surrounded on all sides by that tall black stone wall, easily as large as the kingdom of Tykus. But in stark contrast to Tykus's countless buildings and cobblestone streets, this place was lush with trees and shrubs, short green grass dotted with wildflowers serving as verdant streets. Long wooden buildings with curved roofs dotted the landscape, some over sixty feet long and twenty feet tall. Other buildings seemed to be built into the earth itself; indeed, wherever there was a hill, the entrance to an underground building could be seen. And in some of the larger trees, treehouses had been built. Not the simple, small treehouses one might expect, but huge structures built across numerous trees, with wooden bridges connecting them.

And spread throughout the landscape were five huge spires made of black stone, vines crawling up their sheer walls. Each had to be over thirty stories tall, and tapered into sharp pyramidal peaks at the top.

Hunter stared at the magnificent view, then realized his mouth was open. He shut it with a *click*.

"Wow," he breathed, glancing at Xerxes. He couldn't read the guy's expression, as usual.

"Agreed," Xerxes signed.

A group of men walked out of one of the long wooden buildings nearest Hunter and Xerxes, then started running toward them. The men were unarmed, with tanned skin and long black hair. They were wearing loincloths…and little else.

"Incoming," Hunter warned, taking a step back and reaching for the hilt of his longsword. But Xerxes shook his head.

"HOLD," he ordered.

Hunter obeyed, forcing himself to relax as the men ran toward them. They slowed as they reached Hunter and Xerxes, stopping a few feet away. Which was a bit too close for Hunter's comfort.

"Hello!" one of them greeted, smiling broadly and raising one hand. "I'm Kip."

"Hunter," Hunter replied, pointing at himself. "This is Xerxes," he added.

Kip and the others nodded…and promptly took to staring at Xerxes.

"What are you?" Kip asked the big guy.

"He's an Ironclad," Hunter answered. Kip frowned.

"Never seen one like him before. Was he made?"

Hunter frowned.

"Excuse me?"

"Was he made, or was he born?" Kip clarified. Hunter glanced at Xerxes, who just stood there looking down at them.

"Made," Hunter admitted.

Kip and the other men nodded…and proceeded to stare at Xerxes for a long, increasingly uncomfortable moment.

"Is this the Kingdom of the Deep?" Hunter inquired, breaking the silence. Kip blinked, turning to him.

"Yes," he confirmed. "This is our home. What is yours?"

"I uh," Hunter began, then stopped. He could say that Tykus was his home, but these guys probably didn't get along with the kingdom. "I'm from Earth."

Kip frowned, glancing at his fellows. Then he shook his head.

"I don't understand."

"I came through the Gate," Hunter clarified. "From another world."

Kip's eyes widened, and he broke out into a huge smile, reaching out and grabbing Hunter by the wrists. Hunter resisted the urge to jerk his arms away…and decapitate the guy with his sword.

"An Original!" Kip exclaimed. He turned to his fellows. "From the Great Turtle, like our Ancestors!" Kip turned back to Hunter. "Tykus didn't get you?"

"They did," Hunter admitted. "But I escaped."

"Ah," Kip replied. "This is good, this is good. Come!" he ordered, pulling Hunter forward. "The Elders will want to meet you!"

Hunter glanced back at Xerxes, who merely shrugged, stomping behind Kip and Hunter as Kip dragged Hunter forward. At first Hunter thought that Kip was going to take him to the long building the men had come out of, but they passed to the right of it, continuing down a wide street of short grass and flowers. The air was fragrant with the flowers' sweet perfume, and Hunter's alarm at being pulled along by total strangers soon gave way to a pleasant contentedness. Vi's training made it instantly clear what was going on; the environment was changing his mood, even with his helmet on. Either Kip's enthusiasm was affecting him, or the surrounding environment was. Either way, it was a good sign; people here were generally happy…and happy people didn't brutally murder strangers.

Typically.

Not that Hunter was particularly worried; these men were unarmed, and Xerxes could wipe the floor with them. And if they really threatened Hunter, Hunter could always unleash Zaggie on them.

He allowed himself to relax, giving in to the emotions around him.

"So this is the Kingdom of the Deep, huh?" Hunter asked. He looked around. "Where is everyone?"

"Hmm?" Kip replied.

"Where's all the people?"

"Most are in the Shrine of the Ancestors," Kip answered. "There aren't many people here," he added. "Less than a thousand."

"Not much of a kingdom," Hunter opined.

"Most don't choose the Ancestor spirit," Kip explained.

"The what?"

"The Elders will explain," Kip reassured.

Hunter glanced at Xerxes, who shrugged, and they followed Kip and the other men as they made their way deeper into the kingdom. Far in the distance – in what appeared to be the center of the kingdom – there was a lake with a large island in the middle of it. And on that island was a large ziggurat-like structure, made of the same black stone as the walls and the spires.

"What's that?" Hunter asked, gesturing at the ziggurat.

"The Shrine of our Ancestors," Kip answered. "That's where we're going."

Hunter glanced around; there were no more of the long buildings, nor the treehouses he'd seen earlier. Instead, small hills flanked the grassy path they walked on, large pits dug in the sides of them.

"I'm surprised you just let us in," Hunter admitted to Kip. "You guys don't have much in the way of defenses," he added. Kip frowned.

"Pardon?"

"You have the wall," Hunter clarified, "…but there's no gate. No guards. And you don't have any weapons," he added, gesturing at Kip. "What if Tykus attacked?"

"There is more to the Kingdom of the Deep than your eyes see," Kip replied. "And the Guardians protect us."

"The Guardians?"

"Hope you never see them," Kip stated. "Anyone who does, it is the last thing they see."

Kip offered no more explanation, bringing Hunter and Xerxes through the hilly terrain. The land leveled out as they got closer to the lake ahead, allowing Hunter a better view of the area to either side. A quarter-mile to his right, massive trees grew, large birds perched atop them. One of the huge black spires shot upward from within this forest; he spotted countless ledges on each side of the spire, with more birds perched there. Lots of them. And they weren't small either.

"I hate birds," Hunter grumbled.

"Mom too," Xerxes signed. Which was true. Hunter had forgotten about that; Mom had always hated birds – and spiders – viewing them with an unwarranted suspicion. Trips to the beach had been great fun for Dad, but for Hunter and Mom, the festivities had always carried a dread of seagulls descending upon them like vultures, tearing them apart piece by bloody piece.

"You hate 'em too?" Hunter asked. Xerxes shook his head.

"NO…FEAR FOR…SELF," he replied. "ONLY…FAMILY."

"Ah."

Kip glanced back at Xerxes with surprise.

"You talk?" he asked. Xerxes grunted, but nodded.

"SOME."

Hunter watched the birds in the distance warily, trying to figure out what kind they were. But they were too far away.

"What're those?" he asked, pointing at them.

"Birds," Kip answered.

"What kind," Hunter clarified, trying to keep the sarcasm out of his voice.

"Many kinds," Kip replied. "We celebrate all spirits here."

"Spirits?"

Kip glanced at him sidelong, a frown on his face.

"You do not understand spirits?" he asked.

"Nope."

"Everything has a spirit," Kip explained, gesturing all around him. "The grass at our feet. The birds. Anything that flies, crawls, swims, digs…even us," he added, gesturing at himself and Hunter. "We have human spirits. Others have animal spirits. And most choose to have many spirits."

"Many spirits?"

"You will see," Kip promised, patting Hunter on the shoulder. "The Elders will teach you."

They reached the edge of the lake them, stopping at the shore. Kip put a hand to his mouth, emitting a shrill whistle. Moments later, Hunter saw a rippling in the water ahead of them; something emerged from its surface, coming right for them. It looked for all the world like a huge turtle shell, easily twenty feet in diameter.

Then he saw a huge turtle head pop out of the water. Or rather, a turtle-ish head. Instead of having eyes on the sides, they were facing forward…and the thing had a face of sorts. A squat nose, and a mouth with short, stubby white teeth. And tiny ears on either side of its head.

It looked vaguely…human.

The creature swam up to them, stopping at the shore. Then it spun around slowly, until it was facing away from them. Kip hopped on its back, gesturing for Hunter to do so as well. Hunter followed, hopping onto the turtle's shell, and Xerxes did as well. To Hunter's surprise, the massive turtle handled their weight easily, and immediately began swimming toward the island in the center of the lake, leaving the other men behind.

"What is this thing?" Hunter asked.

"A great turtle," Kip replied. He grinned. "Not as big as the turtle you lived on," he added.

Hunter frowned. His mother was black – or had been, before becoming an Ironclad. But she'd also been part Native American, from the Wampanoag tribe of Massachusetts. They believed that the Earth was a huge turtle, and that everyone lived on its shell. It made sense that these people would know of the Great Turtle, he supposed. The Gate to this world was in Massachusetts, after all…and before the pilgrims came, Massachusetts would've been populated by natives. They must have come through the Gate long ago, creating the Kingdom of the Deep.

"Its face looked almost human," Hunter noted. Kip nodded.

"Sassamon took the spirit of the turtle long ago," he explained, kneeling down and patting the turtle shell. "And that of a Giant. He is very old…one of the oldest in the kingdom. Some say he will never die."

"Wait, you're saying he was *human* once?"

"He has the spirit of a human," Kip replied. "According to legend, his grandparents were human, and accepted the spirit of the turtle. Sassamon took the spirit of a Giant."

"By spirit you mean the traits of things," Hunter deduced.

"In a way," Kip agreed. "The Elders will tell you more."

The turtle – Sassamon – took them slowly across the lake, eventually reaching the shore of the island. They disembarked, and Sassamon turned about, vanishing below the surface of the water. Kip strode toward the ziggurat – the Shrine of the Ancestors – motioning for Hunter and Xerxes to follow. The Shrine occupied a large space – it was at least a hundred yards squared – but was only five or six stories tall. The entrance was a small rectangular doorway, but with no door. Stairs led downward into darkness beyond. Kip brought them to this entrance, then stopped, turning to face them.

“Stay here,” he stated, holding up one hand. “Do not enter until I come for you.”

“Where are you going?” Hunter asked. Kip smiled.

“Inside,” he replied. “To speak with the Elders. No one enters without their permission…and no one leaves the kingdom without their blessing.”

“Wait,” Hunter said. “What’s that supposed to mean?”

“Anyone can come into the Kingdom of the Deep,” Kip answered. “But no one may leave without the Elders’ approval.” His smile faded. “And that,” he added, “…is seldom given without sacrifice.”

Chapter 3

Dominus rested on his belly, prickly blades of grass stabbing his flesh. He lay there, the side of his head on the ground by the small pond he'd drank from what seemed like hours ago. Or maybe days. He'd passed in and out of consciousness countless times, with each slip into the dreamworld acting as a blessed respite from his pain. The agony that had begun to consume him, the feeling of tiny hot needles pricking his flesh over and over again. A symphony of pain that had replaced the numbness he'd experienced before.

He lay there, staring at the grass waving in a warm breeze before him. At the trees beyond. There was a strange sweetness in his mouth, almost like honey. The taste summoned an all-too-familiar feeling that seized him, gnawing at his belly.

Hunger.

Dominus stirred, reaching out with one hand and gripping the base of a clump of grass. He pulled it free, roots and all, shaking it a little to get rid of some of the dirt. Then he brought it to his mouth…and ate. It was bitter, his mouth so dry that it made it almost impossible to swallow. He turned to the pond, crawling up to the water and drinking.

He chewed some more, then swallowed, trying not to gag.

In this way he continued, pulling up grass, tearing leaves from their stalks. Eating small mushrooms growing in the dirt. Consuming everything around him, then drinking. Eating and drinking until he could consume no more. Then he lay back down on the grass, utterly exhausted.

And then, mercifully, sleep took him.

* * *

Dominus opened his eyes.

He was lying in the grass, a few meters from the pond now. He frowned, pushing himself onto his hands and knees…and to his surprise, he found he could do so. The movement made him lightheaded, and he stopped moving, closing his eyes and waiting for the sensation to pass.

Then he opened his eyes, staring down at his hands.

They were black no longer, his charred flesh replaced by smooth, pale skin that clung tightly to his bones. They were skeletal, but whole.

I'm healing, he realized.

It was only then that he remembered the Ironclad's head. That wondrous artifact that had saved him from certain death so many weeks ago, giving him the power to heal…and even to regenerate his amputated hand. The gift that had slowly begun to give him his youth again…for a steep price. For now he was corrupted, no longer welcome in Tykus, the kingdom he'd spent his life protecting. He was a criminal now, a man without a home.

Dominus paused, then shifted to a sitting position, looking down at himself. He was utterly naked, his paper-thin flesh draped over his ribs. The terrible pain and pins-and-needles sensation that had accosted him earlier was gone. Now he felt no pain whatsoever…only hunger, triggered by that strange sweetness that once again coated his tongue.

The hunger grew within him, demanding to be fed.

He ignored it, trying to focus. Trying to remember the last thing that'd happened to him, before…this. An image of King Tykus came to him, of the Seekers who'd been sent to assassinate the man. He remembered saving Tykus, then being confronted by Duke Ratheburg. Tykus had killed Ratheburg, sparing Dominus's life…and giving him a chance at a new one. Tykus's final words came to him.

You will stand outside the kingdom, its eternal champion. You will ensure that we endure, that I endure.

Dominus closed his eyes.

I am the beekeeper.

He opened them, staring at the pond ahead, then rising slowly to his feet. His muscles were weak – terribly weak – but he managed to stand without losing his balance. The hunger pangs grew more insistent, and he knew that he would have to give in to them. The Ironclad's power of regeneration was his now, and it demanded to be fed. In doing so, he would continue to heal.

Dominus looked down at his body again, at his bare chest. An image of a sword – *his* sword – plunging through his back, the bloodied tip emerging from his chest, came to him.

Farkus!

His butler had murdered him…or tried to. Had stabbed Dominus through the heart for the crime of dealing in wild artifacts, those forbidden by the kingdom. Farkus had stabbed him, then…

Burn the body, he'd said. *Please.*

A chill ran down Dominus's spine, and he lifted his gaze, clenching his fists at his sides. He spotted a large patch of charred grass nearby, and knew that this was where he'd been burned. Where he'd been left to die.

Killed by a damn peasant, he thought, gritting his teeth.

His first instinct was for revenge. He could kill Farkus easily, at least once he was fully healed. But he discarded the idea as quickly as it'd come. Succumbing to a desire for petty revenge would not serve him, not in the long run. He was dead now, at least officially. In trying to kill Dominus, Farkus might have given him an unintentional gift. The butler would spread the news of his death, and the kingdom would pronounce him thus. No one would come to hunt him down.

He could start over...start the new life that Tykus had offered him, and protect the kingdom from the outside. Let Farkus have his victory; Dominus could hardly fault the man. After decades of being exposed to Dominus's will, and nights spent in Dominus's ancestral shrine, Farkus had for all intents and purposes *become* Dominus. The old Dominus, that was. A man disgusted with who he'd become.

Yes, he would let Farkus live. He had to focus on preserving the kingdom now.

Dominus felt another chill run through him, remembering the night the Guild of Seekers had attacked the kingdom. They'd attacked the prison first, undoubtedly freeing their master, High Seeker Zeno. Farkus had given Zeno's second-in-command the Ironclad's head...which meant that Zeno was almost certainly in possession of it now, assuming he'd fled Tykus. It was possible that the Guild of Seekers had managed to overrun the kingdom and overthrow King Tykus, but Dominus had to have hope that this was not the case. The wise king had not seemed afraid, after all. In fact, Tykus had admitted to planning the whole thing, knowing full well the Guild would attack...and that they would use the secret, ancient tunnels beneath the Acropolis to carry out that attack.

The same tunnels Dominus had used to escape the city, emerging well beyond the Deadlands before making the long trek back to the Castle Wexford, his former home.

Dominus felt the hunger return, more pressing this time. He resisted the urge, knowing full well he would give in to it shortly. That he would soon become an animal, scouring the forest for anything he could keep down.

Zeno has the head.

If that was the case, then the leader of the Guild of Seekers constituted the single greatest threat to the kingdom of Tykus. With it, Zeno could become as powerful as Dominus...and could raise an army of immortal Seekers to overthrow the kingdom. Dominus had to find Zeno and take back the head before this happened. But the only people who might know where the man was were the highest-level Seekers...and one other person.

Dominus grimaced, taking a tentative step forward, feeling his legs wobble as he did so. He steadied himself, then took another step, spotting a thick cluster of mushrooms growing from the base of a nearby tree. His mouth watered at the thought of eating them, and he gave in to his desire, hobbling over to the mushrooms and kneeling before them. Tearing into them, he stuffed the mushroom caps in his mouth, chewing vigorously. This time he needed no water from the pond, his mouth having regained its ability to make saliva.

He ate until he could eat no more.

Then Dominus sat back on his heels, feeling vaguely disgusted with himself. A former duke reduced to a beggar. A wild man scrounging for food, naked in the wilderness.

Quite the fall from grace, he mused.

But he knew better than to equate a man's possessions with his station. Any man could wear the robes of a duke, but a duke needed no finery to play the part. His mind was his greatest weapon, and he would use it to his advantage.

He returned his thoughts to the Ironclad head, and to High Seeker Zeno.

There were only two possibilities: Zeno had been caught within Tykus, and the head had been disposed of…in which case Dominus need not worry. Or that Zeno had escaped, and was in possession of the head. In that case, there was one person who might know where the man was. Someone who had no love for Dominus, former Duke of Wexford…and who was every bit as dangerous as Zeno himself, possessed of a keen, devious mind and the ice-cold heart of a merciless killer.

The one-and-only Lady Camilla.

Chapter 4

The sun was directly overhead by the time Sukri and Dio stopped following the banks of the River Ormr, the wide, serpentine river whose shore Lady Camilla's mansion had been built upon. They'd left the mansion yesterday morning, trekking silently along the riverside for a whole day, then setting camp in the nearby woods. Dio had set a brutal pace, bastard that he was…and had demanded a repeat performance today.

Sukri glared at the man's back, following him from behind.

Asshole.

Dio wore the standard red and black leather suit and similarly colored mask of Lady Camilla's Seekers, the men and women she hired to retrieve artifacts and Ossae for her wealthy clients. The prick was also Camilla's personal bodyguard…and had been ordered to train Sukri to become one of her Seekers. A dick move by the Lady, considering Dio had also murdered Sukri's best friend Gammon in cold blood.

Psychopathic bitch, she grumbled to herself.

And cold blood was all that ran through Dio's veins. The last few days had taught her that much. Sukri was an Empath, able to sense the emotions of almost everyone around her. This meant of course that her emotions could change on a whim, mirroring anyone she was near…but that she could also tell what other people were feeling, as long as she monitored her *own* feelings. Hour after hour of traveling and sparring with Dio had revealed no emotion coming from him other than cold indifference…and on occasion, contempt. She'd have sworn he was part snake.

Sukri's stomach grumbled.

"We gonna eat anytime soon?" she inquired, hopping over a fallen tree trunk. Dio said nothing…which meant no. She hadn't been allowed to eat since last night. "Okay," she grumbled. "I'll just starve to death."

"Hardly," Dio replied, his cold, flat voice sending a chill through her.

"What's *that* supposed to mean?"

"You're soft," Dio answered. Sukri's eyebrows rose.

"You calling me fat?" she inquired.

Dio said nothing…which meant yes.

"Prick," she muttered, not even caring if he heard. Still, she glanced down at herself. She was barely over one-and-a-half meters tall, with lightly bronzed skin and long dirty-blonde hair tied into thick braids that fell over her shoulders. She was certainly a bit curvy – a fact that made her quite popular with the guys – but she wasn't even close to being fat. Well, maybe compared to Dio, but the guy was built like a goddamn statue. She could practically see his damn veins through his tight-ass uniform.

They fell into an uncomfortable silence, making their way through the forest, each step bringing them closer to their final destination: The Kingdom of the Deep. She'd heard of the place, of course…everyone in Tykus had. Lots of rumors about it, anyway. Supposedly they were all primitives, allowing the corruption of the forest into themselves. The Kingdom of the Deep was where all of Camilla's Seekers trained; why that was the case was beyond Sukri, but it wasn't like she had much of a choice in the matter. She *had* to go there with Dio. If she tried to return to Tykus, she'd be killed by the Guild of Seekers.

Without the Lady, she was as good as dead.

"How far away is this place anyway?" Sukri groused.

No answer.

She sighed, giving up on questioning Dio and focusing on keeping pace with him. Minutes turned into hours, an endless parade of trees passing by as they went. Eventually Dio stopped, dropping his backpack to the ground. Sukri stopped as well, watching as Dio pulled out two wooden staves tied to the side of the pack. Her heart sank.

"Can we at least eat first?" she pleaded.

Dio handed her a staff, then picked up the other one, facing her. Without warning, he attacked, swinging the staff at her temple.

Sukri rushed to block, their staves striking with a loud *thwack*. Dio stopped, nodding at her…and promptly swung at her temple. Again. She blocked it, and Dio followed up with a second attack, thrusting at her belly. Sukri blocked this as well; after hours of sparring every single day, she was getting better at avoiding having the absolute crap beaten out of her. Which Dio still managed to do, every single day.

Dio stopped, nodded, then attacked again, starting with the same two attacks, then adding a third – an upward swing right between Sukri's legs. This time, she was too slow; his staff slammed into her crotch, taking the breath right out of her. She stumbled backward, dropping her staff and falling to her butt on the forest floor.

"Fuck!" she swore, gritting her teeth against the pain. She glared up at Dio. "What the hell is wrong with you?"

He just stood there, waiting.

"Ass," she spat, taking a breath in, then getting to her feet. "Hitting me in the goddamn pussy."

"Were you planning on using it?" Dio inquired.

"Not with you," she retorted.

"Again," he ordered…and promptly attacked. Same three strikes, and this time Sukri was damn sure to block the groin strike. Dio stopped, nodding at her…and did it all over again. Each time she succeeded in blocking all of his attacks, he added another one. Each time she failed, he repeated the string of attacks. They did this until he'd done twenty in a row. Which was five nasty bruises later, not counting the one on Sukri's crotch. As usual, Dio said next to nothing, teaching by doing…and by forcing Sukri to respond.

When they were done, Dio took Sukri's staff, tying it to his pack alongside his and slinging it over his shoulder. Then they continued their march through the woods.

Sukri grimaced as she followed behind him, her crotch still throbbing, not to mention her right thigh. She glared at his back, imagining herself whipping her staff right between *his* legs.

And then slitting his throat like he'd slit Gammon's.

She grit her teeth, ignoring the pain as she walked. There was no point in complaining, certainly not to Dio. And complaining wouldn't do her any good anyway. What she needed to do was train every day until she was as good as Dio. Until she was *better.*

And then – and *only* then – would she get a chance to get back at Dio and Lady Camilla. To get her revenge…and avenge Gammon.

* * *

Hunter and Xerxes stood before the entrance to the Shrine of the Ancestors. Beyond was a short hallway with black stone walls, floor, and ceiling, and narrow stairs that plunged into darkness below. Kip had left them minutes earlier, taking the stairs downward…and leaving them alone on the island. Hunter stood with his arms crossed over his chest, feeling more and more uneasy as the minutes passed. It wasn't just because of Kip's warning about the Elders potentially not allowing them to leave the kingdom; he was also utterly ignorant of the wills that might have been absorbed into the temple's walls. Or the ground at his feet, for that matter. He had a strong will, it was true, but he was all-too-aware of the danger powerful wills posed. That was why he was here in the first place, after all…to stop Zagamar's will from annihilating his.

"Think he's coming back?" Hunter asked Xerxes.

"USE…SIGNS," his brother admonished.

"Coming back?" Hunter signed. Xerxes shrugged. If the big guy was nervous, he sure didn't show it.

Suddenly he spotted Kip ascending the stairs. The man stepped out of the entrance, stopping before them and flashing them his customary smile.

"Come!" he urged. "The Elders want to meet you." With that, the man went back through the entrance, taking the stairs down again. Hunter glanced at Xerxes, who followed behind Kip…or at least tried to. The ceiling was a foot too short for the huge Ironclad, and too narrow to fit his broad shoulders. Xerxes had to duck down and pull in his shoulders a bit just to fit through. Hunter followed close behind, and Xerxes glanced back at him, signing with one hand.

"If I get stuck," he signed, "…cut my arms off."

"Sure thing," Hunter signed back with a smirk.

The stairs descended a good twenty feet into the earth, the light from the entrance quickly fading. It became so dark that Hunter couldn't see a thing, and he put a hand on either wall to steady himself. Eventually he spotted a dull, flickering red glow ahead, revealing the bottom of the stairs. When he reached this, he saw a long, rectangular tunnel ahead, flickering torches bolted to the walls at regular intervals. Symbols were carved into the walls, but Hunter could only make out those closest to the torches. They were crude pictorials of people engaged in various activities, such as dancing, hunting, and…other natural activities.

"Don't think they're Catholics," Hunter mused, smirking at a few of the more interesting symbols as they traveled through the tunnel. "Might learn a few things from these, eh bro?"

"NO," came the guttural reply.

Hunter chuckled, and they reached the end of the tunnel, which branched left and right. Kip took them rightward down a short section of tunnel, which soon opened up into a large underground chamber. This was far better lit than the tunnels, with a huge bonfire in the center of the room and torches bolted to the walls all around the periphery of the room. The ceiling was about twenty feet high, with a gap directly above the bonfire leading to a chimney-like structure that carried the smoke up and away.

And sitting cross-legged before the bonfire was an elderly man, his bare back facing them. His long white hair was tied back into a ponytail, adorned by two long feathers. Kip stopped at the man's side, kneeling before him.

"They're here," he notified.

The old man got to his feet with Kip's help, turning to face Hunter and Xerxes. He was old – at least in his eighties – but stood tall, his shoulders set back and his chest thrust out proudly. Bells on his soft tan boots and pants jingled as he moved. He was surprisingly muscular, his bare chest chiseled even if his skin hung loosely from his flesh. He raised a hand at them.

"Greetings," he said in a deep, surprisingly strong voice. "I am Sannup, Elder of the Temple. I have the spirit of the Ancestors within me." He lowered his hand, nodding at Kip. "Leave us," he requested.

Kip bowed, then left, going back through the tunnel they'd come through. Sannup turned to face Hunter.

"You are Hunter," he stated. "You come from Turtle Island?"

"I do," Hunter confirmed.

"Kip tells me your spirit is strong."

"That's what I've been told," Hunter agreed.

"And this is…Xerxes?" Sannup inquired, turning to the Ironclad. Xerxes grunted. "Kip says he is your brother?"

"He is," Hunter replied. "He was…conceived on Turtle Island, and was born here."

"You have many spirits," Sannup observed, stepping toward Xerxes and studying him. The old man put a hand on Xerxes' chest, feeling the armor there. "Very strong," he observed.

"VERY," Xerxes agreed.

"Hmm," Sannup murmured, stepping back from Xerxes. "Tell me…why are you here?"

"We want to travel to the Deep," Hunter explained. Sannup's eyebrows rose.

"Really?" he replied. "Why?"

"I have…something inside of me," Hunter confessed. "A powerful will that will destroy me if I don't stop it."

Sannup frowned, eyeing Hunter for a long moment.

"Explain," he requested at last.

Hunter hesitated, then did so, recapping his adventure to the Crypt of Zagamar, and the disastrous results. When he was finished, Sannup lowered his gaze, looking troubled.

"What?" Hunter asked.

"We call the spirit you carry 'Hobbomock,'" he explained. "A spirit of death. He created the pukwudgie, the demons that tried to destroy the world…and that destroyed the great tribe that lived in the kingdom you now call Tykus."

"You know of him?" Hunter asked. "Of Zagamar?"

"Oh yes," Sannup confirmed. "His tale has been retold for generations. An old tale, older than your kingdom. You have every right to fear Hobbomock."

"Tell me about it," Hunter muttered. "That's why I have to travel to the Deep."

"We do not usually allow this," Sannup retorted.

"But…" Hunter began, but the old man raised a hand for silence.

"But in your case," Sannup continued, "…I will make an exception. If Hobbomock's flesh is within you, his spirit cannot be allowed to grow. The Deep will stop him…or you will die in the attempt. Either way, Hobbomock will be stopped."

"Cheery thought," Hunter grumbled.

"To have Hobbomock conquer you is death," Sannup countered. "We Elders sacrifice much of our spirits to those of our ancestors, but this is our choice. It should not be forced."

"So I can go to the Deep?" Hunter asked. Sannup nodded.

"You have my permission."

"Great," Hunter replied. "We should get going then," he added, nodding at Xerxes. But Sannup shook his head.

"Not yet," he countered.

"What?"

"Before you *do*," Sannup stated, "…you must *learn*."

"I don't understand."

"What do you know about the Deep?" Sannup inquired.

"It locks in traits," Hunter answered. "Makes it so you can't be changed anymore."

Sannup frowned, considering this for a moment. Then he stepped forward until he was standing a foot from Hunter, and placed one wrinkled hand on Hunter's shoulder. He closed his eyes for a long moment, then opened them, stepping back.

"You have others' memories," he deduced. Hunter hesitated, then nodded.

"I do," he agreed. But surprisingly, despite Sannup's touch, he hadn't received any visions from him. Which meant that Sannup didn't radiate memories…and therefore had to be able to absorb them. A rare trait…one that only Hunter and Xerxes possessed. Or so they'd thought. "You do as well," he guessed.

"Yes," Sannup admitted. "Not as well as you. From you I sense nothing." He smiled. You have a rare gift, Hunter. It is…very special to us in the Kingdom of the Deep."

"Why is that?"

Sannup sighed, glancing back at the crackling bonfire behind him.

"On Turtle Island, everything has a spirit," he explained. "The trees, animals, humans…everything that crawls or flies, burrows or gallops. But only one type of spirit can live in a person." He turned back to face them. "A man can have the spirit of a woman, and a woman that of a man. A lucky few are even born with two spirits, a man and a woman in one. But these are always human spirits, always of the same animal type."

Hunter nodded, saying nothing.

"So, on Turtle Island," the Elder continued, "…we can revere the spirit of a wolf, or the thunder bird, or the snake. But we can never know what it is like to *be* them. We can never truly understand them. So our wisdom is limited."

"Makes sense," Hunter replied.

"Here," Sannup continued, raising his arms to either side, "…one spirit can be in many bodies, and many spirits can be in one body. We can take in the spirit of the wolf, and see as they see. Feel as they feel. We can understand them, see them as one of *us*. That wisdom is sacred, and it is why most of us take in the spirit of others."

"But you're…"

"Human, yes," Sannup agreed. "I have taken in the spirit of my ancestors, the humans from Turtle Island. Their bones live here, in this temple, and give us their spirits. Kip has done the same…the human spirit is what we have chosen. That is our great sacrifice, to never know the spirit of other creatures."

"You *want* to be like an animal?" Hunter inquired. Sannup smiled.

"Of course," he replied. "One cannot treat their fellow creatures with contempt if they allow wild spirits into themselves. Everything has a spirit, and to become one with the world, one must allow the world into oneself."

"Ok," Hunter conceded. "But you worship the Deep, right?"

"We revere it, yes."

"But the Deep locks traits in," he pointed out. "It prevents things from absorbing traits…spirits. Why revere it if it stops you from being able to do that?"

Sannup chuckled, shaking his head.

"The Deep is the Creator," he explained. "It does not lock in traits, as you say. It combines the spirits and flesh of creatures, making them *one* spirit. *One* flesh. It creates new spirits."

"But my mother," Hunter protested. "She went to the Deep and locked in her traits." He explained what had happened to his mother, how she'd been transformed into an Ironclad, her traits locked in forever. Sannup shook his head.

"Her traits were not locked in," he countered gently. "She was what you call a Legend, the strongest of the spirits, and the most selfish. Such spirits refuse to take in other spirits, yet seek to destroy all other spirits they come in contact with. When she combined with the beetle, her spirit and the beetle's spirit became *one* spirit…one that, as she is a Legend, cannot be changed."

"So if she hadn't been a Legend?"

"Then she would have been able to be changed," Sannup concluded.

Hunter stared at the man, feeling his heart sink.

"So it won't work," he realized. "Even if I go to the Deep, I won't be able to stop Zagamar."

"Incorrect," Sannup countered. "Hobbomock's spirit will fuse with yours in its current state, and his spirit will no longer be able to destroy yours. But you will still be able to take in new spirits."

"But if Zagamar's spirit is Legendary," Hunter retorted, "…won't *I* become a Legend?"

"No," Sannup answered. "His spirit is small within you. You will retain the strength of your own spirit."

"All right, we better get going then," Hunter decided.

"Tomorrow," Sannup stated. "You may leave tomorrow. Today I request that you study the five Temples in our kingdom."

"The what?"

"The great black towers you see," Sannup clarified. "They mark the locations of the five Temples. Each is home to the spirits of different creatures. The insects, the birds, the reptiles, the mammals, and the fish…and throughout our kingdom, the plants."

"Ah."

"You are still human," Sannup continued. "Before you go to the Deep, consider taking the spirit of a wild thing within you. You have the rarest gift, to experience a creature's memories. You should not waste it."

"Okay," Hunter agreed. It was the only way he was going to get this guy to let him go to the Deep, after all…and it was just one more day. "Let's go, Xerxes," he added.

"No," Sannup retorted.

"Pardon?"

"He does not go."

"Why not?"

"He has already accepted an animal spirit," the Elder explained. "You have not."

"Okay…"

"Go to each of the temples," Sannup requested. "Learn of the world around you. And if you choose, take an animal spirit into yourself so that you might gain its wisdom and its strength."

Chapter 5

The creature moved over the fallen leaves and branches of the forest floor, blending in with the trees and bushes around it. For although it had been an animal once, it now resembled a walking bush itself, twigs and leaves sprouting from its four bark-covered limbs. It moved slowly, its wooden joints creaking with every step.

It vaguely remembered what it had been years ago, before curling up and falling asleep near a copse of unusually large trees. Before it'd woken up to find itself transformed.

A cool breeze rustled the leaves protruding from its back and limbs, a few of the leaves falling off their stems and floating away. Many of them had turned red and brown, a sign of the winter to come. It would be the creature's third winter in its current state. Soon its limbs would stiffen further, its root-like feet plunging into the earth. Its mind would begin to slow, then wander off into a dreamlike state. A sort of sleep that would continue until the arrival of Spring, when it would become alive once again.

The breeze brought a strange scent to its nostrils. Something the creature had never smelled before.

It paused, staying perfectly still, knowing that any would-be predator would ignore it. They always did, assuming it was just another bush. It heard the *crunch, crunch* of footsteps approaching from ahead and to the right, and stared off into the forest, not even blinking.

Something dark made its way through the thick vegetation far ahead, barely visible between the trees and bushes. Something that walked on two feet. The creature had seen such beings before, and a part of it remembered them fondly.

But still it remained utterly still, watching as the dark figure made its way across its field of vision. The thing moved with a terrible quickness, zipping by and vanishing into the forest to the left.

Minutes later, the creature stirred, stepping slowly toward the path the dark figure had taken. Eventually it reached the path, lowering its head and sniffing at the ground. There were red spots on the leaf-litter, forming a trail leading where the black figure had gone.

It was blood.

The creature paused, lowering its head further and licking at one of the red drops tentatively.

A voice called out from behind.

The creature froze.

It strained its ears, but heard nothing save for the wind rustling through the leaves and the chirping of birds overhead. Still it waited, knowing that its best defense was to stay utterly still.

Minutes passed.

The creature raised its head slowly, plodding forward, following the trail of blood. The dark figure was long gone, and it did not fear the figure's return.

Voices cried out in the distance.

The creature froze again.

Minutes passed, and again, there were only the usual sounds of the forest. At length the creature continued to move, staring down at the bloody trail before it. A sudden hunger pang gripped its belly, and it paused, surprised by the feeling. It rarely needed to eat, as long as it spent enough time resting in the sun.

But now hunger called to it, demanding to be fed.

It stared at the bloodied leaves on the forest floor, then lowered its mouth to them, snatching them up and chewing slowly. Then it moved a little further, eating more of the bloodied leaves and swallowing them.

But the hunger was not appeased.

The creature stepped forward, more quickly now, gathering up more blood-spattered leaves into its mouth, barely chewing them before swallowing. But with each mouthful, the hunger only grew.

And when the voices returned, far-away yet growing louder with every passing minute, the creature didn't even bother to stop, following the bloody trail as it ate, without knowing – or caring – why.

* * *

When Hunter and Xerxes emerged from the entrance to the Shrine of the Ancestors, they found Kip waiting for them. Their jubilant guide took them back across the lake with the giant turtle Sassamon's help, reaching the opposite shore in a few short minutes. Kip turned to Xerxes then.

"I will show you a place to stay," he offered. "Hunter, you can go to each of the five Temples. When you're done, come back to the entrance to the kingdom. I will bring you to a wigwam to sleep in."

Hunter nodded. He knew from going to pow-wows with his mother as a kid that a wigwam was a dome-shaped hut used by the natives.

"How do I get to the Temples?" he inquired. Kip smiled.

"Just look around," he answered. "The towers will show you the way."

"Alright," Hunter agreed. He turned to Xerxes. "See you around I guess."

Xerxes nodded, clapping Hunter on the shoulder…and nearly throwing him to the ground. Hunter caught himself, grimacing at his smarting shoulder…and watched as Xerxes chuckled.

"Really gonna miss you," Hunter grumbled.

Kip and Xerxes left him then, and Hunter sighed, looking around. The nearest spire was the one he'd studied before, with all the birds flying around it. He stared at it uneasily; Sannup had requested that he visit *all* of the Temples before he be allowed to go to the Deep. Hunter might get away with skipping one, but then again he might not. There was no point in testing that theory…they were on a time-crunch, after all. He sighed, starting the long walk toward the bird-spire.

Might as well get this over with.

It wasn't long before the scenery changed from grassy fields with occasional trees to a dense forest. The trees here grew much taller than the ones he'd seen before, rising well over a hundred feet above the forest floor. Hunter spotted more huge birds perched on the uppermost branches. It was almost certainly his paranoia – he was too far away to even see their faces – but he could almost swear they were staring at him.

A narrow path through the forest led to the spire ahead, and Hunter took it, trying to ignore the fauna above. Eventually he spotted a large black stone building in a clearing ahead, much like the Shrine of the Ancestors. But this one was considerably larger, and the huge black spire rose up from its center. Birds were perched on short ledges all the way up the spire…*huge* birds.

Great, he muttered to himself. *Just great.*

It took all of his courage to continue walking toward the building, and when he did, a bird leapt from its perch high above, swooping down…and gliding straight at him!

Hunter cursed, pulling his longsword free from its sheath. But the bird slowed abruptly, landing a few yards from him.

"No need for your sword," the bird stated calmly.

Hunter blinked.

For the bird was not a bird at all. Or at least, not completely. Its feet were part human, part talon, with long toes ending in short claws. Its legs were mostly human, although the knees bent backward instead of forward. It had a humanoid torso, but with a chest that was narrow and pulled outward. And its face was almost completely human, save for striking yellow eyes. But instead of hair, fine white feathers graced its scalp, and most of its body was also covered in feathers. And its wings were utterly massive, far longer than human arms…which it didn't have.

"You can put your weapon away," the bird-man insisted. Hunter blinked, then looked down, seeing his sword still in his hands. He sheathed it, returning his gaze to the…thing.

"What…?" he began.

"My name is Pukwa," the bird-man greeted. He gestured with one wing at the building behind him. "Welcome to the Shrine of Wobsacuck."

"Uh…" Hunter mumbled, clearing his throat. "Wobsa…what?"

"Wobsacuck," Pukwa repeated. "It means 'eagle.' A shrine to all birds."

"Ah."

"I assume the Elders sent you here," Pukwa continued. Hunter frowned.

"How'd you know that?"

"I watched you come into the kingdom," Pukwa answered. "And follow Kip to the Shrine of the Ancestors, and then come here." He smirked. "I *can* fly, you know. And we who take the spirit of birds have excellent vision."

"So you really do have eagle-eyes," Hunter joked rather lamely. Pukwa chuckled.

"Literally," he agreed.

"Sannup sent me to each of the shrines to check them out," Hunter informed. He glanced at the building ahead. "You know where the entrance is?"

"Of course," Pukwa answered. "But you won't be able to get to it on your own."

"Why's that?"

"It's on the roof."

Hunter frowned; the roof surrounding the spire was a good four to five stories up, and the spire had to be hundreds of feet tall.

"There a ladder or something?"

"No," Pukwa answered. "I'll have to fly you up."

"Oh hell no," Hunter blurted out.

"Hmm?"

"I'm not flying up there," he stated.

"Why not?"

"What if you drop me?" Hunter asked. Pukwa chuckled.

"I've carried a lot heavier," he reassured. "I'll grab your arm and bring you up."

"No thanks," Hunter replied. "I'm good. I'll just skip this one and go…"

Pukwa leapt into the air, his huge wings swooping down, a blast of air striking Hunter. Before he knew it, the bird-man's talon-feet had gripped his right arm, latching on with incredible force. With a few beats of his wings, Pukwa shot up into the air…bringing Hunter with him.

"Oh SHIIIIIT!" Hunter yelled, kicking his legs as the earth dropped out from underneath him. Pukwa took them higher, his powerful wings bringing them upward until they were well above the five-story roof of the shrine ahead. Then Pukwa spread his wings out wide, gliding down toward the rooftop. The roof came at them with terrifying speed, and Hunter cried out again, bracing for impact. But at the last moment, Pukwa slowed their descent, and with a few beats of his wings, dropped Hunter gently on the rooftop, releasing his vise-like grip on Hunter's arm. Pukwa landed beside Hunter, gesturing at a doorway at the base of the spire ahead.

"There's the entrance," he informed. "Come on," he added, walking toward it, "…I'll show you around."

Hunter followed behind Pukwa, rubbing his right arm where the man's talon-feet had gripped it. They made it to the entrance, and Pukwa tucked his wings close to his body, stepping inside. Much like the Shrine of the Ancestors, there were stairs leading downward. These, however, spiraled downward for a short distance before opening up into a large room, the stairs turning rightward to descend alongside the nearest wall. The room was octagonal in shape, and perhaps a hundred feet in diameter, with a ceiling fifty feet up. Hunter and Pukwa had emerged near the top.

"Wow," Hunter blurted out, stopping in his tracks. There were dozens of people down below, some of them bird-men hybrids like Pukwa, and others appearing completely – or mostly – human. The hybrids were of many different types, some as short as four feet tall, others over eight. Some had brown feathers, others had black, and still others had white or gray. A few even had beaks, much to Hunter's surprise.

"Come on," Pukwa prompted. "The stairs are more difficult for me, so I'll fly down." He did just that, leaping off the edge of the stairs and gliding to the floor far below. Hunter watched him, then made his way down the stairs. Not without some jealousy; it took him a whole lot longer to reach the bottom and meet up with Pukwa. From here, he could see that there were wide hallways leading away from the room at each wall of the hexagon.

"So," Hunter stated, glancing around. "What now?"

"Each shrine has a central hub like this room," Pukwa explained. "The hallways lead to the rooms where our people choose and acquire spirits, and the many floors below-ground house the spirits themselves."

"Okay…"

"Come," Pukwa urged, tapping Hunter's back with one wing, then walking toward the nearest hallway. Hunter followed alongside the man-bird, glancing at other people as they went. Some of them had wings instead of arms, while a few had wings *and* arms.

"Why do some of these people have arms?" he asked.

"There are many ways to acquire spirits," Pukwa answered. "I chose to be closer to a bird and forgo my arms. Others wish to keep theirs."

"What do you mean by 'many ways to acquire spirits?'" Hunter pressed as they stepped into the hallway. There were several men and women within, all of them gazing at various birds bolted to the walls. Dead birds, of course, stuffed in an impressive feat of taxidermy. These were quite large, although Hunter didn't recognize most of the species.

"You will see," Pukwa replied. He gestured with one talon-foot at the wall to their left. "These are the larger birds of prey…those that hunt other animals. That is what your people call a bald eagle," he added, gesturing at one of the displays. "I chose its spirit. That," he continued, pointing at another display, "…is a type of falcon, and that is a type of condor."

"So if you see a bird you like, you can absorb its traits?"

"You can share its spirit, yes," Pukwa agreed.

"And the spirits are below-ground."

"Correct."

"So their bones are down there?" Hunter inquired. Pukwa nodded. "But what if my…spirit is too strong to be changed?"

"Your spirit is strong," Pukwa stated. "But the spirits below are the strongest."

"You mean they're all Legends?"

"Yes," Pukwa confirmed. "Over the millennia, we have collected powerful spirits of almost every species of bird."

"Wow," Hunter mumbled. And to think that the kingdom of Tykus was all excited about having the bones of *one* Legend. He glanced at Pukwa as they continued down the hall. "But if they're Legends, won't people just be turned into birds? How can you control the process?"

"We have perfected it," Pukwa replied. "We have many ways to transmit spirits. You can gain the eyes of an eagle, or its wings, or its feet, or all of these things…whatever you choose."

Hunter stopped, and Pukwa stopped with him.

"You're saying that – if I wanted to – I could grow wings? And fly like you?" Hunter asked. Pukwa smiled.

"Of course."

Hunter stared at the bird-man for a moment, then turned back to the exhibits, staring at a few of the birds. One of them caught his eye; a large bird with a wingspan that had to be seven feet long. It had pitch-black feathers on top of its wings and white feathers – with the occasional black-striped feather – underneath.

"What's that?" he asked.

"A harpy eagle," Pukwa answered. "They were found to the south on Turtle Island. They are very strong, and are great fliers. They fly between trees with great speed."

"Nice."

They continued down the hall, until at last they reached the end. There were so many birds that they all began to blur together.

"The owls and kites are on the next floor up," Pukwa explained. "The third floor has the hawks, and the fourth the condors and vultures."

"That's a lot of birds," Hunter grumbled. He was surprised that he wasn't more paranoid here, being surrounded by things he hated. But they weren't alive…which is probably why he hadn't run out screaming. He hesitated, stepping toward one of the last exhibits…another eagle-like bird. "Can I touch it?"

"Gently," Pukwa answered.

Hunter stopped a few inches from the eagle, taking off his helmet. Then he bent down, touching his forehead to the top of its head and closing his eyes.

And jerked back with a gasp.

"Whoa," he breathed, shaking his head. Pukwa frowned.

"What's wrong?"

"I…absorb memories," Hunter explained. "I could feel myself flying…diving down toward the ground to kill a rabbit." Pukwa's eyebrows rose.

"You can sense memories?" he asked. "That is a rare gift."

"It was a hell of a rush," Hunter admitted.

"Do you want to see more birds, or would you like to see how we acquire spirits?"

"The second," Hunter answered, putting his helmet back on.

* * *

Pukwa led Hunter to the fifth floor of the shrine, where – instead of the usual exhibits – there were long hallways with rooms on either side. The rooms were small, the walls, floors, and ceilings covered by sheets of compressed wood. In the center of each room was a wooden cot; Pukwa brought Hunter to a room occupied by a woman. To Hunter's embarrassment, she was utterly nude, and lying face-up on the cot. A bird-man with arms was standing over her, taking long strips of what looked to be bark and wrapping them around her legs.

"Will she mind if…" Hunter began, gesturing at the woman.

"She does not mind," Pukwa said. "Watch."

More sheets of bark were wrapped around her legs, spiraling up to her groin. Then her pelvis and abdomen were covered, stopping below her breasts. The bird-man attending her took a wide sheet of bark, turning it upside-down, then grabbing a brush from a nearby wooden table. He dipped it in a clay jar of thick, clear liquid, painting the underside of the bark carefully.

"The bark absorbs spirits poorly," Pukwa explained. "It will protect her legs and body from the effects of the bird-spirit."

Hunter nodded. It made sense; Master Thorius and Vi had taught him that wood absorbed and transmitted traits poorly, which was why most of the buildings in the Outskirts had been made of wood…as had the paper-thin walls of the Guild of Seekers.

The bird-man attending the woman finished painting the clear gel onto the bark, then flipped it right-side-up, having the woman stand up while he placed it carefully over her breasts.

"The liquid was exposed to the spirit of a bird," Pukwa explained. "The chest muscles are needed to use one's wings. She wants to keep her arms," he added, gesturing at her bark-wrapped arms. "She will need to double her chest muscles and back muscles, one on top of the other. One set will move her arms, the other her wings."

"So her chest is exposed to the liquid, but nothing else is?" Hunter guessed.

"Her back will be," Pukwa corrected. "The wings are like arms, and will grow from a second set of shoulder blades on top of the first. Watch," he added.

The rest of the woman's body was wrapped…and then a layer of what looked to be peat moss was glued to the bark everywhere…and a second layer of bark was wrapped around her body. And then a third.

"They will use many layers," Pukwa explained. Each layer helps block the spirits."

Hunter nodded again. Subsequent layers did protect against the transmission of wills…a fact Master Thorius and Vi had also taught him. Each time a trait was absorbed by a substance, the power of that trait was diminished considerably. With multiple layers of different materials, very little of one's will would be able to be transmitted.

"You guys really have this figured out," Hunter murmured. Pukwa smiled.

"We have been perfecting this art for over ten thousand years."

Hunter gave a low whistle, then watched as the bird-man took a smaller brush, dipping it in the clear gel and gently painting the woman's closed eyelids. He took a wooden mask then, placing it on her face.

"This will give her the sight of a bird," Pukwa explained. "The mask helps prevents her nose from becoming a beak."

Hunter turned to Pukwa, noting the man's yellow eyes.

"What is it like?" he asked. "Seeing like a bird."

"I have eagle-eyes," Pukwa replied. "My vision is far sharper than yours, and I can distinguish between similar colors better, and I can spot a rabbit from over two kilometers away."

"Cool."

"I also have two set of eyelids," Pukwa continued. A thin, translucent membrane covered his eyes suddenly, then opened again. "I can see through them reasonably well even when I blink."

Hunter nodded turning back to the woman on the table.

"Why's everything wood?" he asked.

"To prevent the floor and walls and ceiling from absorbing spirits," Pukwa replied. "The wood will be disposed of after the procedure, and new, fresh wood will be put in its place."

"I take it the wood's…spirit is weak?"

"It is," Pukwa confirmed. "We do not want our birds turning into trees."

Hunter smirked at that, watching for a while longer. Then he began to fidget.

"What now?" he asked.

"If you are done," Pukwa answered, "…then you can go to another shrine. If you want, I can fly you."

Hunter considered this, then shook his head.

"Thanks, but I think I'll walk."

Chapter 6

It'd been days since Dominus had left the pond where he'd awoken, making his way through the deep forest on the long journey to Lady Camilla's mansion. The going hadn't been made any easier by the fact that he was utterly naked, rocks and sticks underfoot jabbing at his vulnerable flesh. Not to mention the blood-sucking mosquitos. If there was any consolation, it was that his newfound ability to heal seemed to prevent him from getting bug bites, and any scrapes or other minor injuries healed within the hour. He foraged as he went, eating whatever he could. Wracked by hunger – his body still emaciated – he stuffed himself with mushrooms and leaves, hardly worried about getting sick or poisoned. He'd heal from that too, he knew. And after being burned alive, any discomfort such things caused would seem mild in comparison.

It was the wild wills *within* the plants he consumed that worried him. What they might be doing to him. How they might be changing him. His will was strong, but there had to be more powerful wills within the forest; if he were to consume a Legendary mushroom or plant, his doom would be sealed. He had to be extremely careful, making sure to check if there were clusters of identical-looking plants…a sign of a powerful will exerting its power on the organisms around it.

So it was that he traveled, one foot in front of the other, trying to enjoy the feeling of his bare feet on the forest floor, as Tykus had instructed him to. To feel connected to the land, to the things around him. One foot in front of the other, day after day, until the days blended together. By the time he reached the shore of a wide river, he'd lost track of just how long he'd been walking for. It was, he knew, the River Ormr…the river upon whose banks Lady Camilla's mansion had been built.

Dominus paused before the river, looking upstream, then downstream. He doubted that Farkus had brought him more than a few kilometers away from the Castle Wexford before dumping his charred body…which meant that he was almost certainly downstream of Lady Camilla. He turned left, following the river upstream.

Onward he went for another few hours, stopping every once and again to take a drink of water from the river. He felt stronger than he had yesterday, his body having filled out a little with each passing day. And it would get even stronger, he knew. For, though he was over seventy years old, his skin was now that of a much younger man. Not only had the Ironclad's head given him the power to regenerate, it'd also reversed the ravages of time, slowly transforming him into a younger version of himself. He was perhaps fifty now, by the looks of his reflection in the river. His hair was gray mixed with blond, what little of it he had after being set on fire.

King Tykus's words came to him then.

Be what I can never be…eternal, one life extending forever into the future, gathering the wisdom we so desperately need.

An impossible charge, to be expected to approach anything close to that great man's wisdom. But Dominus would do as his king requested. He would try.

It was nearly sunset by the time he saw a clearing ahead…and the unmistakable five-story-tall U-shaped building beyond. A white stone building with blood-red shingles composing its roof, it was similar to the Lady's family's former residence in the Acropolis, before they'd fled to the countryside during the civil war. But Camilla had made it her own, transforming her family business from simple academics to a bustling hub for the buying and selling of wild artifacts. Artifacts that, had she possessed in the kingdom, would have earned her the death sentence many times over.

Dominus resisted the urge to grimace, knowing that he was now guilty of the same crime. Neither one of them was welcome in Tykus…ever again.

He paused before the end of the forest ahead, staring at the mansion, then down at himself. He was utterly nude…hardly a state in which to seek audience with a Lady. But there was no choice. He took a deep breath in, then stepped out of the trees, forcing himself to stand tall. Dignity was a state of mind, after all. Striding all the way up to the fence surrounding the mansion, he stopped before a closed gate, watching as the silver-armored guard beyond stared at him.

"Get lost," the guard ordered, waving Dominus away.

"I am here for an audience with Lady Camilla," Dominus declared. The guard stared at him, then burst out laughing. He waited patiently for the man to finish, doing his best to give the guard an imperious glare.

"Get outta here," the man replied at last.

"The Lady would not be pleased if she learned of your having turned me away," Dominus warned.

"Oh yeah?" the guard inquired. "And who should I say is requesting her presence?" he added mockingly. Dominus considered the ways in which he could answer this question.

"Duke Dominus of Wexford," he answered.

That shut the guard up.

"Hold on," the man muttered, turning around and walking up to the double-doors leading into the mansion, guarded by two more men. He went inside, and several minutes later he returned, walking up to the gate. He unlocked it, gesturing for Dominus to step through. "The Lady will see you," he stated.

Dominus stepped through the gate, making his way up to the front double-doors. He glanced to the right, seeing a huge silver statue of a snake-like creature with innumerable legs like a centipede set back in a field of crops beside the stone path. It was several stories tall, coiled upon itself. A remarkable likeness of the Lady's signature animal, the horned serpent – a creature both revered and feared by the denizens of the Kingdom of the Deep.

He reached the front double-doors, waiting as the guards standing before them opened the doors, allowing him to step through into the foyer beyond. It was a spacious room, the ceiling some seven meters above supported by large red beams. The floor was made of polished cherry, the walls painted a deep red, the Lady's signature color. A fine establishment, if rather plain compared to Dominus's castle at Wexford. *Former* castle.

He strode across the room toward another set of double-doors ahead. The guard accompanying him gestured for him to stop a few meters before the doors. Moments later, they opened, and a woman stepped through them, flanked by two masked men in black and red uniforms. She was tall and slender, and wore a long, blood-red dress that showed off her every curve. Of which she possessed many, in all the proper proportions. A dark red corset studded with rubies glittered as she strode toward Dominus, her ample cleavage threatening to spill out of its deep V-cut. Long black hair spilled down her back in thick waves, the occasional gray hair all that hinted at her true age. For she was striking beautiful…and she clearly knew it.

"Dominus," she greeted, stopping a few meters from him and inclining her head slightly. Then her gaze dropped to his groin, lingering there for a moment. "Your sword is unsheathed," she noted. "Are you planning on stabbing me?"

"Camilla," Dominus replied. "Give me some clothes and I'll put it away."

"If you insist," she stated. "You look…sick," she noted. "Are you all right?"

"Nothing a few good meals can't fix," he answered.

"To what do I owe the pleasure of your visit, Duke of…?"

Dominus suppressed a grimace. She was intentionally leaving out his former duchy…a particularly clever way of saying that he was duke of nothing at all. Which meant she knew of his 'murder' by Farkus's hand…and almost certainly knew how he'd survived the attempt. Like her or hate her, Lady Camilla was incredibly resourceful…and possessed of a formidable intellect. Two traits that made her exceedingly dangerous.

"I came here," he replied, "…to make you a deal."

CHAPTER 7

Hunter sat down on a small boulder at the shore of a large pond, glancing up at the sun. It'd swung across the sky, now well on its way to falling toward the horizon. There were still a few hours of sunlight left by his estimation, which was rather surprising considering the sheer amount of stuff he'd done throughout the day. He sighed, kicking off his boots and wiggling his aching toes.

After the shrine with the birds, he'd gone to the next shrine...one with reptiles of all kinds. There'd been underground pools where turtle-people got to swim around, and lizard-men that could climb walls and had prehensile tails. The shrine after that had been filled with insects and arachnids. If there was anything Hunter hated more than birds, it was spiders; he'd spent as little time there as possible. The mammalian shrine had been far less bizarre...and not very interesting, other than a few cat-women he'd seen. Their lithe, nude bodies covered in silky fur had been oddly appealing. He'd been caught staring more than once, and had moved on quickly thereafter.

The final shrine he'd visited had been the underwater one...a black stone building like the others, but set beneath a large lake, the shrine's black spire emerging from the water. Someone resembling the creature from the black lagoon had helped him, recommending that he remove everything but his underclothes. Hunter had done so only under the assurance that no one would be interested in stealing his stuff; the fish-man had then helped swim Hunter to a small stone dock at the spire. A doorway there at the base of the spire had led him down – below the surface of the water – to a shrine similar to the others. Except with pools everywhere. Thank goodness the place had been waterproof, with plenty of breathable air. After gazing at more than a few men-fish, crab-men, and even a jellyfish-woman hybrid, Hunter had had quite enough. Being able to breathe underwater seemed like a cool ability, but gills looked ridiculous on people. He didn't consider himself to be particularly vain, but even he had his limits.

One interesting thing he'd learned was that all of the lakes and ponds in the Kingdom of the Deep had underground homes or habitats where the fish-people lived…and that the sea was only a few miles away. Citizens wishing to absorb saltwater spirits started their metamorphosis here, then were brought to the sea to complete it.

Hunter yawned, stretching his arms up above his head, then looking around. He spotted the first spire he'd visited in the distance. Birds still circled it, gliding lazily in the cooling air. He closed his eyes, recalling the short memory he'd absorbed from the dead eagle earlier, remembering what it felt like to fly.

It'd been pretty damn cool.

He was struck by the sudden urge to go back to the shrine, even if just to look at the birds again…and to talk to Pukwa. He wanted to see more of the transformation process…to see how it all actually worked over time.

"Might as well," he mumbled to himself. He wasn't supposed to meet up with Xerxes back at the entrance until sunset, after all.

He slipped his boots back on, making the long walk back to the Shrine of Birds. He was nearly there when a familiar bird-man flew down to meet him.

"Hello again," Pukwa greeted, landing a few feet from him and folding his wings behind his back. "Did you enjoy the other shrines?"

"Some yes, some no," Hunter admitted. Pukwa chuckled.

"I know what you mean," he agreed. "The Shrine of Insects is not to my liking."

"Mine either."

"Although a few of my colleagues consider it a buffet," Pukwa added with a wink, glancing up at the other birds. Hunter smirked.

"If they eat spiders, I'm all for it."

"Some do," Pukwa admitted.

"I'd like to go back up if you don't mind," Hunter stated. "I was hoping to see more of the…uh, spirit transfer process." Pukwa raised an eyebrow, his eyes twinkling.

"You're drawn to our shrine?"

"Little bit."

"I'll take you up," Pukwa agreed.

He swooped forward and upward, grabbing Hunter's arm as before and lifting him off the ground. Seconds later, they landed on top of the building, and walked back in through the small entrance. Hunter found himself back in the huge main room, and took the stairs all the way down to the bottom, meeting Pukwa there. They made their way up to the fifth floor again, stopping before one of the small rooms there. A man was being wrapped as they watched…but the sheets wrapped around his arms were being painted with that clear gel.

"He wishes to have only wings, not arms," Pukwa explained.

They watched the wrapping process, and then Hunter turned to Pukwa, eyeing him for a long moment. Or more specifically, eyeing his wings. To be able to fly…it was pretty damn tempting. And not just for traveling. If he could fly, Tykus's soldiers wouldn't be able to reach him, other than crossbowmen and archers. And if he flew high enough up, they wouldn't be able to reach him at all. Any advantage he could get in the upcoming war would not just benefit him…it could save the lives of his friends and his new people, the Ironclad.

"Yes?" Pukwa asked, snapping Hunter out of his reverie.

"Uh," Hunter mumbled, realizing he was still staring at the bird-man. He turned back to the man being wrapped on the table. "So, hypothetically, if I wanted to do this, would I be able to?"

"Of course," Pukwa answered, breaking out into a big smile. "We would be honored to have you among us!"

"Really?" Hunter pressed. "I could just…do it?"

"Yes."

"How much does it cost?" he inquired. Pukwa laughed.

"We don't use money here," he replied. "That is for other kingdoms. Everyone works to help each other. Those who are honorable may take on the animal spirits we have collected."

"How do you know I'm honorable?" Hunter pressed. Pukwa smirked.

"The Guardians can see memories, like you."

"The Guardians?" Hunter asked. Kip had spoken about them earlier.

"Suffice it so say that you are welcome here."

"Ah."

"If you wish to take the spirit of a bird, you must choose one," Pukwa informed. "Then we can begin."

"When?"

"Whenever you like," Pukwa answered. Hunter paused. He was going to leave with Xerxes tomorrow for the Deep.

"I have to leave tomorrow," he confessed.

"You can start the process today," Pukwa replied. "Your spirit is strong, so we can use a more powerful extract. We can also use needles coated in the extract to put the spirit in your body. This will speed up the process, and the wrappings will only have to stay on for a day or two."

"Needles?"

"An alternative to painting the wrappings," Pukwa explained. "If done properly, the wrappings aren't necessary. But it is painful."

Hunter considered this. If he was really going to go through with this, he'd have to go the quicker route, especially if the Deep was going to lock in his traits afterward. And there was no doubt in his mind that Xerxes wouldn't approve, which means he had to hide it from the big guy until it was too late for the brute to do anything about it.

"Pain I can take," Hunter replied at last. He'd experienced awful, painful deaths many times, at least in the memories he'd absorbed from the animals and people he'd killed. A little acupuncture was nothing.

"We puncture the bone," Pukwa warned. Hunter hesitated.

"You got any pain medication?"

"We have alcohol," Pukwa offered. Hunter smirked.

"That'll do."

* * *

The wooden cot was stiff and uncomfortable, but not as uncomfortable as being stripped and lying belly-up in front of the bird-woman attending him, not to mention Pukwa, who had chosen to stay to watch the process. Being rather spectacularly gifted in the groin department, Hunter had noticed the bird-woman peeking more than once. It didn't help that she was young and quite attractive, and that people here generally didn't wear shirts. Or that she was perilously close to his groin as she wrapped his uppermost thighs with the first layer of bark. To his chagrin, there was a definite – and obvious – change in blood flow when her hand accidently brushed his member as she finished wrapping his left leg. He ordered it to reverse course immediately…and it defied him.

Most definitively.

Hunter grimaced, glad that the warmth in his cheeks would not be visible to those watching due to the darkness of his skin. He caught the bird-woman admiring the show, and his cheeks burned even hotter. To think that Pukwa was watching! The thought made his body reverse course rapidly, and soon the problem was resolved. The bird-lady resumed her work, wrapping his groin region next. Which started the process all over again.

Oh for Christ's sake!

Upward she went, wrapping his belly, then stopping just underneath his pecs. She switched to wrapping his arms then, and his hands. The bird-lady was quick but gentle, and soon only his chest and back were left unwrapped, as well as his head.

Then came the peat moss, and another layer of wrapping. And then more moss, and more wrapping.

The process took quite some time…which gave Hunter plenty of time to second-guess his choice. He'd rushed into the decision, after all. And for what? Was he *really* going to grow a pair of wings? How would he sleep? How would he swim? What if he hated them…could he just cut them off? But he'd have two sets of shoulder blades, and two sets of pec muscles.

His heart started to race. He suddenly felt claustrophobic, wrapped like a goddamn mummy in this small-ass room.

What the hell are you doing?

"All right," Pukwa stated, breaking Hunter's train of thought. "Sit up…time for your medicine."

Hunter sat up stiffly, and the bird-lady handed him a clay jar filled with liquid.

"What's this?" he asked.

"Alcohol," she replied with a smile.

"Ah," Hunter mumbled.

"Drink up," she prompted, putting a hand on his upper thigh. She was still smiling…and it was suddenly very clear that there was intention behind that smile, and her touch. He found his gaze dropping to her bare breasts, and he blinked, trying to focus on her eyes. But he was already growing again, giving her wrapping skills a run for their money.

"Cheers," he stated…then took down the drink in a few rapid gulps.

"Oh my," she murmured, putting a hand to her mouth.

"Well, he's definitely not going to feel any pain," Pukwa declared with a smirk. "At least not until tomorrow."

The bird-woman pushed Hunter gently back down, and then asked him to roll onto his belly. He did so, laying face-down on the cot. He could hear her doing something off to the side, but he couldn't see her. It wasn't long before his head began to swim rather pleasantly.

"This is nice," he murmured.

"Don't move," he heard the woman order.

"I'll do anything you say," he replied with a smile, slurring his words a little. "Damn, but that was some strong shit," he added.

And then he felt a sharp pinch in the back of his left shoulder.

"Ow!" he blurted out, stiffening. He felt a hand on the back of his head, massaging his scalp gently.

"Shhh," the woman murmured. "Let it happen."

"First time I've been penetrated," he slurred, chuckling at his own joke. "Can't say I…ow!"

There was another pinching sensation, then another, all in his left shoulder. But the alcohol had its effect, and he found the pain markedly less as the minutes passed. Or rather, he just didn't give a damn about the pain anymore.

Again and again came the pinching, going from his left shoulder all the way to between his shoulder blades, then to the right. Then came a much stronger pain at his shoulder blades. He grimaced at this, but said nothing. Eventually they had him turn onto his back. The room spun for a bit afterward, eventually settling down. He saw the lady-bird standing over him, and this time he abandoned all decorum, staring at her marvelous top.

"You," he slurred, giving her a big smile, "…are beeeyoootiful."

"Aww," she replied, smiling down at him angelically. "Thank you."

"I mean it," he insisted. "I'm not just saying it 'cause I'm drunk." He grinned sheepishly. "No, yes I am. I just *thought* it when I wasn't drunk. But now I'm saying it."

"You're beautiful too," she replied, patting him on the chest.

"You got a boyfriend?" he inquired.

"No."

"Good," Hunter replied.

She grabbed a long needle then, dipping it into a clay pot. Then she placed the needle over Hunter's bare chest.

"Hold still," she ordered...and plunged the needle into his pec.

"Ooo," he breathed, processing this new pain. He watched her pull the needle out, then dip it in the pot again. Then he decided it would be best to close his eyes. He felt more pinching as she methodically punctured his entire chest, wincing the most as she went over his breastbone. Then, at long last, she was done. She finished by wrapping his chest and back, after which she had him sit up. Slowly.

"You did well," the bird-lady stated.

"Thanks," Hunter replied. He got off the table – with Pukwa's help – and turned to face her. "Hey, I never got your name."

"You will," she replied with a little smile, "...if you come back."

Hunter gave her a lopsided grin, and Pukwa walked him out of the room, guiding him across the long hallway toward the stairs to the lower levels. The combination of the alcohol and the stiff wrappings made the going slow, but eventually they exited the shrine, emerging onto the roof. Pukwa flew Hunter all the way across the kingdom to the entrance, a nausea-inducing flight. It was all Hunter could do to stop himself from decorating the landscape with the contents of his stomach.

Pukwa dropped Hunter off at the entrance to the kingdom, and he found Xerxes waiting for him there. He stumbled up to his brother, giving him a big, sloppy smile.

"Hey bruh," he greeted, slapping the big guy on the shoulder. "Howzit...going?"

Xerxes stared down at him.

"WHAT...THIS?" he asked, gesturing at Hunter's wrappings.

"I'm drunk," Hunter replied.

"WHAT THIS?" Xerxes repeated, jabbing his wrappings with one big finger.

"Got a...massage," Hunter answered. "Acoo...puncture," he added helpfully. Xerxes grunted.

"WE...GO."

And with that, the big lug picked Hunter up, carrying him in his arms and walking toward one of the round huts nearby. The wigwams. Xerxes entered one of them, lowering Hunter onto a pile of soft animal furs on the floor.

“Hope you got your own room,” Hunter mumbled, “…‘cause you ain’t spooning me, I’m telling you that right now.”

And with that, he fell fast asleep.

Chapter 8

The next morning was not good.

Hunter woke to Xerxes stomping into his hut, the sound heralding the arrival of a pounding headache. He groaned, rolling away from the big guy…and was immediately hauled to his feet. It took a moment for Hunter to remember where he was…and more distressingly, why he was wrapped up like a goddamn mummy.

"Shit," he muttered, staring down at himself. His entire chest and upper back were sore, not to mention his shoulders.

"GO…NOW," Xerxes ordered…and turned about, stomping out of the hut. Hunter rubbed his eyes, then realized that his brother wasn't going to wait up for him. He ran after the guy, his wrappings making the going a bit difficult.

"Hey, wait," he protested. "My stuff!"

Xerxes lifted one arm into the air, holding up Hunter's pack. His sword and bow were strapped to it.

"My clothes in there?" Hunter asked.

"YES."

Hunter sighed, falling into step next to his brother. He couldn't tell which was worse, the soreness from the literal needling he'd taken, or the headache from the "pain medicine" Pukwa had given him. Or the embarrassment from whatever dumb shit he'd told that nice bird-woman when he was drunk.

Or the fact that he'd gone and done something really, *really* stupid.

Fuck.

He stared at his feet as they made their way across the Kingdom of the Deep, toward the opposite end of the entrance they'd come through the day before. Apparently there was an exit leading to the Deep.

Couldn't've just gotten a damn tattoo, he muttered to himself. *Noooo. You had to get yourself a fucking pair of wings!*

He contemplated tearing his wrappings off, but the fear of having more parts of him turn into a bird stopped him. There was nothing he could do now…other than hope that the fact that he'd only been in this world for a few months would prevent the procedure from actually working. Some of his body still hadn't incorporated the substance of this world, after all. That meant that parts of him shouldn't be able to absorb traits.

Hunter sighed, walking in silence beside his brother, who thankfully kept the pace relatively slow. They circled around the huge lake in the center of the kingdom, eventually reaching the black stone wall that encircled the kingdom. There were indeed stairs leading up to an arched entrance there, and they soon passed through the archway and out of the Kingdom of the Deep.

"Well that was interesting," Hunter grumbled. The land beyond was a dense forest, and Xerxes took them due west. "What'd you do all day yesterday?"

"EAT."

"Anything else?" Hunter inquired.

"SLEEP."

"Sounds like you had a swell time," Hunter muttered. Xerxes glanced at him.

"What happened to you?" he signed, pointing a finger at Hunter. "What's this?" he added, gesturing at the wrappings still…well, wrapped around Hunter. Hunter grimaced.

"Ever done something stupid when you were drunk?" he asked. Xerxes shook his head, and Hunter frowned. "Ever *been* drunk?" Another shake of the head.

"LIVED IN…CAVE."

"Ah, right."

Xerxes gestured at Hunter's wrappings again. It was clear the big guy wasn't going to let it go.

"I got suckered into letting a nice bird-lady give me a spa treatment," Hunter explained. Xerxes did the Ironclad equivalent of raising an eyebrow…not that he had any. "She was cute. *Really* cute."

Xerxes considered this.

"HAVE…SEX?"

"Unfortunately no," Hunter replied. Xerxes chuckled, slapping Hunter on the back…and sending him stumbling forward. He caught himself, gritting his teeth at the fresh wave of pain the slap had added to his already sore back. "She offered to if we came back," he added defensively. "I think."

"Then we go back," Xerxes signed with a big smile. Hunter couldn't help but smile himself.

"Aww, thanks bro."

"SEX…GOOD," Xerxes opined. Hunter grimaced, remembering his ordeal with Trixie…and with Lady Camilla.

“Sometimes,” he muttered. Xerxes nodded in agreement.

They continued onward through the forest, neither man or beast speaking for a long moment. Then Hunter turned back to Xerxes.

“How long until we get to the Deep?” he inquired.

“Two, three days,” Xerxes signed.

Hunter nodded, trying to recall what Pukwa had told him. The bird-man had said it’d be fine to take off the wrappings within a day or so, if he remembered correctly. He’d keep them on for longer, of course. Mostly out of paranoia, but also to hide any…changes from his brother for as long as possible. If there *were* any changes. A part of him doubted that anything would happen.

Onward they went, trekking through the seemingly never-ending forest for a few hours. Eventually they came to a stream, and stopped to drink…and to rest Hunter’s legs. Xerxes, on account of his incredible ability to heal, seemed to never tire. Like, *never*. Hunter supposed it made sense; any damage to Xerxes’ muscles would be nearly instantly repaired, after all.

Hydrated and quasi-rested, they continued through the forest. Hunter’s hangover gradually abated, and even the soreness in his back didn’t seem so back anymore.

“Is it easier to talk after you’ve been with me for a few days?” Hunter inquired. Xerxes nodded. “That’s good.” He paused. “Hey,” he added. “You got a girlfriend or something?”

“MANY.”

“Oh ho!” Hunter exclaimed, slapping Xerxes on the lower back and grinning mischievously. “Xerxes the player!” Xerxes just stared at him uncomprehendingly. “It means you get a lot of ass,” Hunter clarified. Xerxes nodded at this.

“MUCH…ASS,” he agreed.

“Lucky bastard,” Hunter said. Then he raised an eyebrow. “Got any kids?”

“YES.”

“Oh yeah? How many?” Hunter inquired. Xerxes shrugged, and Hunter chuckled, shaking his head. “Wow. That’s…wow.” He smiled up at his brother. “You know, you’re all right.”

“YOU…TOO.”

He felt a burst of happiness, and realized the emotion was as much Xerxes’ as it was his. He smiled, feeling at peace for the first time in a while. To think that he’d had a brother all this time…a big, monstrous lug with a heart of gold waiting for him…

It was really, really nice.

They fell into a comfortable silence, each enjoying each other’s company without having to speak. Hunter went into a kind of trance, counting his footsteps to a thousand, then starting over again. By the time they stopped again, the sun was directly overhead. Xerxes set Hunter’s pack down, and

Hunter eagerly took out some rations to eat. He hadn't had anything since last night, after all. He sat down, happy to rest his legs and chow down. When he was done, he squirmed in his wrappings. His chest and back were getting awfully itchy, almost certainly from him sweating underneath the layers of bark. He had half a mind to tear the wrappings off, but ignored the urge.

They continued onward until sundown, stopping in a small clearing to eat dinner. Hunter gathered wood for a small fire, and the two brothers sat before it, enjoying the heat of the flames. Or at least Hunter enjoyed it. With his brother's thick armor, he wasn't sure if Xerxes even noticed the change in temperature.

"Hey," he said. "Can you feel anything through your armor?"

"YES."

"So your armor has nerves in it?" Hunter pressed. Xerxes shrugged. "Can you feel me touching you?" he asked, brushing his fingertips lightly on Xerxes' armored forearm.

"Yes," Xerxes signed.

"Huh," Hunter replied. He realized then that he hadn't absorbed much in the way of memories from the guy. They both could absorb memories, which meant that neither of them transmitted memories very well. "What do you think about the war coming up?" he asked.

"I…FIGHT," Xerxes answered. "I…WIN."

"Fair enough," Hunter replied. "But it's easy to be confident when you're frickin' invincible."

"TRUE."

"Speaking of which, I could use a bit of that goo of yours," Hunter stated, glancing at the glowing blue mane running from Xerxes' head down to form his tail. "Mom was almost killed when she went to the Deep." Which was true; she'd only survived being transformed into an Ironclad because she'd fused with the strange organisms that had given her the power to regenerate first. "If I happen to get a bug on me, I'm screwed."

"YOU GO…NAKED," Xerxes replied.

"Don't look," Hunter warned with a devilish grin. "I don't want you to feel inadequate down there you know." Xerxes gave him a look, then glanced down at his own groin, putting one pair of palms together, then spreading them outward. A lot. "Bullshit," Hunter retorted.

Xerxes grinned, reaching down to his armored groin, and Hunter jerked his gaze away.

"Whoa, whoa!" he exclaimed. "No need to prove it. I believe you." Xerxes chuckled, and Hunter shook his head. "Guess you take after Dad too," he grumbled. Figures that's what they would've inherited from the big prick.

The both stared at the fire for a while, until Hunter yawned. He stretched his arms over his head, then took his sleeping bag out of his pack, spreading it out on the ground. Then he laid down, watching as Xerxes did the same.

Without the sleeping bag, of course. Being covered in the equivalent of platemail had a few side-benefits.

"You sleepy?" Hunter asked, knowing that Xerxes was, like the beetles he'd partially become, naturally nocturnal.

"Not yet," Xerxes signed.

"Teach me some more sign language then," Hunter urged. He'd gotten by mostly because Xerxes spelled everything out. Xerxes nodded, walking his brother patiently through sign after sign until Hunter's eyelids were too heavy for him to keep open. Then, turning away from the soft glow of the dying campfire, Hunter went to sleep.

* * *

The next morning, they resumed their trek through the woods…after Hunter shot down a few birds and harvested some vegetables and nuts from the surrounding area. He couldn't help but feel mildly guilty about killing the birds – it seemed rather traitorous – but according to Pukwa he'd chosen a bird of prey for his wings. That, and the fact that he was starving, was justification enough.

After a couple of hours, he found himself walking behind Xerxes instead of beside the big guy, a fact that didn't seem to bother his brother. Hunter found himself obsessing over his wrappings, which were even less comfortable today than they'd been yesterday. His back and chest were itching like mad, and the wrappings around them felt far too tight. Removing them was awfully tempting, and he would've done it if he weren't terrified about what he might find underneath.

Hunter tried to distract himself from the thought, studying the scenery around him. The forest here was different from the one they'd traveled through to get to the Kingdom of the Deep, the trees far taller. The ground was littered with decomposing pine needles, their pungent scent reminding him of Christmas. This effectively prevented anything else from growing, which made it much harder to determine which trees might have strong wills, since they all looked roughly the same. Xerxes hardly seemed concerned, and Hunter faked his brother's attitude. Besides, if there *was* a strong-willed tree – even a Legend – they'd only pass by it briefly. Setting up camp near one, however, would be a tragic mistake.

Eventually they did set up camp, just as the sun started to set. It was in a small clearing, and Xerxes used his four hands to dig up a great deal of the earth around the campsite, piling it along the edges. This effectively removed any strong-willed organisms from the clearing. Then they went to sleep.

* * *

"You getting deja-vu?" Hunter asked Xerxes as they walked.

They'd been hiking through the woods for a good few hours that morning, and the forest had ended abruptly, opening up into wide open fields, the ground rocky with sparse tufts of grass. Occasional trees dotted the landscape, their trunks gnarled and their branches twisted, unlike the stately tall trees behind them. The ground angled upward ahead, a dense fog obscuring their view.

Xerxes grunted, signing "yes."

"Me too," Hunter replied. He could swear he'd been here before, and in a way he had…through his mother's memories of her trip to the Deep. This was the same foggy landscape from her memories; he looked back the way they'd come, seeing a familiar scene: rocky landscape leading down to the forest miles away…and far, far in the distance, the five spires of the Kingdom of the Deep. "We're getting close," he warned.

Xerxes grunted, then stopped, glancing at Hunter for a long moment.

"What?" Hunter asked. Xerxes pointed to his glowing mane.

"Time to drink," he signed.

"You mean drink your gel?" Hunter pressed. Xerxes nodded.

"DEEP…DANGEROUS," the big guy explained. "YOU DIE…MOM MAKE ME…DIE."

"That'd be tough," Hunter replied with a smirk. "Vi cut your head off and you came back."

"NOT TOUGH…FOR MOM," Xerxes countered with a smirk of his own.

"But what about Zagamar?" Hunter asked. "What if this whole thing doesn't work?"

"WE…KILL YOU," Xerxes answered.

"How comforting," Hunter grumbled. "Love you too bro." Xerxes chuckled.

"LOVE YOU," he replied. "NOT…ZAGAMAR."

"Fair enough," Hunter conceded. "So…how we gonna do this?"

Xerxes pointed at Hunter's sword, then at his own glowing mane. Hunter drew his sword, placing the tip near his brother's mane, then hesitating.

"Just cut here?"

Xerxes grunted, grabbing the blade with one armored hand and jabbing the tip into his own mane. It took a surprising amount of force to penetrate the thick membrane; glowing blue gel oozed out onto the blade. Hunter withdrew the blade, and the wound closed almost instantaneously, the flesh knitting together before his very eyes.

"DRINK," Xerxes ordered.

Hunter scooped up the goop from the flat of his blade, holding it in his hand.

"So am I gonna…

"DRINK."

Hunter shrugged, then brought his hand to his mouth, gulping down the thick fluid…and nearly gagging.

"It's warm!" he complained, making a face. "And salty. Oh god," he added. "Think I'm gonna throw up."

Xerxes ignored him, continuing up the rocky incline toward the wall of fog ahead. Hunter grimaced, rushing to keep up with the big guy's long strides.

"So is this gonna make me heal real quick from now on?" he asked. Xerxes shrugged.

"No idea," he signed. "Probably a little faster, not a lot."

"So I'll still be able to die," Hunter ventured.

"LITTLE…HARDER."

"Vi heals quick," Hunter countered. She'd taken a few bone-crunching hits during their assault on the Castle Wexford a few days ago, and healed rapidly.

"SHE DRINK…MANY TIMES," Xerxes explained. "ABSORB…TRAITS GOOD."

"So you let her swallow your salty fluids over and over?" Hunter inquired with a wink and a nudge. Xerxes, to his credit, ignored him. He suddenly missed Vi's banter, which was almost always terribly inappropriate.

They continued their trek upward, falling into a comfortable silence as the fog enveloped them. Through the veil of gray they went, ever forward and upward. Hunter's upper back and chest – which were still itching like yesterday – began to burn. At first it was relatively mild, but it soon worsened, until it was almost unbearable.

"Damn," he swore, coming to a stop. He rubbed the left side of his chest; it seemed swollen, heat radiating from the wrappings still covering it. The wrappings felt as if they were tightening around his chest, squeezing the air right out of him. He tried to take a deep breath, but found he couldn't. "Shit."

"WHAT…WRONG?" Xerxes asked, stopping in front of him.

"Damn wrappings are too tight," he answered. The pain in his chest and back worsened, accompanied by terrible itching. He swore again, clawing at the wrappings. "Get this off me!"

Xerxes obliged, hooking his massive fingers in the wrappings and tearing them off one-by-one, exposing Hunter's chest and belly. Hunter looked down, seeing his pecs grossly swollen like a bodybuilder's…and beet-red.

"Aw shit," he exclaimed, staring at them in disbelief.

"WHAT THIS?" Xerxes demanded.

"I don't know," Hunter answered. "She…they poked me with needles," he added. "Maybe I got infected."

Xerxes twisted Hunter around 180 degrees, then tore away the wrappings from his back. Hunter heard a sharp intake of breath.

"What?" he asked. The tightness around his chest was gone…but the pain was not. He turned to face Xerxes, then reached around with one hand, feeling the back of his left shoulder.

There was something soft there…a small, fuzzy patch. It was remarkably tender.

"What is it?" Hunter asked. Xerxes glared down at him, grabbing him by the shoulders.

"WHAT…YOU DO?" he demanded.

Hunter considered lying again, then lowered his gaze.

"Something stupid," he admitted.

"*WHAT?*"

"I kinda asked a bird-guy to give me wings."

Xerxes stared at Hunter, his black eyes widening. Hunter sensed his brother's shock, and grimaced.

"I was drunk," he explained. "I…"

"YOU…BIRD?" Xerxes interrupted incredulously, letting go of Hunter's shoulders and taking a step back.

"I saw them flying," Hunter protested. "I thought it'd, you know, be…cool. To fly."

Xerxes just shook his head slowly.

"Did I mention I was drunk?" Hunter asked rather lamely. Then the pain in his back worsened, feeling as if his shoulder blades were on fire. "God *damn* that hurts," he exclaimed. "Why the hell is it hurting so much? It wasn't doing this before!"

"GOO," Xerxes answered.

Hunter stared at him, not comprehending.

"HEAL QUICK," his brother clarified. "GROW…QUICK."

"What's growing?"

"WINGS."

"You're saying I've got *wings?*" Hunter blurted out, reaching around and feeling the fuzz on his shoulder blade again. There was something long and hard beneath the fuzz.

Then it *moved.*

"Aw shit," Hunter mumbled. It was a bone he was feeling. A wing bone. "Oh shit oh shit…"

"CALM."

"Easy for you to say," Hunter retorted. "You're not the one growing fucking wings!"

"YOU…WANTED."

"I was *drunk,*" Hunter yelled.

"NO MORE…DRINK."

"Thanks for the tip bro," Hunter grumbled. "Super helpful right now." He let go of the wing, running a hand through his short hair. "Okay, we can fix this," he reasoned. "Cut them off."

Xerxes blinked.

"Here," Hunter urged, unsheathing his sword and holding it out for his brother. "Take it and cut them off."

"NO."

"Just do it," Hunter insisted. "Make it quick. Maybe I should lay on the ground so you can hold me down with a couple hands while you do it." He started to crouch, but Xerxes lifted him right back up.

"NO," Xerxes repeated.

"Come on," Hunter pleaded. "If you put pressure on the…"

"NOT…WORK."

"Not work?" Hunter retorted. "Not work? Why in the hell not?"

"DRANK GOO," his brother explained. "CUT OFF…COME BACK."

A chill ran down Hunter's spine, and he stared up at his brother wordlessly for a long moment. Then he swallowed in a dry throat.

"Come back?" he asked. Xerxes nodded. "You mean regenerate?" Another nod.

Hunter lowered his gaze, staring at his feet.

"Well fuck."

"FUCK," Xerxes agreed.

They both stood there in the dense fog, neither of them saying anything for a long, long time. At length, Xerxes stirred, putting a hand on Hunter's shoulder.

"IT…OKAY."

Hunter glanced up at him, feeling utterly defeated.

"No it's not," he muttered.

"IS TOO."

"I'm a goddamn *bird*," Hunter retorted. Xerxes patted his shoulder.

"JUST…WINGS," he soothed. "NOT SO…BAD."

"Easy for you to say," Hunter retorted. Xerxes just stared at him. "Ah," he mumbled. "Right. Sorry." He sighed, kicking a small stone down the rocky slope. "Sorry I didn't tell you," he added. "I thought you'd get pissed." Xerxes smiled.

"Wish I could fly," he signed.

"Don't think I'd be able to carry you," Hunter replied. And despite himself, he smiled back. "Thanks for being so understanding." Xerxes shrugged.

"FAMILY," the big guy reminded him. Hunter nodded.

"Family."

Hunter sighed, peering through the fog around them.

"Guess we should get going," he ventured.

"STILL…HURT?"

"Oh yeah," Hunter answered. And it did, a burning pain that throbbed like a toothache. Every heartbeat sent another burst of pain through his back. His chest still hurt too; his pecs looked massive. No wonder his wrappings had gotten tight. Pukwa had warned him that he'd develop a second set of pecs under his first, one that allowed him to flap his wings. And another set of shoulder blades. He gazed down at his pecs, cupping them in his hands.

"Damn," he said. "I look *jacked.*" He frowned then. "Guess I should take off the rest of these wrappings," he added. "You got my clothes?" Xerxes gave him the pack he'd been carrying. "All right, turn around," Hunter ordered. "Don't need you getting an eyeful, if you know what I mean."

Xerxes obliged, and Hunter tore off the rest of his wrappings, getting back into his pants. He hesitated when it came to his shirt, however; with his growing wings, he'd need a few alterations. And his breastplate, well…he'd have to have one specially made for him when he got back home. He pulled on his shirt, then told Xerxes to turn around, handing the big guy his sword. A few deft cuts later, and his little baby wings fit through nicely. He picked up his pack with his bow lashed to it, slinging it over his shoulder…and howling in pain as it struck his tender wing.

"God *damn,*" he swore, dropping the pack. "Wow."

Xerxes chuckled, taking the pack and slinging it over his own massive shoulder. And held on to Hunter's bow. Hunter sighed.

"This," he muttered, "…is gonna take some getting used to."

Chapter 9

The sun was setting in the forest when the creature awoke, curled up on the forest floor underneath a large tree. A terrible pain in its belly had woken it, an ever-present hunger that could never be appeased for long. It'd spent the last few days tracking the dark figure, the one that'd left the trail of blood earlier. Its scent was on the ground and the leaves it'd brushed past, an unmistakable odor that led ever forward through the woods.

The creature grunted, getting to its feet.

It moved much more quickly than it had days ago, its limbs far less stiff now. Much of the bark covering it had cracked and fallen away, revealing smooth black skin underneath. Its joints ached, a constant, throbbing pain it had learned to endure. It continued forward, following the scent of the one it was compelled to follow.

The creature ate as it trotted through the forest, pulling leaves from the brush and dead leaves from the ground. A constant stream of food to keep the hunger at bay.

Voices called out, startling the creature. It paused to listen for a moment, then continued forward, ignoring them. The voices came, but they meant nothing. They were not from outside. They were *inside.* Memories, vague and fragmented. Alien. The creature paid them no mind.

Hours passed.

The creature continued tracking the Dark One, not knowing why it was doing so. All it knew was that it *had* to.

Suddenly there was a rustling sound ahead. The creature froze, its heart beating rapidly in its chest. It was not afraid; its heart just beat faster now, even when it was resting.

It sniffed the air, a whiff of something strange but familiar reaching its nostrils. A hint of the Dark One, mixed with something else. Its sense of smell was duller now, though its other senses seemed more keen.

Something stepped out of the bushes ahead, sniffing the ground. A dog…or something like it. Its hair was all-black, patches of fur missing on its body. Its legs were too long for its body, its head flatter, with sunken black eyes. Its flesh stuck to its ribs as if it were starving.

The dog-thing turned its head, spotting the creature. Then it turned away, following the same trail the creature was, eating leaves greedily as it went.

The creature paused, then followed behind the dog-thing. Somehow it knew that the thing was not something to be feared. That it was an ally.

They were brothers now, drawn to the Dark One. They *were* the Dark One, but…not. And they had to find Him, and follow Him. He would make them better.

The creature followed close behind the dog-thing, both of them making their way through the woods. Following the scent of their master.

* * *

The sun was barely over the horizon by the time Sukri spotted a break in the forest ahead, the morning having barely begun despite hours of following Dio after a far-too-early start to their day. Beyond the forest was a short grassy field, a stone bridge beyond crossing a wide chasm. The bridge led to a huge black wall in the distance. Five dark spires pierced the sky beyond this wall. They had finally arrived at their destination…the fabled Kingdom of the Deep.

Sukri stared at the arched entrance to the kingdom beyond the bridge, goosebumps rising on her arms. She'd heard countless stories of the kingdom while growing up in Tykus, tales of corruption beyond imagination. Men and women exposing themselves eagerly to wild artifacts, engaging in bizarre rituals. Sacrificing children to strange gods, turning into half-humans and eating babies. Much of it had to be hyperbole, of course, but every legend held a kernel of truth. The Kingdom of the Deep was the antithesis of everything the kingdom of Tykus stood for.

Here they worshipped nature, not humanity. Chaos, not order.

"So what exactly are we going to do here?" Sukri asked Dio, trudging behind the silent Seeker.

"You'll see."

Sukri sighed, having known that was exactly what he'd say. It was just about all he'd said for the last few days that they'd been traveling. Dio was the worst conversationalist she'd ever met, having no apparent need or desire for human connection. She'd met blocks of wood that were more emotional than he was.

"Tell me about the kingdom," she pressed.

"The Kingdom of the Deep is where all of Lady Camilla's Seekers train," Dio answered. "Technically we're Seekers of the Deep acting as independent contractors for the Lady. All potential Seekers must register with one of the five shrines there."

"What shrines?"

"You'll see," came the reply.

Sukri sighed, stepping onto the wide stone bridge and following Dio across it to the archway beyond. They passed through, a wide set of stairs leading them upward. They reached the top…and were rewarded by a spectacular view: a huge, lush wilderness entirely enclosed within a circular stone wall. Occasional buildings dotted the landscape, some built atop trees, others on the ground. And five huge, black stone structures with tall spires reaching toward the sky, taller than any building Sukri had ever seen.

"Wow," Sukri breathed, taking it all in. She glanced at Dio, whose expression was flat, as usual. "This is it?"

"Yes."

"Where's the…everything?" she pressed, looking around. There weren't any people that she could see. And no castles, and not many buildings, really. Not much of a kingdom.

"You'll see."

"You know, sometimes I think that's all you know how to say," Sukri groused. "One of these days it'd be nice if you, you know, actually *told* me something."

"All Seekers of the Deep have to register at one of the shrines here," Dio stated, gesturing at one of the spires in the distance.

"Okay…"

"All of the Lady's Seekers are Seekers of the Deep," Dio continued. "So you need to register."

"Fine," she replied. "I'll register."

Just then, a group of bare-chested men ran toward them, their hair long and straight, their skin darkly tanned. They reached Dio and Sukri quickly, stopping before them. One of them stepped forward, raising one hand upward.

"Greetings," the man stated. "Welcome back, Dio." He glanced at Sukri. "Who is your guest?"

"I'm Sukri," Sukri replied.

"I'm Kip. Good to meet you," the man stated, flashing her a warm smile. Sukri smiled back.

"See Dio?" she said, turning to her dour teacher. "That's what they call a 'smile.' You might want to try it sometime."

"What brings you here?" Kip inquired.

"She wants to register," Dio answered. Kip's smile broadened.

"Excellent!" he exclaimed. "Does she know which shrine she'd like to register with?"

"No," came Dio's reply.

"Then I will bring you to each of them," Kip decided. "And you can make your decision," he added, turning to Sukri. "Come!"

Sukri glanced at Dio, who inclined his head slightly. Kip grabbed her hand, pulling her away from Dio and toward one of the spires far in the distance. She allowed herself to be led without resistance, eager to get away from the cold-hearted bastard.

"What are the shrines?" she asked. "Those spires?"

"Yes," Kip answered. "Each spire marks one of the five shrines. Each shrine houses the spirits of the five categories of spirits: the mammals, the birds, the reptiles, the water-dwellers, and the insects."

"Spirits?"

"Everything has a spirit," Kip explained. "And spirits can be shared."

Sukri nodded, realizing that Kip was talking about wills. Everything living had a will, and wills could be transmitted and absorbed. It was just another way of describing the same phenomenon.

"How do I register?" she inquired.

"You must accept one of the spirits within a shrine," Kip answered. "Then you can be registered as a Seeker of the Deep."

Sukri stopped, forcing Kip to stop as well. She put her hands on her hips.

"What'd'you mean I have to 'accept one of the spirits?'" she demanded. Kip frowned.

"Dio did not tell you?"

"Dio doesn't say *shit*," she answered. Kip grimaced.

"I should not be surprised," he admitted. "He took on the spirit of the snake, among several others."

Sukri blinked.

"What?"

"Dio took on the spirit of a snake," Kip repeated. "His mind is as cold as a snake's blood.

"That explains a lot," Sukri grumbled.

"I can show you each of the shrines," Kip offered. "You can choose whatever spirit you like."

"Wait a second," she stated. "You're saying I *have* to absorb an animal's will?"

"Or a plant, if you choose," Kip confirmed. "We have many…"

"No."

"Excuse me?"

"No," she repeated. "I'm not doing it."

"You'd better," a voice behind her said. She whirled around, finding Dio standing there.

"The hell?" she nearly shouted. "You scared the crap outta me!" Her armpits itched, as they always did when she was unpleasantly surprised.

"You want to be the Lady's Seeker," Dio stated, "…you have to register."

"But Camilla said I could stay myself." Sukri protested. "How is this any different than having to wear one of the Guild's damn medallions?"

"If I may," Kip interjected. She turned on him. "The Seekers of the Deep are a part of nature," he explained. "To be a part of the world, you have to understand that your spirit is part of a much larger whole."

"I got it," she retorted. "I don't need to turn into a snake to…"

"No register," Dio interjected, "…no job. Then you're on your own."

Sukri turned to face her teacher, swallowing in a dry throat. She didn't' need him to explain what would happen if she refused him. If she refused the Lady. Camilla was the only person standing between her and the Guild of Seekers; without the Lady's protection, Sukri was good as dead.

"Fine," she muttered, turning to face Kip. "Show me the damn shrines then."

"We only ask that you take a part of an animal spirit within you," Kip insisted apologetically. "You still get to keep your mind if you choose."

"Great," she muttered. "Let's get this over with."

* * *

The first shrine Kip took Sukri to was the one with all the insects in it. It didn't take Sukri long to finish that particular trip; a few insect-human hybrids was all it took to convince her that she didn't want any insects inside of her. Or rather, insect-spirits. The next shrine they visited was underwater, and had a bunch of fish-people in it. Breathing underwater seemed cool, but again, fish-people looked ridiculous, except for the mermaids. They were sexy as hell, but not having legs was a deal breaker.

The bird shrine had been pretty interesting, and she'd given some serious consideration to becoming one of the bird-people there. But as awesome as being able to fly might be, it wasn't compelling enough for her to want to sprout a pair of wings. The lizard shrine she skipped altogether, having already seen an example of it in Dio. That left the shrine with the mammals.

And it was there that Sukri found what she was looking for.

"Damn," she murmured, staring at one of the cat-women leaning against a tree within the huge main room of the shrine. The woman was curvy in all the right places, and utterly nude. Short gray fur covered her body – barely – and a long tail whipped about of its own accord. She had mostly human hands and feet, but with long retractable nails, and small pointed ears. Sukri watched the woman climb up the tree with ease, sitting leisurely on a branch some twenty feet up.

"You like?" Kip inquired. He'd gamely escorted her to each shrine, and unlike Dio, seemed to enjoy every moment of her company. If the man ever stopped smiling, she hadn't noticed it yet.

"*Oh* yeah," Sukri replied. "She's sexy as fuck."

"Hmm?"

"I like," she clarified.

"Do you want to talk to her?" Kip pressed.

"Love to."

Kip approached the tree, speaking with the cat-woman, who leapt gracefully off the tree branch – falling twenty feet! – and landed in front of them without any problem at all. She smiled at Sukri, extending a hand-paw.

"Greetings," the woman said. Sukri shook it; the woman's hand was surprisingly warm, and furry with fleshy pads. "Welcome to the Shrine of Mammals."

"Hi," Sukri replied. "I'm Sukri." Up close, the woman was even more beautiful, with big, shimmering golden eyes and a cute button-nose. Her teeth were slightly sharpened, and she had long black whiskers. "Damn you're cute," Sukri blurted out.

"Thank you," the woman replied with a smile. "I'm Kayla. I curate the feline exhibit. You caught me on my break."

"I'm Sukri."

"Why don't I leave you two alone," Kip offered.

"Good idea," Sukri replied. Kip smiled, then left them. The cat-lady – Kayla – eyed Sukri curiously.

"What brings you here, Sukri?" she inquired.

"I'm becoming a Seeker of the Deep," Sukri answered. "Apparently I have to choose a, uh, spirit."

"Well then," Kayla replied with a little smile. "You've come to the right place. Her tail flicked from side-to-side, seemingly of its own accord. "I can show you around," she offered.

"Sure."

They walked toward one of the hallways that came off the main room like spokes on a wheel, and Kayla gestured at some stuffed animals mounted on or near the walls. They were dogs and wolves of various kinds, as well as foxes and coyotes. As interesting as they were, Sukri found herself looking at Kayla more than at what Kayla was showing her. The woman walked with a casual grace, each movement fluid and effortless. She held herself with utter confidence, which – combined with her remarkably slender yet curvy body – made her impossible *not* to watch. They'd gotten halfway through the canine exhibit when Kayla glanced at Sukri.

"See anything you like?"

"You," Sukri stated bluntly. Kayla arched one eyebrow…or rather, what would have been her eyebrow. She had fur everywhere, after all.

"Hmm," she murmured, a little smile playing at her lips. "Would you rather I show you the feline exhibit?"

"Hell yes," Sukri replied immediately. Kayla chuckled.

"Very straightforward," she observed. "I like you already. Follow me."

Kayla led Sukri further down the hallway, then took stairs to the next floor up. Sukri walked up the stairs behind Kayla, admiring the woman's shape. She had small but well-muscled shoulders, her back tapering like a "V" to her tiny waist, which immediately flared out to generous hips and a rather remarkable butt. Her legs were long and extremely well-developed…which explained how she'd jumped twenty feet down from that tree earlier without getting hurt.

"Where are you from?" Kayla inquired as they reached the next floor. The cat-woman continued up the next flight of stairs toward the third.

"Tykus."

"We don't get many people from there," Kayla admitted. "What's it like?"

"Not great," Sukri answered. "Not for people like me."

"People like you?"

"People who're different," Sukri clarified.

They reached the third floor, and Kayla stepped into another hallway. This had to be the feline exhibit; stuffed cats of all kinds lined the walls. Kayla stopped, turning to face Sukri.

"You'd like it here," she said with a smile, her golden eyes twinkling. "We love people who are different."

"I like what I've seen so far," Sukri admitted. Kayla raised an eyebrow.

"Oh really?" she inquired. "What's been your favorite part?"

Sukri hesitated, but only for a moment.

"You," she admitted.

"Hmm," Kayla murmured, turning away from her and strolling down the hallway. She gestured at the exhibits. "These are the housecats," she explained. "The larger cats are further down…the panthers, leopards, lions, tigers…and so on." Sukri nodded, following beside Kayla. There were more types of felines than she'd ever imagined…many of which she hadn't seen before. Pets were rare in Tykus, only the weakest-willed animals allowed to live there. Animals – and plants – were specifically bred to be as weak-willed as possible, to prevent corruption of the masses.

They finished their perusal of the exhibits, and Kayla turned to Sukri.

"Any questions?" she inquired.

"Which one did you choose?" Kayla inquired.

"The Chartreux," Kayla answered.

"What made you choose that?"

"I liked the way they looked," Kayla admitted. "Their golden eyes and beautiful fur. And…" She paused, reaching out and touching Sukri's arm. "Chartreux are *very* affectionate," she added with a little smile. "We love to play, and to please…and be pleased."

Sukri swallowed, finding herself – for once – at a loss for words.

"We tend to form very powerful bonds with our masters," Kayla continued, sliding her hand down the side of Sukri's arm, then dropping it. Sukri frowned.

"Your masters?"

"The one we pair-bond with," Kayla explained. "We protect them, serve them, and lavish them with attention…and expect the same in return."

"Oh," Sukri replied, relieved. "I thought you meant you were like, subservient or something. That's not me."

"Sometimes yes," Kayla replied. "Sometimes no. We're cats," she added with a smirk. "We do what we want."

"And how do you…do it?"

"Pardon?" Kayla asked.

"Uh, change into…you," Sukri clarified, feeling the blood rush to her cheeks.

"I thought you meant something else," Kayla replied, continuing to smirk. "But it doesn't change my answer. I'll show you."

With that, Kayla turned back down the hallway the way they'd come. Sukri stared at her retreating form, her face feeling hot. She swallowed in a suddenly dry throat, rushing to catch up to the woman…but trailing a few feet behind. She hardly wanted Kayla to see her blushing, and what's more, she had no idea how to feel. She'd crossed over to the other side a few times in the past, and for the most part had enjoyed the experience. But someone like Kayla…

God damn, she thought, staring at the woman's figure as she walked.

They went up to the fifth floor, which consisted of many small rooms. Most were empty, but Kayla brought them to one that was not. A woman was lying down on a wooden cot in the center of the room, another cat-lady methodically wrapping what looked to be thin strips of bark around the woman's legs.

"What're they doing?" Sukri asked. Kayla explained the process; this woman had requested to gain the claws of a cat only. A fact that surprised Sukri; she hadn't imagined that she could choose to gain a single part of an animal, after all. Not that the idea interested her; Kayla's full-body transformation was far more intriguing.

Sukri watched them work, then glanced at Kayla.

"You're saying that – if I wanted to – I could be like you?" she asked.

"Of course."

"What can you do?" she pressed.

"I can climb trees and many other structures," Kayla answered. "And jump several times my own height. I have a very good sense of smell, and I can move silently. I have excellent night vision, quick reflexes, and I never get cold."

"And you have claws," Sukri noted. "Are they useful in a fight?" Kayla smiled.

"Very."

"Anything else I should know?" Sukri asked.

"We're carnivores," Kayla answered. "So if you're opposed to eating meat, that might be an issue." Sukri smirked.

"Never been an issue for me," she quipped. "Are you…glad you did it?"

Kayla put a hand on her hip, giving Sukri a look.

"I wouldn't go back," she replied. "Ever." Sukri smiled, mulling it over. And finding herself gazing at Kayla's body once again. This time, however, she didn't try to hide her fascination.

"Do cats kill snakes?" she pressed.

"Of course."

Sukri turned back to the woman on the cot, watching as her upper thighs were wrapped with that strange bark-like material.

"I gotta admit," she stated, "…I'm tempted."

"What would help you make your decision?" Kayla inquired. Sukri smirked at her.

"You," she answered. "And a whole lot of alcohol."

Chapter 10

After what seemed like an hour of careful hiking up a steep incline, the rocky terrain leveled off fifty feet ahead, the omnipresent fog lifting a bit to reveal what lay ahead of Hunter and Xerxes. It was exactly as Hunter remembered from his mother's memories; bones littering the ground as far as the eye could see, with trees growing in dense clusters among the rocks. Or rather, what *appeared* to be trees. As he got closer, Hunter saw that they were all screwed up. Some were covered in fleshy tumors, while others were covered in scales or feathers; one was even covered in something resembling skin.

Most of the corpses littering the terrain appeared long-dead, but as they continued forward, fresher corpses were visible amongst the bones.

"Weird," Hunter murmured, staring at the corpses as he passed by. They were all screwed up as well, just like the trees. Mish-mashed parts put together like an interspecies Frankenstein. Birds with lizard tails, a dog with multiple pairs of wings and the legs of an insect sprouting from its body.

"Getting close," Xerxes signed.

"Got that," Hunter muttered. He gave the corpses and skeletons as wide a berth as possible, hardly relishing the thought of absorbing their memories. Memories of their deaths were usually the first ones he experienced, and judging by how they looked, none of them had experienced a peaceful passing. Thank goodness for his helmet, which offered a degree of insulation from the wills of others. "This place freaking you out?"

"Yes," Xerxes signed.

"At least you're immortal," Hunter pointed out. Xerxes smirked.

"IMMORTAL NOT…GOOD HERE."

"Good point," Hunter conceded.

A few minutes later, he spotted the ruins of an ancient stone building amidst the fog to their left. Just a few columns and a crumbling archway, strange fleshy growths clinging to the stone. The smell of decay grew thicker as they walked, making Hunter feel a little nauseous. That, combined with the throbbing in his back and chest, was making for a miserable hike.

"How do my wings look?" he asked his brother – not for the first time. It annoyed him that he couldn't see them.

"GROWING," Xerxes replied.

"No wonder why I'm so hungry," Hunter grumbled, his stomach growling so loud that Xerxes had to have heard it. They'd already stopped for a snack twice since drinking Xerxes' goo, and he resisted the urge to eat again. Their rations were limited, after all. If his wings wanted to keep growing, they'd have to be satisfied with being fueled by his fat.

Suddenly Xerxes stopped.

"What…" Hunter began…and then Xerxes shoved him bodily to the side. A huge *thing* burst out of the fog toward them, slamming head-on into Xerxes, right where Hunter had been a split-second ago. Xerxes flew backward, disappearing into the fog behind them.

"Xerxes!" Hunter cried, falling to the rocky ground. He scrambled to his feet facing the…thing that had attacked Xerxes. A massive snake head turned to face him, gazing down upon him. It was easily twenty feet high, with a long, coiled body that was mostly hidden by the fog. Huge insectoid wings sprouted from its back at odd angles, misshapen insect legs dangling from its sides, many of which were broken. Patches of what looked like bark interrupted its scales, and every movement caused the bark to crack, blood oozing from the wounds.

The thing hissed, its huge maw gaping open, revealing dripping white fangs as long as Hunter was tall.

Then its head burst forward right at him!

Hunter leapt to the right, but he was too slow. The creature's lower jaw grazed his legs, the impact sending him spinning around madly. He landed on his right hip, and the creature's head lunged at him again. This time there was no time to dodge out of the way; he could only watch as the monstrosity's gaping maw came right at him.

And then Xerxes slammed into the side of the snake's head, deflecting it at the last second.

Hunter scrambled to his feet, backing away from the thing and drawing his sword.

The snake recovered, swinging its head sideways at Xerxes, tossing the Ironclad bodily to the side. Hunter's pack flew off Xerxes' shoulder, and Xerxes vanished once again into the fog.

"Run!" Hunter shouted, turning and following his own advice. He looked back, seeing the giant snake coming after him, slithering on the rocky ground, its insect-like limbs snapping and tearing free from its body. It shrieked, lunging at Hunter, who juked to the side. He felt its head smash into his left shoulder – his left *wing* – sending him careening to the ground.

His wing *howled* in pain.

Hunter gasped, scrambling to his feet just as the snake's head reared back, its jaws opening wide. It lunged forward again…just as Xerxes leapt on top of Hunter's back, shoving him belly-first to the ground.

Darkness descended on them both as the snake's mouth engulfed them, surrounding them in cool, slimy wetness.

Hunter realized his sword was still in his hand, and gripped the hilt with both hands, thrusting it blindly upward. His guts wrenched as the snake's head thrashed from side-to-side, its mouth opening. He slipped out, falling a few feet to the ground below, Xerxes tumbling out after him.

They both got to their feet, facing the humongous monster. Hunter lifted his sword…and realized he didn't have it. It was still embedded in the creature's palate.

The snake drew back from them, arching way up, its cold, alien eyes locking on Xerxes. Then it lunged right at the Ironclad, swallowing Xerxes whole.

Hunter swore, backpedaling rapidly. The snake's head lifted off the ground, its mouth partially open. Hunter spotted his brother inside, one of the snake's giant fangs having impaled Xerxes straight through the belly, the razor-sharp tip emerging from Xerxes' back.

Xerxes gripped the fang with one pair of hands, pulling himself *up* it, impaling himself even more. Then he reached out with his second pair of hands, grabbing Hunter's sword from the roof of the creature's mouth and flinging it down on the ground near Hunter. Hunter picked it up, glancing at the snake, then at his sword.

"Yeah, no," he grumbled. He might as well attack the snake with a toothpick. The snake's mouth snapped shut, and it turned to face him.

Shit!

Hunter backpedaled, knowing there was no way in hell he was going to be able to outrun this thing. And there was no way in hell *he* was going to kill it.

But he knew someone who could.

He turned his focus inward, concentrating on his hunger. On the pain in his left wing where the snake had struck him. Pictured a dark, musty tomb, a huge black statue emerging from the base of a black skull.

Za-ga-mar!

Thousands of voices chanting his name. Soldiers standing in the ruins of city after city, exalting their leader. A god among men.

Za-ga-mar!

Hunter grimaced, feeling that *other* within him growing, flowing out of the dark cervices of his mind. Forming a churning, powerful current that threatened to overtake him.

Za-ga-MAR!

He stepped *outside* of that current, watching as it passed by. Then he dipped his psychic toes within its waters, far enough removed to be safe from the Legend's overwhelming power, but connected enough to be able to control the man.

Or so he hoped.

Time slowed, and at the same time his heart began to beat faster, his pulse pounding in his ears. He studied the giant snake slithering toward him, its massive body undulating slowly.

Product of the Deep, he knew instantly. *Snake, giant, insects, trees combined. In pain. Lashing out.*

His eyes scoured his surroundings, locking on the pack laying on the ground a few dozen feet ahead and to his left. At the bow and quiver lashed to it. He felt Zagamar sigh within him, shaking his head at Hunter's stupidity.

The snake reared its head back slowly, its mouth starting to open. Preparing to strike.

Hunter waited.

Then it lunged forward in slow-motion, its eyes closing, its mouth opening wide as it attacked!

Hunter leapt to the left, jumping and tucking his knees to his chest as the beast struck the ground to his right, then straightened his legs, kicking off the side of the snake's jaw…and flinging his sword right into the beast's eye. It struck true, the blade burying itself into that monstrous globe, clear fluid gushing out of it.

The beast jerked its head back with a shriek.

Hunter used the momentum from having kicked off the beast to launch himself toward the pack in the distance, landing on the rocky terrain and sprinting toward it. He skid to a stop before it, grabbing the bow and one arrow, then turning to face the beast.

It swung its head to track him with its remaining eye, lunging at him.

Hunter nocked an arrow and let it fly in one smooth motion, then tossed the bow aside while the arrow was still sailing through the air.

It struck the creature in its remaining eye, plunging into the orb.

The snake slid to a stop, swinging its head from side-to-side madly. It rolled onto its back, thrashing wildly, its wings breaking under its weight. Blood poured from the wounds, soaking the stones below.

And then there was a loud *crack*.

The snake's entire body shuddered, then went still.

A moment later, the creature's mouth opened slightly, and none other than Xerxes stepped out of it. The big guy was entirely covered in blood, the snake's broken-off fang still impaling him. Xerxes grinned at Hunter, grabbing the fang with a few hands and yanking it straight out of him. The hole through his belly began to close immediately.

"GOOD…FIGHT," Xerxes decided, walking up to Hunter and putting a huge hand on his shoulder. "YOU…HURT?"

Hunter *shoved* Zagamar out of his consciousness, and to his relief the Legend returned into the dark crevices of his mind, silent and powerless once more. But it took a little more effort than it had the last time he'd conjured the guy…the importance of which was not lost on Hunter.

Zaggie was growing stronger within him.

"Not bad," Hunter answered, feeling his heart slow, his metabolism going back to normal. He felt even more famished now than he had earlier. "Just my wing," he added. His left wing still smarted from the snake hitting it.

"IT HEAL," Xerxes reassured.

"Let's get going," Hunter muttered, walking up to his pack and tying the bow and quiver to it, then handing it to Xerxes. "Before Zagamar steals any more of my soul."

And with that, they left the giant snake's body behind, continuing their trek through the swirling fog toward the Deep.

* * *

The Deep was just as Hunter remembered. Or rather, just as it'd been in the memories he'd gained from his mother.

He and Xerxes stood at the edge of a narrow, rocky ledge with thick moss growing on it. A mere yard ahead, the ledge ended abruptly, leading to a straight drop down into a truly massive pit in the earth. It was like looking down into the crater of a volcano…if that crater were several miles wide and so deep that it seemed to travel to the center of the earth itself. To Hunter, already not one for heights, it inspired equal parts awe and fear.

"Whelp," Hunter stated, turning to Xerxes, "…this is it."

Xerxes grunted in agreement, then glanced down at Hunter.

"TAKE…OFF," he ordered, gesturing at…well, at all of Hunter.

"Huh?"

"CLOTHES."

"You want me to take off my clothes?" Hunter asked, raising an eyebrow. Xerxes nodded. "Seriously?"

"REMEMBER…MOM."

"Touché," Hunter conceded. Mom had gone down into the Deep with an ironclad beetle stuck under her shirt, and had paid for it dearly. The Deep would fuse any wills around Hunter to him, meaning that the fewer wills he had around him, the better. "Turn around," he ordered.

"WHY?"

"'Cause I don't want you laughing at my dick," Hunter replied. Xerxes chuckled.

"NO…LAUGH," he replied. "FEEL…SORRY."

"Ha ha," Hunter grumbled. "Asshole."

But Xerxes did as he was told, and Hunter stripped off his clothes until he was entirely naked. Then Xerxes promptly turned back around.

"Bro, what the hell?" Hunter blurted out, covering his groin hastily. Which took both hands.

"GOOD…SIZE," Xerxes reassured, patting him on the shoulder. "PROP…PORTIONAL."

"Gee thanks," Hunter muttered. But there was no way around it; he had to climb down, so he might as well get comfortable being butt-naked in front of his brother. He glanced down the pit again; there were relatively flat, rocky ledges protruding from the wall of the pit directly below, some of them quite small, others large enough to fit a few dozen people on. The nearest ledge was about twenty feet down, and the next-closest was to the right of the first, at least sixty feet down. This supported a small pond that glowed a faint blue, as well as the roots of a large vine crawling up the side wall…all the way up to the ledge they were standing on now, to their right. A single blue, glowing stripe wound around this vine, glowing faintly in the waning sunlight.

"Mom took that vine down," Hunter noted, eyeing the vine. "She went into that pool."

"NO…GO."

"Not into the pool, I know," Hunter agreed. "And I should avoid the glowing moss surrounding it too," he added. There was a good foot or two of blue glowing moss on the ledge surrounding the pool. It contained the same micro-organism that had turned Mom – and Xerxes – into regenerating immortals. A little bit of healing was great, but growing a big blue mane and a tail was a little much. "I can just go down to that ledge above the pool," he reasoned. "That should be enough."

"HOW…KNOW?"

"I don't know," Hunter admitted. It was an excellent point. How *would* they know when they'd been exposed enough to the Deep? "Guess I gotta just go and hope it's enough."

Xerxes paused, then nodded in grudging agreement. There was no other way.

"Get on my back," Xerxes signed. "I'll climb down."

"Hold on," Hunter countered. "Give me a minute."

Xerxes did so, and Hunter stared down the pit. This was it…he was at the Deep. Once he went down there, there was no telling what might happen. He could fuse with Zagamar's will, compartmentalizing the Legend forever like they'd planned. But what if Zagamar's more powerful will took over? Would he still remain himself? Or would he be like Zagamar was now, trapped in his own body, unable to control himself?

It was entirely possible that, by going down there, Hunter was essentially committing suicide.

Of course, the only other option was to leave this place and let Zagamar take over slowly, destroying Hunter's mind piece by piece until there was nothing left at all.

Hunter grit his teeth, taking a deep breath in, then nodding at Xerxes.

"Okay."

The big guy knelt down, and Hunter climbed onto his back, wrapping his arms around the guy's armored neck. Xerxes went up to the vine, grabbing ahold of it and swinging his legs over the abyss. Hunter glanced down…and immediately regretted it.

"Ohhh shit," he muttered, closing his eyes and taking a deep breath in. "Be careful buddy, I can't fly yet."

Xerxes was careful, and with his four arms he had no trouble at all climbing down the vine. They were about a third of the way down went Hunter swore.

"Stop!" he shouted. Xerxes did so. "Go back up," he ordered. "If we go down together, we might get…combined."

Xerxes nodded, climbing back up and depositing Hunter atop the ledge next to the vine.

"I have to go alone," Hunter realized. He squared his shoulders. "All right. Wish me lucky big guy."

Xerxes leaned down, grabbing Hunter with all four arms and giving him a big hug. And picking him right off the ground in the process. Then, mercifully, he set Hunter down.

"Love you too little brother," Hunter said.

He took a deep breath in then, making a point not to look into the abyss he was about to hang over. He climbed onto the vine, remembering everything he'd learned about rock-climbing from his mom and dad. Avid spelunkers, they'd brought Hunter along during their expeditions ever since he'd been old enough to climb.

Here goes, he thought.

He shimmied his way down the vine until he was hanging over the pit, focusing on the next handhold and foothold to the exclusion of everything else. And focusing on taking his time. His life quite literally depended on it.

It wasn't long before his foot touched down on the rocky ledge below, and he let go of the vine, finding himself on a small rocky ledge twenty feet above the glowing blue pool. The ledge sloped downward to his left, leading to the rocky shore surrounding the pool. He had another powerful sense of deja-vu; it was almost exactly as his mother had remembered it.

"Okay," he told himself, taking a step forward. "Now I just have to…"

And then there was pain.

Agony tore through his chest all the way to his back, as if his flesh was being ripped open. He screamed, doubling over, then falling onto his side on the rocky ledge. He gasped, curling up into the fetal position.

The pain was unbearable.

The tearing sensation turned into a burning feeling, as if his chest and back were on fire. He shrieked, the awful sound echoing through the massive pit.

Hunter's vision blackened, the world starting to spin.

He clutched onto the ledge, digging his fingertips into the rock, holding on for dear life. Faster and faster the world spun, until he puked.

His pain grew. Beyond anything he had ever experienced. Beyond any memory of the terrible deaths he'd absorbed. Beyond imagination.

At that moment, if he could have, he would have ended it. Would've leapt into the gaping pit below.

And then, as quickly as it had come, the pain stopped.

Chapter 11

Sunlight splashed across the small bedroom, setting the messy sheets on the narrow bed in the corner aglow. Zac yawned, keeping his eyes closed against the bright light. He let himself wake up slowly; a luxury he could only afford right after the harvest each year. Luckily his family had finished harvesting in record time, thanks to the machines he'd invented. His inventions were an antidote to the mind-numbing work in the fields, and never ceased to amaze his parents and neighbors.

He basked in this leisurely morning, stretching his arms up and out.

It felt *glorious.*

Zac felt a familiar weight on his belly, his cat Zooey in her usual spot. She was always on him or near him, his constant companion. He felt the vibrations of her purring, and put a hand on her back to stroke it. But instead of her long fur, he felt soft, warm skin under his fingertips.

He jerked his hand away, his eyes snapping open.

There, curled up on his belly, was Zooey, fast asleep. But something was terribly wrong with her. Her fur had fallen out in large clumps, her skin below the same olive color as his. And her ears were rounded, her face weirdly flat.

And the fingers on each paw where too long. In fact, they looked like…

"Zooey?" he blurted out.

She opened her eyes, revealing perfectly round pupils.

Zac cried out, scrambling to the head of the bed. Zooey startled, leaping off his bed.

"Honey?" a muted voice called out from behind his door.

"Mom!" Zac yelled.

The door burst open, and his mother ran into the bedroom, looking frantic. And Zooey slipped right between her legs, bolting down the hallway beyond.

"Zac? What's wrong?" she asked.

"It's Zooey," Zac answered. "Something's wrong with her."

"What?"

"I don't know, but it's really bad," he told her. They both stepped out of the room, looking down the hallway. His parents' bedroom door was cracked open…and Zooey was nowhere to be seen.

Suddenly, there was a shout from behind that door, followed by a *crash*, and Zooey shrieking. Zooey burst out of the door, bolting past Zac and Mom into Zac's room.

Dad stepped into the hallway, his eyes wide.

"What's wrong?" Mom asked.

"It's that damn cat!" Dad nearly shouted. He ran a hand through his thinning hair. "It's a god-damn freak!"

"Honey, I…"

"It's *changed*," Dad interrupted, giving her a significant look. They both paused, then stared at Zac. Zac frowned.

"What?" he asked.

Dad took a few steps back, pulling Mom with him. Zac took a step toward them.

"Stay back," Dad ordered.

"What are…"

"I said stay back!" Dad shouted.

"Honey…" Mom began, giving Dad a pleading look. "He's only twelve."

"Don't 'Honey' me," Dad snapped. "And you know that's when this happens!"

"Maybe it isn't what you think," Mom pressed. Dad glared at her.

"Did you *see* that thing?" he retorted. Then he pointed at Zac. "It's turning into *him!*"

"But Zooey was normal last night," she protested.

"That's the damn *point*," Dad shot back. He swallowed visibly, his jawline rippling. "You need to leave, Zac. Grab your things and go."

"But Dad…" Zac stammered.

"No buts," Dad interjected. "Get your shit and get out."

"But *why* Dad?" Zac pressed. "I didn't do anything wrong!"

"I know," Dad conceded. "But you can't live here anymore. You can't…" He swallowed again. "You can't see us anymore."

Zac just stared at him, feeling numb. He turned to Mom, giving her a pleading look.

"Oh Zac," Mom moaned, tears running down her cheeks. "Oh baby, I'm so sorry."

"I can't believe this," Zac muttered. "What did I do?"

"It's not what you did, son," Dad replied. "It's…what you are. Now get your things and go. Don't make me ask you again."

Zac hesitated, then turned away from them, stepping back into his room. Zooey was there, laying on his bed, staring back at him with those freakish eyes.

They looked…human.

He put on his clothes, then grabbed more clothes, stuffing them in the pack he kept in the corner of his room. His mind raced, ticking off the things he'd need. He filled the pack with his spare coins, some snacks, and a blanket, then stepped out of his bedroom. Mom and Dad weren't there; he continued down the hallway, hearing a *thump* as Zooey jumped off the bed, trotting behind him. They went into the living room, and Zac spotted Mom and Dad in the kitchen.

Dad had a butcher knife in his hand.

Zac froze.

"We love you, son," Dad stated, holding the knife in front of him. "But you can't come back. Ever."

Zac stared at the knife, then at him.

"If I ever see you again," Dad added, his eyes moist, "…I'll kill you."

Zac's lower lip trembled, his vision blurring. He turned away from them, going to the front door and opening it. He glanced back at Mom one last time, then stepped through the doorway.

Mom began to wail.

Zac took a deep breath in, feeling something brush against his legs. It was Zooey.

"Come on Zooey," he said, his voice cracking. He reached down to pick her up, clutching her to his chest. And began to walk.

Five minutes later, as he was following a narrow dirt path up a small hill, Zac turned back to look at his parents' small house, nestled within huge fields of recently harvested crops.

It was on fire.

* * *

Zac gasped, jerking out of his dream.

He found himself laying on his belly in the dirt, surrounded by half-eaten bushes and tall trees. It took him a moment to realize that he'd been dreaming. He got on all fours, then tried to stand up.

And promptly toppled over, landing on his side on the forest floor with a *thump*.

He grunted, trying to sit up, but his body wouldn't move the way he wanted. His center of balance was all wrong. He looked down at himself…

…and gasped.

For he was utterly naked. Not only that, his skin was black, and covered in places with something that looked like thin bark. His knees were bent the wrong way, like an animal's, and his hands…

His eyes widened.

They were like paws, but with long fingers that terminated in sharp black claws.

Then he remembered the awful truth. Remembered the first time he'd seen the Dark One in the woods. Remembered sniffing his blood, then licking it. The hunger, the voices. Remembered following the Dark One, and finding others that did the same.

I'm not Zac.

The horrible realization twisted his guts, making him feel nauseous. He closed his eyes, taking a deep breath in, then letting it out.

I'm not Zac, he repeated.

These were the Dark One's memories, not his. He was inferior. An animal. A copy.

He made me better.

The creature stood on all fours, sniffing the air around it. Its sense of smell was even duller than it'd been yesterday. But its mind was sharper, faster. It knew words now, even though it could not yet talk.

The Dark One will help me, it knew. *I'm an animal now, but He will make me better.*

The creature caught the scent of another like him, and started forward through the forest to follow it. His belly ached with hunger, that ever-present *need* that he struggled to fulfill. Onward he went, pulling off the leaves of the bushes around him, eating as he made his way through the forest.

Toward the Dark One. Toward the boy who'd been called Zac, and renamed himself Zagamar.

He will make me better, the creature repeated. Better than the animal he still was, and better even than the humans who'd rejected the Dark One. The humans that would inevitably turn against him, to try to stop him. To kill him for the crime of being different.

Zagamar would make *everyone* better.

Chapter 12

Dominus sat across from the Lady Camilla, at the other end of a long wooden table. He leaned back in his chair, noting how uncomfortable it was. A detail the Lady had certainly seen to, as well as the excessive length of the table. One to make him uncomfortable, the other to accentuate the distance between them.

He supposed he should be thankful she hadn't forced him to sit there naked.

"You're looking better," she observed. Dominus supposed he did after his bath, fresh clothes, and a substantial meal. "Aren't you filling out nicely."

"Thank you for your hospitality," he replied, shifting his weight in his uncomfortable chair. She waved his thanks away with one hand.

"Think nothing of it," she insisted. "We may not always get along, but we *are* contemporaries. Or rather, we were."

Dominus suppressed a grimace, absorbing yet another jab at his fall in station.

"You of all people must understand that titles are less important than a man's qualities," he chided.

"Or a woman's," Camilla agreed, giving a little smile. "You wouldn't be here if I wasn't valuable to you," she added. "Tell me…what good are you to me?"

"I have information," he answered.

"Information," she countered, "…is *my* area of expertise."

"You don't have a monopoly on the truth," Dominus retorted. "I have information you might find…extremely compelling."

"Do tell."

Dominus smirked.

"And what do I get in return?" he inquired.

"You're fed," she replied. "And clothed. And I haven't done Tykus the favor of telling them their favorite corrupt former duke is still alive and well."

"I'm far too valuable for you to waste me like that," Dominus countered. She arched an eyebrow. "I was Duke of Wexford for longer than you've been alive," he pointed out. "I know more about the inner workings of the kingdom than any man, other than Tykus himself. And my ability to heal is only one of countless traits I've absorbed over a lifetime."

"Fair enough," she conceded. She knew as well as he did that the Dukes of Wexford went back six thousand years. In that time, they'd accumulated countless priceless Ossae, including those of the greatest warriors, tacticians, and intellectuals who'd ever lived. All of them concentrated into the person sitting before her. "Give me your offer."

"Is Zeno still alive?" Dominus asked. Camilla frowned.

"That's not an offer."

"Is he?" he pressed. She shrugged.

"Perhaps. Your offer is…?"

"My offer is immortality," he declared.

She stared at him for a long moment, then leaned forward, her cleavage practically spilling from her corset. She gave him a little smile, resting a pale elbow on the table and cupping her chin in her hand.

"You've got my attention."

"I am immortal," Dominus stated. "I will never age. I can heal from any wound," he added. Not exactly the truth, he knew, but there was no point in informing Camilla of his weaknesses. "If you help me, I will provide the same abilities to you."

"You're referring to this special Ironclad head you acquired?" she asked. Dominus nodded. Of course she would have found out about it. "And what am I to provide in return?"

"Zeno."

Camilla leaned back in her chair, considering this.

"Why?" she pressed.

"He is a threat to the kingdom," Dominus answered. "And he conspired to assassinate the dukes and King Tykus himself."

Camilla laughed, the melodic sound echoing through the large room.

"Oh Dominus, ever the patriot," she mused. "Your kingdom rejects you and sentences you to death, yet still you protect them?"

"I have my reasons."

"Very well," she decided. "Zeno's head for the Ironclad's. A fair exchange."

"I keep the Ironclad's head," Dominus countered. "After we use it to grant you immortality, I will destroy it."

"Destroy it?"

"It's too dangerous," Dominus reasoned. "In the wrong hands, its power would be devastating. Or would you like your enemies to have immortal armies?"

"Fair enough," she agreed. "I agree to your terms. There's only one…complication."

"And that is?"

"I know exactly where High Seeker Zeno is," she revealed. "But we may find it rather difficult to reach him. It seems he's gone into the Crypt of Zagamar."

Dominus stared at her mutely. At length, he cleared his throat.

"I see," was all he could manage.

"My men constantly surveil the Crypt, of course," she continued. "My scouts saw him trying to enter the other day. A few tried to stop him, but of course Zeno killed them. He hasn't come out since." She sighed. "He's probably dead."

"Perhaps not," Dominus retorted. Zeno had the Ironclad head…a fact that Lady Camilla didn't need to know. If he told her, she could go after Zeno herself and acquire the head without him.

"Are you suggesting I send my men in the Crypt after him?" the Lady inquired, crossing her arms over her chest.

"Of course not."

"If Zeno didn't survive the Crypt, then you already have what you want," the Lady pointed out.

"If," Dominus agreed.

"You're saying you actually believe he might still be alive?" she inquired incredulously. Dominus gave her a grim smile.

"I'm saying its likely."

"Then you know nothing about Zagamar," she retorted. Dominus smirked.

"I know enough."

"There's something you're not telling me," she accused. She stood then, walking toward him, towing her chair behind her. Then she sat down a few feet from him. Dominus understood the importance of the move; the distance between them was smaller now. She was ready to work together.

He paused, considering his options.

"Tell me," Camilla urged, leaning forward and putting a hand on his thigh. This gave an unfettered view of her spectacular cleavage. That, plus the warmth from her hand, was surprisingly effective in achieving its intended goal.

Dominus resisted the urge to squirm, surprised at his body's reaction. He hadn't been able to…rise to the occasion in over a decade. A consequence of the terrible disease that had slowly choked his blood vessels, causing his legs to rot.

"Zeno has the head," he said at last.

Camilla frowned, leaning back in her chair, her hand slipping from his thigh.

"I see," she murmured. "That does complicate things."

"If Zeno is dead, the head is still within the Crypt," Dominus reasoned. "We can't allow anyone else to get it."

"If it's in the Crypt of Zagamar, no one else *will* be able to get it."

"My offer stands whether Zeno is alive or dead," Dominus told her. "The Ironclad head still represents the greatest threat to the kingdom, and to us. We have to retrieve it."

"What's your plan?"

"My will is strong," Dominus replied. It was a fact, not a boast. "I will go to the Crypt and retrieve it."

"Daring," Camilla murmured, clearly surprised…and impressed. "You'll probably die."

"Will I?"

"Ah yes, your immortality," she replied. "If Zeno has the head, then he may be as immortal as you are."

"I possessed it for weeks," Dominus countered. "Zeno has had it for days at most."

"When Hunter when into the Crypt, he found his sword useful in getting through the trials there," Camilla revealed. "It was Vi's originally. Consider it my gift to you."

"The Original went into the Crypt?" Dominus stated incredulously.

"It must have slipped my mind to tell you."

"Right," he grumbled.

"The boy also told me everything he encountered there," Camilla admitted. "I'll debrief you. Perhaps knowing the Crypt's dangers will help."

"I appreciate it."

Camilla stared at him for a long moment, a slight smile curling the corner of her lips.

"How can I trust you to honor your part of the deal?" she inquired.

"You have my word."

"How comforting."

"Feel free to send your men with me," Dominus offered. "If I attempt to double-cross you, have them kill me."

"I could do that anyway, and have the head for myself," she pointed out. "Assuming they could kill you, which I highly doubt."

"I could kill you now, take the sword, and get the head," Dominus countered. "But I won't."

Camilla arched an eyebrow, propping one elbow on the table and giving him a mysterious smile.

"And why won't you?" she inquired.

"Because I understand the value of relationships," Dominus answered. "And if we work together, we'll be far more powerful than if we don't."

"Mmm."

She stood then, gesturing for him to do the same. He did so, and she stepped up to him – far too close for his comfort – leaning in until her lips brushed up against his ear. He smelled her perfume, faint yet tantalizing, and again he felt his body respond. A strange and powerful sensation after years of absence. Promising something he hadn't felt in…

"You have yourself a deal," she murmured, her breath hot in his ear. She stepped back then, smiling at him in that maddening way of hers. "To relationships," she added, holding out the back of her hand.

Dominus held her hand, leaning down to kiss it.

"To relationships," he replied.

CHAPTER 13

The sun was just beginning to set beyond the tall black stone walls of the Kingdom of the Deep, a cool breeze caressing the land. Sukri stumbled on the wide grassy path leading away from the large treehouse she and Kayla had just come down from, a sprawling, multi-level tavern. They'd left the Shrine and gone to the tavern for a few drinks…all part of Kayla's promise to get Sukri drunk before returning to the Shrine. Sukri felt Kayla's soft, furry arm around her waist, and turned to look at the cat-woman. She was absolutely beautiful, her exotic golden eyes slanting slightly upward, her short gray fur thick and luxurious. Her gaze fell to the woman's lithe body, which had curves in all the right places.

"You," she said, slurring the word slightly, "…have an *amazing* ass."

"Thank you," Kayla replied.

"Can I…?" Sukri inquired. Kayla's lips curled into a smile, and she nodded. Sukri slid her hand down the small of the woman's back, resting her hand on the prominent bulge of her left buttock. "Damn," she murmured. "You're all muscle!"

"Takes a big butt to jump as high as I do," Kayla explained.

"How high *can* you jump?" Sukri inquired. Again she slurred her words a little. Not for nothing, but the drinks they made in that tavern had been *amazing*. And strong, even for Sukri.

"Over three times my height," Kayla answered. "Maybe four."

"Wow," Sukri murmured. She kept her hand on Kayla's butt, enjoying the feel of it as they walked. She ran her fingertips up and down it's gentle curve, feeling the short, soft fur there. Heat radiated from Kayla, she found; the woman had to be a few degrees hotter than Sukri. "You feel really warm," she said.

"We have a higher body temperature than humans."

"Yeah," Sukri replied with a grin. "You're hot as hell."

Kayla only smiled, and they continued their walk through the kingdom. Eventually Sukri recognized that they were close to the main entrance.

"Where we going?" she asked. "Thought we were going back to the Shrine."

"We will," Kayla reassured. She led Sukri toward a small hut ahead, what they apparently called a wigwam. Kayla brought Sukri to the entrance, gesturing for her to enter. She did so, finding a surprisingly spacious interior with animal skins lying on the floor to one side. Kayla sat down on them in one graceful movement, patting the spot to her left. Sukri sat beside her, close enough that their shoulders pressed together.

"This your place?" Sukri inquired, looking around. Her head swam pleasantly.

"It was."

"Was?"

"Before I evolved," Kayla explained. "I only come here when it's raining now. I like to sleep out in the stars."

"Don't you get cold?"

"Do I feel cold?" Kayla countered, putting a hand on Sukri's thigh. Her palm had fur on most of it, with a small hairless section in the upper part of her palm and on each fingertip. And it was very warm.

"How do your claws work?" Sukri asked, shifting her weight uneasily. Kayla held up her other hand, palm down, spreading her fingers wide.

"See your fingertips?" she answered. "Mine are actually pulled backward," she explained. "I can extend them," she continued. Long, sharp claws appeared out of her fur, swinging forward and downward. "Then I can pull them back again." She did so, and the claws swung upward and backward, vanishing into her fur again.

"Always wondered how that worked," Sukri admitted. "Don't claw me," she added with a silly grin. Kayla smiled.

"I would never hurt you," she replied. "Unless you asked me to."

Sukri stared at her, feeling the heat and light pressure of Kayla's hand still on her thigh. A warmth spread down her lower belly into her groin…along with an unmistakable tingling sensation. She swallowed in a dry throat, staring into those hypnotic golden eyes.

"I might, a little bit," she admitted.

She felt a sudden pinprick sensation on her thigh, and looked down, seeing a single claw extending from Kayla's index finger, making a slight dent in her skin.

"Like this?"

"It's a start," Sukri murmured.

Kayla retracted the claw, lifting her hand from Sukri's thigh. She stood then, stepping behind Sukri, then sitting down again so that Sukri was sitting between her legs. Sukri felt the heat of Kayla's belly on her lower back, and resisted the urge to squirm.

"I give excellent back scratches," Kayla said. Sukri felt Kayla's hands slip under her shirt, soft fingertips traveling all the way up to the back of her neck, then trailing down her spine. A chill ran through her, giving her goosebumps.

"Oh," Sukri murmured. Up and down Kayla's fingers went…and then they transitioned from soft pressure to a sudden sharpness. Not painful, but surprising. Sukri stiffened.

"Relax," Kayla murmured.

Sukri tried to, feeling Kayla's claws trailing gently down her back. More goosebumps.

"That," she confessed, "…feels *amazing.*"

"Told you," Kayla said, and Sukri could tell she was smiling. Kayla kept going, and Sukri felt the tension leave her body. At length, Kayla stopped, slipping her hands out from underneath her shirt.

"Aww," Sukri said. "I was just starting to…"

"Take your shirt off," Kayla ordered.

"Excuse me?"

"Take off your shirt," Kayla repeated. "So I can give you a better back scratch."

"Oh," Sukri mumbled. She hesitated, then pulled off her shirt, throwing it to the side. She wasn't particularly shy, having even gone topless in front of Gammon in the past – and reveling in his obvious discomfort.

"You have bruises," Kayla noted. Sukri felt her fingers tracing them.

"My trainer's an asshole," Sukri muttered.

Kayla didn't reply, resuming the back scratch. Sukri sighed, closing her eyes and enjoying it. Kayla focused on the middle of her back, to either side of her spine, then gradually moved outward toward her flanks…which gave Sukri more goosebumps. Then the claws transitioned to soft fingertips again, sliding up her flanks…and grazing the sides of her breasts.

She shivered.

The fingertips went down again, crossing over to the sides of her belly. Sukri felt Kayla lean in, her hot, soft fur pressing against Sukri's back. Up the fingertips went, sliding past either side of her bellybutton, then continuing upward. They reached the undersides of Sukri's breasts, stopping there. Kayla pulled Sukri into her, pressing her chest and belly against Sukri's back. Sukri felt Kayla's breath on the right side of her neck.

"What…" she began, but her voice caught in her throat. She cleared it noisily, her heart pounding against her breastbone. Sukri felt something soft strike her belly gently, and realized it was Kayla's tail. It tickled her bellybutton, then slid up her belly, past Kayla's hands, and flicked across Sukri's right nipple.

Which reacted immediately, feeling almost uncomfortably tight…and making the heat and tingling in her groin intensify. She felt a pulsing there, and shifted her weight a little. Which was a mistake, as she was getting mighty sensitive down there.

Kayla's tail slid up to Sukri's neck, then whipped back down, grazing her nipple again.

"Mmm," Sukri mumbled, squirming in Kayla's grasp. But Kayla only tightened her grip on Sukri's rib cage, just below her bust. Another flick, and Sukri's nipple was painfully erect. "Okay now," she managed to blurt out, leaning forward to try to pull away from Kayla. But the woman was surprisingly strong, pulling Sukri forcefully back against her. "What are you doing?"

Kayla leaned in, resting her chin on Sukri's right shoulder and gazing at her with those big golden eyes. She was smiling.

"Giving you what you wanted," she replied.

"What I…what?"

"I brought you to the tavern," Kayla explained, "…and now this." She pressed her lips against Sukri's shoulder, kissing it. "You said you were tempted to become like me, back in the Shrine."

"Oh yeah."

"I asked you what would help you make your decision," Kayla continued, trailing her tail up Sukri's belly…and flicking her nipple yet again. It was exquisitely sensitive now, and a little painful…but not in a bad way. The tingling and pulsing between Sukri's legs grew more insistent, and she squirmed again. Things were definitely not dry down there anymore.

"And?" Sukri pressed.

"You said alcohol," Kayla replied, "…and me."

"I did say that," Sukri admitted. "Kinda meant that you would tell me all about how awesome it…"

Another flick, this time to the left nipple.

Sukri's breath caught in her throat, and she tried to twist away. But Kayla held her fast…and Sukri felt the slightest pricks of the woman's claws against her ribs.

"*Uh* uh," Kayla chastised. "Stay still."

Sukri froze, her heart pounding in her chest. She was pretty sure Kayla wouldn't *really* hurt her, but the implied danger had its effect. Both nipples were painfully engorged now, and her neck was incredibly sensitive. Kayla shifted, the silky fur on her cheek brushing against the side of Sukri's neck, and Sukri shivered.

"Lie down," Kayla ordered, letting go of Sukri and standing up. "On your belly."

Sukri cleared her throat, glancing back at her.

"Thought you said Chartreux were subservient."

"Do it," Kayla pressed, her tail whipping out and lashing Sukri's back. It didn't hurt much, but it sure got the point across. Sukri obeyed, laying on her belly on the soft animal fur below her. She felt Kayla's fingertips on her back, then sharpness as Kayla brought her claws gently down Sukri's back…all the way to her pants. Sukri felt tugging there.

"What…?"

"Lift up your hips," Kayla ordered. Sukri resisted.

"Um, I'm not wearing any underwear."

"Neither am I," Kayla reminded her.

Sukri hesitated, then lifted her hips, and Kayla pulled her pants down over her butt, then slid them down and off her legs. Sukri felt the cool night air on her bare posterior, and felt incredibly exposed. She had the sudden, powerful urge to get up and get dressed, and leave the wigwam behind. But she felt Kayla's hands on her lower back again, claws trailing over her buttocks and down the back of her legs.

More goosebumps.

Her hands slid up Sukri's legs and buttocks, and then Sukri felt the claws come out. Down they went, making her shiver. Kayla slid her hands up Sukri's inner thighs, then back down, caressing them.

Then she got up, circling around to kneel by Sukri's head.

She ran her soft, furry fingers through Sukri's scalp, kneading it gently, then focusing on Sukri's neck and upper back. Sukri felt herself relaxing; Kayla was good with her hands, and it'd been a long time since Sukri had been touched.

"Turn over," Kayla ordered.

Sukri hesitated, then did so, turning onto her back, looking upward. Kayla knelt just beyond her head, leaning over her, a smile on her lips.

"What are you…" Sukri began, but Kayla pressed a finger against Sukri's lips.

"Shhh."

Kayla cupped Sukri's temples gently in her hands, then got down on all fours, leaning in and pressing her lips against Sukri's forehead. Her lips, like the rest of her, were warm to the point of being hot.

"I…"

Kayla leaned down a little further, pressing her lips against Sukri's. They felt incredibly soft, the smell of her fur surprisingly pleasant. Kayla held the kiss for a moment, then pulled away a few centimeters. Her golden eyes seemed to stare right through Sukri.

Then she leaned in again, kissing Sukri…and biting her lower lip gently. Sukri felt Kayla's tongue flick across her lip. To her surprise, it was soft.

"Thought you'd have a rough tongue," Sukri said after the kiss ended. Kayla smiled, leaning in again and kissing her. This time their mouths opened, their tongues mingling gently. No, her tongue was *definitely* not rough.

"I kept it soft," Kayla admitted. "For a reason."

"What's that?"

Kayla didn't answer, kissing Sukri again. It felt marvelous, this slow, sensual kissing. Kayla took her time, rushing nothing. It made Sukri feel positively giddy…and more drunk than she already was.

Kayla pulled away for a moment, eyeing Sukri with an expression she couldn't read.

"What?" Sukri asked.

"Have I helped you make your decision?" Kayla inquired.

"Mmm, maybe," Sukri replied. "I could use a little more convincing."

Kayla smirked, leaning down and kissing Sukri again. Then she crawled forward a few centimeters, on all fours, until her breasts were right over Sukri's face. She leaned down, kissing Sukri's breastbone, then her upper belly…and continued downward, licking Sukri's bellybutton.

Sukri swallowed, her heart *thumping* in her chest, her whole body tingling.

Still lower Kayla went, crawling so her own belly was brushing up against Sukri's nose. Sukri felt Kayla's mouth on her lower belly, that soft tongue trailing down even further. Ever-so-slowly, centimeter-by-centimeter, until it was perilously close to the pulsing between her legs. Sukri squirmed, her hips bucking uncontrollably, wanting nothing more than to meet that tongue. Yearning for it.

But Kayla kept her lips just above, torturing Sukri…all the while sliding her lower belly over Sukri's nose, until her own groin was positioned right above Sukri's face. Sukri stared upward, feeling Kayla's lips on her skin, her legs trembling.

"Touch my butt," Kayla murmured.

Sukri complied, reaching around and cupping Kayla's buttocks. She squeezed them, then pulled Kayla toward her, feeling the woman's lips touch hers. They were hot…incredibly so. Sukri kissed them, then flicked her tongue between them.

"Mmm," she heard Kayla murmur, feeling Kayla's buttocks contract under her hands.

And then Kayla's lips slid downward, and Sukri felt hot wetness there, meeting the pulsing in her groin. She gasped, tensing up, her hips bucking again. Kayla kept her mouth on her, flicking her tongue gently against Sukri.

"Mmm," Sukri murmured. "Oh!" she gasped, turning her head to the side and shuddering. Kayla continued to work on her, slowly and gently at first, then faster. Sukri returned the favor, matching Kayla's movements. She felt Kayla react, grinding her hips into Sukri's face, moaning as Sukri went faster…and going faster herself. Sukri felt a mounting pleasure between her legs, one that grew with every second. She groaned, gripping Kayla's butt tightly and taking Kayla fully into her mouth. She felt Kayla tense up, felt Kayla's tongue go faster, heard the woman moan again.

The pleasure grew, and as it did, Sukri went faster, feeling Kayla do the same. Sukri tensed up, pulling her hips up, her pleasure growing stronger. She was getting close.

Kayla gave a muffled moan, her hips bucking once, then again. She tried to pull her hips away from Sukri's mouth, but Sukri pulled her in, crushing Kayla's pelvis against her face. Faster she went. Harder.

Kayla's body went rigid…and her mouth went mad, her tongue working relentlessly on Sukri. Sukri felt her pleasure rise, and tried to pull her hips down away from Kayla, but it was no use. She had no chance against Kayla's assault. There was no escaping the inevitable.

She felt Kayla's hips convulse rhythmically against her…just as her own pleasure peaked.

Sukri stiffened, holding her breath…and holding back the inevitable torrent that awaited her. Then she gasped, letting go, giving in to the ecstasy. Kayla did not relent, even in the throes of her own ecstasy, bringing Sukri wave after wave of pleasure until she was capable of no more.

Even then, as Kayla's mouth lifted from her groin at last, Sukri felt a rhythmic pulsing there, the aftershocks of her rapture.

Kayla pulled away from Sukri, crawling backward, then leaning down and kissing Sukri full on the lips. She pulled away, smiling at Sukri.

"Are you convinced?" she inquired.

"Sold," Sukri replied.

CHAPTER 14

Hunter lay on his side on the cool rocky ledge sixty feet below the edge of the Deep, his knees curled up to his chest. Sweat dripped from every pore in his body, his heart pounding in his ears. Remembering the ungodly pain that had stopped just seconds earlier. Torture beyond anything he could have imagined. He closed his eyes, taking deep, slow breaths, collecting himself. Then he straightened, out, rolling onto his belly and standing up.

Or at least he tried to.

A heavy weight pulled him backward as he stood, and he stumbled, nearly falling off the narrow ledge. He grabbed onto the thick vine next to him, holding onto it for dear life.

Jesus.

There was no pain now. No itching. Hunter looked down at his naked body, seeing huge pecs there. They looked even larger than before, but were no longer red or irritated-looking. He spotted a flash of white to his right, and turned his head to look at it.

A chill ran down his spine.

They were white feathers, he realized. Long white feathers attached to a large wing. A *very* large wing. He felt a twitching sensation in his back, and saw the wing move.

Oh shit.

He looked to his other side, seeing another wing there, spreading out at least five feet to his left, if not more.

Oh shit oh shit…

He fought against a rising panic, forcing himself to take slow breaths. Closing his eyes, he recited the mantra Vi had taught him.

Emotion is temporary.

There was another twitching sensation in his back, and the sound of rustling feathers.

Emotion is temporary, he recited. *Action is forever.*

He grimaced, opening his eyes and staring at the vine before him.

"You acted," he muttered. "And now it's forever."

He let go of his death-grip on the vine slowly, adjusting to the new weight on his back. There was the slightest of breezes, and he felt himself being pulled backward. He grabbed onto the vine again, feeling the air flowing over his wings, its touch a gentle caress.

I can feel my wings!

Hunter paused, focusing on his right wing. On the feeling of the breeze flowing over it. He tried moving it; the limb of the wing felt like a second pair of arms, he realized, complete with a shoulder, elbow, wrist, and hand. He tried moving at the shoulder, as if he was bringing his elbow away from his body…and the wing flared outward.

Holy shit.

Hunter bent at the elbow then, and the wing pulled inward a bit. He extended the elbow, and the wing flared out to the side again. Moving the "fingers" moved the last third or so of the wing, including the tip. And the movements were extremely difficult, requiring all of his concentration…and they were still bumbling and awkward, his movements shaky.

It was *freaky.*

"HUNTER!" he heard a voice shout from above.

He glanced up, seeing Xerxes leaning over the edge of the abyss, looking down at him.

"YOU…OKAY?"

"Fine," Hunter shouted back. "Other than I'm a *fucking* bird."

"CLIMB…UP?"

"Don't have a choice, do I," Hunter shot back. It wasn't like Xerxes could climb down here and get him, after all. They'd end up getting merged by the Deep. As much as he liked his brother, he couldn't see himself inside of the guy. He sighed, starting the long climb up to the top. The weight of his wings made it awkward, so he took his time, making sure his handholds and footholds were secure before continuing.

A gentle breeze whipped around him…and nearly tore him right off the vine.

"The hell?" he swore, holding onto the vine as tightly as he could. He glanced back, seeing his wings flared outward. He tried tucking them in – by pulling his "arms" to his sides and bending the "elbows" – and his wings tucked all the way in to his back. The force threatening to pull him off the vine vanished. He focused on keeping his wings in this position, continuing the climb up the vine. It was enormously difficult, holding his wings like this; he felt like a toddler when he moved them, with no coordination whatsoever. Eventually he made it to the top, Xerxes helping to pull him well clear of the edge of the pit. Xerxes stared at him for a long, silent moment.

"Don't say anything," Hunter grumbled, feeling another breeze try to catch his wings. He moved further from the edge of the pit; the last thing he needed was a strong wind to blow him into the damn abyss.

"LOOK…PRETTY," Xerxes offered, ignoring Hunter's demand. Hunter shot him a murderous look.

"What did I just say?"

"LIKE…*ANGEL*," Xerxes continued, breaking out into a big grin.

"Oh for Christ's sake," Hunter grumbled.

Xerxes chuckled, and Hunter took a few steps back from the Deep. His wings were like trying to carry an umbrella in a strong wind. Any little breeze – unless he kept them tucked in – could push him around. A strong breeze might send him flying away like a damn kite.

He sat down, concentrating on his wings again. If he flexed his pecks – pulling his "arms" in – his wings flapped, pulling forward directly in front of him. And, he noted, it made his chest look even bigger. If he did the opposite – like trying to pull his arms behind him – the wings went all the way back. They really were like a second pair of arms. A bumbling, awkward pair.

"YOU…OKAY?" Xerxes asked. Hunter sighed.

"This is gonna take some getting used to," he admitted. At least he knew the Deep had worked on him. His change had been abrupt and monumentally painful, like his mother's. He stood up, getting dressed – after more extreme modifications to his shirt, of course – and faced his brother. Xerxes was staring at him. Just…staring.

"What?" Hunter demanded, feeling rather self-conscious.

"WANT…SEE YOU…FLY."

"I can barely move the damn things," Hunter grumbled. "I feel like a toddler trying to walk for the first time." He turned away from Xerxes, starting the long walk back to the Kingdom of the Deep. "Gonna be a long time before I'm flying, if I ever even *learn* how to fly."

Xerxes walked beside Hunter, looking down at him with a big grin. He touched Hunter's left wing, running his hand over the feathers.

"FUN TO…WATCH…TRY."

"Ha ha," Hunter grumbled, tucking his wings in as best he could, pulling it away from his brother's touch. "Let's just get back home."

* * *

The trip back through the veritable graveyard of skeletons surrounding the Deep – failed experiments of the monstrous pit's strange power to fuse creatures together – was thankfully less eventful, no more creatures daring to attack them. After making their way back down the rocky hill to the forest, the sun had already started to set. They made camp in the usual fashion, laying on the ground to go to sleep. Having wings made sleeping awkward for Hunter; it was almost impossible to sleep on his back, and he hated sleeping on his belly. He eventually found a comfortable position laying on his side, draping one wing over his face.

Then, mercifully, he slept.

The next morning, Xerxes woke them both up early, and they continued their trek through the woods. Hunter took the opportunity to practice moving his wings, folding them and spreading them out, and putting them in various positions in-between. Breezes were annoying…that is, until he took the opportunity to see how he could interact with them. He soon found that if he leaned over and spread his wings, tensing them up when strong breeze blew right at him, it would push him backward…but also nearly pull him off the ground. Xerxes caught him practicing this, and stopped.

"What are you doing?" he signed.

"Just experimenting with the wind."

"Wind?" Xerxes pressed.

Hunter frowned, then realized that, with his armor, Xerxes probably couldn't feel breezes very easily. Or maybe Hunter was just more sensitive to the wind because it affected his wings so profoundly.

"Watch," he prompted. There was a pretty strong breeze blowing toward them; he leaned into it, spreading his wings all the way out and pulling them forward a little. The wind caught them, and Hunter slid backward, his toes dragging across the grass.

Xerxes grunted.

"I bet if I flap my wings once, I might even be able to get off the ground," Hunter ventured.

"Do it," Xerxes signed.

"Alright," Hunter agreed.

He waited for another breeze, then spread his wings out again. The breeze pulled him back, and he felt it fill his wings. He pulled his wings forward again, using his chest muscles…and promptly lifted a couple feet off the ground.

"Whoa!" he cried, folding his wings back. He fell to the ground, stumbling backward. "You see that?"

"AWE…SOME," Xerxes confirmed.

"Damn right."

"Again," Xerxes signed. Hunter complied, repeating the performance…and even flapping his wings a little more powerfully. He flew up a good three to four feet, sailing backward…and kept his wings open this time. He glided gently to the ground.

"Yeah!" he exclaimed, feeling positively giddy. "You see that? That was amazing!" Xerxes chuckled. "You know, getting these wings might not be so bad after all," Hunter admitted.

"AGREE."

Hunter tried a few more times, and then the breeze died down, much to his disappointment. He folded his wings, and they continued their trek.

Minutes turned into hours, and before long the sun was shining directly overhead. They stopped to eat, much to Hunter's relief. After summoning Zagamar yesterday – and growing a pair of wings – he never seemed to stop being hungry. Their limited rations made foraging a necessity, and Hunter even found himself accepting hunks of mushroom that Xerxes got for them. It was gross – something no civilized person would normally eat – but it calmed the hunger pangs.

Onward they went, talking on occasion, but mostly enjoying each other's silent company. Xerxes was perfectly happy to talk when talked to, and to be silent otherwise. It was actually rather pleasant, getting to spend time with his brother. The guy was far smarter than he appeared to be, communicating deftly and elegantly when signing…even if he did seem like a dumb, knuckle-dragging brute when he spoke. Hunter recalled his first meeting with Xerxes, when he'd arrived in Varta, and wondered for the umpteenth time what would've happened if Tykus had never gotten him. He never would've been fooled into thinking he'd killed his own mother and brother, and never would've gone to Lady Camilla to get revenge. Which means he never would've drank Zagamar's liquified brains…and had to go to the Deep. He'd probably have ended up with his mom and brother, no wings, no Zagamar…and no Vi.

Of course, that hadn't happened. And honestly, he was glad. Despite everything, things had turned out all right.

"Love you big guy," Hunter said, patting Xerxes on the lower back as they walked. Xerxes gave him a questioning look. "I just…I'm glad I went through the Gate. Getting to meet you, well, it's one of the best things that's ever happened to me."

Xerxes smiled.

"BEFORE…YOU, HEART…HALF. NOW…WHOLE."

Hunter smiled back. A few minutes passed, and Hunter noticed the ground sloping sharply downward ahead, leading to flatter ground a few dozen feet below. They stopped at the edge of the slope.

"Be careful," Xerxes signed. "Don't break a leg."

And then promptly jumped down the hill, rolling wildly to the bottom.

"Must be nice being invincible," Hunter grumbled. He hesitated at the top, peering over. Sliding down on his butt was probably the safest way to go.

Unless…

He spread his wings out, eyeing the bottom of the hill. If he spread his wings out and ran down the steep slope, he might just be able to glide down the hill. Of course, if he lost control, he'd have to tuck his wings and roll down. Which meant he'd probably break a wing. Xerxes had given him some goo, but there was no guarantee he'd heal very quickly. Of course, the big guy could always just take some more goo and spread it over the wound…

"COME," Xerxes urged from the bottom.

"Yeah yeah," Hunter grumbled.

He tensed his wings, then leaned forward, hesitating a moment longer. Then he stepped off the edge, running down the steep slope.

"Ahhhh!" he yelled, his guts doing somersaults as the air caught his wings suddenly. He felt them fill with air, and he leaned forward, his feet lifting off the slope. The ground pulled away quickly, dropping out from beneath him as he glided through the air.

Crap!

He resisted the urge to fold his wings, holding them in their spread position. Forward and downward he glided, until the ground leveled out. He passed directly above Xerxes, at least a dozen feet above the guy's head…which meant he was flying a good twenty feet above the ground. And right toward the tall trees ahead.

"Crap!" he shouted, pulling his wings in…and dropping like a stone. He swore, re-opening his wings, feeling them catch the air like a parachute a few feet above the ground. Seconds later, his feet struck terra firma, and he stumbled to a stop.

Hunter stood there, hands on his knees, his wings safely tucked on his back. Sweat dripped from his forehead, his armpits itching a little. Like they usually did when he got the crap scared out of him. He heard heavy footsteps behind him, and a deep chuckle.

"CLOSE…CALL," Xerxes noted. Hunter grimaced, turning to face his brother.

"Remind me never to do that again," he grumbled. Xerxes chuckled again.

"You'll get used to it," he signed. "Don't stop practicing."

"Easy for you to say," Hunter muttered. "Let's go," he added, walking toward the trees. "We have a war to prepare for."

Chapter 15

Rain poured from the dull gray sky in a steady downpour, making the canopy of leaves overhead tremble violently. It formed deep puddles on the forest floor, filling Zac's boots and soaking through his clothes. He shivered in the cold, hugging himself tightly in a vain attempt to keep warm.

You okay, Zooey?" he asked, glancing back.

Zooey nodded silently, walking behind him. The clothes he'd taken from home were far too big for her, his jacket able to serve as a cloak of sorts. She glanced up at him, her face pale from underneath her hood.

Zooey wasn't really Zooey anymore.

She'd continued to change as they'd traveled together, her hair falling out completely, save for her eyebrows and eyelashes, and the top of her head. Her limbs had grown longer, and – having eaten everything in sight for the last few days – she'd grown significantly bigger. Nearly three feet tall, she walked as he did. And talked. Her claws were nearly gone.

She was practically human.

"Want to ride on my back for a little?" he asked.

She nodded again.

Zac stopped, crouching down, and felt her jump on his back, wrapping her arms around his upper chest. He stood back up, then continued forward through the woods.

Lightning flashed high above, a burst of dull light amidst the gray.

"How are you feeling?" he asked.

"Cold," came Zooey's reply. Her voice was like his, but higher pitched, and more feminine. She could easily pass for his twin sister if she wasn't so short.

Zac hesitated.

"Do you still remember…being a cat?" he asked.

A pause.

"Yeah."

"Sorry," he offered. It'd become clear what he was, after seeing Zooey's transformation. His parents had understood it before him. They'd known what he was. Normally he would've figured it out long before anyone else. He'd always been smarter, after all. His whole life, people seemed…slow.

But this time *he'd* been slow. Because the truth had been too terrible to contemplate. What he was. And what that meant.

Zac pushed the thought away, gritting his teeth.

"Why?" Zooey asked.

"Hmm?"

"Why sorry?" she clarified.

"I…for what I did to you," he explained. "How I've changed you."

He felt Zooey squeeze him, felt her cool cheek against his.

"It's okay," she murmured.

"That's what I would say, even if it wasn't true," he pointed out. He always said he was okay, even when he wasn't. Something he never told his parents, but had confided in Zooey many, many times…when she'd still been a cat.

"I like me better now," she insisted. "I can talk to you, and understand you." She paused. "Now I understand everything you used to tell me, back when I was…me."

Zac swallowed, feeling uneasy. He'd confessed a lot to Zooey over the years. Everything.

"I'm different now," she continued. "You made me better."

He wiped his eyes with the back of his sleeve, hoping Zooey would think it was because of the rain. Minutes passed, until he spotted a clearing in the distance. Zac veered toward it, and moments later they emerged from the forest.

They were on a large hill, he realized…and the ground sloped downward ahead, leading to a valley below. A small town was nestled there, barely visible in the rain.

"There!" he said, relief coursing through him. "Maybe there's an inn or something."

"We don't have much money," Zooey warned.

"We'll make more," he countered. "I can always build things for people."

"True."

"We have enough for a night," he added. "Unless you want to sleep in the rain." Zooey grimaced. As a former cat, the idea clearly didn't appeal to her.

"All right," she agreed.

They made their way down the hillside, reaching one of the larger buildings. A three-story building with a sharply-angled roof. He found the sign. Lionfare's Inn, it read. Zac put Zooey down.

"Hide your…" he began, but Zooey was already pulling her hood well over her head, hiding her face from view. He grabbed the door handle, pulling the door open and stepping through. A small lobby greeted him, the innkeeper standing behind a tall counter. It was an older man, in his fifties or early sixties.

Zac studied him, taking in every detail.

He had graying hair, bald on top and thinning at the sides. Few wrinkles, indicating a life spent mostly indoors. Well-groomed beard and mustache. A man who prided himself on his appearance, even if he was overweight. Clothes wrinkle-free, without stains. But rough hands, with callouses. He did labor, likely carpentry. A good skill for a man who owned an inn, to be able to build and repair furniture.

The counter was polished, without many scratches. Recently sanded. The innkeeper prided himself in the appearance of his inn as well. A man who spent more time in the world than in his head.

Unlike Zac.

In a split-second, Zac finished sizing the man up. Just in time for the man to glance up at them. The innkeeper's eyes went from Zac to Zooey, then to Zac again. Clearly suspicious.

"What'd'you want?" he growled.

"A room for the night," Zac answered. He stepped up to the counter, but the innkeeper stopped him with a gesture.

"Hold on," he ordered. "Back a few steps."

Zac paused, then obeyed.

"What's a couple kids doing out in the rain at night?" the man inquired.

"We're orphans," Zac explained. "Our house burnt down. Our parents…" He swallowed, lowering his gaze and shaking his head.

"Uh huh," the innkeeper replied. He inclined his head at Zooey. "Take off your hood."

"Why?" Zooey asked. The innkeeper rolled his eyes.

"Because if you don't, I kick your ass out," he answered.

Zooey glanced at Zac, who nodded. She reached up, pulling her hood back.

The innkeeper's eyes narrowed.

"She's my sister," Zac explained.

"I can see that."

"We just need a room for one night," Zac stated, dropping a few coins on the counter. "Will this be enough?"

The innkeeper glanced at the coins, inspecting them. Then he reached down behind the counter, putting on a pair of gloves and taking the coins.

"Your room is outside," he declared. "In the shack to the left." He handed Zac a key. "Leave it like you found it."

Zac smiled, nodding his thanks, and they left the inn, running through the rain to their room. It was indeed a shack, separate from the inn itself. A precaution against powerful wills, he knew. There was a small pen attached to the shack surrounding by a little fence, probably for chickens or some such.

They reached the shack, and Zac unlocked the door, opening it and stepping inside.

"Oh," Zooey muttered, covering her nose. The room was small and dusty, and cheaply made. Far from the quality of the main building.

Disposable.

There was a bed in one corner of the room, and Zac pointed to it.

"You can sleep there," he offered. "I'll sleep on the floor."

"There's enough room for both of us," Zoey countered.

"You sure?"

She nodded. They stripped off their wet clothes, and Zac hastily retrieved his blanket from his pack, handing it to Zooey. She was older than him, six in cat years and maybe double his age in human years. And as such, she was…developed.

"Thanks," she murmured. They laid down on the bed together, and Zac stared up at the ceiling, letting out a sigh.

"This is nice," he murmured.

"I think we overpaid," she countered. He smiled, turning to gaze at her.

"Thanks for coming with me," he stated.

"Didn't have much choice," she countered. "Our…your parents would've killed me."

"You didn't know that at the time," he pointed out. She smiled back at him.

"True."

Zooey reached out, running a hand through his hair. The stubs of her claws felt good on his scalp.

"You're…special, Zac," she stated.

"Because I'm a…"

"Because of this," she interrupted, putting two fingers on his forehead. She lowered them to his chest, just to the left of his breastbone. "And this."

He swallowed past a lump in his throat.

"They were afraid, Zac," she continued, staring into his eyes. "They loved you, but they loved themselves more."

Zac rolled onto his back, his vision blurring. He wiped his eyes with the back of his hand, taking a deep, shuddering breath.

"If they'd known you like I do, they wouldn't have been afraid," she insisted, running her fingers through his scalp again. "I'm lucky to share this," she added, pointing to his forehead, then his heart again.

"Thanks Zooey," he mumbled. She leaned in, kissing him on the cheek.

"Thank *you*," she replied.

"For what?" he asked.

"For making me better."

***

Sukri opened her eyes groggily.

She was lying on her side on a bed of animal furs, in a small room with thatched walls. There was something pressed against her face; she reached up, touching it…and realized that it was something rough but slightly flexible.

A mask.

She stared at her hand, realizing that it was completely wrapped in a yellow-brown material.

What the hell?

Sukri frowned, looking down at herself. Her entire body was covered in the same material. Even her feet. She wracked her brain, trying to remember what'd happened to her. How she'd gotten…

She felt movement against her back, and then an arm draped across her chest. A slender arm covered in short gray fur.

She froze.

It came to her then, her memories of the night before. Getting drunk at the tavern, then going back to the wigwam with Kayla. Their…night together. Then their repeat performance a half-hour later. And again, and again.

Sukri touched the mask covering her face again, running her fingers over it.

Kayla'd taken her back to the Shrine afterward, guiding her to the fifth floor of the place. She remembered lying down in a small room, on a wooden cot. A woman wrapping her up like a cocoon. And then…

Then it got hazy.

She gazed at the wall ahead, recognizing it. She was back in Kayla's wigwam. They must have come back here after the…procedure.

Shit.

She looked down at herself again, at the wrappings covering her. Imagined herself covered in fur. A bolt of fear went through her.

You've done some stupid shit when you were drunk, she told herself. *But this…*

The thought of lying here was suddenly too much for her to bear. She had to move.

Sukri sat up, twisting around to look at Kayla, whose arm slipped off of her. Kayla opened her eyes sleepily, gazing up at Sukri. She smiled, reaching out and stroking Sukri's arm.

"Hey you," she purred.

"Hey," Sukri mumbled.

"You okay?"

Sukri didn't answer, staring down at Kayla. At her golden eyes and gray fur, her pointed ears. Imagining herself looking like that. Not being *herself* anymore. She had the sudden urge to tear off her wrappings…and would've done so if Kayla hadn't sat up, cupping Sukri's face between her warm, furry hands.

"Hey," Kayla said, staring into her eyes. "It's okay."

"I don't…"

"Shhh," Kayla interjected, leaning in and kissing Sukri on the lips. Sukri allowed this, swallowing past a lump in her throat. "You're going to be okay," Kayla reassured.

"I think I made a mistake," Sukri confessed, moisture blurring her vision. "I…"

"This is normal," Kayla insisted calmly, running a hand over Sukri's head. Which was also wrapped.

What have I done?

"You're going to freak out," Kayla stated, her tone soothing. She leaned in, kissing Sukri again. "Everyone does."

"You did?"

"I did," Kayla confirmed. "It's part of the process."

"Of turning into a cat?"

"Of saying goodbye," Kayla corrected. Sukri frowned. "To become something else, we have to say goodbye to what we were," Kayla explained.

"But I like who I am," Sukri insisted. Kayla arched an eyebrow.

"Do you?"

Sukri hesitated. She'd spent her whole life not liking who she was. Wanting to be something more. That's why she'd been so dead-set on becoming a Seeker. And she'd dragged Gammon into it with her.

And that'd turned out just *great.*

Now she was under the Lady's thumb…and she had no choice in that matter either. This – doing what she'd done – was the first choice she'd made in a long time that'd been *hers*. Maybe not the best choice, but she'd made it.

"No," she confessed.

"This is your chance to reinvent yourself," Kayla said, smiling at her. "I was scared too, but I would never go back now. Being me," she added, gesturing at her herself, "…is wonderful."

"You are pretty wonderful," Sukri admitted.

"So are you," Kayla replied.

"You don't really know me."

"I can tell you're a good person," Kayla countered. "Cats are very good at reading people."

"I've done some bad things," Sukri confessed. An image of Udeln came to her…her fellow Seeker candidate. The innocent man she'd been forced to slaughter, slicing his throat open and watching him die. And the young boy High Seeker Zeno had forced her to kill.

Things she could never tell another soul. No one would love her if they found out what she'd done.

"That doesn't make you a bad person," Kayla retorted. "It makes you human."

"You don't understand what they made me do," Sukri muttered, tears dripping down her cheeks, she tried to turn her head away from Kayla, but the woman turned Sukri's head gently back to face her.

"This is a new beginning," she insisted.

"No it's not," Sukri retorted. "Dio's just going to turn me into a killer like he is. I can't…I don't have a choice."

"Dio is your trainer?"

"Yeah," Sukri confirmed. "You know him?"

"Yes," Kayla answered. "Everyone knows of him. He's a formidable warrior…a Seeker of the Shrine of the Reptiles."

"He's a snake all right," Sukri grumbled. "He murdered my friend."

"I'm sorry," Kayla murmured, stroking the side of Sukri's mask. "But you don't have to stay with him. The Kingdom may take you in."

"What?"

"Apply for citizenship here," Kayla urged. "The Kingdom of the Deep can protect you. Dio wouldn't dare go against us."

Sukri hesitated, daring to hope.

"I can do that?"

"You can," Kayla confirmed. "Just register with the Shrine of Mammals and ask for citizenship. You'll need a citizen to vouch for you, so I'll come with you."

"You'd do that for me?"

"Of course," Kayla answered, smiling at her. She leaned in and kissed her again, and this time Sukri kissed her back. "Cats hate snakes."

Sukri smiled at that.

"Guess I'll fit in," she ventured. "So that's it? I just apply?"

"Yes," Kayla confirmed. "If you pass the initial screening, the Elders will read your memories to confirm your character."

Sukri froze.

"What?"

"They'll read your memories," Kayla repeated.

"They can do that?" Sukri asked.

"Yes."

Sukri swallowed in a dry throat.

"Maybe I shouldn't do this," she confessed. Kayla gave her a reassuring smile, putting a soft, warm paw on her arm.

"It will be okay," she insisted.

"I don't know," Sukri muttered. "It's all happening so fast. I…I need to think about it."

"Of course," Kayla agreed.

"And about…this," Sukri added, gesturing at her wrappings. "I mean, I *love* the way you are," she added, "…and I'm sure I'd love being like you too, it's just…"

"It's okay," Kayla interjected. "You're allowed to be unsure."

"Were you?"

"I was," Kayla confirmed. "I almost changed my mind. But I didn't. I faced my fear. I faced the unknown. And now my body is different…I can do things I could never do before. But my mind is still the same…mostly."

"Mostly?"

"Chartreux are affectionate and loyal," she explained. "And playful, like I said before. We're pleasers, and love attention. You end up absorbing that. It really isn't a bad thing."

"I enjoyed it last night," Sukri admitted with a rueful grin.

"Would it help you relax if I…pleased you?" Kayla inquired. Sukri hesitated, glancing down at her wrappings. Her groin was covered.

"I'm kind of wrapped up."

"Those are easy to get off," Kayla said, leaning in and kissing her, then pushing her gently down onto her back. She crawled backward, kissing Sukri's wrapped belly. "People *do* have to pee, after all."

"I guess it wouldn't hurt to take my mind off of things," Sukri reasoned. Kayla didn't reply, focusing on removing the wrappings around her groin. "So that's how you do it," Sukri murmured.

Kayla finished taking off the wrappings, proving that they *were* easy to get off. And moments later, that Sukri was too.

Chapter 16

Dominus walked down the crushed stone path to the gate protecting Lady Camilla's mansion, the footsteps of two of the Lady's Seekers following behind him *crunching* with each step. He reached the gate, the guard standing by it opening it for him. He continued onward, the Seekers trailing behind him.

Dominus knew full well their real purpose: reconnaissance. And potentially to ensure that Dominus kept his end of the bargain. Of course, she could also be planning to have them kill him after he retrieved the head...or even before, if she felt he was too dangerous to keep alive.

Not that he was worried. Every contingency was accounted for, with a strategy for dealing with each of them.

Camilla would expect no less from Dominus, of course. It was the never-ending game they'd been playing their entire lives, plans within plans, attacks and counterattacks, a shadow war between members of the aristocracy...and former members. A game they played as much for the thrill of it as for any marginal advantage they might gain over each other. A game Camilla was very good at.

But Dominus was better.

He continued onward toward three horses tied to stakes ahead, feeling the weight of his pack on his back. A few large meals had filled him out considerably, his regenerative powers quickly converting the flesh he'd consumed to flesh of his own. He was even stronger now than before he'd been impaled and burned, able to carry his pack and sword – while wearing leather armor – without losing his breath.

It was remarkable.

They reached the horses, mounting them and turning to where the forest met the shore of the River Ormr. The Seekers led the way, both having acted as scouts around the Crypt of Zagamar in the past. They reached the shore, riding parallel to the river for a kilometer, then turning right down a wide dirt path through the forest. Though winter was still months away, many of the lower branches of the trees were bare, the underbrush gone. The forest was unusually quiet, the *clop, clop* of the horses' hooves the only sound. It gave Dominus time to think…and to plan.

If this mission was successful, then the Ironclad head would be destroyed…at the expense of a much more powerful Lady Camilla. Assuming he kept his promise and delivered the head to her. Doing so would strengthen their partnership, one that could be valuable to him. But he also needed to think in much larger timeframes now; with a life potentially extending into infinity, did he really need to try to consolidate power at the risk of creating an equally eternal enemy?

So many options, each with consequences that would ripple through the centuries ahead.

He sighed, eyeing the two Seekers riding side-by-side a few meters ahead of him.

A dark shape leapt out from the trees to the right, slamming into the rightmost Seeker and throwing him off his horse.

The Seekers' horses squealed, rearing up on their hind legs, nearly throwing the second Seeker off. Dominus's horse balked, backing away from the shadowy figure grappling with the first Seeker. A small black beast with long arms and legs.

It tore into the Seeker's face, ripping off his mask and plunging its thumbs into his eye-sockets, twisting the orbs free from the man's face with a muted *pop*…and eating them.

The Seeker *screamed.*

The second Seeker dismounted, drawing twin scimitars and rushing up to the beast, slashing at it. It dodged, leaping off the first Seeker and throwing itself at the second.

The Seeker side-stepped, whipping his scimitars in a vicious angle downward, slicing off the beast's arm at the elbow.

The creature spun, clawing the Seeker's face with its remaining hand, knocking the black and red mask off the man. Then it grabbed its own severed arm, whipping it around like a club and smashing the Seeker in the temple.

Dominus leapt off his horse and sprinted at the creature, his sword already in his hands. The monster whirled to face him…and Dominus's breath caught in his throat.

Its face was human…or rather, humanoid. It had black skin interspersed with patches of what appeared to be bark, and a face that was slightly too long, its eyes sunken. And had long fingers and toes ending in vicious-looking black claws.

It snarled at him, leaping right at him!

Dominus let his body go loose, allowing his reflexes to manifest themselves. His sword was a blur, slashing at the creature's throat…but the thing moved even faster than him, dodging out of the way, then lunging at him again. Dominus side-stepped, thrusting his sword right into the thing's flank, burying it in the thing's flesh.

The creature ignored the wound, grabbing the blade with its remaining hand and yanking it out of Dominus's grasp, tossing the blade into the forest.

Dominus cursed, backpedaling as the creature growled at him, blood pouring from its wounded flank.

Then it attacked, raking at Dominus's face with its claws.

Dominus blocked the blow with one forearm, kicking the thing in the chest. But the creature was too fast, dodging out of the way…and throwing Dominus off-balance. He stumbled, and the beast raked at Dominus's ear.

He felt a sharp pain there, followed by hot wetness pouring down the side of his neck.

Dominus grunted, blocking another swipe at his face, then feigning another kick. The creature dodged…and Dominus elbowed it right in the temple.

It stumbled to the side, dazed.

Dominus leapt on the thing, shoving it onto its belly and pinning its remaining arm behind its shoulder blade. He reached around its neck with his other arm, getting it in a chokehold.

He *squeezed.*

The creature struggled, thrashing wildly, nearly throwing Dominus off of its back. But Dominus held on, tightening his chokehold and pulling backward so hard the creature's back arched.

Its windpipe *cracked.*

There was a gurgling shriek, and the thing flailed wildly for a few more moments. Then it slowed, and stopped, slumping to the ground.

Dominus held the chokehold for a full minute longer, then let go, stumbling backward. He stared at the dead creature, then reached up to his right ear. There was nothing there…just a bloody flap of tissue. The thing had torn his ear off.

He stood there for a moment longer, his heart *thumping* in his chest, then turned, seeing the two Seekers lying on the ground. One with no eyes, the other groaning and trying to stand, a large gash on his temple.

Dominus went into the forest, retrieving his sword. Then he stopped before the eyeless Seeker. The man was no use to the Lady now…or to him.

He plunged his sword into the man's heart.

The other Seeker got to his feet, turning to stare at Dominus…and his fellow Seeker. The man's jaw dropped open.

"What did you…" he began.

"He was good as dead," Dominus interjected coldly. "Get your horse."

Dominus went to retrieve his own steed, taking a few minutes to find it standing on the dirt path. He mounted it, riding back to the Seeker, who'd managed to retrieve his.

"What was that thing?" the Seeker asked.

"I don't know," Dominus admitted.

"It moved so fast…I've never seen anything like it."

"Me neither," Dominus confessed. "We need to be cautious."

He started his horse forward, continuing the trek down the wide path. The Seeker hesitated, then followed after him.

"What are you doing?" he demanded. "We have to go back!"

"Do we?"

"Your ear is ripped off," the Seeker reminded him.

"I'll be fine."

"What if there are more of them?" the Seeker pressed. "We…"

And then they both froze.

For there, not a half-kilometer away, was another one of the black creatures. It crouched on all fours in the middle of the path, turning its grotesque head to face them. It was slightly different than the last one they'd seen, with thicker, shorter limbs and a short tail. But it too had inky-black skin, with sunken eyes and sharp claws.

It stared at them.

Dominus heard rustling to his right, and spotted another black shape emerging from between the trees there. Another one of the creatures…but much larger. As big as a bear…and covered in black, patchy fur.

More of them appeared, coming out from behind the trees, all of them staring at Dominus. Over a dozen of them.

Dominus yanked on his reins, pulling his steed back the way they'd come and kicking his heels into the horse's flanks. Hard. He broke out into a gallop, leaving the Seeker behind.

"Hey!" he heard the man shout.

Dominus steered down the wide path back toward the Lady's mansion, glancing back to see the Seeker galloping after him…and the black creatures swarming onto the wide path after them. Some ran while others galloped, but they all moved with frightening speed.

Damn!

He leaned down, kicking his horse to go faster. It gladly obeyed, its hooves thundering on the ground below. The creatures bolted down the path after them; some of them fell behind, but a few managed to keep pace with Dominus and the Seeker…and were steadily closing the gap between them.

The Seeker pushed his horse to the limit, managing to catch up to Dominus, riding alongside him.

And behind them, a few of the larger creatures closed in, now only a few meters away.

They're going to catch up, Dominus realized. And if they ate him, even he wouldn't be able to come back from it.

He glanced at the Seeker beside him, then leaned to the side, shoving the man off his horse.

The Seeker screamed, striking the ground and tumbling a few meters. Before he could even get to his feet, the creatures were upon him.

There was a blood-curdling shriek, and then silence.

But only a few of the monsters stopped to consume the man. Most continued the chase…now only a meter away from his horse's rear hooves. Dominus swerved to the side, slowing for a split-second. The creature reached his horse's flank, and Dominus leaned over, unsheathing his sword and slashing at the beast in one smooth movement.

His blade struck true, and the creature shrieked, falling and tumbling on the path. Dominus sped up, leaving the thing behind. The plan had worked, but two more of the things were closing in fast…and the other ten or so were following far behind.

Dominus turned forward, kicking his horse again, spotting the River Ormr in the distance.

Only a little farther…

He heard the rhythmic grunting of the beasts behind him, growing louder by the second. His horse's breath came in short gasps, foam leaking from the sides of its mouth. It wouldn't be able to hold this pace for long.

Reaching the shore of the river, Dominus turned left, galloping toward the mansion in the distance. The black beasts followed, slipping and sliding in the sand, creating some distance between them.

Yes!

But they recovered quickly, running along the edge of the forest where the footing was firmer, to Dominus's left.

He felt his horse starting to slow, and slammed his heels into its flanks. It sped up…but eventually began to slow again. Dominus screamed at it, slamming his heels into the horse again and again, watching as the creatures closed in, now directly flanking him. But they didn't veer in.

Yet.

They're waiting to get ahead, he realized. *They're compensating for the poor footing near me.*

A chill ran through him, and he recalled their grotesque humanoid faces.

They're intelligent.

The mansion was less than a quarter-kilometer away now, the gated fence and the statue of the horned serpent visible…as was the single guard at the gate.

"Hey!" Dominus shouted, waving his arms. "Hey!"

And then one of the creatures veered in, leaping at Dominus!

Dominus's sword came out in a flash, slicing at the creature's face without so much as a thought. It howled, slamming into the horse's left flank, then tumbling away. Dominus's horse stumbled to the right…toward the rapidly-flowing water of the river.

Dominus yanked on the reins, steering the horse to the left, but it was too late.

He leapt from the horse, sheathing his sword in mid-air, then landing on his feet, sprinting toward the mansion even as his horse stumbled into the water. A few of the black monsters leapt on it, pulling it from the water and tearing it apart.

The rest came for *him.*

Dominus swore, pumping his legs as fast as he could, aiming for the gate ahead. He waved his arms again.

"Open the gate!" he cried. He was less than a hundred meters away now, the beasts catching up to him rapidly.

He saw the guard behind the gate hesitate, peering out from between the metal bars.

"OPEN THE GATE!" Dominus screamed.

He heard a loud grunt behind him, and his body burst into action, unsheathing his sword and leaping into the air, twisting 180 degrees. He saw one of the beasts leaping at him…just as his blade sliced through its neck, blood spraying from the wound.

It dropped, the other beasts leaping over its body, rushing after him.

Dominus twisted another 180 degrees in mid-air, landing and continuing his sprint without so much as a pause. He barreled toward the gate, watching as the guard opened it.

Ten meters…fiver meters…

He felt something slam into his back, and he stumbled through the gate, falling and somersaulting on the crushed stone path, then leaping to his feet. Black beasts smashed into the gate even as the guard tried to close it, flinging it open and throwing the guard to the ground. They leapt on the man, tearing at his flesh with manic glee.

Dominus ran toward the front double-doors ahead, watching as they opened…revealing Lady Camilla.

"Help!" Dominus cried, rushing toward her. More beasts trailed behind him, over a dozen of them inside the gate now.

Camilla brought something up to her lips – a whistle – and blew.

Dominus heard rumbling to his right, and turned to see the huge statue of the horned serpent there.

It was *moving.*

The huge serpent uncoiled, its eyes opening. It turned toward the creatures chasing Dominus, opening its huge maw, a long tongue snaking out of it.

Dominus reached the steps up to the front porch of the mansion, and the Lady stepped back, letting him through…and shutting the door immediately, locking it.

Bam!

One of the beasts slammed into it, rattling the door.

"Come," Camilla stated calmly, leading Dominus up to the second floor of the mansion. There were no windows on the first floor, thank goodness…almost certainly as a precaution against such an attack.

They went upstairs, stepping up to a window on the second floor. It gave a perfect view of the front yard…and of the horned serpent and the beasts within it.

The creatures swarmed the serpent, leaping on it and tearing at its scales.

"What if…" Dominus began, but Camilla put a hand on his arm.

"Relax Dominus," she soothed. "Enjoy the show."

He watched as the beasts tore at the serpent, trying to pry the scales off its long body…with no success. The serpent roared, flopping onto its back and rolling around, crushing several of the creatures under its massive weight. A few of the beasts managed to leap off in time, and the serpent went after them, rearing its head back, then snapping them up in its massive jaws.

"See?" Camilla said, smiling at him and patting his arm. "You've got nothing to worry about. Well, except for your ear."

Dominus grimaced, bringing a hand up to his right ear. Or where it used to be. The bleeding had already stopped.

The horned serpent finished off the last of the creatures, flinging their corpses out of the fenced-in yard. Lady Camilla turned to Dominus.

"Would you be so kind as to open the window?" she inquired.

Dominus did so, pulling it open. Camilla brought the whistle to her lips again, and the horned serpent immediately stopped its rampage, returning to its original spot and coiling back on itself.

"Well then," she stated, turning away from the window. "You can start by telling me what happened to my Seekers."

Dominus nodded absently, watching the scene below. The creature whose throat he'd slit was lying just outside the fence now. He swallowed in a dry throat, remembering how close he'd been to death.

And then, minutes after Camilla and Dominus had left the window, the creature's limbs twitched, and it got up, glancing at the mansion, then galloping back toward the forest.

CHAPTER 17

It was morning by the time Hunter and Xerxes spotted the tall black spires of the Kingdom of the Deep in the distance, a full two days after emerging from the Deep. And it was about two hours later before they finally reached the curved archway serving as the entrance to the kingdom. After spending the better part of a week hiking, Hunter's feet were sore, his ankles chafed by his boots. Not as badly as he would've imagined, possibly because his body was getting tougher. Or maybe Xerxes' goo had helped him heal a bit faster, to keep up with the wear and tear. Still, he was glad to finally be out of the woods.

"Man, I could use a drink," Hunter told Xerxes as they crossed into the kingdom. "Not alcohol," he added. "Just some water. And a nice hot meal."

"No mushrooms?" Xerxes signed with a smirk. Hunter made a face. He'd had far too many mushrooms on the way back…and familiarity had definitely bred contempt.

"Maybe I can get Pukwa to show me how to use these things," Hunter ventured, flapping his wings a little. He'd tried gliding a few more times, but only for small drops, no more than five feet or so. He hardly noticed the weight of his wings anymore, and had practiced moving them throughout their long journey. They didn't feel alien to him anymore, but they were still a bit awkward.

"NO…TIME," Xerxes countered.

"At least a meal then," Hunter pressed. Xerxes nodded, and they set out toward the human side of the kingdom, which was of course on the opposite end of the kingdom, by the other entrance. They made their way over the grassy terrain, following the curve of the circular lake in the center of the kingdom, then continuing onward toward the other end. Eventually they reached the treehouses, wigwams, and longhouses at the human side. They were passing by one of the wigwams when Hunter nearly collided with two people exiting the small hut.

"Whoa, sorry," Hunter apologized, taking a step back. It was a cat-woman and another person – it looked like a woman – wrapped up like a mummy, with a wooden mask held to her face by more wrappings around her head.

"Not a problem," the cat-woman replied. She appeared to be the same cat-woman he'd seen when he'd visited the Shrine of Mammals with Pukwa days ago. "Didn't I see you in the Shrine a few days ago?" she inquired.

"Yeah, that was me," Hunter confirmed. "Nice uh, bumping into you again."

"Hunter?"

Hunter turned, realizing it'd been the masked woman who'd spoken. She was staring at him, her mouth open.

"That's me," he confirmed. "Do I know you?"

"It's Sukri!" she cried, practically throwing herself at him. She gave him a big bear hug, then pulled away. "I can't believe you're still alive!" she exclaimed. "And you got wings!"

"Yeah, well, I do crazy shit when I'm drunk," he admitted sheepishly.

"That makes two of us," Sukri replied. She noticed Xerxes then, and jerked backward, staring up at him in horror. "Holy…"

"Don't worry," Hunter reassured. "This is Xerxes. He's my brother."

Sukri stared at Xerxes, then at Hunter.

"Your brother's an Ironclad?"

"Long story," Hunter admitted.

"PLEASED…MEET YOU," Xerxes greeted, extending a hand. Sukri glanced at it suspiciously.

"Yeah, I'm good," she stated. "I had a friend get his arm ripped off by one of you…your kind. People. Whatever."

Xerxes shrugged, clearly not offended.

"I don't see the resemblance, Crispy," Sukri admitted.

"My mom's an Ironclad too," Hunter said. "Like I said, long story."

"She's alive?" Sukri asked. "You found her?"

"Sure did," Hunter confirmed. "What're you doing here?" he asked. "And where's Gammon?"

Sukri hesitated, lowering her gaze. She shook her head.

"Dead."

"What?" Hunter blurted out. "How?"

"Dio murdered him," Sukri muttered. "Slit his throat just for the hell of it. After we surrendered. Lady Camilla all but forced me to become her Seeker, then made me come here with Dio."

Hunter took this in, feeling numb. He hadn't known Gammon for long, but the guy'd been a sweetheart…and loyal to a fault.

"I'm sorry," he mumbled.

"Me too, Hunter."

"Sorry for pushing you out that window," Hunter added, scratching the back of his head sheepishly. He'd shoved her out of a window of the Lady's mansion when he'd been possessed by Zagamar. "I uh…wasn't myself."

"Yeah, about that," Sukri replied, putting her hands on her hips. "Dick move, Hunter."

"I was…possessed."

"That's a new one," Sukri grumbled. "Points for creativity."

"I was. It's a long story," he insisted. "I'll tell you all about it, promise." Then he frowned. "Where's Dio now?"

"Not sure," Sukri admitted. "Kayla here says if I become a citizen, Dio can't touch me."

"Bet the Lady won't like that," Hunter ventured.

"The bitch can suck it," Sukri retorted. Hunter grimaced; As much as he hated Camilla, sucking was one thing she'd excelled at.

"What about the Guild of Seekers?" he inquired. "Won't they come for you?"

"Yeah, they kinda want me dead," Sukri replied. Hunter smirked.

"That makes two of us."

"Well look at us, Hunter," she exclaimed. "Ever imagine we'd get into all this trouble?"

"You, yes," Hunter replied with a grin. "You were *always* getting into trouble."

"The Guild of Seekers won't be able to harm you here," Kayla interjected. "We should get going," she added. "Before Dio comes to find you."

"Too late," a voice behind them grumbled.

Hunter turned, seeing a slender, muscular man in a tight leather uniform standing behind them. A black and red uniform with a grotesque mask covering his face…and an unforgettable silver bo staff on his back. Hunter's blood went cold.

"Speak of the devil," Hunter muttered. "Xerxes?"

Xerxes grunted.

"If this guy tries anything, tear him apart. Slowly."

Xerxes grunted, stepping between Hunter and Dio. Nearly four feet taller than the Seeker, Xerxes loomed over the man, his four hands clenched into fists. Dio just stood there, ignoring him.

"Let's go," Dio ordered, his eyes on Sukri.

"Fuck off," Sukri retorted.

"Wrong answer," Dio growled.

"You have no right to force her to go with you against her will," Kayla interjected calmly. "She wishes to gain citizenship."

"She's not a citizen yet," Dio retorted.

"It is illegal to intervene in a person's attempt to gain citizenship," Kayla countered. "If you attempt to do so, you will incur the wrath of the

Elders…and the Guardians." She crossed her arms over her chest. "Even you cannot hope to win against them."

Dio considered this.

"The Lady will not be pleased," he warned.

"Her pleasure is no concern of ours," Kayla replied.

"You sure about that?"

"Quite."

Dio stared at Kayla for a long, uncomfortable moment, then turned to Hunter.

"You and I have unfinished business."

"I don't think so," Hunter retorted. "Go back to your bitch before you get hurt, little man."

"See you real soon," Dio said. Then he stepped around Xerxes…or at least he tried to. Xerxes stopped him with one giant palm on his chest.

"KILL…NOW?" he inquired, glancing at Hunter.

"Probably not such a good idea here," Hunter decided. "Outside is good."

"See you outside then," Dio promised…and swatted Xerxes' hand away, striding past them all and making his way toward the exit. Hunter watched him go.

"Asshole," he muttered.

"I…GO," Xerxes said, stomping after Dio. "BE…BACK."

"What're you doing?" Hunter demanded. "Hold up!"

"GO…KILL."

"Wait a second, would ya?" Hunter insisted. Xerxes paused, turning back. "We can kill him later. Promise."

Xerxes sighed, clearly disappointed. But he stomped back up to them.

"I like your brother already," Sukri ventured, smiling up at Xerxes. Xerxes smiled back.

"HUNTER…TELL ME…ABOUT YOU."

"Oh yeah?" Sukri asked. "What'd he say?"

"LIKES…YOU."

"Aww," Sukri replied, glancing at Hunter. "I know boys push girls they like, but out of a third-story window? That's a bit much, Hunter."

"I didn't…never mind," Hunter grumbled. "We gotta go."

"Where?" Sukri asked.

"Back home," he answered. "I live with the Ironclad now…and Vi."

Sukri's eyes widened.

"I thought she was dead," she protested. "The Lady said…"

"She's alive and well," Hunter interrupted.

"Huh."

"It's nice to see you," he said, smiling at her. "By the way…what spirit did you choose?"

"Give it a few days and you might just find out."

"That mean you're coming with us?" he asked.

"I don't think so," Sukri answered, glancing at Kayla. Kayla smiled, putting a hand on Sukri's shoulder. She turned back to Hunter, shaking her head. "No, I'm staying here."

"Fair enough. See you around, Sukri."

"See you," Sukri replied, leaning in and giving him one last hug. Hunter turned to leave then, Xerxes walking at his side. "Hey, wait," Sukri called out after them.

"Yeah?"

"Dio's probably waiting for you," she warned.

"Oh I know," Hunter replied. "We're gonna kill him."

Xerxes perked up.

"Watch out," she warned. "He's really good. I mean *really* good."

"Not worried," Hunter reassured her. "I'm not gonna kill him. *He* is," he added, patting Xerxes on the arm.

"He might not be able to," Sukri cautioned.

"Yeah he will."

"How do you know?"

"Trust me," Hunter insisted. "Come on big guy. Guess we'll have to wait a little bit longer for that meal."

"Wait!" Sukri said, running after them…as best as she could in her wrappings. "If you're gonna kill him, I ain't missing it."

"By all means, tag along."

"Sukri," Kayla called out after them. "Your citizenship…" Sukri stopped, turning to face her.

"I'll be back," she promised. "I just wanna see this."

Kayla smiled, then leaned in, kissing Sukri full on the lips. And kept kissing her. Hunter's eyes widened, and he glanced at Xerxes, who seemed equally intrigued. After a long moment, they pulled away from each other, and Sukri waved goodbye to Kayla, following Hunter and Xerxes. They made their way toward the archway marking the entrance to the Kingdom of the Deep, taking the stairs down to it and passing through. The long, wide bridge greeted them, crossing the deep chasm below. Sure enough, Dio was standing at the other end of the bridge waiting for them. They stepped onto the bridge, making their way toward him. Hunter and Xerxes stopped some twenty feet away from the guy.

"Go on big guy," Hunter prompted. "Kill."

Xerxes smiled…then stomped after Dio, barreling toward the Seeker.

"Hunter…" Sukri began, putting a hand on his shoulder…but Xerxes was already halfway to the Seeker and closing in fast.

Dio just stood there, hands at his sides.

Xerxes reached the Seeker, reaching out with all four hands…and Dio leapt to the side, his staff somehow appearing in his hands. He whipped it at the back of Xerxes' knees.

The blade at the end of the staff bounced off Xerxes' armor.

Xerxes slid to a halt, pivoting and lunging at Dio again. Dio ducked to the side, swinging at the exact same spot behind Xerxes' knee.

Again it bounced off.

Dio followed up immediately by leaping into the air and bringing his staff down on the top of Xerxes' head. Hard.

The armor there scuffed a little, but remained intact.

Xerxes crossed one pair of arms over his chest, smirking down at Dio.

Dio took a step back, and Xerxes went at him again, reaching out to grab him. The Seeker moved like a blur, dodging aside and using the momentum to chop viciously at Xerxes' hands. This time the deadly blade at the end of the staff managed to chop through Xerxes' armor.

A few fingers fell to the ground.

Xerxes grunted, staring at his amputated fingers, then lunging at Dio again. Again the Seeker dodged, lopping a few more fingers off.

"Hunter!" Sukri exclaimed, gripping Hunter's arm. Hunter patted her hand.

"It's okay," he reassured. "Watch."

Xerxes balled his hands into fists, swinging wildly at the man.

Dio dodged each swing effortlessly, his staff a blur as he counterattacked, four hits to Xerxes' every attempt. Not a single blow touched Dio…but every strike hit Xerxes. Xerxes roared, trying to grab the staff out of Dio's hands, but Dio was far too quick, the *thwack, thwack* of his staff hitting the Ironclad echoing off the wall behind Hunter. Eventually Xerxes stumbled backward, scowling down at Dio, who faced him fearlessly…then lunged at the big guy, his staff whirling so quickly that Hunter couldn't follow it.

Xerxes stumbled backward onto the bridge, Dio's staff hitting him so fast and hard that he had no time to recover. He fell onto his butt on the bridge, and Dio grunted, swinging his staff at Xerxes' temple…and striking it so hard that Xerxes' head snapped to the side with a loud *crack*.

Xerxes fell onto his left side, his limbs jerking uncontrollably.

Dio stared down at the Ironclad, then stepped over him, coming right for Hunter.

"Shit," Hunter swore, unsheathing his sword. "Get back!" he ordered Sukri.

"I can't leave you," Sukri retorted.

"You armed?"

"No…"

"Then get back!"

Dio lunged at Hunter…and passed right by him, grabbing Sukri and throwing her back toward Hunter. Sukri fell into him, and they tumbled onto the bridge. Hunter swore, scrambling to his feet, facing Dio.

The Seeker strode toward them, now standing between Sukri and the Kingdom of the Deep.

Hunter focused inward, feeling his hunger, his anger. He stoked it, willing forth the voices from the past. The Legend within him.

Za-ga-mar!

A chill ran through him, and he took a step back, then another. Dio closed the distance between them, his staff gleaming in the sun.

Za-ga-mar!

Time slowed, Dio's footsteps seeming to take an eternity to rise and fall. Hunter felt Zagamar's mind within his own, instantly evaluating the situation. Plotting each possible action, taking it to its logical conclusion.

Need more data.

He feigned a thrust at Dio, at only a fraction of the speed Zagamar was capable of…but plenty quick for a regular human. Dio dodged to the side, thrusting the butt of his staff right at Hunter's belly. To anyone else, the attack would've been lightning quick, but to Hunter, it was almost tediously slow.

Hunter took a step back, bending at the waist, Dio's staff missing him by an inch.

Dio followed up immediately by swinging the butt of his staff up at Hunter's chin. Hunter leaned back, the blow missing him again by a fraction of an inch. Another attack, another dodge. Again, and again. And again.

Dio stopped, taking a step back, staring at Hunter silently.

Hunter smirked.

And then Dio went ape-shit.

He swung his staff twice as fast as before, each thrust and slash blending into the next in a vicious string of attacks. Hunter's mind raced, calculating the trajectory of each attack and dodging and parrying every last one of them.

Then Dio's foot came out between attacks, managing to connect with Hunter's belly.

Hunter stumbled backward, bending forward at the waist…and Dio came right at him. Hunter dodged and parried desperately, only barely managing to deflect each blow. He felt Zagamar's frustration…and the world slowed even further, his thoughts coming so fast he couldn't follow them, his heart pounding rapidly in his chest.

Play-time's over.

He went on the offensive, counterattacking every attack Dio attempted, slashing, thrusting, and kicking…and setting Dio back on his heels. The Seeker barely managed to block each counterattack.

And then he turned to run.

Hunter lunged after Dio…and right into the Seeker's mule-kick.

The blow struck Hunter right in the chest, knocking the wind out of him. He flew backward, landing on his back on the bridge, his helmet bouncing off the hard stone.

His vision blackened.

Hunter groaned, rolling onto his side, his heart pounding far too quickly, his lungs screaming for air. He gasped, struggling to get to his feet, but his limbs felt like jelly.

Metabolism too high, he sensed Zagamar thinking. *Temporary lack of air untenable.*

He watched as Dio stepped toward him, saw Sukri leap in-between them, waving her arms at Dio.

"Don't!" she cried. "Stop!"

Body failing. Energy consumption too high. Must abort.

Hunter *shoved* Zagamar back into the recesses of his mind, the world speeding up instantly. He got to his feet, clutching at his chest.

Dio pushed Sukri aside, lunging at Hunter!

And then a huge black shape leapt over Hunter's head from behind, slamming into Dio and shoving him backward.

"Xerxes!" he heard Sukri cry.

Dio stumbled backward, then rolled into a backwards somersault, springing to his feet. Xerxes roared, rushing at the Seeker. Dio dodged, beating the Ironclad back with a flurry of blows, then ran back toward Hunter, his staff gleaming in the sunlight. Sukri intercepted the Seeker, but Dio shoved her to the side…right as Xerxes slammed into him from behind.

Dio stumbled forward…and Sukri flew to the side, right toward the edge of the bridge!

Hunter burst toward Sukri, who fell onto her side, then slid head-first over the edge of the bridge.

No!

He lunged after her, landing belly-first on the bridge, grabbing at her legs. He caught her by the ankle…

…and promptly slid off the bridge with her.

Shit!

His gut wrenched as they fell from the edge into the canyon, plummeting toward the river hundreds of feet below. The wind howled in his ears as they accelerated, tearing at his clothes.

Shit shit shit!

And then he felt a sudden jerk as he spread his wings out reflexively, feeling them fill instantly with air. He nearly lost his grip on Sukri's ankle.

Wings!

Hunter spread them out fully, tightening his grip on Sukri. They were gliding now, accelerating rapidly forward through the canyon. He glanced down, seeing the river still hundreds of feet below…and in the distance, the canyon began to narrow sharply, from about a thousand feet across to less than a hundred.

"Shit!" he heard Sukri scream.

He focused on the canyon ahead, aiming for the center as it narrowed. The walls closed in on either side…and up ahead, the canyon curved gently to the right.

Okay, he told himself. *You got this.*

Hunter pulled his right wing in, trying to turn rightward…but that just caused him to barrel-roll instead. He swore, extending both wings, righting himself.

"Hunter!" Sukri warned. The curve was coming up quickly…and if Hunter didn't turn, they'd smash into the cliff wall ahead. He focused, trying to twist his core to force himself to turn, but this didn't work either.

The curve was only a hundred yards away now…and closing in fast.

Think!

He remembered flying on planes back on Earth, looking out of the window as the plane was turning. A flap on the back of the wing would go up and down to do it. Which meant that turning required increasing resistance to air flow on one wing…the right one. So to do that…

Hunter rotated his right wing backward, as if he were rotating his arm to make it go palms-up. He felt an immediate *push* on his right wing, turning him rapidly to the right…way too far. He glided toward the rightmost canyon wall.

Shit!

He reversed the action, rotating his left wing back – more gradually this time – and turned gently to the left. The curve in the canyon was only fifty feet away now; he rotated his right wing slightly, turning gradually to the right, following the oncoming curve…and made it through, reaching the straightaway beyond.

Yes!

His elation was short-lived, however. There was a left turn a few hundred feet away…one much sharper than the last.

Hunter focused, practicing turning left, then right. He was still picking up speed as he dropped gradually downward; he needed to slow down if he was going to make it through the turn ahead. He tried rotating *both* wings backward…and felt the wind shove him back powerfully. His stomach lurched as he decelerated…and as he promptly began to lose altitude, plummeting toward the river far below.

He rotated his wings forward, accelerating forward again…and slowing his descent as he resumed gliding. Experimenting with different wing positions, he found a good compromise, gliding at a reasonable speed toward the turn ahead without losing altitude too quickly.

The turn approached, a near-ninety-degree turn leftward. The canyon had narrowed further, now a mere fifty feet wide here, giving him little room for error.

He took a deep breath in, waiting for the turn…then rotated his left wing back, turning sharply with the canyon. He came perilously close to the leftmost canyon wall, his wingtip only a few yards away. But he managed to level off, gliding gently to the center of the canyon again.

Yes!

They were only a hundred feet above the surface of the river now, and the cliff walls on either side were considerably shorter ahead. Hunter was only a few yards below the tops of them. If he could gain a little altitude, he could land on them.

He tried flapping his wings, and immediately regretted it. His wings flapped at different times, their movements uncoordinated, and this seriously disrupted his equilibrium.

"Careful!" Sukri shouted over the howling wind.

"Sorry," Hunter yelled back. He abandoned his plan, focusing on gliding safely in the center of the canyon. Luckily the canyon walls dropped even lower ahead, not even fifty feet high. Which meant that he could easily fly over them.

Hunter did just that, turning right and gliding out of the canyon. There was dense forest ahead, hardly a suitable landing area. He scanned the terrain, spotting a clearing amidst the trees. But how was he going to land with Sukri dangling head-down?

"Swing up," he shouted at Sukri. "Grab my arms!"

She grunted, doing a sit-up and grabbing his forearms.

"I'm gonna let go of your legs," he warned. He did so, and her hands slid down his forearms, stopping at his wrists. He grabbed her wrists as she gripped his, then turned toward the clearing, rotating his wings backward as they drew closer. They were only twenty feet above the treetops now, and dropping quickly.

"We're not gonna make it!" Sukri cried.

"Hold on," Hunter ordered. He rotated his wings forward, picking up speed, thirty feet from the clearing now.

Twenty…ten.

He felt a jolt as Sukri's leg smacked against the top of a tree, and struggled to keep himself flying straight. She struck another tree, then another…and then they were in the clearing!

Hunter rotated his wings back sharply, decelerating rapidly…and dropping Sukri to the ground. She fell the six feet to the ground below, and Hunter zoomed past her, gliding another few yards before his feet touched the ground. He stumbled to a stop, folding his wings behind him.

"You did it!" Sukri cried, rushing up to him and practically leaping into his arms, squeezing him tightly. He hugged her back, and they held each other for a long moment before Sukri disengaged. She stared at him shaking her head with a mix of disbelief and awe. "I didn't know you could do that," she exclaimed. Hunter smirked.

"That makes two of us."

And then his legs wobbled underneath him, and he turned to the side, leaning over and puking his guts out.

CHAPTER 18

Zac awoke to the sound of banging on his door.

He jerked up into a sitting position in his bed, and Zooey bolted upright beside him. They were in the shack they'd rented from the innkeeper, and sunlight was streaming in through the windows.

There was more banging on the door, making dust rain down from the ceiling.

"What…?" Zooey blurted out.

"Get dressed," Zac stated, leaping out of bed and pulling on his clothes hurriedly. They were still a little damp from the night before. He grabbed the blanket from Zooey, shoving it in his pack, then went to the window, looking out.

The innkeeper was standing far away from door, using a long wooden pole to bang on it. And there were other men standing behind him.

Armed men.

Zac looked down, seeing the fenced-in pen attached to the shack. Chickens were walking about. Or what had once been chickens.

Zac swore, backing away from the window.

"We have to leave," he declared. "Now."

Zooey nodded once, not even questioning him.

"Out the window?" she proposed. There was another window at the other end of the room. He nodded, and they both ran to it, opening it and crawling through.

Then they ran.

Zac heard shouting from behind, and looked back over his shoulder to see a few of the men coming around the side of the shack, pointing at him and gesticulating wildly. The innkeeper came into view, dropping his long pole.

Someone handed him a crossbow.

"Oh sh…" Zac blurted out, grabbing Zooey and pulling her close to him as they ran. There was a short fence ahead, and they leapt over it. Zac landed on his feet, but Zooey stumbled forward suddenly, falling onto her belly.

A crossbow bolt protruded from her back.

"Zooey!" Zac cried, yanking her to her feet. Her eyes were wide, her mouth open in a perfect "O."

He looked back, seeing the innkeeper chasing after them, reloading the crossbow as he ran.

Zac gathered Zooey in his arms, running toward the hill they'd come down the night before. He saw the forest atop it, and his mind raced.

Trees will provide cover. Make us harder to track. Innkeeper is overweight, won't be able to keep up.

He reached the foot of the hill, charging up it as fast as he could. Glancing back, he saw the innkeeper rushing after them. The man stopped at the base of the hill, lifting his crossbow to aim.

Zac switched to a zig-zagging pattern.

The innkeeper fired, the bolt shooting toward them. It buried itself in the side of the hill to Zac's left, missing him by less than a foot. He heard the innkeeper curse.

Needs to reload. Almost to the trees.

Another bolt flew over Zac's right shoulder.

Come on…

He reached the tree line, weaving between the wide trunks. Glancing back, he saw the innkeeper bounding up the hill after them. But the man slipped on the still-wet grass, sliding back down the hill on his belly.

Still Zac ran, clutching Zooey to his chest, until he could run no more.

He collapsed by a broad tree trunk, setting Zooey down. Her face was deathly pale, her breath coming in short gasps. He propped her against the tree, kneeling before her.

"Okay Zooey," he stammered. "Okay. We're okay."

Then he spotted the sharp, bloody tip of the arrowhead jutting out of her chest.

"Zac," she gasped. She coughed, pink, bubbly spittle trickling out of the corner of her mouth.

"Oh Zooey," he moaned. "Oh no Zooey, no, no…"

"Zac," she repeated, breaking out into another fit of coughing. Her face twisted in pain, and she grit her teeth, squeezing her eyes shut.

"I'm so sorry Zooey," he whimpered. "I didn't…"

"It's okay," she mumbled. "It's okay Zac."

"No Zooey, it's…"

"They'll never…accept us," she interrupted. She put a cold hand to his cheek. "You know…that."

"But…"

"It's not your fault," she said. "Not…your fault."

"It is," he insisted. "You were right, we never should've gone in that inn."

"…not you," she gasped. "Not your fault. It's…them."

He blinked tears from his eyes, feeling them trickle down his cheeks. She gave him a weak smile.

"I got to be…you," she murmured, stroking his cheek. "Got to…" She coughed again. "You're…special, Zac. You're…"

"I'm a freak," he retorted.

"You're…better," she countered. "Make them see, Zac. Make them…better."

"Zooey," he said, holding her hand against his cheek. "Don't leave me."

She grimaced, shifting her weight against the tree.

"Thirsty," she mumbled.

And then her breathing slowed, her eyes staring off into space.

"Zooey?"

He put a hand to her cheek, tapping it gently. But she didn't respond.

"Zooey?" he repeated, tapping harder. "Zooey!"

No response.

Zac stared at her, his whole body going numb. She took another breath in, her chest barely rising. A horrible gurgling sound came from her throat, more pink foam dripping from her mouth.

It was the last breath she ever took.

* * *

The creature jolted awake from its dream.

It gasped, feeling a terrible pain in its throat, and in its side. It was sprawled on its back on the forest floor, the leaves high above swaying in a stiff breeze. It took a moment for the creature to recover from the dream. And for it to remember what had happened.

How the human had stabbed it and strangled it, crushing its throat.

It grunted, rolling onto all fours and running a hand over its throat. The flesh there was intact, its voice box no longer crumpled.

How?

The creature looked around, spotting the corpse of a man dressed in a black and red uniform laying nearby. The human whose eyes it had torn out. Hunger seized the creature, and it walked up to the corpse.

And ate.

An hour later, it finished gorging itself, stumbling away from what remained of the human. Lowering its head to the forest floor, it sniffed the footprints there, smelling the same scent it'd smelled on the human who'd nearly killed it.

The humans were *always* trying to stop them. The Dark One and anyone who dared to follow Him. Who dared to receive even a small portion of His essence.

The creature spotted movement in the distance, and turned toward it. There were shadows lurking between the trees, more of the Dark One's followers. One of them glanced at the creature, nodding slightly. The creature nodded back, then began to follow the others.

Though the memories it shared with the Dark One were vague and ephemeral, it remembered what had happened long ago. First the humans had sent bounty hunters to stop Him. Then towns had risen against Him, amassing small armies to find and kill Him. When that'd failed, the towns had sought help from the cities, sending larger forces.

And then entire kingdoms had sent their armies.

But they'd been too late, the humans. They'd underestimated Him. Underestimated how quickly he could turn their own armies against them, by giving their soldiers a taste of his will. For he was better than them, and he made his soldiers better by sharing his gift with them. The gift of his intelligence, and of his perspective.

The humans were weak and stupid, always reacting instead of acting. Always letting their fear control them.

But with each victory, the Dark One had become less and less afraid.

And now that He was reborn, there was nothing that could stop him.

Chapter 19

Dio dodged out of the way of the black-armored beast's clumsy attacks, punishing it with a string of blows from his staff. He turned back toward the Original, sprinting toward the boy. The girl – Sukri – tried to get in-between them, and Dio shoved her to one side.

And then felt something ram him from behind right as he did so.

Dio stumbled, shoving Sukri far harder than he'd planned, and watched as she careened toward the edge of the bridge. He managed to keep his balance, seeing the Original dive for her, grabbing her by the ankle…and sliding right off the edge of the bridge with her. Dio lunged toward them, but it was too late.

They were gone.

He heard the *thumping* of the black beast's footsteps behind him, and spun around, whipping his staff at its head, snapping it to the side. Then he followed that with a string of blows so quick that the creature struggled to block even half of them with its four arms.

Dio finished with a vicious chop down on top of the thing's head, stunning it for a moment. Then he turned to look over the edge of the bridge.

The Original was gliding gently over the canyon, the girl dangling below him. Dio grimaced, feeling a flash of irritation. He'd never failed Mother before.

She would not be pleased.

He heard the beast coming for him, and sent the thing reeling with a vicious combination of blows, targeting areas with thinner armor. Fingers, toes. Its face and eyes. To its credit, it managed to block many of the blows, but Dio still managed to lop off a few more fingers.

It was slow. Slow mind, slow body. Just like everyone else.

The creature roared, charging at Dio, who dodged to the side easily, swinging his staff in a powerful arc at the back of its knees. It bounced off, but the armor there cracked; Dio followed up with another three attacks, the armor sinking in under the force of his blows. The last strike bit into its flesh, blood spurting from the wound.

No mobility, no chance.

The beast emitted a low growl, limping away from Dio. It circled around him, then lunged at him again, its four arms out wide to grab him. Dio ducked into a roll, evading the thing's grasp and swinging at the back of its knees again. His staff bounced off the thing's armor.

Which was intact.

Dio backed away, staring at the creature's legs. Its armor there was pristine, the wound he'd created earlier gone. Vanished.

The beast turned to face him, its black eyes glittering in the sunlight. Dio studied it, noting its fingers. The one's he'd cut off earlier.

They too were intact.

How?

The creature leapt at him again, and Dio dodged, raining another devastating series of attacks upon it. This time he focused on its face, striking it again and again, then going after its legs when it tried blocking its face with its hands. It stumbled backward, and his staff was a blur as blow after blow struck true, chipping away at the thing's armor. Black fingers fell to the floor, blood dripping from its forearms where his staff managed to crack its armor.

Dio followed with a vicious jumping back-kick right to its chest, sending it stumbling backward. It fell, landing on its back…and he leapt right on top of it, chopping down at its face with his staff. The cruel edge of its blade sank into its face with a *crunch*, splitting it in two.

The creature roared, grabbing Dio's staff and tearing it from his hands. Or at least it tried to; Dio moved with the staff, keeping his grip on it. He stomped on the beast's ruined face then, over and over, until it let go of his weapon.

It rolled onto its side, then onto its belly, rising to its feet.

And as Dio watched – before the Seeker's very eyes – the wounds knitted together, the creature's flesh becoming whole once more. Fresh armor grew underneath, pushing the broken pieces outward like a molting snake shedding its skin. Even its fingers grew back.

Within seconds, it was whole again.

Dio backed away, a chill running through him. A feeling he hadn't felt in years came to him then. One he hated in others, and even more so in himself.

Doubt.

He circled the beast slowly, twirling his staff. The monster didn't attack, only rotating to face him as he circled. Dio glanced at the edge of the bridge, circling until it was right behind the creature.

Then he burst forward, his staff a blur as he attacked.

The beast curled its arms inward, blocking the rain of blows, its armor cracking under the barrage. Still Dio pressed forward, pushing the beast toward the edge of the bridge. Toward the sheer drop hundreds of feet below.

But it dodged to the side suddenly, backing away from the edge, toward the end of the bridge opposite the Kingdom of the Deep. The beast was clearly intelligent. And its armor had already repaired itself.

He lunged at it again, driving it backward, trying to force it to the left to push it toward the edge. But it corrected course each time, absorbing each attack, no longer even attempting to attack now.

It's tiring me, he realized.

And he *was* tiring. He had stamina many times that of an ordinary man, but even he had his limits. The beast was wearing him down, waiting for him to make a mistake. It could take anything he threw at it, and it knew it.

Dio swung his staff in a wide arc, smashing it against the thing's temple…then turned and bolted toward the Kingdom of the Deep.

He heard rhythmic grunting behind him, and turned to see the beast barreling toward him, running with shocking speed…and closing the distance between them rapidly.

Dio skid to a halt, turning and whipping his staff at the creature's skull. It blocked the blow with one arm, lunging at him. He ducked under its arms, turning toward the Kingdom again, but the beast caught up to him, shoving him from behind. Dio fell into a quick somersault, leaping to his feet and reversing direction, ducking under the beast's arms and running across the bridge in the opposite direction.

The beast followed tirelessly, running after him, closing in fast.

It was then that Dio realized there was no running from this thing. He couldn't kill it. It was a juggernaut, an unstoppable force.

And it was going to kill him very soon now.

Unless…

He made the decision instantly, never faltering, never doubting. There was no fear.

Dio swerved to the left, running right to the edge of the bridge, and jumped.

CHAPTER 20

The air in Camilla's underground cipher room was cool and moist, a consequence of the water constantly flowing into and out of it. For a cipher room was designed to stop traits from powerful artifacts and Ossae from spreading. This was usually accomplished by setting artifacts on pedestals protruding from a pool of constantly flowing water. The water absorbed any radiated traits, carrying them away quickly…and preventing contamination of the surrounding area. This cipher room was underground, so it would remain hidden, and was not connected to the mansion. Having to carry powerful artifacts through her home would risk contaminating the building…a risk Camilla dared not take. It was not nearly as large as Dominus's cipher room, only seven meters squared. Water poured down each of its four stone walls, flowing into a pool several feet deep that formed the floor of the room. Stone pillars rose up from the bottom of the pool to protrude a half-meter from the water, forming stepping stones across the pool to a central, raised platform four meters squared.

And on this sat a wooden table upon which laid the corpse of one of the black creatures that had attacked Dominus, its dead eyes staring at the ceiling above.

Camilla stepped across the stepping stones toward it, dressed in a special full-body suit made of alternating layers of woody fibers and cloth. A disposable suit that would protect her from short-term exposure to another's traits. Dominus had been given a similar suit, and followed behind her, stopping beside the table.

"Tell me Dominus, what do you think of this?" Camilla inquired.

Dominus studied the creature. It was little over a meter in length, with long arms terminating in what looked to be a cross between a paw and a hand. It had a long torso and legs, its thick hide midnight black. What little fur it had sprang haphazardly from patches on its chest and back.

But its face was mostly human.

"Likely an animal exposed to a strong-willed human," he deduced. The creatures had varied in size and the details of their fur and limbs, but all had shared identical humanoid traits. But the black skin was odd; it was not the chocolate brown of the Original's skin, but rather pure black. A skin tone not found in people…supposedly.

"Agreed," Camilla replied. She stared at the thing's face for a long time, and Dominus frowned at her. She seemed distracted.

"What is it?" he asked. She glanced up at him.

"Hmm?"

"What are you hiding?" he demanded. She gave a rueful smirk.

"Ever the observant one," she murmured. "You're a dangerously clever man."

"I'm only a danger to my enemies."

"Mmm, yes," Camilla replied. She turned back to the beast. "You of course have heard the story of the founding of Tykus?"

Dominus didn't bother answering.

"When Tykus came through the Gate to this world, he believed it to be Svartálfaheimr, the world of the Svartálfar."

"The dark elves, yes," Dominus replied impatiently.

"Well, the Elders of the Kingdom of the Deep have records that go back to that time period. They tell a story of a devil they call Hobbomock, an evil creature that created an army in his image. An army of black-skinned monsters that ravaged the world."

"The dark elves," Dominus repeated.

"Yes. They say Hobbomock was actually human once, a man with a powerful spirit…a Legend. He conquered many peoples, coming to rule the kingdom upon whose ruins Tykus was built. But Hobbomock was greedy, and went to the Deep to increase his power. It is there that he became a devil…one with enormous power, but with a hunger that could never be sated."

She swallowed visibly, her eyes glued to the creature's sunken eye-sockets.

"Hobbomock's power was his curse, and it spread to every living thing he touched. An army of dark elves was created, and their hunger nearly devoured this world. That hunger killed Hobbomock, decimated his empire, and nearly destroyed the Kingdom of the Deep."

She hesitated then, taking a deep breath in. Her face was deathly pale, he realized, beads of sweat glittering on her forehead despite the cool air. Dominus turned to the beast, staring into its sunken eyes. A chill ran through him.

"You mean Zagamar," he stated grimly. "Hobbomock is Zagamar."

"That is what I believe," she admitted. "And the dark elves were the creatures exposed to Zagamar's will. Hunter…the Original…described a terrible hunger that overwhelmed him when he went into the Crypt."

"From Zagamar's will."

"Correct," she replied. "Which lends evidence to my conclusion. And if Zeno went into the Crypt and consumed Zagamar's flesh…"

"Then these creatures…" Dominus muttered, swallowing in a suddenly dry throat.

And then the beast's eyes snapped open, and it lunged at Camilla!

Camilla tried to duck out of the way, but the beast slammed into her, throwing her backward into the pool. Then it turned to Dominus, its sunken eyes narrowing. Dominus's sword was already in his hands, held out before him.

The creature's neck veins pulsed rapidly, its eyes flicking from Dominus's sword to the exit of the cipher room. Camilla swam toward the exit, pulling herself onto one of the stepstone-like pillars.

The beast growled, then leapt *over* Dominus's head, landing behind him…and bounding over the stepstones after Camilla!

Dominus chased after the creature, slashing at its back. Blood sprayed from the wound, and it spun on him, lashing out with a flurry of attacks with its vicious claws. It moved incredibly fast – faster than anyone Dominus had ever seen – and even his incredible reflexes had difficulty defending against them. The beast managed to rake him across the face, and he swore, stumbling backward.

Then it pounced on him, throwing him onto his back on the stone floor.

Dominus tried to thrust his sword upward into the thing's belly, but it pinned his arm to the floor, ripping the sword from his hands and tossing it backward. He grabbed its neck, squeezing as hard as he could. It went wild, raking its claws madly across his face, chest and belly, ripping hunks of flesh out of Dominus.

The pain was excruciating.

Blood spurted from Dominus's wounds, the creature digging madly into Dominus's chest. Its claws cut through his muscle and met bone, grating against his ribs.

Still Dominus squeezed, pushing his thumbs up into its windpipe, trying to crush it.

And then it jerked forward, a silver blade bursting through its chest and burying itself into Dominus's breastbone.

The beast went still, slumping on top of Dominus.

Dominus groaned, trying to roll the beast off of him, but his arms wouldn't work properly. He looked past the monster, seeing Camilla standing over them, his sword in her hands. She pulled the weapon free, then rolled the beast off of him.

He looked down, seeing his own rib cage exposed, the muscles of his chest utterly destroyed. Nausea threatened to overcome him, and he closed his eyes, resting his head back against the stone below.

"Dominus, are…oh," Camilla gasped, putting a hand to her mouth. She knelt down, staring at his gruesome wounds. "Can you…?"

"I'll heal," Dominus replied. "Eventually." He opened his eyes, giving her a weak smile. "Thank you."

"Thank *you*," she countered. "It was going after me before you stopped it. It would've killed me."

"I know."

"You could have let it," Camilla noted. "And taken my mansion. No one would have been able to stop you."

"I know," he repeated.

"Why didn't you?"

Dominus sighed, staring up at the ceiling. He felt woozy from all the blood he'd lost. His mind was almost certainly not working correctly. But for the moment, he didn't care.

"I don't have anyone anymore," he admitted. She didn't respond, and he swallowed past a lump in his throat. "Everything I had is gone," he continued. "My son. My title. My castle. My…"

He choked on the word, suddenly hating himself for baring his soul.

"Your what?" Camilla pressed gently.

"My wife."

"Right," Camilla murmured. "She died in the fire."

Dominus nodded. Of course she'd heard the story…the version everyone else knew. But only *he* knew the full story.

He closed his eyes, seeing a small boy holding a broken lantern, cheeks wet with tears.

Just a mistake, Conlan. It's not your fault.

He pushed the thought away, opening his eyes. It was pointless to obsess about the past. A moment of weakness he would not allow again.

"I can't move my arms."

"I'll send for help," Camilla promised. She stood then, walking back toward the entrance.

"Camilla," Dominus called out after her. She turned to face him. "You could kill me now if you wanted to."

She paused, then gave him one of her maddening smiles.

"Now why would I go and do a thing like that?" she inquired. "I'm far from done with you, Dominus…former Duke of Wexford."

"What are you going to do with me?" he asked bluntly. The words came out slurred, and he felt even dizzier now.

Camilla walked back up to him, kneeling down and putting a hand on his cheek.

"I'm going to use you, Dominus," she answered. Her lips curled into a smirk. "And you're going to like it."

She stood then, walking to the exit.

"Wait!" he called out after her.

"Yes?"

"Cut off the beast's head," he advised. "And burn the body…make the fire hot. Scatter the ashes."

"As you wish, my Duke," Camilla replied, giving a slight curtesy.

And then she vanished beyond the exit, leaving Dominus lying on the cool stone floor, in a pool of his own blood.

* * *

Hunter and Sukri walked side-by-side through the forest, fallen leaves and twigs crunching under their feet with each step. They'd left the clearing Hunter had landed in a few minutes ago, after he'd finished emptying the contents of his stomach. They'd followed the river upstream, hoping to get back to the bridge – and Xerxes – but the way was blocked by steep cliffsides. They'd been forced to go around. *Way* around. And there was no guarantee how far around they'd have to go before they reached a path that would lead to the Kingdom of the Deep…or if it was even possible from here.

"You sure your brother's gonna be okay?" Sukri asked.

"He's fine, trust me," Hunter reassured. "He's invincible."

"Except he isn't," Sukri retorted. "Dio cut his fingers off."

"That's nothing. Xerxes regenerates. Vi cut his head off and he just grew another one."

"Seriously?"

"Yup."

"Well shit," Sukri mumbled. She glanced at him as they walked. "Still can't believe you flew like that," she admitted. "Thanks again for saving me, by the way."

"This make up for when I pushed you out the window?" he inquired. Sukri gave him a look.

"Yeah, about that," she grumbled. "What was with you then, anyway?"

"Long story," he replied. He gave a brief recap of his journey to the Crypt of Zagamar, and what'd happened to him there. And how Vi had taught him to unleash Zagamar to enhance his fighting skills.

"Damn, Hunter," Sukri replied when he'd finished. "You're an even bigger mess than I am."

"*Oh* yeah."

"So you…unleashed Zagamar when you fought Dio?" she asked. He nodded. "Thought you'd learned to fight like that from Vi," she admitted. "That was damn impressive. Fucking amazing, actually."

"Still lost."

"Yeah, but still. Holding your own against Dio is impressive." She hesitated. "So…this Zagamar is taking over your mind?"

"Not anymore," Hunter replied. He explained how he'd gone to the Deep to prevent Zagamar's influence from growing. And how it'd made his wings grow almost instantly to full length…a clear sign it'd worked.

"So you chose a bird, huh?" Sukri mused. She glanced at his wings enviously. "Not gonna lie, I'm kinda second-guessing my pick now."

"What'd you choose?"

"To be a cat-woman," Sukri answered. "Like Kayla."

"That woman we met earlier?" Hunter asked. She nodded. "I remember seeing her in the Shrine of Mammals when I was trying to decide what to be." He grinned. "Thought she was…"

"Sexy as fuck?"

"Actually, that's exactly what I thought. Like, word-for-word."

"Yeah, me too," Sukri admitted. "And now here I am," she added with a sigh, gesturing at her wrappings.

"You went for the…full effect?"

"Yeah. I was kinda drunk," she confessed. Hunter chuckled.

"Me too." He paused. "And there was this hot chick who did the procedure. I wasn't about to say no."

Sukri glanced at him, arching an eyebrow.

"Did you…?"

"No," Hunter replied. "Wanted to. But no."

"Huh," Sukri murmured. "Funny. A hot chick convinced me too."

"Kayla?"

"Yup."

Hunter raised an eyebrow, grinning at her.

"Did you…?"

"Like I'd tell you," she scoffed.

"Well, I'm going to pretend you did," he replied. "In fact, I'm gonna imagine it tonight."

"You gonna wank off to it?" Sukri teased. Hunter shrugged.

"I might just do that."

"Pfft. Men," she grumbled.

"Can you blame me?"

"Hell no," she replied. "I'd do the same." She shook her head ruefully. "Guess we're still two peas in a pod, huh? Nice to see that some things haven't changed."

"Yeah," Hunter agreed. "You're still the same old Sukri."

She grew quiet, staring at her feet as she walked.

"What?" he asked.

"I'm not the same old me," she muttered. "Not even close. The Guild made sure of that."

"What do you mean?"

"Those medallions they gave us," she explained. "They fucked with my head. Made me…do things. Bad things. And now look at me," she added, gesturing at herself.

"If it makes you feel better, I thought I murdered my own mother and got my brother and Vi killed."

"But you didn't," Sukri countered.

"Yeah, well, I hated myself for weeks after what I did. I thought about committing suicide. I didn't even want to live with myself, much less anyone else." He put a hand on her shoulder. "I know what it's like to do something terrible, something you think you can never come back from."

"No you don't," she retorted, pulling away. "You didn't do something terrible. You just thought you did."

"Yeah, but I know what it's like to *feel* like I did."

"Not the same," she muttered, lowering her gaze.

Hunter suppressed the urge to push the issue, letting it go. After a long, uncomfortable silence, she glanced up at him, smiling with her eyes but not her lips.

"Guess we're both pretty fucked up, huh?"

"Yeah," he agreed.

"I miss the old me," she mused. "When the most I had to worry about was my shitty job."

"Literally," Hunter quipped. They'd been in waste management, after all. "If there's one thing I've learned, it's that there really isn't anything such as 'me' here. We're ourselves and a bit of everyone we meet. We just have to be careful who we choose to interact with."

"Ain't that the truth," Sukri muttered. "Remind me not to join a frickin' cult again."

"Yeah, and don't get all your friends to do it too."

She punched him in the shoulder. Hard.

"Low blow, asshole," she grumbled. "Thanks for reminding me how I got everyone I cared about killed."

"Dio killed Gammon, not you," Hunter retorted. "And if anyone got Kris killed, it was me. Master Thorius wouldn't have sent us on that suicide mission if it weren't for me, remember?"

"True," she admitted. "So…what's two screw-ups like us gonna do now?"

"Well, you can always come live with me," Hunter offered. Sukri raised an eyebrow at him.

"Little forward, don'tcha think?"

Hunter blushed.

"I mean with the Ironclad," he clarified. "My mother is invincible like Xerxes. And we have a whole army, not to mention Vi. No one will be able to hurt you with them protecting you."

"I don't know," Sukri replied. "Kayla offered to have me stay in the Kingdom of the Deep."

"With her?" he asked. She hesitated.

"Kinda. Yeah."

"Is that what you want?" he pressed. She shrugged.

"I don't know," she admitted. "A part of me does." Hunter grimaced.

"Guess I can't compete with that."

"Hey now," Sukri admonished. "Don't sell yourself short, Hunter. You're not half-bad-looking yourself you know. Kinda had a crush on you back in Tykus."

"You know, I was wondering about that," Hunter admitted. "When us and Gammon went for Starfuckers, you knew Gammon wouldn't drink them." He didn't know at the time, but the drinks had been exposed to feelings of lust…and anyone drinking them would get all hot and bothered.

"Oh hell yeah," Sukri replied. "I was totally trying to get in your pants. Until I felt that whore's stench on your bed…what was her name again?"

"Trixie."

"I didn't want to be like her, you know? I wanted it to be…"

"Real?" Hunter inquired.

"Yeah."

She went quiet then, shaking her head slowly.

"I get it now," she said. "Gammon was in love with me for years, and never told me. But when he got his chance, he refused to date me. Said he was a Polarizer, and didn't want to think that he could make me love him just by my absorbing his love for me whenever we were close. He wanted it to be real too."

"Sorry," Hunter mumbled.

"Well, *we're* both Empaths, so I guess we don't radiate emotions well. So we don't have to worry about that," Sukri reasoned.

"That a proposal?" Hunter inquired with a devilish grin. Sukri's eyes dropped to his body.

"Well, you *do* have really nice pecs now," she admitted. "Frickin' bulging out of your shirt, by the way."

"They flap my wings," he explained.

"I don't give a shit what they do. I just like the way they look."

"Gosh, you're so deep."

"Ha ha," Sukri grumbled. "If we ever date, I'm gonna treat you like a piece of meat. Just warning you."

"Oh no," Hunter mock-complained. "Not that."

"And I expect *you* to do the same," she continued with a smile. Hunter chuckled, leering at her. Which wasn't hard to do; even with multiple layers of wrapping covering her body, her generous curves were still easy to appreciate.

"Hey, if you end up looking like that cat-lady, I won't be able to keep my hands off you," Hunter warned. Sukri smiled, but the expression soon faded, and her gaze dropped to her feet. At length, she glanced at Hunter.

"Let's just…keep things friendly for now, okay?" she proposed. Hunter smiled.

"Deal."

They walked in silence then, the twigs and fallen leaves littering the forest floor crunching under their boots, each step bringing them closer to the Ironclad lair. And what Hunter suddenly hoped very much would become Sukri's new home.

CHAPTER 21

It was sunset by the time Hunter and Sukri decided to quit for the day, ending their hours-long trek through the woods. They'd spent most of the day trying in vain to find their way back to the Kingdom of the Deep. Hunter had climbed a few hills, scoping out the terrain, but it hadn't been particularly helpful. Then he'd tried using the sun as a compass to guide them. There was no direct route available given the steep cliffs in-between them and their destination, forcing them to try to circle around. The more they did, the harder it became to keep track of where they might be. And with the sun setting, it was nearly impossible for Hunter to figure out where they were going.

In other words, they were lost.

Hunter picked a clearing for their camp, gathering brush and sticks for a fire, then lighting it. He gathered stones to place around the fire – they would radiate heat long after the fire had died – and got to work building a lean-to. Sukri helped when she could, then stood there, watching him, a funny look on her face.

"What?" he asked.

"It's just…you're doing all this," she replied. "How did you learn this stuff?"

"Vi taught me."

"It's impressive," she admitted. "The guild didn't teach me anything…I mean, other than making me absorb skills and stuff."

Hunter smirked, finishing the lean-to, a small shelter with an angled roof made of leaves propped up on some thick, straight branches.

"Vi hated the way the guild taught," he said. "She thought learning things by doing them was best, and absorbing skills should only be used to enhance your foundation."

"Yeah, well, obviously she was right."

Hunter sat before the fire, emptying his pockets of the various edible leaves, roots, nuts, and vegetables he'd collected along the way.

"You really going to eat those?" Sukri asked. "They could be strong-willed."

"Nah," Hunter replied. "I checked for that."

"How?"

"I only pick plants that are at the edge of a cluster," he explained. "Plants in the center of a cluster of similar-looking plants probably have the strongest wills. But those at the edge have to be weak-willed if the plants beyond them don't look like them."

"Ohhh," Sukri replied. "Well shit, that just makes sense."

"Yup."

"Let me guess…Vi taught you that?"

"Of course," he confirmed. "Vi taught me everything." He realized that he missed her very much. It'd been about a week since he'd seen her. Sukri sat down next to him, putting her hands close to the fire. They enjoyed the heat and crackling of the flames for a bit, and then Sukri turned to look at him.

"She seems really awesome," she stated. Hunter smiled.

"She is," he agreed. "She saved my life. And not just because she prevented me from dying." He paused, choosing his words carefully. "Vi was the first person in my life who refused to give up on me. And the first person that wouldn't let me give up on her."

Sukri lowered her gaze, staring at her lap.

"Wish I knew what that was like," she muttered. Hunter put a hand on her shoulder.

"Gammon never gave up on you."

Sukri grimaced.

"Yeah."

She turned to him then, her eyes glittering in the light of the fire.

"Would you ever give up on me?"

"No," Hunter replied. Sukri glared at him.

"I mean it, Hunter. I'm being serious."

"I am too," Hunter insisted.

"You answered awfully quickly."

"Sukri, if there's one thing I've learned, it's that I should never give up on my friends," Hunter explained. "I got Vi, my mom, Xerxes, and now you. And that's it. That's…"

"What?"

"That's my world. That's everything I care about, right there," Hunter concluded. "I don't have anything else. Just the clothes on my back, my sword, and you guys."

Sukri swallowed visibly, staring into the fire for a long, long time. Then she scooted closer to Hunter, pressing her shoulder against his, and wrapping an arm around his waist. She rested her head on his shoulder.

"You really love Vi, huh?" Sukri asked.

"Yeah."

There was a pause.

"Did you guys ever…?"

"Oh hell no," Hunter replied, giving her a look. "She likes women."

"Oh. Good."

"Besides," he added with a grin, "…she'd break me." Sukri arched an eyebrow.

"And I wouldn't?"

"Okay, you can move away now," he stated, scooting away from her. She punched him in the shoulder – which was already pretty sore from her punching it a dozen times earlier that day – and then promptly pulled him right in beside her, laughing at him.

"Don't worry," she soothed. "I'm tough on the outside, but once you get past that…"

She leaned in, her face inches from his, her eyes searching his. Her scent was intoxicating, unlike any woman he'd smelled before. It smelled like home.

"You mean once I get *inside*?" he quipped, butterflies flitting in his stomach. She pulled back, rolling her eyes.

"You got a lot better chance at that if you shut up," she grumbled.

"Yes ma'am."

Sukri leaned in again, staring at him for a long moment, then leaning in all the way, pressing her lips against his. He responded, kissing her back. She was surprisingly gentle, not forceful like he remembered when they'd made out a little back in the Outskirts. Back then she'd seemed rushed, as if she was just trying to get to the sex. His bed – with Trixie's will contaminating it – was probably to blame for that.

Now she took her time, leaning in and kissing him softly, savoring the moment. She bit his lower lip gently, then released it…and then opened her mouth, exploring his with her tongue.

It felt *amazing*.

She pushed him backward, lowering him onto his back under the lean-to, then crawling on top of him. Then she hesitated.

"This okay with your wings?" she asked.

"Yeah."

She smiled, resting her chest and belly on his…and her pelvis on his extremely engorged groin.

"Sorry," he mumbled. She smirked.

"Must be doing something right."

"You are," Hunter agreed immediately.

She put a finger to his lips, then leaned in, grabbing his head in her hands and pressing her mouth firmly against his. Again she explored him, with her tongue and her hands. Her mouth tasted as good as she smelled, and each kiss made him feel positively giddy, a tingling sensation spreading through him. He'd never felt anything like it…not with Trixie, and certainly not with the Lady. That'd been lust. Sex, pure and simple. But *this*…

Sukri pulled away, running her fingers down his chest, then cupping his pecs in her hands. She kneaded them gently, smiling to herself, then let go, staring at him. He frowned.

"What?"

"You feeling what I'm feeling?" she asked.

"I um…I don't know," he admitted. "But I've never felt anything like this before."

Sukri gave him a look.

"You just telling a girl what she wants to hear?" she pressed. "I need you to be honest with me," she added, her tone deadly serious.

"Your mouth…your smell, it just…" Hunter began. "I can't explain it, but *damn*."

"Right?"

She rested on top of him again, kissing him slowly, taking her time. Forcing *him* to take his time. To enjoy it. To relish it. And despite her groin pressed again his, and the urgent pressure in his member, for the first time in his life Hunter didn't care if they had sex.

All he wanted was this.

She continued to kiss him, grabbing the sides of his helmet and trying to pull it off. He stopped her, giving her a rueful look.

"Might not want to do that," he cautioned. She frowned, pulling back a little.

"Why not?"

"I can, uh, absorb memories," he admitted.

She jerked back suddenly, the blood draining from her face.

"What?" she blurted out.

"It happens less when I have my helmet on," he explained.

"You can absorb my memories?" she pressed, backing away further and getting to her feet. Hunter grimaced.

"Not with my helmet on," he insisted. She stared down at him, then shook her head.

"I can't do this," she blurted out.

"Wait, what?"

She turned away from him, going to the opposite side of the fire, then sitting down. Hunter stared at her from across the campfire, then sat up.

"What's wrong?" he asked.

"Nothing."

"Sukri…"

"I'm going to sleep," she muttered, laying down and turning on her side away from him. Hunter stared at her in utter confusion, then laid back down himself under the lean-to.

Okay...

And though neither of them said anything more that night, it was a long time before either of them fell asleep.

***

Dominus sighed, staring up at the white ceiling far above his head, red wooden beams running just underneath it at regular intervals to support it. The mattress underneath him was soft but firm, one of the most comfortable he'd ever laid on. But after more than a day of rest, he was getting antsy. Camilla had indeed called for help after the ordeal in her cipher room, her guards coming to carry Dominus back to the mansion. Her physician, a portly man by the name of Phelbus – a man whose competence was slightly outmatched by his confidence – had tried to tend to him. Dominus had turned the man away, suffering Phelbus's insistence that Dominus would die without his help with uncharacteristic patience.

Eventually Phelbus had left, giving Dominus time to focus on what was truly important: food.

He'd consumed every meal brought to him, and within hours asked for more, much to the amazement and curiosity of Camilla's staff, who had never seen someone eat so much in their lives. But Dominus had lost a great amount of tissue during the attack, and if he didn't eat, his body would take from itself to heal him, pulling resources from his other muscles. He was going to need his strength...especially if Zagamar had truly returned.

Dominus knew all-too-well what a true Legend could do.

An avid reader, particularly of history, Dominus had learned of Legends in the past, both human and otherwise, who had risen throughout the ages. Transforming everything and everyone around them, they were like a plague, bringing destruction wherever they went. No one could remain themselves around them for long.

The histories told of Ganitar, a bull who'd been born to a poor farmer many kilometers from the kingdom centuries ago. It'd transformed its own mother, and every cow in its stable...and the farmers...into itself. The grass it slept on, the animals it drew near. Everything became Ganitar. The surrounding towns had no idea until it was too late, countless bulls stampeding through the land, eating everything in sight. An entire year's worth of crops was destroyed, and no one knew which one of the bulls was Ganitar, as they all looked the same. No one knew which bull to kill.

The kingdom of Tykus had acted, slaughtering every cow outside of its borders, using archers to shoot them from afar. Not a single cow remained after they were done, and their bodies were heaped in a pit, then buried. No one would dare eat their meat, for fear of it being Ganitar…and becoming the Legend reborn.

To think what might have happened if twenty men had consumed the Legend's meat, all of them becoming the Legend itself, with only a slightly-lessened ability to transform everything around them…

The door to his room opened, and Lady Camilla stepped in. She was wearing one of her usual risqué dresses, a black gown with a deeply plunging V-neck.

"I would have expected a lady to knock," Dominus grumbled. She walked up to the foot of his bed, putting a hand on her hip and smirking at him.

"I was hoping to catch you…enjoying yourself," she replied.

"My arms don't work yet."

"A shame," she murmured, circling around to stop at the right edge of his bed, sitting down on it. She glanced at his chest – which was wrapped in bandages, leaving his belly bare – then put a hand on the mattress, inches from his right hip. "You must be terribly frustrated."

"I've got other things on my mind."

"I've found that one's mind works far better if one's body is taken care of," Camilla lectured. "You can't ignore the needs of the flesh without consequence, Dominus."

"I've ignored them quite well for the last twenty years," Dominus retorted.

"Mmm," she murmured. "You were an old man then, and very sick." She lifted her hand from the bed, placing it on the bony protrusion of his pelvis. It was warm, and to Dominus's surprise, it had an immediate and powerful effect on him. He felt a long-forgotten pulsing in his groin. "Tell me Dominus," she continued, "…could you even unsheathe your…sword for all those years?"

Dominus grimaced, trying to swipe her hand from his pelvis. But of course his arms didn't work, his chest muscles still only having partially regenerated. She smirked, glancing down at his groin. It was impossible not to notice the effect she'd had on him.

"Only a fool equates impotence with manliness," he snapped.

"My apologies," Camilla replied, lifting her hand away. "I didn't realize you were so sensitive about it."

"I'm not."

"Well you're certainly not an old man anymore," she pointed out, glancing at his still-swollen groin. She paused then, giving him a curious look. "Has it affected your mind?"

Dominus blinked.

"What?"

"Your youth," she clarified. "Your body is growing younger. Is your mind?"

"I still remember everything," he stated, more defensively than he would have liked. "I'm still myself." Still, he'd never considered that his *mind* could be changed by the Ironclad's power. The thought was instantly sobering…and terrifying.

Had he changed?

"I was just curious," Camilla replied.

Dominus nodded absently, focusing inward on himself. He hadn't been monitoring his feelings or thoughts as closely as he used to…and he'd found himself having racy thoughts more and more often, particularly when he was around her. Powerful urges that had all but vanished a decade ago, now roaring back to life.

An annoying – and dangerous – distraction

"We don't have time for games," Dominus reminded her. "Or have you forgotten about Zagamar?"

"Ah yes," Camilla muttered. "That."

"The beast that attacked me was dead before it arose," Dominus declared. "I cut its throat myself."

"I know," Camilla replied. "My men checked its pulse before bringing it into the cipher room, of course. It had none."

"You understand the implications, of course."

She sighed heavily, then nodded.

"Zeno must have absorbed some measure of the Ironclad's regenerative abilities before being taken over by Zagamar," she deduced. "And Zagamar has passed that ability on to his underlings."

"Precisely," Dominus agreed. "Which means we are in grave danger."

"I agree," she replied. "I've already sent scouts to the Kingdom of the Deep to alert them. I suggested they go on the offensive immediately, before Zagamar's hordes get too numerous to handle."

"My plan exactly," Dominus concurred. She smirked.

"Brilliant minds think alike."

"I have to warn Tykus as well," Dominus pressed.

"I'll send a messenger."

"No," Dominus retorted. "I'll go myself." Camilla frowned.

"Dominus, are you forgetting…"

"That I'm supposed to be dead? Yes," Dominus interrupted.

"And you *will* be if you go back," Camilla pointed out.

"Keep in mind that I'm not stupid," Dominus grumbled. "I have my ways."

Camilla considered this, then sighed.

"And how exactly do you expect to *reach* Tykus?" she inquired. Dominus grimaced; she had a point. They'd barely gotten a few kilometers from the mansion before running into the Svartálfar. Or rather, the creatures that had been somewhere between animals and the dreaded dark elves.

"How are your messengers getting to the Kingdom of the Deep?" Dominus shot back. Camilla smirked.

"By flying, of course," she revealed. "Or do you forget that I'm not constrained by Tykus's silly laws?"

Dominus hesitated, considering this.

"Can you fly me out?" he asked. "At least to the Fringe?"

Camilla smiled, putting a hand on his bare belly, her palm resting well below his belly button. Again, he felt himself growing…and felt the head of his member pressing against the bottom of her wrist.

"For a price," she replied.

"Name it," Dominus shot back.

"I want to know who your contacts in the Kingdom of the Deep are," she declared. "The ones you always used to outbid me when you were Duke."

Dominus considered this. Without the power of the Duchy – and the vast fortune it had provided – those contacts were now useless to him.

"And?" he pressed. With Camilla, there was always more.

"I want access to the hidden stashes of artifacts you've acquired. And the location of the Kingdom's stash of illegal artifacts."

Dominus grimaced. The Kingdom did indeed have illegal artifacts held outside of the Kingdom in various locations.

"For mere travel?" he retorted. "No."

"In return, I offer my…services," she pressed. "I can satisfy those annoying urges you've…re-acquired."

"So now you're offering to be a whore," he noted. She smirked.

"Oh, *so* much more than that, Dominus," she countered. "I'm offering you a stake in my business empire. Say…twenty percent?"

Dominus paused. It was a proper incentive for him. As business partner, he'd take twenty percent of the profits from the Lady's acquisition of his own artifacts and the Kingdom's stash. He would be instantly – and considerably – wealthy. This would also position him relatively close to Tykus, allowing him to effectively serve as its protector.

"Sixty percent," he countered. She arched an eyebrow. "Your personality is strong, but you absorb traits well," he reminded her. She frowned.

"And how do you know that?"

"The Kingdom has a dossier on every person of interest," he revealed.

"Ah. Your point?"

"If I stay with you, you may absorb some of my healing ability," he noted. She gave a rueful smile.

"Always so perceptive," she mused. Dominus gave a tight smile back. He knew very well that her offer to…take care of him served more than to satisfy her own peculiar appetites. The intimacy allowed for substantial transfer of traits…one that Dominus would normally never allow. And with the Ironclad head missing – or gone – Dominus was her only chance at achieving immortality.

"Thirty percent," she countered. "I've worked too hard not to retain a majority stake."

Dominus tried to reach out to offer a hand, but of course his arm didn't move. He grimaced.

"Deal," he agreed. She smiled at him.

"We'll make it official once you can sign the proper documents, she stated. Then her smile broadened, and she reached into her cleavage, pulling out two long, black leather straps. They were restraints, he realized. "I'm going to tie your legs to this bed," she declared. Dominus frowned, feeling his member pressing harder against her palm. He was annoyed at his body for betraying him…and at the same time, intrigued.

"For how long?"

"When your arms finally work again, you can untie them," Camilla replied. "Until then," she added, lifting her palm up, then sliding her fingertips down past his bellybutton, until they were perilously close to his erection. Then she rested her palm down on it, making it pulsate reflexively. "You're mine."

Chapter 22

When Hunter awoke under the lean-to the next morning, the campfire had long since died. The sun was peeking through the trees just above the horizon, and Sukri was just waking up, stretching out her arms tiredly. Hunter got up, nodding at her, then packing up their stuff. They didn't say much to each other.

It was more than a little awkward.

"We're lost," he declared. "The ocean is north of Tykus, so I think we should find the river and follow it downstream. All rivers lead to the ocean, after all."

"Did Vi teach you how to find your way in the wilderness?" Sukri asked.

"Of course."

"Then I'm in your capable hands," Sukri replied.

The river was to the west, and Hunter noted the direction of the rising sun, then left the clearing, entering into the forest once again. Sukri followed alongside him, and they hiked for a few miles before they heard the rush of running water in the distance. They followed it, eventually reaching the edge of a cliff. The River Ormr was a thirty-foot drop below. They walked parallel to it downstream then, neither of them saying anything as they walked. Hunter wanted to talk with her – to try to understand what'd happened the night before – but decided against it. She clearly didn't want to talk.

Hours passed, and eventually Hunter slowed, then stopped.

"Wait a sec," he said.

"What?"

"This place looks familiar," he stated. The river had gotten much narrower, and quite a bit shallower, more of a stream now. It'd branched a few times, the main river having gone further west. Hunter had followed the shallower branch on a hunch; he'd learned to trust his hunches, given that the majority of them were, at their root, memories he'd absorbed from others. There was a hill in the distance, and a smaller stream leaving a cave in one side of the hill to join the larger stream.

It was the back entrance to the Ironclad lair…the one he and Vi had taken when they'd found the lair the first time!

"Come on," Hunter urged, leading Sukri toward the cave entrance. She followed reluctantly.

"You gonna tell me what's going on?" she asked.

"This is the Ironclad lair," he explained. "We're here!"

He strode up to the entrance to the cave, walking alongside the banks of the smaller stream. There were several Ironclad guarding it, and they turned to regard Hunter and Sukri as they approached.

"Good afternoon," Hunter signed, smiling at the Ironclad.

"Good afternoon," one of them signed back. "Who is she?"

"A friend," Hunter signed in reply. The Ironclad nodded.

"Welcome back," it signed. "I will bring you to the Queen."

One of the Ironclad led Hunter and Sukri into the shallow stream, climbing into the cave, then continuing forward along the left side, as Hunter had done with Vi weeks ago. They followed the Ironclad through the underground maze, eventually reaching the large curved tunnel leading to the central cavern.

"This is where your mom lives?" Sukri asked as they passed countless Ironclad guards lining each wall of the tunnel.

"Yup."

"Bringing me home to meet the fam already, eh?" she quipped. "You move fast."

Hunter ignored her comment, and eventually the tunnel opened up into a huge domed cavern. One with a hole in the ceiling far above, a waterfall cascading down to a pool in the center. A ring-like waterfall surrounding and obscuring a rocky island in the middle of the pool.

Hunter led Sukri to the edge of the pool.

"Stay here," he requested. Then he stepped down into the pool, feeling its current try to pull him leftward. He resisted this, walking toward the waterfall ahead. A blue glow emanated from it; Mom was home, of course. "Mom?" he called out.

The light grew brighter, and then a dark figure emerged from the waterfall, stepping down into the pool. It was an Ironclad even taller than Xerxes, with long black tendrils sprouting from its head like hair, some glowing bright blue like Xerxes' mane. It was clearly female, with breasts jutting out of its thorax; tendrils of glowing blue membrane extended down its arms and legs like veins. It was Neesha, queen of the Ironclad…and his mother.

"Hey Mom," Hunter greeted, pulling his wings as far in as possible. But there was no way to hide them. She stared down at him…or more specifically, at his wings.

"Hunter, what did you do?" she demanded.

"Nice to see you too," he replied lamely. She glared at him, crossing both pairs of arms over her thorax.

"What did you *do*," she insisted. Hunter sighed, spreading out his wings.

"A bad thing," he admitted.

"You turned into a *bird*?" she blurted out incredulously, taking a step back. Hunter shrugged.

"I was drunk."

"You were drunk," she repeated.

"They said I had to choose a spirit," Hunter explained.

"So you chose a bird?" she exclaimed. "You know I hate birds!"

"So do I," Hunter reminded her. "Didn't you always tell me to face my fears?" he added rather lamely. She gave him a withering look.

"Hunter…"

"Hi there," Sukri interjected, waving at Neesha. "I'm Sukri."

Neesha turned to Sukri, as if seeing her for the first time.

"Who is this?" she demanded.

"My friend," Hunter answered.

"Not for nothing, those wings saved our lives," Sukri informed her. "I got shoved off a bridge. Hunter caught me and flew me to safety."

Mom considered this.

"That's nice," she decided. "We'll cut them off."

"Yeah, about that," Hunter grumbled. "I kinda swallowed Xerxes' goo beforehand."

"It just keeps getting better," Mom muttered. "So I'm going to have to live with this?"

"Afraid so."

Neesha sighed, eyeing Hunter's wings with disgust, then shaking her head.

"Fine. Did you make it to the Deep?"

"Yeah. Zaggie can't take over anymore."

"Good," she replied, clearly relieved. "Where's your brother?"

"We don't know," Sukri piped in. "Last thing we saw, he was fighting one of Lady Camilla's Seekers near the Kingdom of the Deep."

"Then he's probably looking for you," Neesha guessed. "I'll send some Ironclad to fetch him."

Just then, Hunter heard footsteps behind him, and turned to see a very familiar woman striding toward him. She wore a suit made of dark brown leather, countless bones embedded in the fabric, and the face-part of a human skull at her chest. She had light brown hair cut so short she was almost bald, and large green eyes that twinkled as she approached.

"I leave you boys alone for a couple days," she declared, stopping beside Sukri at the edge of the pool. "…and look at what happens. Nice wings, Hunter. You look like a fairy."

"Hey Vi," Hunter greeted sheepishly, climbing out of the pool to stand before her.

"Hello," Sukri greeted.

"Who are you?" Vi inquired.

"Remember when you first met me?" Hunter asked. Vi nodded.

"You were with a girl, a big guy, and the guy who got his arm ripped off," she recalled.

"Right," Hunter confirmed. "This is the girl."

"I'm Sukri," Sukri greeted. Vi turned to her, looking her up and down. Particularly focusing on the down.

"Nice ass," she complimented.

"Thanks," Sukri replied. "Your ass is amazing." Vi smirked.

"Yeah it is."

"Hunter's told me a lot about you," Sukri added. "He really loves you, you know."

"I know," Vi replied. "The feeling is mutual," she added, wrapping an arm around Hunter's shoulders and squeezing affectionately. "Good to see you, kiddo. Not going to lie, I was a little worried about you."

"I had Xerxes to protect me," Hunter replied with a smile, squeezing her back. "I missed you too by the way." He turned to Mom. "How's the war planning going?"

"It's planned," she answered. "We'll wait for your brother to return, then storm the kingdom."

Vi pulled away from Hunter, putting her hands on her hips and eyeing him critically. "In the meantime, we've got work to do."

"Huh?"

"You went and got yourself a pair of wings," she explained. "So now I have to teach you how to use them."

"Pfft," Hunter scoffed. "What would *you* know about flying?"

"You doubting me?" Vi shot back. Hunter grimaced. He'd done so many times in the past, and she'd always proven herself right. "That's what I thought," she stated.

"Can you train me too?" Sukri asked. Vi considered this.

"We'll talk," she decided. "I need to get to know you first."

"Thank you for considering it," Sukri replied.

"Don't kid yourself, Sukri," Vi retorted. "I might just be keeping you around 'cause I'll get to look at that ass all day long."

"I'll be sure to give you a show then," Sukri replied. "Consider it payment for services rendered." Vi smirked, giving Hunter an approving look.

"I *like* her," she exclaimed, slapping him on the side of his shoulder…hard enough to nearly knock him off his feet. He'd forgotten how strong she was. "Follow me, both of you," she added, making her way toward one of the tunnels off the main cavern. Hunter glanced at his mother.

"Go on," Neesha urged. "I'll see you later."

"Bye Mom," he replied. "Love you." He turned about, following Vi and Sukri.

"Love you…ugh, those *wings*," Neesha groaned. Hunter grinned, spreading his wings out all the way just to torture her. It must have had an effect; he heard splashing, and glanced back to see that his mother had returned to the island beyond the waterfall.

"Well then," he declared. "That went better than I expected."

* * *

The sky was overcast when Hunter, Vi, and Sukri emerged from the front entrance of the Ironclad lair, passing a few dozen Ironclad guards surrounding the entrance, then turning rightward. The grass was jet-black, each blade crunching under their feet as they walked. A consequence of the Ironclads' will exerting itself on the grass over time. The grass had died long ago, the beetle shell covering each blade preventing them from absorbing sunlight. A reminder that, as with the Deep, not all combinations of wills were survivable.

"How're you doing?" Hunter asked Vi as she followed them further into the woods.

"Busy," Vi answered. "I've been working with your mother to organize the attack on Tykus."

"Wait, you're…?" Sukri asked, glancing at Hunter.

"Yeah, we're taking Tykus down," Hunter explained. "They were planning on destroying us, but there was some sort of attack on the kingdom a few days ago."

"It was the Guild of Seekers," Vi revealed. "They were caught smuggling illegal artifacts. The Kingdom raided them and jailed High Seeker Zeno, so the guild struck back. And hard, from what our scouts have reported."

"Wow," Hunter murmured. "They really attacked Tykus?"

"Yep," Vi confirmed. "Some people think they even made it into the Acropolis, although the Kingdom denies it. But according to one of my sources, all the dukes were murdered."

"Damn," Sukri said, giving a low whistle.

"Wait," Hunter interjected. "Even Dominus?"

"That's right," Vi confirmed.

"How do you know all this?" Hunter pressed.

"I…interrogated a high-level military officer leaving the Kingdom to return to the military base in the Deadlands," Vi explained.

"Ah." He paused. "Did he survive your interrogation?"

"That would be a no."

They reached a familiar wide dirt path leading up a steep slope ahead. It was the same path Vi had led Hunter to when he'd first reunited with Xerxes. She walked up it, Hunter and Sukri following behind.

"Where are we going?" Sukri inquired.

"To the top of this hill," Vi answered. "I need to see what Hunter can do with those wings of his."

"He glides pretty well," Sukri offered. She described her harrowing plunge from the bridge, and Hunter's heroic actions in saving her.

"Not bad," Vi had to admit. "Not many people would've been able to pull that off. You kept calm under pressure Hunter. I'm proud of you."

"I had a good teacher," Hunter replied with a smile, putting an arm around Vi's shoulders and giving her a squeeze. She smiled, tousling his hair affectionately.

So you know how to glide. Can you fly?" Vi asked.

"No, haven't gotten there yet."

"We'll watch you glide first," Vi decided. "Then we'll work on flying."

"How do *you* know how to fly?" Hunter asked.

"I don't," Vi confessed. "But I'm gonna figure it out."

They reached the top of the hill, and Vi stopped, turning to look back down it.

"Okay," she stated, gesturing down the hill. "Glide."

Hunter nodded, unfurling his wings. He braced himself, feeling a slight breeze against him; even this threatened to pull him backward. He leapt upward and forward, feeling his wings catch the air instantly, the downward-sloping path dropping away gradually as he glided down the hill. Soon he was a good thirty feet in the air; despite his previous experience, he still got butterflies being so high up. The thought that one wrong move might send him plummeting to the earth still terrified him. He ignored his fear as best he could, remembering to rotate his wings backward to slow himself as he neared the bottom of the hill. There was forest ahead; he rotated his left wing, circling gradually to the left, spiraling downward. Eventually he straightened out, touching down at the base of the hill.

Nice and easy, he thought, feeling rather proud of himself.

Then he had to walk all the way back up.

"That was *pretty*," Vi exclaimed as he reached the top again. "Not bad, Hunter. Not bad at all."

"Thanks."

"You actually learned that pretty quick," Vi admitted. "I know a few bird-people from the Kingdom of the Deep. It usually takes a long time to get used to your wings."

"I kinda had to learn or die," Hunter replied ruefully. Vi grinned.

"Best way to learn."

"It's pretty much her teaching method," Hunter told Sukri with a wink. Vi ignored him, gesturing down the hill again.

"Alright, now I want you to start gliding down a few meters, then beat your wings and fly backward and land right where you started."

Hunter took a deep breath in, then nodded.

"Alright."

He stepped to the very edge of the slope again, unfurling his wings, then leaping down as before. Again, his wings filled with air, and he started gliding down, picking up speed quickly. He rotated his wings back to slow down, then beat them like he was doing a chest fly at the gym, bringing his wings together in front of him. He launched upward and backward…and promptly began to fall.

Hunter swore, spreading his wings out to his sides again…and started gliding down the hill.

"Beat 'em!" Vi shouted from behind.

Hunter did so, beating his wings once, then again, feeling himself launching backward and upward as he did so. But the minute he stopped, he started to fall again. He grimaced, beating his wings again and again, sweat dripping down his forehead and into his eyes. Then he realized he was directly over Sukri and Vi.

"Good!" Vi exclaimed. "Now get down here."

Hunter complied, beating his wings a few more times, then gliding in a tighter circle than before, landing on the hilltop a few yards away. He strode up to them, wiping the sweat from his forehead.

"That's hard," he admitted.

"That's what happens when you beat it," Vi quipped. Hunter rolled his eyes, and Sukri smirked. "So you can glide, and you can gain altitude," Vi continued. "We're getting there."

"What next, master?" Hunter inquired.

"Now you glide all the way to the base of the hill and fly back here without touching the ground," Vi answered. Hunter nodded, facing the edge of the slope again, then spreading his wings and leaping down. The ground dropped from beneath him, and he picked up speed rapidly, the wind howling in his ears. He was well above the treetops when he reached the end of the slope, and he turned gently to the right, circling around until he was facing Sukri and Vi. He was about halfway down the hill altitude-wise.

Okay, he told himself. *Here goes.*

He tried rotating his wings back a little, then beat them, and felt himself rise up a little bit…but he also lost some forward momentum.

You're not trying to fly backward, he reminded himself.

He rotated his wings back to neutral, then flapped them again, and this time he gained altitude without sacrificing much speed. Again and again he flapped, flying a little higher each time…all the while careening toward the slope ahead.

Uh oh.

He flapped harder and faster, rotating his wings back as he did so to slow down…and promptly smacked feet-first into the slope. He stumbled, landing belly-first onto the dirt.

"Well damn…" he began – and then a gust of wind struck him, filling his still-open wings and flinging him backward. He panicked, spreading his wings out desperately…and gently glided back onto the slope. This time he folded his wings immediately behind his back.

And heard Vi's laughter from ahead.

He sighed, hiking up the path back to the top. He'd made it about three-quarters of the way up, he found. When he finally reached Vi and Sukri, Sukri patted him on the shoulder.

"You're doing great," she reassured…holding back a smirk.

"Actually that was terrible," Vi corrected. "But you'll do better next time. One piece of advice…keep your legs up and behind you."

"Huh?"

"You're letting your legs hang down," Vi explained. "It's creating way too much drag. Keep 'em up and together. Or pull your knees to your chest. You know, like a bird."

"Right, got it."

He waited to catch his breath for a moment – flapping his wings wasn't too hard, but walking up that damn hill was – and then leapt from the edge again, spreading his wings out. He started gliding down again.

"Legs!" Vi shouted.

Hunter grimaced, realizing his legs *were* hanging beneath him. He kicked them backward, straightening his legs and pulling them together so his knees touched, as if he were diving.

And felt himself immediately pick up speed, accelerating rapidly!

"Whoa!" he blurted out, pulling his legs down reflexively. He slowed, tilting upward a little. Then he steeled himself, throwing his legs back again…and immediately sped up. He lost a lot less altitude this time, sailing well above the treetops at the bottom of the hill. He turned, being careful to do so gently at such a high speed, then made his way back up the slope.

Okay, he told himself. *That worked.*

He beat his wings experimentally, making sure to keep his legs up this time…and felt himself gaining altitude smoothly. He broke out into a grin, feeling positively giddy. Beating his wings slowly and powerfully, he gained more and more altitude, this time nearly making it to the top of the slope before having to slow down abruptly, landing on the slope side. Thankfully he managed to keep his balance.

"All right Hunter!" Sukri cried, running up to him and giving him a big hug. "That was awesome!"

"Yeah it was," he agreed. "That really worked. Thanks Vi."

"And you questioned me," Vi quipped, grinning at him. He gave her a rueful smile.

"All right, I admit it. You were right."

"Never get tired of hearing it," Vi replied. "Now go and land all the way at the top like I told you to."

Hunter did so, repeating his performance…and this time sailing well over Vi and Sukri's heads on his way back, landing a good thirty feet behind them.

"Good," Vi stated, clapping him on the shoulder when he'd walked back to them. "Easy part's over now."

"Huh?"

"Take my bow," she ordered, slipping her bow off her back and handing it to him, then securing her quiver to his waist. "Time to make you dangerous."

CHAPTER 23

Dominus's hips bucked as his will broke, hours of Camilla's maddeningly slow, ceaseless seductions bringing him past any ability or desire to hold off, to deny her that which she most desperately wanted: to see him lose control. To see Dominus, the former Duke of Wexford, give in to her at last.

He moaned, his hips bucking again and again, sweat pouring from his body, his heart pounding in his chest.

It was ecstasy.

At last the waves of pleasure ended, and he looked down, watching as Camilla met his gaze, her eyes twinkling. She would have given him that maddening smirk of hers…if her mouth had not otherwise been occupied.

She lifted her head, letting him slip out, and his member fell hot and slick against his belly.

"Mmm," she murmured, sliding upward sinuously, her breasts and belly sliding against his skin. She leaned down, kissing him on the lips…or at least trying to. He turned his head to the side, making her pout. "Awww…after all that, not even a kiss?" she inquired.

"You got what you wanted."

"And so did you," she retorted with a smile, sitting back, resting her groin against his. "Or are you going to pretend you didn't want that?"

"The crude desires of the body do not reflect the desires of my mind."

Camilla stared at him…and promptly burst into laughter.

"What?" Dominus demanded.

"You," she answered, shaking her head. "You're so…quaint."

"Quaint?"

"Mmm," she replied, shaking her head and smiling at him. Her long hair fell over her shoulders, draping across her ample breasts. "So *repressed.* Tell me Dominus…how many women have you slept with?"

Dominus grimaced.

"I don't have to justify that with an answer."

"That's answer enough," Camilla countered. "Poor Dominus. Wasting all your gifts following Tykus's regressive laws. Think of all the *pleasure* you could have."

"A distraction," Dominus shot back.

"Is it?" she inquired. "I seem to do quite well despite all my…distractions." She leaned down, kissing him on the neck. "In fact, I find it clears my mind." She smiled at him again, trying to kiss him on the lips. He turned his head away again, and she nibbled on his earlobe instead.

"Camilla…"

She sucked his earlobe into her mouth, biting it gently, then letting go, kissing his neck again. He tried to ignore her, but he felt a familiar stirring in his groin, his member somehow – impossibly – awakening. It grew, hardening against her groin…and she slid her pelvis against it rhythmically.

"Dominus," she stated incredulously, her eyes widening. She looked down, watching as he grew to his full length. "Oh my," she murmured. "I wonder if it works?"

She slid her hips up to his belly, then slid down, and Dominus felt her body engulf him in hot, tight wetness. He gasped, not expecting it…and she moaned, taking him in completely.

"Oh *Dominus*…"

She ground her pelvis against his, riding him slowly. She rested her head next to his on the bed, her breath hot against his ear.

He felt the unmistakable rise of his pleasure, coming as readily as if he hadn't just orgasmed moments ago. Its power and urgency surprised him, and he stiffened.

"Stop," he ordered.

But she didn't stop, grinding against him even harder, her breath coming in short gasps. He felt his pleasure rise with hers, and tried to push her away from him. But his arms were weak, his muscles still in the process of healing.

"Camilla!" he snapped.

She gasped, her whole body stiffening, her breath catching in her throat. Moments later, he felt a rhythmic pulsing around his member, contractions so powerful that they threatened to push him out. Still she ground against him, his pleasure rising dangerously high, approaching the unthinkable.

"Stop!" he cried.

She did stop then, staring down at him, her skin glistening with sweat.

"What is it darling?" she inquired.

"If you don't want a baby, I would suggest releasing me," he replied. She took a moment to process this, then smiled.

"I wouldn't worry about that," she reassured. Still, she slid him out of her. "I didn't realize you were so close." She gazed down at his erection. "Were you always so…virile?"

"No," Dominus answered truthfully. It had to be the Ironclad's strange power, he realized. Allowing him to recover almost instantly from being spent.

"This," Camilla murmured, shifting the angle of her pelvis, then sliding it down on top of his member, "...could be interesting."

He felt himself pressing against her flesh, then felt him slide into her again. Except this time it was even tighter. He grunted.

"Camilla," he blurted out, but she put a finger to his lips.

"Relax," she soothed, bringing him into her fully.

He moaned, that single movement nearly bringing him to completion. Dominus looked down, seeing himself within her...but most definitely not in her womb. He stared as she began to ride him again, hardly believing what was happening. What they were doing was illegal in Tykus, an abomination for which he would have been stripped of his Duchy.

But as she moved expertly on him, he became lost in his pleasure, resting his head back on his pillow and closing his eyes. And moments later, when she brought him quickly to his second of many orgasms to come that day, he cried out in ecstasy, not even bothering to hold back anymore.

* * *

Dominus pulled on the last piece of armor that Camilla had given him, a fine metal breastplate. It was quite comfortable, as was the rest of his armor. He gazed at his reflection in the full-length mirror in his suite's master bathroom, hardly recognizing himself. For he had almost no gray hair at all, and his skin was that of a young man, now in his forties at most. After days of robust eating, he'd filled out remarkably well, his body stronger than it'd been in decades.

He felt...good.

Dominus heard footsteps behind him, and saw Camilla entering the bathroom in the mirror's reflection. She was dressed in a mixture of leather and chain-mail armor, a uniform that offered a reasonable combination of protection and mobility...while somehow still managing to showcase her remarkable figure. She smiled, stepping right up behind him and wrapping her arms around him, her hands on his chest.

"You look dashing," she murmured.

"And you look ravaging," he replied. This earned him a smile, and she let go of him, standing to one side and gazing at him silently. He allowed this, surprised at how calm he was feeling. After their marathon of sex the previous day, he'd expected to spend a great many days kicking himself for what he'd allowed to happen. To think that he'd been shocked by sodomy; what they'd done after that had only been more and more egregious, a descent into the most depraved acts he'd ever imagined...and more than a few he would *never* have imagined.

But despite their offenses, tomorrow had come. He had eaten breakfast, gotten dressed, and engaged in the normal doings of a civilized man.

And now he felt absolutely fine.

He glanced at Camilla in the mirror, watching her watch him as he tested his longsword, pulling it free from its scabbard, then placing it back in its sheathe. It made him think of what they'd done the day – and night – before. How she'd dominated him, controlling his pleasure and forcing him to give her what she wanted. How she'd broken him down bit-by-bit, destroying his every imaginable inhibition. It made his groin stir just to think of it.

He'd *liked* it.

He took a deep breath in, turning to face Camilla, who continued to watch him silently, a mysterious smile on her lips. To allow her to dominate him…to allow *anyone* to dominate him…would have been unthinkable in the past. Even now, he would never allow such a thing outside of the bedroom.

But he knew full well that things that were forbidden were the most desired…and nothing was more forbidden to a powerful man that to lose control. To *be* controlled.

"And what are *you* thinking?" Camilla inquired, breaking the silence.

"I could ask the same of you."

"Answer and I will," she retorted.

"I was strategizing about how to deal with Zagamar," he lied. She smirked, stepping behind him and wrapping an arm around his waist, putting her hand on his crotch.

"I didn't realize Zagamar affected you this way," she teased.

"Fine," he grumbled. "I was contemplating our…evening together."

"Which part?"

"All of it," he admitted.

"And?"

"I hope you understand that I won't be controlled so easily outside of the bedroom," he warned. She laughed.

"Oh Dominus," she replied, letting go of him. "The bedroom is the one place where anything goes. Where we can be vulnerable…both of us. Equals."

He raised an eyebrow.

"You're saying we're not equals?" he retorted. She gave a little smile.

"I'd dare say you might have even been my superior, back when you were Duke Dominus of Wexford," she replied. "But now?"

"I gave up my title for immortality," he reminded her.

"Granted," she conceded. "You *are* the first man I've ever been with who *was* my equal," she admitted. "I find it…refreshing."

"Our alliance works in both our favors," Dominus noted.

"I agree," Camilla replied. "But if we're going to have an alliance, I have one more…stipulation."

"Such as?"

"Well, seeing as you're the only man who can satisfy my prodigious appetites, I would demand you do so regularly," she proposed.

Dominus hesitated, then nodded. The Ironclad's power had given him the ability to recover rapidly from being…spent, allowing him to copulate again and again for hours on end. And without any of the usual discomfort such an attempt would bring.

"And I would also demand that you allow me my…outside dalliances," she continued. "I'm not one to be owned by one man…or woman."

"Fine."

"Is it?" she pressed. "Most men would get jealous."

"I'm not most men," he reminded her.

"That you're not," she agreed. "Now, about your transportation to the Deadlands. Come with me."

* * *

Camilla led Dominus to the roof of the mansion, where he found a large winged mount standing. It was hybrid between a horse and a bird, equipped with a fine-looking saddle. Other, smaller winged creatures also stood on the roof a ways away from the winged steed, some of them half-bird, half-man. Camilla led Dominus to the winged horse, gesturing for him to mount it.

"This will take you to the Deadlands," she explained. "It already knows the route. Just snap the reins and it will start flying."

"These other creatures, are they scouts?" he asked. Camilla nodded.

"They're how I keep tabs on the Kingdom, and my other allies and enemies. From high up they're indistinguishable from birds, and they have remarkable sight."

"Clever."

And it *was* clever. Camilla was clearly operating on a much more sophisticated level than he'd imagined. And her use of wild artifacts and hybrid creatures – unacceptable in the Kingdom – was clearly a strength, not a weakness. She was changing his perspective…just as King Tykus had urged him to do.

Nature wasn't the enemy…and man was a part of nature. He'd built up walls around himself to keep nature out, and Tykus had started the process of breaking those walls down.

"Are you ready?" Camilla inquired.

"I am," he replied. "How will I get back?"

"Your steed will fly away after you land," she answered. "I can't risk it waiting for you and being found by any scouting parties from the Kingdom. But my scouts will be on the lookout for you. Come to the Fringe a kilometer west of the King's Road and they'll summon the steed for you."

"Thank you," he stated, giving her a rare smile. It felt awkward on his lips. She smiled back.

"You're welcome."

"What will you do while I'm gone?" he inquired.

"I'll coordinate with the Kingdom of the Deep," she answered. "They have considerable resources to combat Zagamar, and a great desire to do so. Hobbomock is their arch-enemy, the devil that threatens to end the world. They'll be our greatest ally."

Dominus nodded, mounting the winged horse. Camilla showed him a special belt system to hold him tight to the harness, and he buckled it, tightening the straps. Then he waved.

"Until we meet again," he stated.

And then he snapped the reins, and the horse bolted, running straight for the edge of the roof!

Dominus gripped the reins tightly as the horse leapt off the roof, spreading its wings wide. His stomach lurched as they fell toward the river twenty meters below, and he clung to the horse desperately, resisting the urge to cry out.

And then the horse beat its wings, their descent stopping, and it soared upward into the air!

The wind whipped through Dominus's hair as they picked up speed, angling away from the river and back toward the forest he'd been ambushed in the other day. They flew over it with remarkable speed, faster than Dominus had ever imagined being able to go. His whole body tingled as they flew further and further upward, the vast expanse of the world spreading out before them.

Endless forest broken by mountains and rivers, Nature in all its majesty.

It was glorious.

Dominus laughed then, feeling giddy as the horse continued to climb higher. He devoured the scenery, seeing the world as he had never seen it, feeling the wind in his hair, the sun on his skin. The horse beneath him, its muscles working as it brought them higher.

He felt alive. *Connected.*

And then the horse slowed its ascent, gliding quickly forward. Ahead, Dominus saw something beyond the forest. A hint of yellow, and then of blue beyond. The Deadlands, and then the ocean. From here, the Kingdom of Tykus was not even visible, a speck in a vast, beautiful world.

And for the first time since he'd left Tykus, venturing out into the world as a new man, he understood what the great king had been trying to teach him.

CHAPTER 24

Zac stepped through the ruins of Eastbrook, a large town at the banks of the serpentine river that cut through the sprawling lands far north of the Kingdom of the Deep, his boots *crunching* on broken glass strewn across one of its cobblestone streets. He saw a cluster of small bodies on the ground ahead, near a stone fountain in the center of the town.

His jawline rippled.

"Barbaric," he heard one of his generals mutter. General Roden, a veteran of Zac's army. His highest-ranking general, ten years Zac's senior. But the man was deferential, as were all the others. They understood Zac's abilities. Abilities they had been given a small taste of.

Abilities that had made them better.

Zac said nothing, walking up to the bodies and kneeling before them. They were children, some no older than two. Covered in blood. Some with their throats slit, others with caved-in skulls.

He sighed.

"To think that they'd rather kill their own children than have them join us," General Roden muttered, shaking his head.

"They didn't love them," Zac muttered, rising to his feet. It was always the same. People desperately spending their lives trying to absorb the wills of their leaders. The aristocrats, the rich. The powerful. Caring nothing for being themselves…until someone like Zac showed up. Someone who threatened to make them different than their peers.

To the parents of these children, being different was clearly a fate worse than death.

He felt a familiar anger rise within him. For he knew damn well that, if these same parents had been offered artifacts carrying the wills of their own elites, they would have gladly used them to change their children. To rob them of their souls.

"Being different is a crime, Roden," Zac stated, turning away from the bodies. He gazed at what remained of the town. One in a long line of towns and cities that had sent their men to kill him. The rulers of the surrounding lands had learned of the presence of a true Legend. Rulers that more often than not only pretended at being Legends, or were copies of Legends that had lived long before.

A true Legend was a threat. They could not let him live, much less create a kingdom of his own…or conquer one of theirs.

"Indeed, sire," Roden agreed.

Soldiers searched the rubble, taking whatever valuables they could find. An army was expensive to run, even for a Legend.

"You know how I feel about that term," Zac grumbled.

"What, sire?" Roden inquired. Zac nodded. "You're worthy of it," Roden insisted. "And your men want you to take up the mantle of kinghood."

"That's what all the other Legends did," Zac retorted. "You see what happens."

"You're different," the general pressed.

"That's right," Zac agreed. "I am."

"What *are* you going to do?" Roden inquired. Zac sighed, watching the soldiers. Many had given up searching the town, and were forming a circle around him. Giving him wide berth, as was their right. Those who wanted his will were welcome to it, and those who did not would never be forced to submit to it.

"I'm going to live forever," he answered. Roden smiled.

"Of course," he agreed. "You're a Legend."

"No," Zac countered. "Not as a copy, Roden. I'm going to find a way to live forever. As a true Legend. And I'll spend my life taking down anyone who does this," he added, gesturing at the bodies of the children on the street, "…to their own people."

"Sire?"

"Making them think that being different is worse than death."

The soldiers began to chant then, raising their swords in the air, surrounding Roden and Zac. Began to chant the name Zac had given himself, years after he'd started building his army. A name that sent fear into the hearts of those who opposed him.

Za-ga-mar!

He stared at them, his loyal men. Each there because they wanted to be. Men from villages and towns all over the land. Poor men. The dispossessed. The discarded. The "others."

Za-ga-mar!

A chill ran down his spine as they called his name over and over, the power he held at once intoxicating and terrifying. A power he had to handle with great care, lest it corrupt him as it had corrupted so many others.

Two soldiers stepped forward, holding young women before them. They were quite beautiful, their hands tied behind their backs, their clothes torn.

"I'd say you deserve a little relaxation, sire," Roden stated, gesturing at the women. Zac hesitated, eyeing the women. They were terrified, their eyes wide, their mouths gagged.

Za-ga-mar!

"Come on sire," Roden pressed. "Live a little before you die."

"Bring them to my tent," Zac decided.

The women were taken away, and Zac watched them go, taking a deep breath in, then letting it out. He would relax this evening. The women would be forced to see to it. And with the repeated gift of his essence, they would turn around. They would gain his perspective, and fear him no more.

No one ever did, after seeing things from his point of view. After realizing the truth.

Za-ga-mar! Za-ga-mar!

He raised a fist into the air, and his soldiers cheered.

* * *

The wind howled in Hunter's ears as he turned gradually leftward, soaring well over a hundred feet above the forest. He looked down, spotting the all-too-familiar path leading up to the hilltop ahead. Sukri and Vi were standing there, watching him as he flew back toward them.

Hunter grabbed an arrow from the quiver at his waist, then nocked it, pulling his bowstring all the way back. At the same time, he rotated his wings backward a little, slowing his flight as he approached the hilltop.

He aimed…then fired.

His arrow shot forward smoothly toward a circle Vi'd painted on a tree trunk to her right…and missed by a few inches, ricocheting off the side of the trunk and burying itself into the grass. Hunter cursed, swinging his legs forward and beating his wings, slowing rapidly and dropping gently to the hilltop beside Vi and Sukri. He retrieved his arrow, putting it back in his quiver and returning to the two women, shaking his head.

"Damn," he muttered.

"You were close," Sukri said. "You're getting better."

"She's right," Vi agreed. "You're getting there Hunter."

Hunter nodded, still feeling disappointed. He'd made that flight at least a few dozen times, and that'd been the closest he'd gotten to hitting that target. The first few attempts had been a disaster; he'd almost fallen out of the sky when he'd tried to focus on using the bow, all the while forgetting to keep his wings out. It'd been like driving a stick-shift for the first time, forgetting about his feet when focusing on the wheel, and vice-versa.

He *was* getting better.

"Go on," Vi prompted. "Gotta hit it if you want to go home."

Hunter sighed, breaking into a sprint and leaping off the hill. With a few beats of his wings, the ground dropped quickly below, and he continued his ascent, feeling for pockets of air that felt right. He couldn't explain why exactly, but when his wings felt full of air, he knew to beat them. Doing so launched him higher and higher, until he was once again over a hundred feet above the downward-sloping path. He glided then, picking up speed rapidly, enjoying the feeling of the wind ruffling his clothes, the utter freedom of being in the air. Away from everything and everyone.

Free.

He waited, then did a U-turn, dipping down and aiming toward the hilltop in the distance. Again he grabbed an arrow, nocking it and pulling his bowstring back as he approached the target.

Remember your breathing.

Hunter took a deep breath in, then let it out, holding his breath and aiming. He paused, then fired.

The arrow flew true, slamming right into the center of the target!

"*Yeah!*" Hunter shouted, slowing quickly to land on the hilltop.

"Nice shot Hunter," Vi congratulated, walking up to him and patting him on the shoulder. "You done good kiddo."

"It *was* a nice shot," Sukri agreed.

"All right guys," Vi stated. "That's it for today. I'm going to go talk to Neesha."

"What should we do?" Hunter asked.

"Anything you want," she answered. "Great work, by the way."

"Thanks."

Vi waved, then walked back down the slope, following the path back to the Ironclad lair. Hunter watched her go, realizing he could reach the bottom in a fraction of the time she could. He stretched his wings out, suddenly glad that he'd taken the plunge, letting Pukwa and that woman convince him to get his wings. As terrified as he'd been of changing, now he couldn't imagine ever going back to the way he was before.

"Damn wrappings," Sukri muttered, scratching at her chest. "Itch like a mother."

"It's not the wrappings," Hunter countered. "It's the new tissue changing and growing. Felt the same thing in my chest and back when my wings were coming in."

"Really?" she asked. She stopped scratching, the blood draining from her face.

"What's wrong?"

"I don't know," she muttered. "I wish I never did it. This whole cat thing. Maybe I should just rip these off."

"I think it's a little too late for that," Hunter replied apologetically. "If you're itching, the change is already happening. It might not end well if you stop it part-way."

"You think so?"

"Yeah," he confirmed. "Probably just end up looking like a really hairy woman."

"Ass."

"But seriously, I felt the same way when my wings were coming in," Hunter confessed. "I totally freaked out…I even told Xerxes to rip them off."

"Really?"

"Yeah. I thought I'd made a terrible mistake. I just wanted to be me again, and not something else. I was scared shitless."

She paused, staring at his wings.

"Would you go back?" she asked.

"Not a chance."

"So you're happy with them?" she pressed. Hunter smiled.

"Did you *see* me out there?" he replied.

"So if you had to do it again, you would?"

"Without question," Hunter confirmed. Still, Sukri looked unconvinced. He put a hand on her shoulder. "Look, I'm still me," he explained. "And I still have you guys. Yeah, I'm not exactly human anymore, but it doesn't really matter."

"Yeah, well you still *look* human," Sukri retorted. "I'm gonna look like a cat."

"And you'll still be you, right?"

"That's what Kayla told me," Sukri admitted. "She said my mind was stronger-willed than my appearance, so they chose wrappings that would be somewhere in-between, so I'd change appearance without getting a cat-brain."

"Thank god," Hunter replied. "Cats can be assholes."

He thought about Charlie then, his own cat back on Earth. She'd been his faithful companion for the last few years, the one creature he'd been able to love unconditionally. The only one that hadn't let him down.

"I had a cat back on Earth," he ventured.

"Yeah?"

"Yeah. I miss her," he admitted. "Hell, I even miss my dad. He turned into a drunk after Mom went through the Gate. He thought he'd let her die. It…broke him."

Sukri nodded, not saying anything.

"I blamed him for years," Hunter mused. "And now I can't even apologize to him. I can't tell him that Mom's still alive." He sighed, shaking his head. "God, I was such an asshole to him."

"But you took care of him?"

"Yeah," he replied. "I guess I was always waiting for him to take care of me for once."

"That's what you've got us for," Sukri replied, putting a hand on his shoulder, then slipping it off rather quickly.

"Thanks," he murmured, forcing a smile.

"You're welcome."

"So," he stated, looking around. "What do we do now?"

"I dunno," she replied. "Kinda wanted to take off these dressings."

"I thought…"

"Kayla said I could take them off after a day or two," Sukri interrupted. "She said since she used the needles, the wrappings didn't need to stay on longer than that."

"You used the needles too?"

"Yeah," Sukri admitted. "Hurt like a bitch. I was really drunk."

"Well, it's been what, a day and a half?" he asked. The sun was nearing the horizon, signaling the rapidly approaching sunset.

"Two days," Sukri corrected.

"Wanna take them off?"

Sukri hesitated, then shook her head.

"Not today," she replied. "I'd rather do it tomorrow."

"Nervous?"

"Hell yeah," she confirmed. He smiled at her.

"I'll still like you, cat or not," he declared. "Hell, if you look anything like Kayla, I'll like you even more."

"She *was* hot," Sukri agreed. Hunter hesitated, eyeing her for a moment.

"Seems like you guys were pretty good friends," he ventured. "More than friends, actually. That kiss was something else."

"Yeah," Sukri murmured. "It's…complicated.

"How so?"

"Kayla gave me my first *out*," Sukri explained. "A way to finally be free of all the shit, you know?"

"By becoming a citizen of the Kingdom of the Deep?"

"Yeah," she replied. "And she…it was good. She was good to me."

Hunter didn't say anything, even though every inch of his being wanted to ask what that meant.

"I don't know," Sukri continued. "I mean, a part of me wants to go back. A big part. But I don't know if I'd just be going back because it's safe, or because I really want to be there."

"With her?"

Sukri glanced sidelong at him.

"Yeah," she admitted. "And it wouldn't be fair to Kayla if I was just going back because it was safe." She sighed, kicking a nearby stone. "I've spent my whole life trying to be something I'm not. I don't want to…I *can't* do that anymore."

"Well, I don't want you to be anything but yourself," Hunter stated. She grimaced.

"Yeah, well if you really knew me, you wouldn't say that."

Hunter put a hand on her shoulder, and she flinched away from his touch.

"Sukri..."

"Forget it," she muttered.

"But..."

"I don't want to talk about it," she insisted. "I'm *not* going to talk about it."

Hunter sighed, then nodded.

"All right," he muttered. "Guess we should get back to the caves then." He hesitated. "Want me to fly you back?"

Sukri glanced at his wings, then his helmet.

"I'll walk," she replied.

* * *

By the time they reached the huge cavern that served as the chamber for the queen of the Ironclad, Vi was already there, standing by the edge of the pool talking with Neesha. And there, standing beside Vi...and utterly dwarfing her...was none other than Xerxes.

"Hey bro!" Hunter greeted, breaking away from Sukri and giving the big guy a big hug. "You're okay!"

"FINE," Xerxes agreed. He glanced down at Hunter and Sukri. "YOU...GOOD?"

"Yeah," Hunter replied. "Just fine."

"SAW...YOU FLY," Xerxes admitted, raising one pair of arms up as if he were flying himself. "LIKE BIRD."

"You shoulda seen me today," Hunter replied with a grin. "I'm getting a whole lot better."

"What happened to Dio?" Sukri asked. "You kill him?"

Xerxes shook his head.

"HE...FLEE. JUMP...IN RIVER."

"That's a long drop," Hunter ventured. "He probably didn't survive it." But Sukri didn't look convinced.

"Don't bet on it," she grumbled.

"We were just discussing our strategy for the upcoming war," Neesha interjected. Everyone turned to face her. Even with them standing on the cavern floor and her wading in the pool, she was still taller than anyone but Xerxes, whose head was level with hers. "Xerxes will start preparing his troops tomorrow, and we'll attack the morning after."

"What's the plan?" Hunter asked.

"A two-pronged attack," Vi answered. "We'll send a small portion of our army to the military base in the Deadlands, and make a real big scene taking it out. That's the distraction."

"All the while sending the bulk of our army under the wall around Tykus," Neesha added. Hunter blinked.

"Under?"

"We've been digging tunnels under the Deadlands for weeks," Neesha explained. "The wall extends ten feet below-ground. We've managed to dig below it."

"So while Tykus is distracted by the attack on the military base – and sends reinforcements to help – the rest of our army will come right out of the ground inside the city, taking it by surprise," Vi finished.

"But what about the Acropolis?" Sukri interjected. "There's a wall around that too."

"DIG," Xerxes replied.

"Blue's right," Vi agreed. "Once we take down everything outside of the Acropolis, we'll have plenty of time to dig underneath the wall."

"And then we confront Tykus," Neesha concluded.

"Confront?" Hunter asked. "You mean kill, right?"

"Not necessarily," Neesha countered. "Tykus and I had an…agreement," she explained. "He agreed to let my people be, and I agreed not to attack his kingdom. But when he gave the dukes the order to wipe us out, he broke that agreement."

"Ok…"

"I've given him ample time to explain himself," Neesha continued. "But he hasn't done so. My only recourse is to attack before the Kingdom does, and face him directly…through Vi."

Hunter turned to Vi with a questioning look.

"I'm going in under the wall with Xerxes and the second group of Ironclad," Vi explained. "We'll storm the Acropolis and I'll confront Tykus."

"Why not just have Mom go?" Hunter asked.

"I'm a Legend honey," Neesha explained. "I can't risk exposing others to my will."

"All right," Hunter conceded. "What do I do?"

"What do you mean?" Mom asked.

"I'm not sitting here while everyone else goes to war," he clarified, crossing his arms over his chest. "I want to help. I *have* to help."

"Hunter…"

"I'm not taking 'no' for an answer," he insisted. "The Kingdom screwed me over. It tried to turn me into an addict, then Dominus tried to kill me…and Vi."

"Remember what I said about revenge," Vi warned.

"This isn't about revenge anymore," Hunter retorted. "It's about protecting my family from these assholes. And making sure that they never do this to us – or someone like us – ever again."

"It's too dangerous," Neesha countered.

"I can fly," he reminded her. "I can shoot down archers and take out key targets without having to risk fighting on the ground."

"You need more practice kiddo," Vi said.

"I'll get plenty tomorrow," he countered. "You can flog me all day."

"Don't need permission to do that," she countered. But she nodded, facing Neesha.

"It's reasonable," she admitted. "Hunter's pretty good. With a little practice, he'd be an asset. And with Zaggie, he'll be lethal."

"Fine," Mom decided. "Have you swallowed your brother's goo?" she asked Hunter.

"Uh, yeah," Hunter answered.

"How many times?" Neesha pressed.

"Once."

Sukri glanced at Xerxes, then at Hunter.

"Something you boys wanna tell me?" she inquired, arching an eyebrow.

"It's…I'll tell you later," Hunter grumbled.

"Do it again," Neesha ordered. "Vi, continue training Hunter."

"Anything I can do to help?" Sukri asked.

"You're not trained up yet, so we're not putting you in this one, sorry," Vi answered. "We'll take off your wrappings tomorrow and I'll start training you too, but for now, just focus on getting lots of rest. You're going to need it."

"All right," Sukri agreed. Everyone said goodbye to Neesha, and Hunter, Xerxes, Vi, and Sukri began the long journey back to the entrance to the Ironclad lair. They emerged from the cave, passing the Ironclad guards all around them.

Then Sukri froze.

"What?" Hunter asked, stopping beside her. He followed her gaze, spotting someone standing beside a tree to their left. A very familiar woman. Well, cat-woman, anyway.

"Hello Sukri," Kayla greeted, walking languidly toward them. She stopped in front of Sukri, leaning in and embracing her.

"Kayla!" Sukri exclaimed.

Chapter 25

The next morning, Sukri stood at the top of the hill they'd spent most of the day yesterday on, Vi and Kayla at her side. They watched as Hunter leapt off the top of the hill, flying high into the air. He gained altitude quickly, flying straight, then circling around, flying back toward the white circles Vi had painted on the tree trunks nearby. Each circle had been painted at different heights, and Vi had instructed Hunter to hit all of the targets in one pass. Sukri watched as he soared toward them, feeling a familiar jealousy come over her.

Should've picked the bird, she thought for the umpteenth time, watching as he shot arrow after arrow at the trees. He zoomed by overhead, having struck two of the five targets.

"Again!" Vi shouted, watching as Hunter circled around again, dropping to the top of the hill and going to retrieve his arrows. His mother had ordered the Ironclad blacksmith to make Hunter a new breastplate, one that would accommodate his wings. The dull black metal reflected none of the bright sunlight streaming down from the sky; it was designed to make him harder to see at night-time.

"He's learning quickly," Kayla noted. The cat-lady had apparently witnessed what had happened at the bridge, and had helped Xerxes track Hunter and Sukri back to the Ironclad lair. She'd offered to stay a while to help Sukri. And, Sukri suspected, to try to convince her to go back to the Kingdom of the Deep to become a citizen there.

"He's a good student," Vi agreed. "Now that he knows how to listen." She turned to Sukri then.

"All right Sukri, time to take off those wrappings."

"Great," Sukri muttered. She looked down at her arms, feeling suddenly apprehensive. "You sure we should take them off now?"

"It will be fine," Kayla reassured. "The transformation will continue now, with or without them."

"I don't know…" Sukri mumbled.

"You're afraid of the unknown," Vi stated. "And the longer you put off facing your fear, the longer it'll have power over you."

Kayla put a furry hand on Sukri's shoulder, giving her an encouraging smile.

"You can do this," she insisted.

Sukri sighed, then nodded.

"All right."

Vi grabbed Sukri's wrist, then took a dagger from her own belt, sliding the blade across the wrappings covering Sukri's forearm. Sukri flinched, but the blade cut through her wrappings without touching her skin. Vi unwrapped the wrappings there, exposing Sukri's forearm.

Sukri's breath caught in her throat.

Her forearm was beet red, a thick carpet of small gray hairs springing from her flesh. She stared at it, swallowing past a sudden lump in her throat.

Shit.

Vi unwrapped Sukri's hand next, revealing a furry palm with small pads of skin showing in the center of her palm and on the tips of her fingers. While her fingers had only had three parts to them before – with two joints – now she had an extra joint beyond her fingertips. This was pulled all the way back, nestled within short hairs sprouting from the backs of her fingers, and at the end of each was a long, curved claw.

She stared at her hand, feeling slightly nauseous.

"Damn," she mumbled.

"You okay?" Vi asked.

"No," Sukri replied. "Think I'm gonna throw up."

"Sit," Vi ordered. Sukri did so, hunching over and staring at the ground. Then she glanced at her exposed hand again.

"Oh god," Sukri mumbled. "Oh god oh god…"

"Sukri…" Kayla began, but Vi held up a hand to stop her. Vi squatted down in front of Sukri and grabbing her by the shoulders.

"Look at me. *Look* at me."

Sukri did so, gazing into Vi's eyes. She realized she was hyperventilating, and tried to slow her breathing. But the feeling passed quickly, a serene calmness washing over her. It was Vi, Sukri realized; she was absorbing the woman's emotions.

"That better?" Vi asked with a smile. Sukri nodded. "Good. You're a sponge for emotion too, just like Hunter," Vi noted.

"Yeah."

"This is scary shit," Vi conceded. "I get it. But you're going to be okay. You're going to get through this."

"Okay."

"Let's do the other hand, okay?" Vi prompted. Sukri nodded, and Vi cut the wrappings at her other forearm, unwrapping them and exposing her other hand. It was identical to the first, complete with the claws at the end. Sukri stared at her hands, turning them over. Then she stretched her fingers out. The fourth section of each finger swung forward, the claws swinging forward and downward with them.

It felt *weird.*

"Those are some great weapons," Vi noted. "I'm sure Kayla will teach you how to use them later."

"Of course," Kayla confirmed. She knelt beside Sukri, giving her a warm smile. "It gets easier," she assured her.

Sukri nodded absently, relaxing her hands. Her claws retracted.

"I'm going to unwrap your arms now," Vi warned.

"Damn it!" came a shout from above. Sukri looked up, seeing Hunter swooping by; three arrows were sticking out of the trees, two having struck their targets, while the third was just above its painted circle. He landed, going to retrieve the arrows.

"Again," Vi called out, returning her focus to Sukri. She unwrapped Sukri's arms up to the shoulders, tossing the wrappings aside. Her arms were also beefy red, and were covered with the same thick carpet of hair, so short that they barely protruded from her skin.

"I'm hairy," Sukri groaned. "I *hate* hair."

"And yet you chose a cat," Vi noted.

"Regretting it now," Sukri grumbled. Then she glanced at Kayla. "No offense," she added hastily. Kayla smirked.

"None taken," she replied. "The in-between stage is always ugly. It will only get better from here."

"Uh huh."

"Hey," Vi interjected, grabbing Sukri by the shoulders. "You're going to be okay. No matter how you look, you're still *you.* You're not in Tykus anymore. You're with us. And no matter what, we'll accept you and support you. Got it?"

Sukri swallowed past a lump in her throat, moisture blurring her vision.

"You sure about that?" she muttered.

Vi frowned at her.

"What's up?" she asked. Sukri shook her head.

"Nothing."

"Bullshit," Vi retorted. "Something's eating you up inside."

"I'm fine," Sukri insisted, trying to pull away from Vi's grasp. But Vi's grip was like iron.

"The longer you put off facing your fear…" Vi prompted. Sukri wiped the moisture from her eyes, meeting Vi's gaze.

"The longer it'll have power over me," she muttered.

"Right."

Sukri glanced at Kayla, who was watching her with those big golden eyes.

"Can you give us a minute?" Vi asked the cat-woman. Kayla hesitated, then nodded, standing up.

"Of course," she replied. She turned about, walking away from them. Far enough away that even with her cat-ears, she wouldn't be able to hear them. Sukri watched her go, then turned to Vi, who was staring at her intently.

"Talk to me," Vi pleaded.

Sukri sighed miserably, lowering her gaze.

"You'll hate me," she muttered.

"Why?" Vi inquired. "Did you kill one of my friends?"

"No."

"Did you steal my shit?"

"No," Sukri repeated.

"Then we're good," Vi concluded. Sukri shook her head.

"The Guild of Seekers," she stated. "They made us…they made *me* do some bad shit."

"You had to kill your fellow students, then murder a few rich kids," Vi stated. Sukri's eyes widened, a chill running down her spine. She stared at Vi incredulously.

"How…?"

"I was a Seeker for the guild, remember?" Vi explained. "I did all that shit too. And a whole lot worse."

"You…did?"

"Oh yeah," Vi confirmed. "And believe me, it fucked me up. Made me wonder if anyone would ever love me if they found out. That's the whole point, sweetheart. The guild's a cult. And the first thing a cult does is separate you from everyone else. Not just physically, but emotionally."

Sukri swallowed, unable to speak.

"They played you, Sukri. They used guilt to control you. And the sooner you learn to forgive yourself, the sooner you'll be free of them."

Sukri nodded mutely, tears welling up in her eyes. She blinked, and they rolled down her cheeks. Vi leaned in, embracing Sukri.

The dam broke.

Horrible sobs came out of her, her shoulders heaving with each one. Vi held on to her, holding her tightly.

"It's okay," she soothed. "You're okay."

Sukri continued to cry. And cry. For how she'd fought with Kris before he'd died. And for what she'd done to Gammon, a man who'd loved her for years, and when she'd finally offered to love him back, he'd refused.

And for herself. For the girl who'd always dreamed of being something special, and had ruined her life – and so many others – chasing that dream.

After a long, long time, the tears slowed, then stopped. Sukri pulled away from Vi, wiping the tears from her cheeks and giving the woman a smile.

"Thanks," she murmured. Vi smiled back.

"You're welcome."

"Hunter was right about you," Sukri said. "You're pretty awesome."

"You have *no* idea," Vi replied with a grin. Sukri chuckled despite herself. Vi stood up, and Sukri joined her. Vi got to work unwrapping Sukri's other arm. "Okay, time for the body."

"Uh," Sukri began. "I'm kinda naked."

"Kinda hoping you were," Vi replied with a devilish grin. There was a series of *thumps* in the distance, followed by muffled cursing. Hunter landed on the hilltop, retrieving his arrows, then walking toward them.

"Hey, whatcha doing?" Hunter asked. Vi turned to glare at him.

"Go away," she ordered.

"But…"

"Go," she repeated. "You can stare at your hairy friend later."

"Wow," Sukri muttered. "Low blow."

Hunter grimaced, but obeyed, launching into the air for another run. Vi unwrapped Sukri's chest, revealing her upper chest, and then her breasts. Normally Sukri wasn't shy in the least, but now she wanted nothing more than to cover up. For her chest was just like her arms…as was her belly.

"Fuuuck," Sukri muttered, shaking her head. "Just…fuck."

"Well, you got a nice rack, I'll give you that," Vi noted. "It's gonna look better once the hair comes in all the way."

"Oh *why* did I do this?" Sukri groaned. Vi ignored her, making her stand up, then unwrapping her pelvis and legs. More red skin, more hair. And something else.

"Oh," Sukri gasped, putting a hand over her mouth. She felt dizzy again, and would've fallen if Vi hadn't grabbed her by the hips.

"Just a tail," Vi reassured. "It's alright."

Sukri twisted around, staring at her butt…and the long tail poking out from just above her butt cheeks. It twitched, utterly by itself.

"Throwing up now," Sukri notified, and promptly kept her word.

There were four *thunks* as Hunter swooped by, and another round of swearing. Sukri barely registered him landing.

"Go away," Vi snapped. "Go fly somewhere far away. We'll finish your training later."

"You okay Sukri?" he asked.

"Go!"

Hunter hesitated, then nodded, leaping off the slope and flying away.

"It'll grow longer," Vi reassured. "Your tail, I mean."

"Great."

"Your feet will make great weapons too," Vi noted. Sukri glanced down at them; they were just like her hands, except her big toe sprouted from the side of her foot now rather than the end. Her foot-claws were even bigger than the ones on her hands, extending and retracting in the same way. "Not to mention you'll be a great climber."

"Awesome."

"Alright, last part," Vi warned. She pulled the mask from Sukri's face, unwrapping her head and neck. Then she stared at Sukri for a long moment.

"Don't tell me," Sukri muttered. "I *really* don't want to know."

"Actually you look pretty cute," Vi admitted. "You kept your long hair. It's coming in gray and black at the roots."

"Least I'm not a blonde anymore."

"Your ears are pointed," Vi continued. "Cute button-nose too."

"Are you just saying that to make me feel better?"

"Hell no," Vi scoffed. "If you looked hideous, trust me, I'd tell you."

"You're so comforting."

"You want comfort, go to Hunter," Vi replied with a smirk. "I don't sugarcoat anything Puss."

"Puss?"

"Your nickname," Vi explained. "You prefer Pussy?"

"It's not bad," Sukri replied. "But I prefer dick."

Vi chuckled, slapping Sukri on the shoulder.

"That's the spirit," she encouraged. "Alright, let's get Kayla over here and have her show you how to use those claws."

* * *

Sukri clung on all fours to the base of a wide tree branch some five meters above the forest floor, her eyes on Vi and Kayla standing below. They were both looking up at her.

"It'll be fine, just jump down," Vi urged.

"And break my leg?" Sukri shot back. "No thanks."

She'd managed to climb up the tree using her claws…a process which had been both easier and harder than she'd imagined. Pulling herself up the tree had been surprisingly easy, but getting used to retracting and extending her claws at the proper times had been tougher. Now she understood why cats had a hard time climbing down things.

"You're not going to break anything," Kayla reassured. "You're a cat."

"I'm not done changing yet," Sukri pointed out.

"Your ass says you're ready," Vi replied.

"What?"

"Your ass," Vi repeated. "Have you looked at it recently? It's spectacularly developed. It means your legs are ready. You can jump higher now, and fall farther."

"I'll climb down."

"Do that and *I'll* break your leg," Vi shot back.

Sukri stared at Vi, suddenly unsure if the woman actually meant it.

"Fine," she grumbled. She retracted her claws – which she'd been using to grip the branch – then sat back on her heels, taking a deep breath in.

Okay.

And then she jumped.

She cried out, falling like a stone toward the ground beside Vi and Kayla, and landed on all fours. Without any pain at all.

Sukri stayed there for a moment, then got to her feet, brushing off leaf-litter from her palms.

"See?" Vi stated with a grin.

"Wow," Sukri murmured. "Yeah, you were right."

"Get used to it," Vi replied with a wink. She turned to Kayla. You think she can jump back up there?"

"Easily," Kayla answered.

"All right," Vi decided, turning back to Sukri. "Jump back up to the branch you just fell from."

"I jumped from it," Sukri countered.

"More of a hop and fall. With a scream."

"You're asking me to jump all the way up to *that?*" Sukri asked incredulously, pointing to the branch. It was five meters up; that would be like jumping to the second story of a building. Higher, even.

"Yep."

"That's impossible," Sukri protested. Vi rolled her eyes.

"We gonna have to do this *every* time?"

Sukri sighed, then looked up at the branch. She squatted down, then jumped…about a meter off the ground.

"Don't hold back," Kayla urged. "Jump as high as you can." With that, Kayla crouched down, leaping upward…impossibly high…and landed right on the tree branch. She smiled down at Sukri. "Come on," she prompted.

Sukri nodded, squatting down again. She took a deep breath in, then pushed off the ground as hard as she could.

And sailed upward nearly five meters, her fingertips brushing up against the bottom of the tree branch!

She fell back to the earth, landing on all fours, hardly believing what'd just happened.

"I did it!" she cried, leaping to her feet and spinning around to grin at Vi. "Did you see that?"

"Good job Sukri," Vi congratulated. "Next time land on the branch."

Sukri felt her excitement wane, and she sighed, looking up at the branch. It seemed far too high up to jump onto. But then again, it'd seemed far too high to even touch with her hands, and she'd done that. She crouched, then leapt, seeming to fly upward. She managed to grab the top of the branch, and extended her claws, clinging to it, her legs dangling in the air.

"Made it!" she cried.

"Land on your *feet* on the branch," Vi corrected. "Like Kayla."

Sukri retracted her claws, dropping to the ground with a *thump.*

Again and again she jumped, each time getting a little higher. Once she got over the fear of jumping higher, she found she could make it all the way to the top of the branch pretty easily. Landing on top of it, on the other hand…

She sailed toward it on her sixth attempt, striking her ankles on the side of the branch and promptly flipping head-over-heels, falling head-first toward the ground. She cried out, whipping her tail around and twisting her torso, and landing harmlessly on all fours.

"Whoa," she breathed, staying there for a moment, then standing up. "You saw what I did with my tail?"

"It's a reflex," Kayla explained from her perch on the branch. "It turns you around so you'll always land on your feet."

And that changed everything.

Without having to worry about landing wrong and breaking her neck, Sukri got bolder, leaping up to the branch with abandon. It turned a frightening task into an absolute blast, seeing just how far she could push herself. By the time Hunter returned from his long flight away, she'd leapt from the ground to join Kayla on the tree branch multiple times.

It felt *awesome.*

"Hey guys," Hunter greeted as he landed a few meters away. Sukri hopped down from the branch, and his eyes widened as he noticed Sukri's nakedness, his gaze immediately drawn toward her more interesting bits. "Damn."

"You like?" Sukri inquired.

"Oh yeah," Hunter replied. Sukri did a little turn for him, and he gave a low whistle. "That ass," he murmured, shaking his head.

"I know, right?" Vi piped in.

"Saw you jumping all the way up there," Hunter ventured. "Pretty awesome."

"Please," Sukri shot back. "This from the guy who can fly."

"Can't climb up a tree though," he pointed out.

"Enough blabbing," Vi interjected. "Hunter, go hit those five targets. No eating until you do."

"Yes master," Hunter replied, bowing deeply, then flying away. Vi turned to Sukri.

"I've seen cat-people jump six to seven meters," she stated. "With a little practice and time to finish your metamorphosis, you'll be able to too."

"Awesome."

"Those claws aren't just for climbing," Kayla pointed out. She leapt down from the branch, landing beside Sukri. "They're very effective weapons. Try using them on that tree trunk," she prompted. "Give it a few swipes."

Sukri walked up to the trunk, then extended her claws, putting them on the trunk and sliding them down. It felt surprisingly good, kinda like the eargasm she got when she used a little stick to scratch the inside of her ear canal. But in her fingertips.

"Harder," Kayla ordered.

Sukri swiped the trunk harder, raking the bark.

"*Harder.*"

She lunged at the trunk, tearing at the bark. Hunks of it tore off; she half-expected to feel pain in her claws, but she didn't.

"Nice," Vi stated. "Now imagine what you could do to someone's face."

Sukri did so, and it was a sobering thought.

"Cats go for the face and the throat," Kayla explained, walking up to the tree trunk and slashing at it with one hand…and leaving deep gouges in the bark. "Take out your opponent's eyes. Claw them out. Then tear through the vessels of the neck and the windpipe."

"Ugh," Sukri muttered. "Sword seems a bit cleaner."

"Go ahead and use a sword," Vi stated, "…but if you lose it, or if an enemy gets in too close, you'll need to learn how to fight close-range. Your claws are a natural weapon."

"And don't forget your feet," Kayla piped in.

Sukri glanced down, extending the claws on her toes.

"When I kick, it's to create blunt-force trauma," Vi explained. "You can do that too – especially with your highly-developed leg muscles – but you also have the option of using them to totally fuck up your opponent. If you're knocked on your back, shred 'em with your feet. I've seen a cat-lady disembowel a man in a few seconds that way."

Kayla nodded in agreement, and Sukri gave a low whistle.

"Wow."

There were four *thumps*, and Hunter swooped by, cursing loudly. He landed, grabbing his arrows, then trying again.

"You can also jump really high, which means you can leap over your opponent, or on top of them. People have a hard time defending attacks from above. And they usually don't realize they can dodge out of the way until it's too late," Vi lectured.

"Got it."

"You don't 'got it' until you've *done* it," Vi retorted. She reached down to a pack lying next to her, withdrawing two practice swords and throwing one to Sukri. "Enough talk. Time for the pain, Puss."

"Great," Sukri groaned. "Had enough of this shit from Dio." Vi snorted.

"Dio ain't fit to wipe my ass," she retorted.

"Really?"

"Damn right. Camilla had me teach him for a while, actually."

"Was he good?" Sukri pressed.

"I'll give him credit, he wasn't bad," Vi admitted. "But his head was all screwed up. Everything he does is for Camilla's love…and Camilla doesn't know *how* to love. I tried to teach him how to love himself, but Camilla wouldn't allow it. So I quit training him."

"What'd he do?"

"Camilla manipulated him, of course. Compared him to me all the time, and never favorably. He vowed to get better than me. Practiced all day every day since then."

"Wow, that's messed up," Sukri muttered.

"Dio's going to spend the rest of his life trying to earn something Camilla can't give him," Vi declared. "And he'll never love himself until she loves him. That's why you've got to find a way to forgive yourself, kiddo. Because you won't be able to love yourself until you do…and if you don't, you'll end up just like him."

Sukri swallowed past a lump in her throat, lowering her gaze to her feet.

"Enough talk," Vi declared, readying her own sword. "Let's see what you're made of, Puss."

Chapter 26

The entrance to the secret tunnel passing far beneath the Deadlands to the Kingdom of Tykus was well-hidden, a slight gap in the rock wall of a large hill. It had been covered by bushes that Dominus had been forced to push through to get inside. A series of ancient traps similar to those protecting Dominus's ancestral shrine had to be navigated, and luckily Tykus had taught Dominus how to do so before Dominus's trek to the Castle Wexford the week before. Now he walked down the pitch-black tunnel, torch-in-hand, making his way back to the Acropolis.

For kilometers the tunnel extended, forever forward and angling slightly downward, toward the crypts deep beneath the ancient fortress. Dominus felt uneasy knowing that he would soon be in the presence of the great king. And at the same time, he yearned for it.

The beekeeper has returned to his hives.

At long last he spotted the end of the tunnel ahead, a rough stone wall. He walked up to it, then turned, stepping heel-to-toe away from it, counting his steps.

Ninety-one, ninety-two, ninety-three.

Coincidentally, the age Tykus had been when he'd died six thousand years ago.

Dominus leaned against the leftmost wall, feeling around for a slight depression there. He felt a stone within the wall give inward, and then a trapdoor above opened up. A guard appeared above the trapdoor, peering down at Dominus. It was one of Tykus's Royal guards, the most skilled warriors in the Kingdom.

Save for Dominus, of course.

The guard let down a rope ladder, and Dominus climbed it, passing through the trapdoor and into another tunnel above. The guard closed the trapdoor, turning about silently and leading Dominus down this new tunnel.

Onward they went, passing through multiple series of heavy locked doors, then through a bewildering maze of smaller tunnels and rooms. These were the crypts below the Acropolis, the remains of the ancient castle whose ruins the Acropolis had been built upon.

Eventually Dominus found himself in the basement level of the Acropolis; the guard led him to the long hallway leading up to the Royal Chambers. More guards lined the walls on either side, all of them staring at him silently.

Dominus paused, then pulled off his boots, setting them aside, then following his guide. Without the numbing presence of his boots, the floor was cold and hard under his feet. He spread his toes out as he walked, enjoying the sensation.

His guard stopped, and he stopped beside the man. A guard standing in front of the huge double-doors of the Royal Chambers turned, placing the end of his hollow scepter into a small hole in one of the doors, speaking into it. A moment later, the doors opened, and a tall young man with long blonde hair stepped through, walking right up to Dominus. It was Tykus himself, reincarnated from the bones of the long-dead king.

"Ah, hello Dominus!" he greeted warmly, reaching out and embracing Dominus. Then the king stepped back, holding Dominus at arms' length.

"My Liege."

"Come now Dominus," Tykus chided. "Did I not ask you to call me by my name?"

"My apologies…Tykus," Dominus stated. "You did." He glanced down at the man's feet, finding that they too were bare.

"You look good," Tykus observed. "I wasn't expecting to see you so soon after what happened to you."

"You heard?"

"Of course," Tykus replied with a smile. "I have eyes everywhere…literally!" He chuckled, putting an arm around Dominus and walking him back down the great hallway, away from the Royal Chambers. "Gave me quite a scare, actually. To think that a future such as yours was nearly nipped at the bud!"

"I woke up in the woods," Dominus explained. Tykus raised an eyebrow.

"I know," he replied, his blue eyes twinkling. "I was there. Or rather, one of me was."

Dominus's jaw dropped open, and Tykus chuckled.

"Who do you think dripped honey in your mouth as you slept like the dead?" he inquired. "And fought off the Seekers searching for your body to steal your Ossae?" He sighed, shaking his head. "A good thing your former guards were so lazy. They laid you down on your belly and threw oil on your back, and set it ablaze. If they'd been more careful, there wouldn't have been enough of you to salvage."

"I see," was all Dominus could muster.

"Never underestimate a man's capacity for laziness," Tykus mused. "We leaders plan for it, don't we? Order a man to do something and he'll do it with the least effort possible. But make the man believe *he* wants something done and he'll move heaven and earth to do it."

"Indeed," Dominus replied. "The essence of leadership."

"Aha!" Tykus cried, slapping Dominus on the back. "Contributing to the conversation…I think we're getting somewhere, Dominus."

"Is that what you've done with me?" Dominus asked, stopping suddenly. "When you made me the protector of the Kingdom?" Tykus stopped with him.

"Did you want to protect the Kingdom before you ever spoke with me?" Tykus inquired. Dominus nodded.

"Of course."

"Then you have your answer," Tykus concluded. He continued their walk, almost at the huge metal double-doors at the other end of the hall now. He made a gesture, and the guards opened the doors before them, revealing a hallway continuing to a wide stairway leading upward ahead. "This place is too sterile," Tykus stated. "Let's go to the gardens."

They walked up the stairs, their bare feet making little noise on the cool stone, and reached the floor above. There were guards everywhere, but none paid them any mind. Dominus felt a sudden pang of dread, half-expecting one of the dukes to be there.

"The dukes are still undergoing their metamorphosis," Tykus stated, clearly sensing Dominus's trepidation and guessing the source of it. The king had never failed to be frighteningly observant. "You have nothing to fear here."

Tykus led them outside of the Acropolis, to a large flower garden. The grass was prickly and slightly wet under Dominus's feet, the sun warm on his skin.

"Ah, that's better," Tykus murmured. He stopped, taking a deep breath in, then letting it out, closing his eyes and letting the sun bathe his face. Then he opened his eyes, turning to Dominus. "How are you feeling, Dominus?"

Dominus paused.

"I…fine," he stammered.

"It's a serious question," Tykus insisted. "How are you feeling?"

Dominus considered the question for a moment.

"I don't know how I should be feeling," he admitted. Tykus burst out laughing.

"There's no should or shouldn't about it," he countered. "Feelings just *are*, Dominus." He gestured at Dominus. "So answer the question."

"I feel…free, but lost," Dominus admitted.

"Then you are," Tykus replied.

Dominus nodded.

"But you didn't come here to chat, did you Dominus?" Tykus deduced. "You're far too businesslike for that."

"No," Dominus admitted. "I came because I have terrible news."

"Go on."

"I have reason to believe that the Svartálfar have returned," Dominus declared.

Tykus's eyebrows knit together.

"I have reason to believe they've returned because of Zagamar," Dominus stated. "He has been reborn."

Tykus stared at Dominus, swallowing visibly. Then he broke Dominus's gaze, staring out at the garden.

"I see."

"I was attacked by a group of Svartálfar," Dominus continued. "We managed to kill them and take one of the bodies to study."

"We?" Tykus inquired.

"Lady Camilla and I," Dominus clarified. Tykus's eyebrows rose.

"Ah."

"The creature was confirmed dead," Dominus continued. "Yet it revived and attacked us. High Seeker Zeno was seen by Camilla's scouts entering the Crypt of Zagamar last week. He was in possession of the Ironclad head."

Tykus sighed, his shoulders slumping a little. He lowered his gaze to his feet.

"Then we," he replied at last, "...are in grave peril."

* * *

The War Room was a long, rectangular underground chamber within the Ironclad caves, a room Hunter had been in before without realizing it. There was a long table in the center of it, with chairs all around. Xerxes and Vi stood at the head of the table, a huge map of the Kingdom laid out before them. There were a few armored Ironclad standing around as well, each of them one of Xerxes' generals. Hunter and Sukri stood to one side, Sukri dressed in a simple shirt and pants. It was all Vi had for her, at least until the Ironclad's resident blacksmith made her some armor. Kayla wasn't there, naturally. A citizen of the Kingdom of the Deep helping to attack Tykus could present a diplomatic nightmare for the two kingdoms.

"Okay," Vi began. "Two of Xerxes' generals will attack the military base before sunrise. The walls are short enough to scale. Take out the sleeping guards first. Create confusion. No survivors, got it?"

Xerxes gave her a nodding grunt.

"At the same time," Vi continued, "...the bulk of our army will go underground." She pointed to dotted lines on the map, tracing them under the wall and into the Kingdom. "According to our calculations, the tunnels end just underneath several buildings in Tykus. The Ironclad will come out of those buildings, and no one will understand how they got there. This'll confuse the crap outta the City Guard."

She pointed at a few marked buildings throughout the city.

"These are the main guard barracks for the City Guard," she explained. "I want these hit simultaneously. Throw firebombs through the windows to force them out, then massacre them. Don't let them organize or things're gonna get a lot trickier."

Another grunt from Xerxes.

"While this is happening, we'll have a group of Ironclad rush to the wall surrounding the Acropolis. Take the western wall here," she continued, pointing to the section of wall to the right. "Dig under the wall and open the gate from the inside to let the rest of the army through. If that doesn't work, they'll have to go under the wall. Either way, we storm the Acropolis."

She turned to Hunter.

"Hunter, you're our eyes in the sky. Your job will be to pick off archers at all these locations," Vi continued, pointing to various ramparts and towers with blue stones marking them. "These are just the ones I remember seeing in the past. You'll need to go early to scope out the rest of them. Take 'em out quick, and make sure to stay out of range of their arrows in between runs. They hit your wings, you're in deep shit."

"Got it."

"When you're done taking them out, fly to the Acropolis and take out the archers on the wall. Wait until the Ironclad start digging, so the archers will be distracted. You'll see me with the Ironclad then; pick me up and fly me on top of this balcony on the Acropolis. I'll go in, make my way to the front door, and make sure they're open for us."

"Okay," Hunter agreed. "I can do that."

"You'd better take those archers out first," Vi warned. "Otherwise I'll be a sitting duck while you're flying me up there."

"What about once we get inside the Acropolis?" Hunter asked.

"Simple," Vi answered. "We kill everyone we see, find Tykus, and corner him. Then I negotiate."

"Isn't he a Legend?" Hunter asked. "If you stay close to him for too long…"

"My suit has lots of layers," she reassured, gesturing at her brown leather outfit. "It's designed to keep me from absorbing wills. Besides, the king is just a clone of the original Tykus. His will probably won't be any stronger than mine."

"What if he refuses to negotiate?" Hunter pressed.

"Then he's going to die."

Hunter shook his head, staring at the map.

"I don't get it," he admitted. "Why negotiate at all? We'll have him outnumbered, his whole kingdom conquered. Why not just kill him and be done with it?"

"Because that's not what your mother wants."

"Yeah, but…"

"No buts," she interjected. "Any questions Blue?"

"NO."

Sukri stirred.

"I have a question," she piped in. "What do I do?"

"Like I said, you're gonna have to sit this one out," Vi replied. "Sleep with that necklace I gave you, and keep training with Kayla. That'll go a long way towards getting you up to par."

"All right," Sukri grumbled.

"That's it then," Vi declared. "Get some sleep guys…you're going to need it. We're waking up a few hours before sunrise."

And with that, they were dismissed.

Chapter 27

The sky was still dark by the time Hunter emerged from the Ironclad cave, Vi, Xerxes, and Sukri walking at his side. A literal army of Ironclad – thousands of them – stood at the ready, saluting silently when Xerxes emerged from the cave. The big guy saluted back, then stopped, turning to Hunter.

"BE…CAREFUL," he admonished.

"I will be big guy," Hunter promised. "Thanks for the extra goo, by the way." He'd done as Mom had recommended, taking another gulp of the blue stuff. It was enough to make him heal slowly from wounds that would otherwise have been fatal, and enough to make him regenerate lost tissue, but nowhere near enough to give him anything close to Xerxes' healing power.

Xerxes put a hand to his own chest.

"HEART…HALF," he rasped. "NOW…FULL." He shook his head firmly. "IF…BROKEN, EVEN MINE…NEVER HEAL."

Hunter swallowed past a lump in his throat, nodding mutely at his brother. Xerxes knelt down before him, wrapping his four arms around Hunter and giving him a gentle squeeze. Then he stood, smiling down at Hunter. Hunter cleared his throat noisily.

"Thanks for everything," he said. "For taking me to the Deep. And…for waiting for me, all those years."

"FAMILY," Xerxes grunted. Hunter smiled up at him.

"Family," he agreed. "Take care of yourself, bro. And take care of Vi."

"Probably going to be the other way around," Vi countered with a grin. "Remember what happened to poor Blue at Wexford?"

Xerxes grunted, punching Vi in the shoulder. Or at least he tried to; she dodged out of the way, kicking him in the side of one knee, causing it to buckle. They both chuckled.

"All right, let's go," Vi prompted. "Hunter, finish saying your goodbyes. Then fly overhead. Remember, take out the archers on the King's Road first. Take advantage of the darkness while you can."

"Yes ma'am," Hunter replied.

"Now give me a hug," Vi ordered. Hunter did just that, and Vi squeezed him so hard it literally took his breath away. "Love you Hunter."

"Love you too Vi."

"Don't you dare die," she warned, giving him a strained smile. "Remember what I said about never giving up on yourself."

"I won't," he promised. "Thanks for never giving up on me."

"Yeah, well, we're family, right?"

Hunter broke out into a big smile.

"I guess we are," he agreed. "I'm honored you think so."

"There's nothing I've given you that you haven't earned, Hunter," Vi replied. She paused, then leaned in, kissing him gently on the cheek. "Bye kiddo."

And with that, Vi turned to leave, Xerxes stomping at her side. The army of Ironclad followed suit, marching behind the two as they made their way into the forest. Sukri raised an eyebrow at Hunter, putting her hands on her hips.

"How come you get to have goo and I don't?" she demanded.

"Well, I *did* offer you some earlier, technically," he quipped. She rolled her eyes.

"Your brother's goo," she clarified.

"You'll have to ask him," Hunter replied. "Although if he gives you his, I'll be jealous."

"Oh yeah?"

"Yeah," Hunter confirmed. He rubbed the back of his helmet, giving her a sheepish look. "I'm, uh…a little confused."

Sukri frowned, and Hunter sighed.

"It's just…we had a really great connection back there, when we made camp after falling off the bridge and all. Then you just…shut down. And shut me out."

Sukri's gaze dropped.

"Look, I understand if you don't want someone absorbing your memories," he continued. "I get it. But with my helmet on…"

"Hunter," Sukri interrupted.

"I can keep it on," he insisted. "I won't absorb much of anything."

"Hunter!" she snapped. Hunter grimaced, his mouth shutting with a *click*. She glared at him for a moment, and then her expression softened. "It's not you," she explained. "It's me."

"What do you mean?"

Sukri took a deep breath in, then let it out, her eyes on her feet. When she lifted her gaze, her eyes were glittering with moisture.

"Take off your helmet," she ordered.

Hunter hesitated, then did so, setting it on the ground beside him. Sukri squared her shoulders, then stepped forward.

"Go on," she stated. "Take my memories."

Hunter hesitated.

"Are you sure?"

"No," she answered. "Do it before I change my mind."

Hunter nodded, then grabbed Sukri's temples, pulling her forehead against his, and closing his eyes.

Images flashed in rapid sequence in his mind's eye.

He gasped, pulling his head away from hers. Then took a step back, staring at her. She stared back almost defiantly, her lower lip quivering.

"Well?" she demanded.

Hunter swallowed, then stepped right up to her, wrapping his arms around her. She stiffened, but he embraced her tightly, rocking backward and forward slightly.

"I'm sorry," he whispered in her ear. She pushed him away, until he was at arms' length.

"Sorry for what?"

"For what you went through," he explained. "For what they did to you. And…what they made you do."

Sukri's face paled.

"You saw it," she stated flatly.

"Yes."

"What I did to those boys," she pressed.

"What they made you do, yes," Hunter confirmed. "And how you felt about it. How it kept you up at night. And how…it made you not want to be close to me." He paused. "Because you were afraid of what I'd think of you if I found out."

"And what *do* you think of me?" she inquired. He lowered his gaze, choosing his words carefully. Then he looked straight into her eyes.

"I think you deserve to be happy for once," he answered.

"You…really mean that?"

"I do," he confirmed. "It's all I want too."

"Hunter, you *are* happy," she retorted. "You've got your family, and Vi."

"True," he conceded. "But I don't have a girl. Honestly, I never have."

"What about Trixie?" Sukri asked, arching an eyebrow. He grimaced.

"That's my point," he replied. "Every woman I've been with was just…using me. It was physical. Just sex, not…love."

"So you want love?"

"Well, yeah," he answered. "Don't you?"

"Sure," Sukri replied. "But it's a little too early to tell me you love me. Makes you seem clingy."

"Not what I meant," he grumbled. "Asshole."

She punched him in the shoulder playfully. But hard.

"Hey!" he blurted out. "Jesus…I forgot about how violent you were."

"Clearly I'm a lot more violent than you thought," she retorted. But she broke out into a smile, putting her hands on his shoulders. "I tell you what," she proposed. "You come back from this whole war thing alive, and we'll give it a shot. Hell, I might even let you give me some of your goo."

Hunter chuckled, shaking his head.

"Deal?" she pressed. Hunter nodded

"Deal."

"Don't forget your helmet," she reminded him.

He reached down, picking it up off the ground and putting it back on his head. Sukri leaned in then, pressing her lips against his. For a while. Then she pulled away.

"Now get out of here," she ordered, shoving him away playfully. "And come back in one piece, okay?"

Hunter nodded, then stepped back, jumping into the air and beating his wings. He'd been practicing taking off from standing for much of the afternoon yesterday; the ground dropped beneath his feet, and he waved at Sukri, flying up until he was a good thirty feet above the treetops, then spreading his wings out and gliding forward. The wind whipped around him as he gained speed, following the Ironclad army marching through the forest below. He overtook them quickly, speeding above the treetops, searching for favorable air currents. The telltale sensation of wind filling his wings signaled his success, and he flapped his wings, flying higher and higher. Within minutes, the ground was hundreds of feet below; he relaxed into a glide again, studying the terrain ahead.

Tykus was north of the Ironclad base; without being able to use the sun as a compass, he had to resort to using the stars. Luckily Vi had taught him how to do so weeks ago. He angled northward, picking up speed, enjoying the feeling of weightlessness. It was truly freeing, being able to fly like this. To know that, on a whim, he could leave the world behind…could go anywhere he wanted, without fear of alien wills transforming him. He couldn't imagine going back to how he'd been before.

Minutes passed, and he spotted the King's Road ahead, snaking through the forest. He followed it, flying so high above that no guard patrolling it would even realize he was there. And if they happened to see him flying, they'd just assume he was a bird. It wasn't long before the deep forest transitioned to the Fringe, heralded by an abrupt change in the vegetation. To think that this trip had taken him hours in the past, even by carriage!

A short while later, he spotted the end of the forest, the vast expanse of the Deadlands ahead. He followed the King's Road, reaching the Deadlands, making sure to maintain altitude. There was a large, walled-off military base a kilometer or so ahead and to the right; he ignored it, following the King's Road toward the Kingdom further north.

It wasn't long before he saw it: the massive wall of the Kingdom surrounding a vast metropolis at the base of a huge hill. And atop this hill, the huge fortress that was the Acropolis, its golden roofs contrasting sharply with its stark white walls. A chill ran through him, the memory of the first time he'd stood on the King's Road, gawking at the great kingdom, coming to him.

He'd been just a kid then. Lost, angry. Resentful. Using sarcasm to hide his insecurities, and to create a wall between himself and anyone else that might actually care.

He smiled, gliding steadily toward the kingdom. It seemed like a lifetime had passed since then, even though it'd only been a couple months at most. And now he was a different person – literally as well as figuratively – with a family and friends that would die for him. And whom he lived for.

Now it was time to wait. He would fly high above the city, looking for all the world like just another bird to anyone watching. But when the Ironclad swarmed into the city, he would show Tykus what he was capable of.

* * *

"Hey!"

Sempton groaned, rolling away from the sound and burying his head into his pillow. He felt a hand grab his shoulder and shake it.

"Wake up!"

Sempton sighed, rolling onto his back and opening his eyes. The short wooden ceiling of the common sleeping barracks was only a meter above. He glanced to his right, seeing a man perched on the ladder of his bunkbed. It was Percy, his bunkmate.

"What?" Sempton grumbled, rubbing his eyes.

"Something's happening," Percy explained. "It's…"

The front door of the barracks burst open, a tall man in full armor striding through. It was Sergeant Mannin.

"All right people," he barked. "Load up and line up! This is *not* a drill. I repeat, this is not a drill!"

Sempton sat bolt upright…and slammed his forehead on the ceiling.

"Ah, *fuck*," he swore, rubbing his head gingerly.

"Come on," Percy urged, hopping down from the ladder. Sempton rolled out of bed, climbing down the ladder to the floor below. Percy was already putting on his armor…as were the other thirty-odd men in the barracks. Sempton followed suit, fumbling to get his breeches on.

"Move it!" Sergeant Mannin yelled. "Go, go!"

Percy finished dressing, and Sempton struggled to catch up, cinching his belt around his waist, his sword at his left hip. He put on his helmet, then followed Percy past the Sergeant and out of the barracks. They emerged into the cool night air, row after row of squat wooden buildings greeting them.

The Deadlands military base was a step up from the shithole the Outskirts had been, but it was purely utilitarian. A semi-permanent town completely surrounded by a seven-meter wall.

All around them, soldiers spilled out of their barracks, rushing into the narrow dirt streets.

Sempton swallowed in a dry throat, his heart thumping in his chest. He glanced at Percy, who glanced back wordlessly, fingering the hilt of his sword. Sergeant Mannin strode out of the barracks, coming to the front of the line of soldiers.

"Get to the north wall!" he shouted, pointing to the left. "Form a line with the others!"

"What's going on?" someone asked. Another soldier shouted, pointing to the north wall a half-kilometer away. Sempton turned, peering into the darkness; the wall was lit by torches, their flames whipping around in the wind.

Then he saw it.

Countless shadows pouring over the wall, appearing atop it and leaping down into the base.

"Form a goddamn line!" Sergeant Mannin screamed, sprinting toward the wall. The other soldiers followed, unsheathing their swords. Percy did too…and Sempton followed behind the man, turning left down the narrow dirt road and running toward the wall. Hundreds of soldiers packed the street ahead of them, all of them rushing toward the shapes plunging into the base. Lit from behind by the torches on the wall, Sempton could barely make out huge figures. Hundreds of them swarming toward them.

Shit.

He slowed, letting soldiers pass him by on either side, watching as the things reached the front of the line of soldiers…and plowed right through them.

"Ironclad!" a voice screamed.

Sempton felt hands shove him from behind, and he stumbled forward, catching his balance. He was pressed forward by the soldiers behind him.

"Go, go!" one of them yelled at him.

He picked up his pace, moving to the left as he went forward, slipping between the other soldiers…and watching as soldiers on the front lines were tossed into the air, their swords flying from their hands. One of the soldiers was lifted by the arms; the Ironclad holding them pulled, tearing the soldier's arms from his body. The man screamed in agony, blood spurting from the stumps of his shoulders.

Shit!

Sempton continued moving forward and leftward, until he reached the edge of the column of soldiers. He spotted a side-street ahead, and pressed forward.

Come on, come on…

He reached the side-street, and ducked down it, hiding behind a few large boxes stacked against the wall of one of the buildings. He paused there, waiting for someone to follow him, or to call him out.

But there was only the sound of marching feet, and of screams and indistinct shouting in the distance.

Sempton crouched there, a hand on the hilt of his sword. He'd never been in battle before, having barely made it out of basic training. Joining the military was supposed to have been his ticket out of the Outskirts, a way to make a decent wage and get exposed to artifacts that would change him. Lighten his skin and hair, and give him a chance at being able to move out of the Outskirts and into Lowtown. To finally make a good wage to support his family.

He sure as hell didn't sign up for this.

There was more screaming, seeming closer now, and Sempton cursed under his breath, glancing around. There was an open door leading into the building he was crouched next to; he ducked inside, closing the door behind him and locking it.

More sleeping quarters greeted him, identical to the one he'd been sleeping in. And to his immense relief, the room was deserted. He paused, looking around the room for somewhere to hide; the only option was under one of the bunkbeds. He walked up to one, laying on the floor and trying to scooch under, but it was too tight a squeeze. Sempton cursed, getting to his feet.

Bam!

Sempton spun around.

"Help!" a voice shouted from beyond the door he'd come through.

Bam bam bam!

"Help me!"

There was a garbled scream, then a loud *thump*. Then silence.

BAM!

The door rattled, the frame around it cracking.

Sempton turned and ran.

He rushed to the rear exit of the barracks, shoving the door open and bursting into the street beyond…and colliding into a group of soldiers. They cursed, shoving him backward onto the dirt.

And then an Ironclad rammed into the group, sending the men flying.

"Shit!" Sempton swore, scrambling to his feet. The Ironclad roared, grabbing one of the soldiers by the throat and tearing out his windpipe. It tossed the man aside, leaping on top of another soldier, tearing off his limbs one-by-one and tossing them aside.

Sempton ran, sprinting as fast as he could down the street away from the soldiers and Ironclad, then ducking down a side-street. He found another building to the right, bursting through the door and slamming it behind him, searching frantically for somewhere to hide. It was a storage facility, armor and weapons hanging by hooks on the walls. He spotted a closet door to his left, and sprinted up to it, opening it and huddling inside, closing the door in front of him.

There was utter darkness.

Sempton lowered himself onto his butt, his heartbeat pulsing in his ears, sweat dripping down his forehead into his eyes. His every breath sounded far too loud, and he focused on slowing his breathing, keeping his ears peeled.

Silence.

He allowed himself a sigh of relief, wiping more sweat from his forehead, then closing his eyes.

There was a muted scream from outside.

Sempton's eyes snapped open.

Thump, thump, thump.

He froze, hearing the sound get closer. It stopped suddenly, right before the closet door, and he hear a snorting sound. Heavy breathing, like a horse's.

Oh shit oh shit…

A warm wetness spread across his groin, and he began to shake uncontrollably, the unmistakable stink of piss hitting him.

The doorknob creaked, and the closet door swung open slowly, revealing a huge black figure. One with two pairs of massive arms.

It reached for him with four hands, and Sempton screamed.

* * *

The air in the wide tunnel leading from the Fringe under the Deadlands was musty, forcing Vi to breathe through her mouth as she followed Xerxes and the other Ironclad down it. A few of the Ironclad carried torches, providing just enough light for the nocturnal creatures to see. Of course, with Xerxes' glowing mane and tail bathing the immediate area in dull blue, Vi had no problem finding her way. Not that she would've anyway, considering the slight alterations she'd made to her eyes long ago.

She heard the literal army of Ironclad stomping down the tunnel behind her, and sped up to walk beside Xerxes.

"You nervous, Blue?" she inquired.

"NO."

"You sure?" she pressed, flashing him a wicked grin. "You can tell me if you are, you know. We can work through it."

Xerxes ignored her, and she chuckled, patting him on one of his huge arms. Xerxes was *never* nervous, at least not in battle. Being immortal certainly helped. She suspected he didn't worry about himself at all. His health, or pain, or wealth, or any of the things that normal people spent their lives agonizing over. Xerxes only cared about his people. And his family.

The guy was the most selfless being Vi had ever met.

She'd heard the old saying many times, that if you wanted to learn someone's true character, give them power. And so many people in the kingdom – Dominus, the other dukes, even her own uncle, who'd used what little power he'd had to rape her as a child – had failed that test. Men who proclaimed to be of impeccable virtue, yet possessed none.

Vi smiled up at Xerxes.

"You're a good man, you know that?" she told him. He glanced down at her as they walked, a questioning look on his face. "You and Hunter are two peas in a pod."

Xerxes grunted.

"He's a good man, but young," he signed. "He worries too much about what doesn't matter. Can't focus on what does."

"He'll learn," Vi replied. Xerxes nodded, signing again.

"Life will teach him."

Vi didn't reply, looking ahead. They were close to the end of the tunnel now. By Xerxes' calculations, the tunnel was a mere foot away from the basement of one of the taverns in Lowtown. The Ironclad ahead of Xerxes and Vi parted to let them through, and Xerxes strode all the way to the end of the tunnel, Vi at his side.

Then the big guy turned, nodding at one of his generals and flashing a few hand signals. He stepped to the side then, and two Ironclad pressed forward, each using their four hands to dig furiously at the wall. The Ironclad were excellent diggers, their armored hands scooping the dirt and rocks away with ease. Sure enough, they reached dull gray stone, the foundation of the building.

Luckily they'd brought warhammers.

Everyone stood back as the two Ironclad swung their hammers, smashing through the wall to reveal a wine cellar beyond. Row after row of wooden shelves with bottles and casks of various alcoholic beverages.

"Nice work," Vi whispered, nodding at Xerxes. The guy's calculations had been perfect; the tunnel had brought them right under the Ironside Inn. "Not bad for an oversized beetle."

Xerxes made another hand signal, and the Ironclad started pouring into the basement. Vi kept to one side, watching as they thundered by.

"Ready when you are, Blue," she stated.

Xerxes paused, then pushed his way into the line, stomping into the cellar. Vi followed, nimbly avoiding being trampled by the big brutes all around her. She passed through the stone wall into the cellar, following the Ironclad up the stairs. There was a scream from the floor above, then the sound of glass shattering and a loud *thud.*

Vi reached the top of the stairs, finding herself in a large tavern. A single body lay on the floor, surrounded by broken glass. Ironclad stomped out of the entrance into the street beyond. Vi followed them, hearing shouts from outside, followed by screams.

She emerged from the tavern into the streets of Lowtown, faint sunlight heralding the arrival of dawn. Scanning the street and the rooftops around her, she spotted two dead guards lay on the street…but otherwise the street was deserted. Xerxes stopped beside her.

"BARRACKS," he growled. He flashed some quick hand signals with each of his four hands, communicating different messages to different generals…all at once. Then he turned to Vi.

"You go west, I go east," he signed. "Just like the plan."

Xerxes turned then, gesturing for his group of Ironclad to follow him as he sprinted down the street, turning left down a side-street. There were many barracks housing the City Guard, most of which would be filled with fresh guards from the shift change an hour before. The two largest ones were to the northeast and northwest; taking them out would hamper the City Guard's attempts at organizing their defenses.

Vi broke out into a sprint, a literal army of Ironclad following behind her as she made her way down the winding streets toward the northeast barracks. She looked up, spotting two archers on the wall surrounding the city.

Damn it Hunter!

She whipped out her bow, nocking an arrow…and watched as both archers jerked, tumbling from the wall. A dark shadow swooped through the sky overhead, and Vi grinned.

Atta-boy, she thought.

Vi put her bow away, spotting a few guards patrolling ahead. They cursed, taking one look at the wave of Ironclad rushing at them…and running.

But they couldn't outrun the Ironclad…and they sure as hell couldn't outrun Vi.

She burst past the beasts, leaving them in her dust and closing the gap between herself and the guards rapidly, ending both of their cowardly – but very practical – lives with the edge of her sword. Then she stared at their lifeless bodies, her jawline rippling. They were just kids…not even twenty by the looks of it.

Wrong place at the wrong time, she thought. They would've run to alert the authorities, she knew. But it was still a waste. Innocent boys paying the price for the games of old rich men.

She spotted another archer on a rooftop ahead, and reached for her bow…right as an arrow slammed into the archer's chest. Hunter flew by, looking Vi right in the eye and giving a thumb's up. She shook her head, giving one more glance at the soldiers she'd killed.

Focus, she told herself.

She broke out into a jog, turning down another street to see a broad three-story stone building ahead. It was the barracks.

A bell tolled in the distance. The emergency alarm to mobilize the City Guard.

"Okay boys," Vi shouted. "Light it up!"

She ran up to the front wall of the barracks, stopping before one of the many large windows there and reaching into her pocket. She pulled out a small bottle filled with oil, its mouth stuffed with fabric, and grabbed one of the torches from a nearby Ironclad, lighting the fabric and tossing the bottle through the window. A few Ironclad did the same, lighting their own firebombs and tossing them through other windows.

An arrow whizzed by Vi's head, smashing a hole through the partially-broken window beside her.

Son-of-a…

Her bow was already in her hands, and she turned in the direction the arrow had come from, spotting an archer in a tower a block away. Who promptly tumbled from the tower, an arrow sticking out of his chest. He fell a few stories, landing on the street with a dull *thud.* Hunter flew by a fraction of a second later, gliding a good ten meters above the rooftops.

There were shouts from within the barracks, smoke billowing from the windows. Seconds later, guards rushed out of the front doors of the barracks and leapt through the windows…right into the waiting arms of a sea of Ironclad.

Vi didn't even have to draw her sword; the Ironclad tore the men apart. Literally.

More guards spilled out of the building, some carrying shields and warhammers. They began to form a line in front of the building, bracing themselves against the wall. Flames appeared in the windows, the smoke growing thicker every second.

Vi unsheathed her sword, striding toward the nearest victim. He turned toward her, lifting his shield and readying his warhammer.

Then slumped to the ground seconds later, his head tumbling from his shoulders.

Vi didn't so much as pause, rushing at the line of soldiers, her sword flashing as she dispatched one guard after another, ducking and weaving, their attacks missing her by a wide margin. They may as well have been toddlers to her, clumsy and slow. There was no challenge in it…only the wholesale slaughter of men who had the shit luck to be in the wrong tribe.

One-by-one they fell, her sword thrusting and slicing at every vulnerable point, every hole in their defenses, until there were none left standing. She ended each of their lives quickly, minimizing their suffering.

It was the best she could do.

More guards rushed out of the entrance, and Vi sheathed her sword, turning away from them. She nodded grimly at the army of Ironclad before her.

"Finish this," she muttered. "I'll meet up with Xerxes."

The Ironclad attacked the fleeing guards, and Vi left them behind, jogging west toward the other main barracks. She was supposed to meet Xerxes there, then go with him up the main stairway to the Acropolis at the top of the huge hill in the center of the city. There were occasional people walking down the streets, morons ignoring the tolling of the bell. She ran past them, reaching the northwest part of Lowtown in a few minutes. Ironclad had already surrounded the large five-story building, smoke pouring from broken windows on the first and second stories.

"Where's Blue?" she asked the nearest Ironclad. They glanced at her, flashing a few hand signals. "Ah," she murmured, looking up.

A window on the fourth story exploded outward, shards of glass flying everywhere as Xerxes smashed through it. He fell toward the street, holding two guards by the napes of their necks. While on fire.

Then he slammed into the street, driving the guards' faces into the cobblestones so hard their heads crumpled.

Xerxes stood, his left leg bent at an impossible angle, the armor at his mid-thigh cracked. It healed quickly, and moments later he stomped up to Vi, flames still licking at bits of debris on his shoulders.

"Bit dramatic," Vi opined. Xerxes gave an ugly grin. "You busy?" she inquired, glancing at the burning building. Bodies of guards littered the street around it, muffled screams coming from inside.

"I…FREE."

She grabbed one of his left hands, turning southward toward the city entrance. He followed beside her gamely, taking one footstep for every three of hers.

"All right Blue," she stated. "Time to climb those stairs and take on the Acropolis. You ready?"

"READY," Xerxes confirmed.

They passed fleeing citizens and the bodies of guards lying on the street, making their way toward the massive stairway near the entrance of the kingdom. The screams of the dying echoed through the air, and Vi sighed, letting go of Xerxes' hand and walking faster.

"Come on," she muttered. "Let's get this over with."

Chapter 28

The wind shrieked in Hunter's ears as he soared toward two archers standing on top of one of the buildings in Lowtown, an arrow nocked in his bowstring. He drew it back, firing, then immediately grabbed another arrow and nocked it to fire again. It felt *right*, and that feeling was validated as both arrows flew true, slamming into their targets. He burst past them, gliding over the city, the buildings passing by in a blur beneath him.

Hunter angled upward, gaining altitude and turning in a slow circle, scanning the rooftops below. He spotted another archer in a guard tower ahead and to his right, their bowstring drawn. Hunter followed the archer's gaze, spotting a line of Ironclad surrounding a large building a block away…and a woman in a brown leather uniform beyond, near the wall of the building.

Vi!

He nocked an arrow, firing it at the archer, right as the archer fired *their* arrow.

The arrow struck the archer in the chest, and he fell from the tower. But the archer's arrow flew right at Vi, missing her by mere inches. He saw Vi grab her bow, nocking an arrow and turning toward the falling guard, then Hunter.

Damn it, he thought, soaring by her. *Never gonna hear the end of that one.*

Hunter focused, scanning the rooftops again, finding another couple of archers atop the main wall around the city. He flew toward them, reaching for another arrow, but his quiver was empty.

Damn.

The archers saw him coming, and they fired at him. Hunter swerved out of the way, but he was too late; one of the arrows clipped his breastplate, ricocheting off.

That *hurt*.

Hunter cursed, fleeing from the archers, dodging left and right erratically. More arrows whizzed by, and he dropped down until he was flying a few feet above the rooftops, putting as much distance between himself and the archers as possible. No more arrows whizzed by; he flapped his wings, gaining altitude until he was a few hundred feet above the city.

Then he scanned the streets, searching for Vi.

The northeast and northwest sections of Lowtown were overrun with Ironclad. Guards from the smaller barracks were advancing toward them from the southern part of the huge city, some flanking huge carriages rolling down the streets.

"The hell are those?" he wondered.

He glided over the city, eventually finding what he was looking for: a figure in a brown uniform sprinting down one of the side-streets toward the northwestern part of Lowtown. Toward a large building surrounded by Ironclad. It had to be the barracks Xerxes had been tasked to take out.

Hunter rotated his wings forward, feeling his stomach flip as he began to dive down toward the city, the wind howling in his ears. Then he leveled out a few dozen feet above the city, zooming over the street leading to the barracks. Vi was already there; he spotted something huge leaping out of the fourth-story window; it was Xerxes, a guard in either hand. His brother dropped to the street, smashing the guards' faces into the cobblestones.

He heard a shout to his left, and spotted an archer on one of the rooftops. Hunter cut to the left, flying at the man. He unsheathed his sword, flying right over the archer and thrusting his blade through the man's face.

The sword was torn from Hunter's hands, and Hunter circled back, landing on the rooftop. The archer was most assuredly dead; he yanked his sword free from the man's face, taking the arrows from the archer's quiver to refresh his own.

Back in business.

He strode to the edge of the roof, peering down at the barracks. Flames roared from broken windows, smoke rising into the air.

Vi and Xerxes left the other Ironclad, making their way south toward the city entrance. Phase three was next…the storming of the Acropolis.

There was a rumbling sound to his right, and Hunter turned to see a long column of guards approaching the Ironclad surrounding the barracks, accompanied by one of the huge carriages he'd seen earlier. From here he could see that the carriage was heavily armored, metal spikes covering its surface.

"Aim!" one of the guards shouted. Six guards grabbed a wide hose extending from the side of the carriage, pointing it at the Ironclad. "Fire!"

A jet of black liquid shot at the Ironclad, dousing them instantly…and forcing them backward. The guards aimed the stream upward, black liquid showering down on the beasts.

"Ignite!" the guard shouted. Hunter spotted a guard holding a torch, and drew his bow, firing an arrow at the man. The arrow took him down…but not before he'd thrown the torch at the group of Ironclad.

Shit!

The black liquid ignited, flames spreading rapidly over the Ironclad. They screamed, their guttural voices piercing the air, setting the hair on the nape of Hunter's neck on end. He watched in horror as his people burned.

God-damn son-of-a…

Hunter fired an arrow at the guard who'd issued the commands, taking him down, then firing another and another, killing the guards holding the hose. The Ironclad not covered in flames backed away frantically from their burning comrades, who ran and thrashed blindly, spreading the burning oil to everyone around them. More and more Ironclad burned, fully a third of them dying horribly in front of Hunter's eyes.

And there was nothing he could do to save them.

A second carriage rolled down the street on the opposite side of the Ironclad, blocking the road and trapping the remaining Ironclad between the carriages. Hunter leapt from the edge of the roof, flying to a rooftop closer to this second carriage, then landing and nocking another arrow. He fired it at the guards picking up the carriage's hose, striking one of them. But another took the guard's place. Hunter shot more arrows, felling a guard with each one, until he had no more arrows left.

"Fire!" a guard commanded.

Oil shot out from the hose, dousing the other Ironclad, who tried to flee from the deluge. But the veritable wall of burning Ironclad stopped them…and any that tried to leap over their burning comrades were ignited themselves. Flames spread quickly over the entire army.

He grabbed the hilt of his sword, seriously considering jumping down and attacking the men. But with the fire and smoke – not to mention the dying Ironclad thrashing about and the prospect of getting doused in oil himself – there was no point in him doing so. The Ironclad were as good as dead, and nothing he could do would change that.

Hunter grit his teeth, watching for a moment longer, then forcing himself to turn away.

You should've…

He stopped the thought immediately, focusing on what he needed to do.

Meet up with Vi. Fly her into the Acropolis.

Running across the rooftop away from the massacre, he leapt off the edge, feeling the air fill his wings instantly. He flew upward and forward, spotting the Acropolis in the distance atop the hill in the center of the city, a long stone stairway leading up to it. Xerxes and Vi were already sprinting up it, a long column of Ironclad following behind them. A veritable army of guards were waiting for them at the top of the stairs…along with another large, armored carriage facing away from the approaching Ironclad.

And as Hunter watched, a door at the back of the carriage swung open, a huge spiked cannonball rolling out…and down the steps.

"Oh *shit,*" he swore, pumping his wings harder. He was still a good half-mile away from the stairs…too far away to do anything. As if there was anything he *could* do.

The cannonball rolled down the steps, picking up speed as it did so, crushing the stone under its incredible weight. It careened right for Vi and Xerxes…and the Ironclad behind them. There was a steep drop on either side of the stairs. Which meant there was nowhere to run.

Xerxes charged up the stairs, passing Vi and sprinting up the rightmost side of the stairway to meet the oncoming cannonball. Xerxes ran right into it, shoving it to the left even as it smashed into him, sending him flying backward and rightward.

The big guy flew thirty feet into the air, then fell another hundred feet to the hillside beside the giant stairway.

Hunter watched as the cannonball rolled leftward and downward, barely missing Vi – who'd moved all the way to the right – and barreling toward the Ironclad. The Ironclad threw themselves at the cannonball one after the other, shoving it further to the left, sacrificing themselves for their comrades further down the stairway. It worked; the cannonball rolled off the stairs, plummeting to smash through a few buildings downhill.

Vi charged the guards at the top of the stairs, the Ironclad army right behind her.

The guards unhooked the carriage from its horses, shoving it down the stairs at the approaching army. It rolled toward Vi, who dodged it easily, making her way to the top…just as Hunter reached the stairs behind her. He landed, folding his wings behind him and drawing his sword, running after Vi.

She reached the first of the guards, her blade whirling so fast it was a blur. Blood sprayed all around her, everyone who dared to get too close paying the ultimate price for their hubris. But she was only one woman, and there were hundreds of guards in her way.

Luckily Hunter hadn't eaten that morning.

He focused on his hunger, letting it dominate his mind. Willing forth visions of an ancient past, of soldiers crying out the name of a fallen Legend.

Za-ga-mar!

A familiar rush of adrenaline came over him, his heart pounding in his chest, his vision growing sharper. Clearer.

Za-ga-mar!

He closed in on the line of guards ahead, time slowing, his mind seeming to lift out of a fog. He reached the nearest guard, watching as the man raised their shield to block. Hunter kicked the man's shield, sending the guard stumbling backward…and at the same time making Hunter do the same. He spread his wings wide, floating down a few steps, then charged at the man.

One slash to the legs and the guard doubled over…and Hunter grabbed him, tossing him down the stairs to be trampled by the oncoming Ironclad.

Then he turned back to face the other guards, watching as Vi mowed through them, moving even faster than he could. He joined her, allowing Zagamar to guide his sword. Men fell to it in a symphony of blood, even as a wave of Ironclad crashed into the guards all around him, tearing the pathetic humans apart. Hunter ducked, dodged, slashed, and stabbed, planning six moves in advance, every movement flowing like a deadly dance.

The guards didn't stand a chance.

A few minutes later – a much longer period of time for Hunter than anyone else – he was surrounded by the bodies of his enemies.

Hunter *shoved* Zagamar out of the forefront of his mind, feeling a shift as he became fully himself once again.

Vi stepped up to him, her arms crossed.

"About that archer," she began.

"Yeah yeah," Hunter grumbled. "I knew you weren't gonna let that go."

She chuckled, patting him on the shoulder, then glancing back down the long stairway. None other than Xerxes was sprinting up the steps toward them. Utterly intact, of course.

"Thanks for saving our necks," Vi said as Xerxes reached them. "Took balls to do what you did."

Xerxes rolled his eyes at the pun.

"All right," she stated. "Let's go dig under that wall and take on the Acropolis. I've got a meeting with a king."

* * *

Hunter wrapped his arms around Vi's waist from behind, then spread his wings. He flew them upward, Vi's weight making it take more difficult than usual. But he managed to gain altitude slowing, rising above the wall surrounding the Acropolis. Ironclad lined the western part of the wall, stones and dirt flying as they dug furiously. Hunter held Vi tightly to him as they rose ever-higher, the Acropolis ahead of them.

"Don't enjoy this too much," Vi warned. "Keep your sword sheathed, m'kay kiddo?"

"Ha ha," Hunter grumbled. "I prefer it consensual, remember?"

She chuckled, the pointed ahead.

"See that balcony over there?" she asked. There was a large stone balcony several stories up on the Acropolis, looking over a large interior courtyard. It was a good twenty feet above them, and perhaps a hundred feet away. "Drop us on it."

"Roger that."

"Huh?"

"Figure of speech," Hunter explained. "Looks like there's two archers on it."

"That's why I'm carrying my bow," Vi replied. She aimed, then fired one arrow, then another, taking them both out. One through the right eye, one through the left.

"Damn you're good," he muttered.

Go faster," Vi urged. They were almost level with the balcony now.

"I'd go faster if you weren't so heavy," he shot back.

"All muscle baby."

"Uh huh," he teased. But of course she was right; her torso was as hard as a rock. He flew a good ten feet above the balcony, then spread his wings out wide, gliding down to it and dropping Vi. She bolted forward, and he landed on the balcony as well, following after her. There was door ahead leading into the Acropolis; Vi opened it, stepping into a wide hallway beyond. The walls and floor were made of slabs of fine granite separated by grout of gleaming gold, the ceiling a good twenty feet above their heads. Armored guards stood on either side of the door they'd opened.

"Stop!" one cried.

Vi cut them both down in a flash of silver, her blade already back in its sheath even before the guards' bodies struck the floor.

"Damn that was pretty," Hunter said, following Vi forward across the hallway.

"Tell that to their families," she retorted.

There were two more guards in the hallway ahead; they unsheathed their swords, intercepting Vi and Hunter. Vi mule-kicked one of them right in the chest, throwing them a good fifteen feet backward. Hunter reached the other guard, faking a thrust at his belly. The guard took the bait, moving to block the attack…and Hunter followed with a second thrust to the man's groin.

The guard crumpled.

Hunter finished the man off, then rejoined Vi, who was busy yanking her sword free from the other guard's neck.

"Incoming," she warned.

More guards were rushing down the long hallway toward them, spilling out of a door at the end of it. There were at least ten of them.

"I take nine, you take the other one?" Vi proposed.

"Uh huh."

The guards rushed at Vi and Hunter, two of them reaching Hunter and thrusting their swords at him. He backpedaled, blocking both swords, but one guard thrust again. Hunter cursed, pulling his wings forward in front of him quickly; this forced him backward, his boots sliding against the granite floor…and the guard's thrust missed him by mere inches.

Hunter batted the sword away, slashing the man's throat open. Then he kicked the doomed guard back, blocking a string of attacks from the second guard.

This guard was clearly better than the first.

Hunter went on the defensive, backpedaling as the guard continued to attack him, each swing and thrust followed rapidly by another. One thrust slammed into his metal breastplate, knocking him off-balance. He grunted, barely blocking a follow-up slash to his throat. But still the guard pressed forward, slashing at Hunter's left thigh.

The blade sliced through his armor there, blood flowing from the wound.

Hunter swore, leaping backward and flapping his wings. This sent him flying up and away from the guard; he sheathed his sword, drawing his bow and firing an arrow into the man's face.

He dropped to the floor, grimacing as pain shot through his left thigh. Then he watched as Vi finished off the last of the other guards, thrusting her sword into their groin. She walked up to Hunter then.

"Wow," he muttered. "Dick move."

"You okay?" she asked, gesturing at his leg.

"Flesh wound," he reassured her. Then he walked up to the guard he'd shot, retrieving his arrow from the man's eye-socket. "After you."

They continued to the door at the end of the hallway, and Vi kicked it open. Another hallway greeted them, one with a long line of doors on either side. And there was a guard posted at every one of them.

Vi burst forward, unsheathing her sword and running for the nearest guards.

Hunter grabbed his bow, firing arrow after arrow at the guards, taking four of them out before any of them got the bright idea to use their shields to block them.

Then he leapt into the air, spreading his wings and flying upward to the ceiling twenty feet above.

Catch me now, he thought with a smirk, nocking another arrow, then firing it at one of the guards' faces as they stared up at him. The arrow buried itself in the man's open mouth.

The other guards raised their shields up above their heads…and were promptly cut down by Vi.

Which made half the guards lower their shields again.

Hunter smiled grimly, firing at the guards who'd lowered their shields, picking them off one-by-one. Then he glided down toward one of the few remaining guards, unsheathing his sword and folding his wings in mid-air. He dropped like a stone toward the guard, chopping down at the man's head.

His blade cut right through the man's helmet…and skull.

"Nice move," Vi said, walking up to Hunter.

"Really got the drop on him," he quipped, jerking his sword free from the guard's head. Vi rolled her eyes.

"Just stop. Please."

They made their way down this new hallway, passing the doors on either side.

"You know where you're going?" Hunter asked.

"Nope."

"You're kidding, right?" he pressed.

"We don't exactly have the floorplans for the Acropolis," she pointed out. "We need to let the Ironclad in, then search the whole place until we find Tykus."

They reached the end of the hallway, which had another door; they went through, finding stairs leading forward and downward to yet *another* hallway. Vi started down the stairs, and Hunter glanced down at his injured thigh, then at the long staircase.

Yeah, no.

He ran off the edge, spreading his wings and gliding down, gently landing at the bottom. They continued down the hallway.

"Jesus," Hunter muttered. "Is this place *all* hallways?"

He heard screaming from ahead, and spotted a whole ton of guards at the opposite end of the hallway. All surrounding a huge black creature with a glowing blue mane and tail.

"Reinforcements have arrived," Vi declared.

And then Xerxes attacked.

Limbs and bodies flew into the air as Xerxes demolished the guards, tearing arms and legs clean off, and even the occasional head. The guards fought back, but it was hopeless. Within moments, they were dead...all except for a few that had the good sense to flee. Those died to Vi and Hunter instead.

"Hey Blue!" Vi called out. Xerxes stomped up to them, what few wounds he'd incurred healing rapidly. He grinned at them.

"HEY."

More Ironclad came through the doorway behind them, congregating behind Xerxes.

"WHAT...PLAN?" Xerxes inquired.

"Go floor to floor, find Tykus," Vi answered. Hunter perked up suddenly.

"It's in the basement level, just below the first floor," he stated. Vi stared at him.

"And how do you know that?"

"My...er, Dominus's memories," he explained. "The ones I absorbed back in Wexford."

"All right then," Vi declared. "Let's do this."

* * *

Xerxes' feet *thumped* on the granite floor as he led Hunter, Vi, and his troops down yet another hallway of the Acropolis. They'd cleared out much of the second floor of the huge building, then gone down to the first, and now the basement level. Thanks to Dominus's memories, Hunter knew they were getting close.

A guard burst out from one of the side-doors in front of Xerxes, and Xerxes bopped him atop the head with one big fist. The man's neck *crunched*, and he fell to the floor, his limbs twitching. Xerxes didn't even skip a beat, continuing down the long corridor.

More guards spilled out of a larger door to the right, armed with greatshields and warhammers.

"For the king!" they cried.

Xerxes broke into an all-out run, barreling toward the guards. There had to be at least thirty of them.

Not that he cared.

He rushed right up to them, leaping head-first into the crowd and smashing into their shields. They flew backward with the force of the impact, knocking down the guards behind them like bowling pins and falling to the floor.

Xerxes leapt on one of them, pummeling their head and chest with his four fists, their facial bones crumpling under the onslaught. He stood up then, feeling swords bouncing off his back and arms, and grabbed the nearest guard's sword by the blade, tearing it out of the man's hands and plunging it into his chest. Right through his metal breastplate.

"Need any help?" he heard Vi ask from behind. He twisted around to look at her, then shook his head, even as more swords *clanged* off his body from all around.

"NO."

Then a warhammer struck him in the middle of the back with a loud *crack*. He stumbled forward, then caught himself, spinning around and backfisting a guard in the temple. The man's helmet caved in, blood pouring down his neck.

Another guard swung their warhammer at Xerxes, smashing him in the back of the head.

That hurt.

His vision blackened, his knees buckling. Another hammer struck him, smashing him in the face.

Anger welled up inside him, growing with every blow. With every fresh burst of pain.

He roared, lashing out blindly, his hands closing on someone's limb. He pulled it taut, then smashed his ruined forehead against it, feeling the limb snap. Pain shot through his skull, but he welcomed it. He *savored* it. Let it feed his rage.

His vision returned, and he found himself on his knees, surrounded by guards.

Xerxes grabbed two of their heads, smashing them together, then flinging them to either side. He tore a warhammer from a guard's hands, rising to his feet and swinging it around in a circle. It struck guard after guard, sending them flying.

Then he chucked the hammer at another guard's head, nearly taking it clean off the man's shoulders.

The rest of the guards fell quickly, and soon Xerxes was standing in the middle of a pile of bodies and severed limbs, covered in blood.

"Not the most elegant display of fighting skill I've ever seen, but effective," Vi declared, walking up to Xerxes and patting him on the arm.

"Nice work bro," Hunter agreed. "Come on."

They went through the large door the guards had come through, finding a wide staircase leading down to a wide hallway. At the end of it were two huge metal doors, both of which were closed. Xerxes ran down the stairs, watching as Hunter glided down beside him.

Not for the first time, he wished *he* had wings.

He reached the bottom of the stairs, then sprinted up to the huge double-doors, ramming into them. And then ricocheting off.

They didn't even budge.

Xerxes grunted, flashing a few hand signals to an Ironclad behind him, one carrying a warhammer. The Ironclad lifted his weapon up and smashed it into the floor right before the doors…but it bounced off with a loud *clang*. The floor immediately underneath the doors was metal as well.

"Break up the granite," Vi suggested.

The Ironclad did so, smashing their warhammer into the granite flooring just in front of the doors. After a few minutes, he'd made a sizable hole. But the metal flooring under the doors extended as far down as the hole did; there was no way to get under.

"Well shit," Vi muttered.

"Now what?" Hunter asked.

"The ceiling," Vi proposed. "If we can get one floor above, and dig through *that* floor, we can get in."

"The ceiling's twenty feet high," Hunter pointed out.

"And you can fly me in," Vi reminded him. "And Xerxes can just go splat and heal."

"And then we open the doors from the inside and let them in," Hunter concluded. "Got it."

Suddenly there was a loud *thunk*, and then a screeching sound of metal on metal from beyond the double-doors. Then another *thunk*, and the doors swung slowly open.

"That won't be necessary," a voice from beyond stated.

Chapter 29

Hunter watched as the huge metal doors opened, revealing a long hallway beyond, the walls lined with guards. And there, standing before them, was a tall, slender man dressed in a simple gold, blue, and white robe. He looked to be Hunter's age, with long blonde hair and a long beard, and the man's sharp blue eyes regarded each of them calmly. Hunter drew his sword, staring the man down.

"And who are you?" he inquired.

"I am King Tykus," the man declared calmly. "And who, may I ask, are you?"

Hunter stared at the man, hardly believing his ears.

"*You're* the king?" he blurted out.

"Yes."

"But…" Hunter protested.

"He's a reincarnation," Vi explained. "The old king died a month or two ago. They exposed some poor kid to Tykus's Ossae."

"That is correct," Tykus agreed. "Please," he added, "…introduce yourselves."

"This is Hunter," Vi replied. "I'm Vi. And this is Xerxes," she added, gesturing at the big guy. "This is our army," she said, gesturing at the Ironclad.

"Welcome," Tykus greeted.

"Are we though?" Vi countered.

"My doors are open."

"Granted," Vi conceded. "But only after we kicked your army's ass."

Tykus chuckled.

"You'll find my army is many times larger than you may have anticipated," he replied. "If I were to wish it, you would not find getting out so easy as you did getting in."

"You sure about that?" Vi retorted.

"Quite."

"So you're saying you just let us in here?" Hunter asked incredulously. "I call bullshit."

"Not at first," Tykus admitted. "Your tunneling under the walls was quite successful, and unexpected. But I ordered the bulk of my army to fall back when I heard who was leading the charge," he added, gesturing at Xerxes.

"Gonna have to explain that," Vi grumbled.

"He's Neesha's boy," Tykus explained.

Vi glanced at Hunter, who glanced at Xerxes. Xerxes grunted.

"Okay, now I'm confused," Hunter admitted.

"If you let us in here, then you're an idiot," Vi stated, crossing her arms over her chest. "We're armed and you're not. I could kill you in a heartbeat."

"Probably," Tykus agreed.

Vi just stared at him.

"You sure you're the 'great' King Tykus?" she asked. "Because so far I'm not impressed."

"To be fair," Tykus replied, "...you haven't taken a chance to get to know me yet."

"Not interested," Vi shot back. "This is purely business." Tykus smiled.

"Business is always personal."

"Spare me the bullshit," Vi grumbled. "Why'd you order the dukes to go to wipe out the Ironclad?"

"You mean the dukes I killed?" Tykus inquired. "They're hardly in a position to execute my orders."

Vi frowned.

"You killed your own dukes?"

Just then, a man sprinted into the great hall through the double-doors; a middle-aged man with short blonde hair, a stern face, and wearing a simple black shirt and pants. He skid to a halt before the assembled Ironclad, his eyes widening.

"Your Highness!" the man cried.

"All except for one," Tykus corrected, smiling at the man. "Hello Dominus."

Hunter's eyes widened, and he stared at the man incredulously, his hand going to the hilt of his sword.

"Wait, *this* is Dominus?" he asked Vi. "I thought he was old. And, you know, dead."

"He was," Vi confirmed. "Blue's head must've changed that."

"What's going on?" Dominus demanded.

"It seems Vi, Hunter, and the Ironclad have moved against us," Tykus replied calmly. "A pre-emptive strike after they received word that the Kingdom was planning to attack them."

"Hey Dominus," Vi greeted, putting her hands on her hips. "Miss me?"

"Step away from the king at once!" Dominus commanded, drawing his sword and glaring at them.

"You killed my friend, asshole," Hunter spat. "Then you tried to kill Vi and my brother!" He strode toward Dominus, his mouth set in a grim line. "And now I'm gonna kill you."

"Whoa there kiddo," Vi said, stepping in front of him and stopping him with an outstretched hand. "Reel it in."

"No," Hunter said, shoving her hand away. "He doesn't get to live after everything he did to us!"

"By all means," Dominus stated, eyeing him coldly. "Make the attempt."

"Enough!" Tykus shouted, his voice suddenly powerful. It cut right to Hunter's soul, stopping him in his tracks. He turned toward the king.

"I don't take…" he began, but Vi cut him off.

"Shut up Hunter," she ordered. "Now."

Hunter's mouth clicked shut. He glared at her, but obeyed. Tykus sighed, turning to Hunter. The king walked right up to him, putting a hand on his shoulder.

"I've lived oh, over a hundred lifetimes," he stated. "And I can tell you that if there's one thing I've learned, it's that revenge is a poison. One that you drink first before handing it to your enemy."

"I'm not letting him get away with what he did," Hunter retorted, pulling his shoulder away.

"Of course not," Tykus agreed. "But killing him would only be necessary if he continued to pose a threat to you. Which, I assure you, he does not."

"Says the man who ordered the genocide of the Ironclad," Vi pointed out. Tykus grimaced.

"I ordered it only to appease my dukes," he replied. "Dukes that I had every intention of…replacing before they had any opportunity to carry out that order. I have no animosity toward your people," he added, nodding at Xerxes. "Or Neesha."

Hunter blinked.

"You know my mother?" he asked. It was Tykus's turn to look surprised.

"You're her son?" he inquired. He had the audacity to laugh. "Oh, what a tangled web you've woven, Dominus!"

"My liege, I…"

"Oh, don't bother defending yourself," Tykus interrupted. "Their minds are already made up." He turned to Vi. "I ordered the Ironclad destroyed knowing full well the Guild of Seekers would turn against the kingdom. I used the opportunity to purge my dukes, strip Dominus of his title, and destroy the guild. Neesha was never in any danger…not that I could ever pose a danger to her."

"What do you mean?" Vi asked.

"Why, she's invincible, naturally," Tykus replied, his eyes twinkling. "And she's a Legend, whereas I am a mere copy of one. If she chose, she could march through Tykus and single-handedly destroy it, changing everyone within into a lesser copy of herself. Including me."

No one said anything. It was painfully obvious that Tykus was right.

"So why," the king continued, "…would I ever attempt to move against her?"

Vi lowered her gaze, shaking her head.

"Well shit," she muttered.

"But…" Hunter began, but Vi shot him a glare. He grimaced.

"I have no animosity toward you," Tykus insisted calmly. "Even though you've invaded my home, killed my guards, and threatened my life. I have every reason to seek revenge on you, wouldn't you agree?" he inquired, raising an eyebrow at Hunter.

Hunter lowered his gaze, swallowing in a dry throat.

"But I understand this was all a misunderstanding," Tykus continued. "And in talking with each other – and listening to each other – we can do far more good than anything accomplished by the edge of our blades."

"I'll give you this," Vi piped up. "You're a smooth talker." Tykus chuckled.

"I assure you there is no artifice in my speech," he replied. "I speak the truth because I have no need for lies. I suspect you're the same," he added. Vi nodded grudgingly.

"Guilty as charged."

"Hunter, I respect your mother," Tykus stated. "She's a fine woman, and I've enjoyed our many conversations over the years. You have a great deal to learn from her." He turned to Xerxes. "Dominus and the guild ordered you to be beheaded," he stated. "My apologies," he added. "This would not have happened under my watch."

Xerxes said nothing.

"Yet you recovered from this injury," Tykus noted. "Are your memories intact?"

"YES."

"Remarkable!" the king exclaimed. "I should like to ask you more questions about this later, if you're agreeable." He turned to Dominus then. "Dominus, it appears that, while I was dead, you created a few unnecessary enemies. I regret that I was not there to counsel you."

Dominus lowered his gaze, clearly ashamed.

"That's it?" Hunter blurted out. "We're just going to forgive him?" Tykus nodded.

"Well of course."

"Hell no," Hunter retorted. "He doesn't get off that easy."

"Easy?" Tykus inquired. "Oh no. I suspect it's going to be quite difficult for him. In any case, we have a great deal more to worry about than each other," Tykus warned. "It seems that the Svartálfar have returned."

"The dark elves?" Vi replied, her eyebrows going up.

"Yes," Tykus confirmed.

"How?" Vi pressed.

"Because Zagamar has returned," Dominus answered. Everyone turned to him.

"What?" Hunter blurted out.

"High Seeker Zeno entered the Crypt of Zagamar," Dominus explained. "And brought your head with him," he added, gesturing at Xerxes. "A few days later, I was attacked by a horde of dark elves."

"You're saying Zagamar was the source of the Svartálfar?" Vi asked. Tykus nodded.

"He was the Legend that created them," he explained. "They are incomplete and inferior copies of him. And now, everywhere he goes, he will be creating an army of clones that will do his bidding."

"Shit," Hunter swore.

"You can say that again," Vi muttered.

"We can only guess as to Zagamar's intentions," Tykus continued, "...but if history is any indication of the future – which it usually is – then we are in dire trouble."

"I don't need to guess at his intentions," Hunter retorted. "I *know* his intentions." Tykus frowned at him.

"Explain."

"Zeno may have gotten to Zagamar, but I got to him first," Hunter revealed. "I drank some of his brains. He's inside of me now."

"Then I'm afraid you are doomed," Tykus replied apologetically. "He will take over your body slowly – you are an Original, after all – but he will dominate you. We cannot have one Zagamar to contend with, much less two. The only solution would be..."

"To go to the Deep?" Vi interjected. "Yeah, already done. Zagamar can't dominate him anymore."

"Ah," Tykus murmured, his eyes brightening. "Excellent!"

"Not so excellent," Hunter shot back. "This guy is a megalomaniac. He's scary smart, and he thinks and moves like everything and everyone else around him is in slow-motion. And he wants to rule the world...to change everything into a version of himself. He thinks he's the pinnacle of human evolution."

"Then we *are* in trouble," Tykus observed. "For not only is Zagamar reborn, but he was reborn with a hint of your power," he explained, gesturing at Xerxes."

"Wait," Hunter blurted out. "You're saying he can *regenerate*?"

"Yes, as can his copies, to a lesser extent."

"Well, we're dead," Hunter declared.

"We're not dead yet," Vi countered. She turned to Tykus. "I assume you have a plan?"

"Of course," Tykus replied with a smile. "I've planned for this contingency for millennia. As I've planned for every potential catastrophic event…including your siege today."

"You *expected* this?" Hunter asked incredulously. Tykus smirked.

"Did I seem surprised?" he inquired. Hunter grimaced. The man hadn't, of course. "I find planning for tragedy to be the most effective antidote for fear," Tykus mused. "Anxiety is nothing more than the fear of being helpless in the face of the future."

Vi crossed her arms in front of her chest.

"Gotta say what everyone else is thinking," she stated. "What the hell?"

"Pardon?" Tykus inquired.

"What's a guy like you doing leading a kingdom like this?" she stated. "You're nothing like these assholes," she added, gesturing at Dominus.

"He's playing us," Hunter guessed. Vi shook her head.

"No. I know when I'm being played," she countered. "This guy's for real."

"A kingdom takes men of all kinds to operate," Tykus answered. "Personality is destiny, and there are many types. Each has a place within the whole, much like the parts that make up our bodies. And even I daresay that none of our bodies would function very well without our…" he added, gesturing at Dominus, "…assholes."

Dominus grimaced at that.

"I…" he began, but Tykus waved him off.

"Suffice it to say that my kingdom – and the world – is in grave danger," the king declared. "The Svartálfar are a much greater threat to me than all of you are," he added. "Most human Legends have the good sense to limit their influence on the world as much as possible. Zagamar does not."

"You're one to talk," Hunter grumbled. Tykus raised an eyebrow.

"Explain."

"You run a kingdom that forces everyone that isn't blonde-haired and blue-eyed to either sling shit in the Outskirts for the rest of their lives or change themselves until they *do* fit in," Hunter complained. "And I was one of them."

"True," Tykus admitted. "But my influence is limited. Or did you believe that this great wall I had built around the kingdom was to keep things out?"

Hunter stared at him mutely.

"If I chose to, I could have expanded this kingdom across the world," Tykus continued. "I could have used my Ossae to transform the world into my likeness, reigning over a vast empire. But I have not done so. My kingdom is limited, self-contained. Even my people do not have access to my Ossae; they are to be used only to reincarnate me, and to create my guards and scouts." He smiled. "I have no more desire to rule the world than you do."

"He's got a point kiddo," Vi conceded.

"I still don't trust him," Hunter countered. He paused, then took off his helmet, stepping up to the king. "If you're telling the truth, you won't mind me absorbing some of your memories."

Tykus gave him a surprised look.

"You have the gift?" he inquired.

"Yes."

"A rare gift indeed, to be able to see things from another's perspective," Tykus murmured. "By all means."

Hunter held the king's temples in his hands, then touched his forehead to Tykus's.

* * *

He found himself standing on a large ship docked at port, a bitter cold wind whipping through the air. Sailors went about their tasks preparing for the upcoming voyage, bringing the last of the rations aboard. A tall man stood on the deck before him, rugged but handsome, a bit of gray in his beard. His father…the greatest man he'd ever met, and would likely *ever* meet.

Father smiled, putting a hand on Tykus's shoulder.

"Good luck Tykus," he said. Tykus glanced back at a burly, brutish man on the other end of the ship, shouting at one of the crew. It was his uncle Thorvald. Tykus grimaced.

"I'll need it, father."

His father chuckled, patting Tykus's shoulder.

"A wolf and a dog never play," he quoted. "But remember: if you fight with a pig, you'll get his stink on you."

Tykus smiled, and his father ruffled his hair affectionately.

"There's a great man inside of you," his father insisted. "It's your job to find him and bring him out."

"Yes father."

"I look forward to meeting the man you'll become," he continued, squeezing Tykus's shoulder. "You're an Erickson," he added. "Make me proud."

* * *

Hunter gasped, stumbling back from Tykus, his eyes snapping open.

"Jesus," he breathed. He felt other memories flash in his mind's eye, and knew without a shadow of a doubt that the king was genuine. He stared at the king, feeling a chill run down his spine. The mere sliver of Tykus's soul he'd experienced had been…indescribable.

"Are you convinced?" Tykus inquired. Hunter nodded.

"He's for real," Hunter declared. As much as he disagreed with the man's methods, he could no longer disagree that Tykus lived up to the reverence his people had for him.

"Alright," Vi decided. "You said you had a plan for every contingency. What's your plan for Zagamar?"

"To defeat him, we have to work together," Tykus answered. "All of us. We must band together as people and as kingdoms, uniting our people against a common threat. And we must strike early. The longer Zagamar has to build his army, the more difficult our task will become."

"Wait, you're asking us to work with *him*?" Hunter blurted out, pointing at Dominus.

"Yes," Tykus confirmed. "That is your penance, Dominus…and your opportunity for forgiveness, Hunter. It is far too easy to commit violence against someone you don't know. That is why nations dehumanize their enemies before attacking them."

"Like you did to the Ironclad," Hunter pointed out.

"To justify building the wall that limits our influence, yes," Tykus replied.

"Ah."

"You will work together, fight together, and protect each other. You will get to know each other's perspectives. And that," he added with a smile, "…is the only way an enemy can become a friend."

"Your Highness," Dominus protested.

"Call me Tykus," Tykus reminded him. "Do you trust me?"

"Implicitly," Dominus answered.

"Then consider this the end of our conversation," Tykus concluded. "Thank you for your consideration," he added, walking up to Hunter, Vi, and Xerxes and shaking their hands. "We will be in touch."

"Uh…how?" Hunter asked.

"I am everywhere," he answered. "Rest assured that one of me will come to you."

Chapter 30

"Zac," a man's voice greeted.

Zac glanced up from the paperwork spread out on the table before him. His faithful general, General Roden, had entered his tent. Old and bent now, but still strong, the man's blue eyes had long since darkened with exposure to Zac's will. They were so similar now that at first glance it would be hard to tell them apart. Still, Zac had never allowed anyone to become as much…him as Zooey had. The general kept his distance as was required, standing at the entrance of the tent.

"Yes?" Zac prompted.

"The men and I have been talking," Roden admitted. "We…don't think this is a good idea."

"I know," Zac replied.

"It's just…" Roden paused, and Zac waited for him to continue. "We're doing so well. We're strong. I'm not sure it's wise to do this right now."

"I know," Zac repeated.

"There's no way to be sure of what will happen," Roden pressed. Zac sighed.

"General," he stated. "I know. I know everything you're going to say. I know every argument you'll make. All of them."

Roden grimaced, lowering his gaze.

"I know," he mumbled. "I just…"

"You care about me," Zac interjected. General Roden nodded.

"We all do, sir."

"And I care about you," Zac replied. "You've been at my side for thirty years, Roden. You've stayed when others betrayed me. When the armies of the three kingdoms threatened to annihilate us."

"Of course sir," Roden replied. "I would do it again. And not just because a part of me is you."

Zac smiled.

"If this fails, take my body to the crypt," Zac stated. "You have my will, Roden. It's all there."

"Yes sir."

"Carry on without me then."

"Yes sir."

"Is that all, Roden?" Zac inquired. Roden hesitated.

"Be careful, sir," he insisted.

"I will."

Roden bowed, then left, and Zac sighed, lowering his gaze to the papers on his desk. Logistics of running his army. Larger now than it'd ever been, but still much smaller than the armies they'd faced in the past…and those they'd fight in the future. But what Zac lacked in numbers, he more than made up for with his mind.

His inventions…and strategy…had won them every battle.

The kingdoms had risen against him, one after the other. Each with a ruler that was, or had been, a Legend like Zac. Each dead-set on stopping Zac from forming his own kingdom. It was always the same.

If they don't belong, subjugate them. If they're strong, destroy them.

And these rulers, these Legends and false Legends, and copies of former Legends…they fooled their people into scrambling to be just like them. And that anyone who wasn't was…unacceptable. Tyranny in its subtlest form.

I will free them all.

He reached out for one of the papers on his desk, a message from the Kingdom of the Deep. One of the few kingdoms that had not tried to stop him…and the self-appointed guardians of the Deep.

We appreciate your request to visit the Deep, but we must deny it. Our allies are your enemies, and while we have no desire to move against you, we will not aid you.

Zac stared at the page, then crumpled it up. He'd already sent a reply, of course. And by the time the Elders of the Kingdom of the Deep received it, it would be too late.

He glanced over at the cage in the middle of his tent, at the creature within. It'd taken him years to find it. A creature with jet-black skin and long, thin arms and legs. It was vaguely humanoid, and moved with incredible speed.

A Makadewa.

They were rare, and difficult to capture on account of their vicious tempers and sheer speed. And this one was rare indeed; a Makadewa with a near-Legendary will, at least for its appearance. Time had taught Zac that while his own mind was indeed Legendary, his appearance was only nearly so. If the Deep truly did merge creatures, he could keep his mind yet gain the Makadewa's speed. And more importantly, its other incredible trait.

It never aged.

The only way for a Makadewa to die was to be killed. And if Zac could find another creature, one with the ability to heal rapidly, or even regenerate, he would become unstoppable. He would never die…all at the expense of a voracious appetite.

Zac stared at the creature even as it stared at him. Then he walked up to it, grimacing at a pain in his right hip as he did so. He'd spent a great deal of time close to the creature, but his body hadn't really changed much. A disappointment. Only the Deep had a chance of merging them, while keeping his body humanoid.

At sixty years old, Zac's time was running out. And he still had so much to do. So much he needed to accomplish.

He'd gone through every contingency, of course. If the melding worked, and he gained the Makadewa's immortality, all would be well. If not, his heightened metabolism would likely accelerate the aging process.

And General Roden would have to take him to the mountain.

Zac hesitated, then grabbed the cage, picking it up and walking it out of the tent. Sunlight streamed down on his face as he stepped outside, and he squinted, waiting for his eyes to adjust.

Standing before them in the distance was a huge mountain, a narrow dirt path leading up to the foot of it. A path littered with bones. There had been a great asylum built here long ago, one that had fallen into ruin. But the bones of the insane remained, their wills as powerful as they'd been in life.

The perfect location for Zac's crypt.

He watched as men wearing large wooden helmets trudged up the path toward the entrance to his crypt, dragging prisoners of war behind them. The able-bodied would be forced to build the crypt's many defenses, and the great tomb itself. And the few insane men and women that Zac had collected over the years, some with wills nearly as powerful as his own…they would serve a different purpose. To protect his tomb from the unworthy.

A tomb that, with the benefit of his great intellect, would withstand the ages, preserving his flesh for eternity.

He glanced down at the cage he held, studying the Makadewa for the umpteenth time. How fast it breathed. How quickly it moved. How it studied him. It'd undoubtedly gained the power of his mind, being so close to him for so long, but its body had not changed.

"We'll be together soon," he promised, smiling at the creature. "You and I. You'll make me better," he added. "And together, we'll make the *world* better."

* * *

It was already early afternoon by the time Hunter, Xerxes, Vi, and Dominus passed beyond the Deadlands to the Fringe, reaching the deep forest beyond. The army of Ironclad had left the city, what remained of the City Guard under orders from the king himself not to intervene. Being accustomed to flying everywhere – at a fraction of the time it took to travel on foot – Hunter found himself impatient and irritated. Which could've very well been because of his trek through the Fringe, absorbing the emotion there. He found that he absorbed less with his helmet on however, just as he rarely absorbed memories when he wore it.

He'd said very little during the trip, and Vi must've noticed.

"What's on your mind?" she asked, walking at his side. Hunter grimaced.

"Something that happened back in Lowtown," he confessed. She waited for him to continue, and he sighed. "The Kingdom set a bunch of Ironclad on fire," he continued. "I tried to stop them, but I was too slow."

"I see."

"If I'd been quicker, I could have…"

"Stop," Vi interrupted.

"What?"

"You heard me," she replied. "I know what you're doing. You're blaming yourself. Beating yourself up. Who's that going to help?"

"It isn't," Hunter answered. "But…"

"You did good Hunter," Vi interjected. "You did a lot of things that saved lives. People die in war. You can't save them all."

"I know."

"But your heart doesn't," she pointed out. "Your heart's the thing I like most about you, kiddo. But you have to learn how to forgive yourself. Take your licks, feel terrible, then learn from it. Be better next time."

He swallowed past a lump in his throat.

"Forgiving yourself is a skill just like anything else," Vi stated. "If you want to lead a big life – a life where your successes matter – then your mistakes are going to matter too."

He nodded.

"Thanks Vi," he mumbled.

"Any time, Hunter."

They walked side-by-side in silence for a while, until Hunter cleared his throat.

"Vi?"

"Yeah?"

"This Tykus," he began, then paused. Since leaving the kingdom, he'd found himself preoccupied with the king's memories. Fragments of thoughts, of book passages. Of stone tablets with precious revelations carved into them. He'd absorbed the memories of many men, but Tykus's were different.

"What about him?" she pressed.

"His memories…it's…" He shook his head. "I can't explain it."

"Try," she urged. Hunter noticed Dominus staring at him, coming closer to listen.

"He's everything he says he is," Hunter explained. "And so much more. We need to listen to him. I mean we *really* need to listen to him."

"You might've absorbed his memories a bit too much," Vi warned. "It can change your perspective."

"No," Hunter replied, shaking his head. "I only got a glimpse, but trust me, that's all I needed. The man is unlike anyone I've ever met. He's better than we are. Better than all of us. Scary smart, Vi. Like Zagamar, except he's a good guy."

"Well, we don't have a choice but to listen to him," Vi ventured. "Zagamar's not gonna stop at destroying the Kingdom. He'll go after us too. The Ironclad, and the Kingdom of the Deep. Everyone."

"AGREE," Xerxes piped in.

"Lady Camilla has already contacted the Kingdom of the Deep," Dominus revealed. Everyone turned to him.

"You've talked with Camilla?" Vi inquired.

"Yes," Dominus confirmed, ignoring Hunter's comment. "We've become allies."

"Figures," Hunter grumbled.

"She may be a manipulative bitch," Vi told Hunter, "...but Camilla's resourceful. We could use her help too."

"I agree," Dominus concurred.

"Well I don't," Hunter retorted. "Or have you forgotten what the 'Lady' did to me?"

"Gonna have to set that aside for now," Vi counseled.

"Like hell I will!"

"Fate of the world depends on it kiddo," Vi argued. "You can tell her to fuck off after we kill the megalomaniacal Legend and his hordes."

"Awesome," Hunter muttered. "This just keeps getting better and better."

They continued in silence, much to Hunter's relief. He found Dominus stealing glances at him, and gave the former duke an irritated look.

"What?" he snapped.

"Your wings," Dominus replied. "I find them...curious."

"What, 'cause I'm 'corrupted' now?" Hunter guessed. Dominus grimaced.

"I am corrupted as well," he countered. "Tykus has taught me the error of my previous...philosophy."

"Well let's all sing 'kumbaya' then," Hunter grumbled.

"What?"

"Look, just because we have to work with you doesn't mean we like you," Hunter said. "You don't get a pass for everything you did to us."

"Naturally," Dominus agreed. "This is an alliance of necessity."

"Glad you get that."

They fell silent, continuing their trek through the woods. It was over an hour later that Hunter spotted a river to their right, and Xerxes led them along its shore until the grass turned black, crunching under their feet. The big guy angled back into the woods then, eventually bringing them to the front entrance of the Ironclad caves. Xerxes flashed hand signals at the many Ironclad guarding the entrance, and they let everyone pass, including Dominus. Hunter followed Xerxes through the maze of tunnels, eventually reaching his mother's chamber.

Hunter froze.

There was a man in a brown cloak standing at the edge of the pool, facing Neesha, who was wading in the pool a few yards away. Neesha glanced at Hunter, Vi, Xerxes, and Dominus. And Dominus stared at Neesha, his jaw going slack.

"Come in," she prompted.

They did so, everyone stopping at the edge of the pool, to the right of the cloaked man. A hood covered his head, his face hidden in shadow.

"WHO…THIS?" Xerxes demanded.

The cloaked man turned to face them, reaching up and pulling the hood down, revealing himself. His hair was short and gray, his face smooth-shaven. Despite his age, he looked terribly familiar.

"Tykus!" Dominus gasped, staring at the man, who smiled.

"Indeed," he replied. "I take it these are your boys, Neesha? And Vi?" he inquired, gesturing at everyone.

"They are," Neesha confirmed. "Tykus and I were just finishing our conversation," she added. "It appears we were mistaken in attacking the Kingdom. My apologies once again, Tykus."

"A terrible misunderstanding," Tykus replied. "I trust you spoke with the king?" he asked, glancing at Hunter and Vi.

"We did," Vi confirmed. "So you're another Tykus?"

"Correct."

"He came here after we attacked the military base in the Deadlands," Neesha explained. "If we'd had the opportunity to talk earlier, none of this would have happened."

"I can guarantee you that the king takes full responsibility," Tykus assured her. "Tell me about your conversation with him," he requested of Vi and Hunter.

Vi told the tale, with Hunter and Dominus providing details along the way. When they were done, middle-aged Tykus sighed heavily.

"I wasn't aware of the return of the Svartálfar," he confessed. "It's been too long since I visited the king…and since I've visited you, Neesha. Lack of communication has led to unnecessary tragedy…as it so often does."

"We have to prepare for war with Zagamar," Vi stated. "Camilla is coordinating with the Kingdom of the Deep, and we're coordinating with Tykus. With their armies and ours, we might stand a chance against this guy."

"I will help, of course," older Tykus stated. He removed his cloak, revealing fine silver chain-mail armor…and a large sword at his hip. Not to mention big, burly arms…at least twice the size of the king's.

"Damn Tykus," Vi exclaimed, reaching over and squeezing his biceps. "You been working out?"

"I come from a people that valued the martial arts," Tykus replied. "Neesha could tell you about them…apparently my father is nearly as legendary in your world as I am in this one."

"You're coming with us?" Hunter asked.

"If you'll have me."

"We would be honored," Dominus declared, bowing before the man.

"We have a goal," Vi stated. "Now we need a plan. How exactly do we plan on taking Zagamar down?"

"His Svartálfar will grow in number every day," Tykus answered. "They are voracious eaters, and will consume everything – plant or animal – that they find. They're excellent fighters, mostly due to their speed and their claws. We must focus on finding and killing Zagamar before he can build a sizable army."

"So we go hunting then," Vi replied. "Where are these dark elves?"

"Zagamar must have emerged from his crypt," Dominus reasoned. "There's a mountain range blocking his way to the west. We spotted Svartálfar at Camilla's, to the east. The Kingdom of the Deep is to the south, and we're…the Kingdom is to the north. Zagamar will either go north or south."

"Likely north," Neesha reasoned. "The Kingdom of the Deep managed to repel Zagamar the first time. He'll remember that defeat. No offense, but your kingdom is an easier target," she added, giving Tykus an apologetic look.

"No offense taken," Tykus replied. "Insisting on remaining 'human' is a significant disadvantage in this context."

"If our armies work together and march south, we can cull the Svartálfar and limit Zagamar's range," Neesha offered. "The Kingdom of the Deep can send their armies north, and we can meet in the middle."

"A pincher attack," Hunter translated.

"I can contact another one of me and have them notify the king," Tykus said. He turned to Dominus. "Your access to the Kingdom of the Deep is through Lady Camilla…you'll need to contact her."

"I will," Dominus promised.

"Hunter, with your wings, you'll be instrumental in locating the Svartálfar," Neesha noted. "I'll need you to scout from the Crypt of Zagamar outward starting tomorrow."

"Got it," Hunter agreed.

"Vi and Xerxes, you'll be in charge of my armies. After Hunter locates the Svartálfar, you'll go in and eradicate them."

"Be careful," Dominus warned. "They're extremely dangerous, even for me."

"In the meantime, Vi, if you could continue to train Sukri?" Neesha requested.

"Sure."

"And Hunter, you'll need to fly Dominus back to Camilla's," Neesha stated. Hunter raised his eyebrows.

"Excuse me?"

"Hunter…" Neesha began.

"You don't want me going back to that bitch," Hunter interrupted. "Because if I do, I'm going to kill her. Unless she decides to make me her prisoner again, which she very well might."

"She will not," Dominus promised.

"You don't know her," Hunter retorted.

"But I do know how she thinks," Dominus countered. "Camilla's a pragmatist. It would be strategically foolish to alienate the son of the queen of the Ironclad…and in doing so, threaten her relationship with Tykus and myself."

"He's got you there, kiddo," Vi pointed out.

"In any case, it will not be necessary," Dominus said. "Camilla has already arranged transport back."

"But Hunter needs to head to the Crypt of Zagamar," Neesha pointed out. "Camilla's mansion is on the way."

"And Camilla has scouts that may have already pointed out some of the locations of the dark elves," Dominus realized. "Hunter will need to know where not to look." He nodded. "Very well."

Hunter sighed.

"Fine," he muttered. "I'll take you."

"Go then," Neesha ordered. "We don't have time to waste."

"Can I at least say hi to Sukri?" Hunter asked. Vi smirked, nudging him with her elbow.

"Hunter wants to *get* some," she teased.

"Fine," Neesha replied. She smirked at Hunter. "Just don't get her pregnant yet, okay?" Hunter's cheeks turned hot, and he glared at her.

"Mom!"

"Not for nothing, your babies are gonna be *gruesome*," Vi quipped.

"I'm leaving now," Hunter declared, turning about and doing just that. He heard laughter behind him, and shook his head, blushing furiously. Even Tykus was joining in on the fun; his laughter was the loudest by far.

Their voices died off as Hunter made his way through the large tunnel leading out of the Ironclad lair, toward the surface…and Sukri.

CHAPTER 31

The sunlight filtering through the leaves and branches of the deep forest was waning by the time Dio reached the banks of the River Ormr. He limped over the wet, packed sand by the shore, his left knee aching after his leap from the bridge to the Kingdom of the Deep. He'd jackknifed perfectly into the water hundreds of feet below, but the force of the impact had injured his knee and the left side of his chest. Every breath hurt, and he found himself having to stop to catch his breath every few minutes.

He was lucky to be alive.

Dio grimaced, following the river as it wound its way toward Lady Camilla's mansion, barely visible in the distance. Mother would not be pleased. Both the girl and the Original had escaped him, a grave failure.

And he was *not* accustomed to failure…nor was Mother accustomed to him failing. Every step closer to the mansion was a step closer to facing her wrath.

He heard a rustling to his left, at the tree line.

Dio kept walking, turning his head slightly toward the tree line, studying it. There was nothing there…not visible to his eyes, anyway. But taking the spirit of a snake – among other things – had given him the ability to sense the heat of living things through organs between his eyes.

And within the relative coolness of the forest, three red-hot shapes moved parallel to him.

He studied them, noting how they kept pace with him. They were hotter than any living thing he'd ever sensed, indicating an exceedingly fast metabolism. A trait found in smaller animals. But these were not small; they were half to three-quarters the size of a man, walking on all fours.

Dio slowed, catching his breath. The creatures slowed with him.

They were stalking him.

Dio stopped, retrieving his staff and turning to face them. The creatures stopped as well, staring at him. He could see them now, with his normal vision. Black-skinned creatures with long arms and legs, their faces vaguely human. Hybrids, but none like he'd ever seen.

He waited, standing there at the shore, staring at them.

They watched for a moment longer, then burst out of the trees, rushing right at him!

Dio whipped his staff at the nearest creature, but it dodged out of the way, moving even faster than he had. He followed up with three more strikes, his staff a silver blur before him. One landed, smashing one of the creatures in the jaw, sending it flying to the ground.

The other two lunged at him from either side.

Dio leapt into the air high above their heads, watching as they collided with each other below him. Then he brought his staff down on one of their backs, the blade at the end severing its spine.

He ignored the sharp pain in his knee as he landed, whirling his staff at the third creature, stringing one attack after the other in rapid sequence.

It ducked and dodged, evading every single attack, then leaping in and slashing at Dio's face with its claws. Dio jerked his head back, the thing's claws clipping his mask and sending it flying from his face.

He counterattacked, kicking it in the throat, then swinging at its temple. The beast ducked back out of range just in time, clutching at its throat, staring at him with sunken black eyes.

Dio stood there, his breath coming in short gasps, each one sending a sharp pain through his chest to his back. The first creature he'd attacked – the one he'd clipped in the jaw – got to its feet, slinking on all fours toward him.

Dio waited.

They lunged for him as one, and Dio backpedaled out of range. But it'd been a feint; one followed with another attack, the other reaching down and throwing a clump of sand at Dio's face. Dio feigned surprise, jerking back and closing his eyes.

Their heat-signatures, of course, were still visible to him.

He side-stepped the first creature's attack, smashing it in the face, then leapt at the second one, attacking at every possible angle, moving quicker than the creatures would've thought possible. His body was utterly relaxed, each attack leading into the next, an endless symphony of death.

The beast tried to evade him, but failed, Dio's staff striking it again and again, cutting it to shreds.

Then he turned to the other one, chopping its head clean off.

He glanced at the third creature, the one with the severed spine. It was watching him.

He decapitated it, and it watched no more.

Dio stood there for a long moment, waiting for his breathing to slow. Then he retrieved his mask, turning back toward the mansion. Continuing along the river, he kept his eyes – and heat sensors – on the forest to his left.

A few minutes later, he spotted more of the creatures, matching his pace and angling from the deeper forest toward the river.

A lot more.

He counted sixteen of them, nearly identical to the ones he'd killed earlier. All of them at the tree line now, staring at him.

Dio pulled his staff from his back, continuing to walk. The mansion was still over a kilometer away, and he was in no condition to run. He stopped, turning to face them, and waited.

He didn't have to wait long.

All sixteen of them burst from the tree line, rushing right for him.

Dio waited for the first ones to reach him, then burst into action, his body and staff moving as one. It whirled so quickly around him that it was impossible for the human eye to follow…and promised death to anything it touched. It struck one beast, then another, fulfilling that promise.

But the others were equally fast, somehow managing to dodge many of his attacks. He killed a third, feeling his breaths coming in shorter gasps, his movements getting slower. One of the beasts managed to get past his whirling staff, ramming into his shoulder.

He relaxed into the blow, letting his body twist with it, and used the momentum to swing his staff hard against another creature's skull.

Another one got through, ducking under his staff and raking its claws down his right thigh. Dio stepped back with that leg, his leather armor tearing, and brought one end of his staff straight down on its head.

Just as yet another one leapt right at his throat.

Dio dropped into a backwards somersault, the creature flying over him as he did so. Then he leapt to his feet, spinning around and slashing the thing's throat.

Something slammed into his back, knocking him forward toward the water.

Dio caught himself, whipping his staff around at his attacker, but it'd already backed out of range. Ten of the enemy were still alive, keeping just out of striking distance.

He clutched his side, gasping for air, feeling suddenly lightheaded. His legs felt weak, and began to shake uncontrollably.

I'm going to die.

The thought came to him without fear, nor surprise. It was a statement of fact, the realization that he had been bested. Uninjured, he could have annihilated these things. But through a series of unlikely events, reality had chosen a different end. He was going to die today.

But he would not go alone.

One of the beasts lunged at him, then drew back…just as another did the same…and a third leapt at him from the side, raking at his shoulder. He thrust his staff at it, knocking it backward…or rather shoving it. His arms were weakening.

And two more jumped on him from the front as he did so.

Dio tried to whip his staff around to take them both out, but he was too slow, and they collided with him, knocking him onto his back on the wet sand. The back of his head sank into cold water, and he gasped, trying to twist to throw the beasts off of him. But they were too heavy.

They raked at him with their claws, slashing at his chest and belly.

Dio bent his knees and dug his heels into the ground, then pushed himself backward, trying to throw himself into the river. The beasts pinned him down, two more grabbing his legs and dragging him back toward the forest. His staff was torn from his hands, his arms and legs pulled taught by four of the things.

And a fifth loomed over him, its grotesque face covered with patches of thin bark, its lips parting in a vicious snarl.

Dio stared at it silently, letting his body go lax.

It was time.

The beast on top of him reached out with one hand, wrapped its long black fingers around his throat. Dio felt its long, sharp claws dig into his flesh on either side of his windpipe, gripping it firmly. The creature leaned in, its breath hissing from between its teeth.

"You are worthy," it rasped. "Join…"

THUMP!

The ground trembled beneath Dio, screams piercing the air ahead of him. The creature twisted around, then leapt off Dio, running forward…and then flying through the air as something massive slammed into it from the side. Dio gasped, struggling to sit up.

And saw a huge silver serpent with innumerable legs rear its head back, lunging forward and snapping up two of the creatures in one gulp.

The horned serpent had burst through the forest, a line of downed trees evidence of its passage. The black creatures swarmed over it, raking at its thick scales. But it was futile; the serpent's hide was far too thick and strong for them, impervious to their attacks. It ended them all, eating, crushing, and trampling them to death until none remained.

Dio stared at the carnage in disbelief, then collapsed onto his back, staring at the bright blue sky above.

Thump-a-thump, thump-a-thump…

He heard the telltale sound of a horse approaching, heard it stop nearby. Someone dismounted. He tried to turn his head to see who it was, but he could not. His body felt numb, and far away, as if it belonged to someone else.

A figure crouched over him, a face filling his vision. A woman with long, dark hair, beautiful eyes and full lips.

A memory came to him, of the same face looking down at him. Of hands reaching for him, spattered with blood. The blood of the men that'd killed his parents.

I've got you, she'd said. *You don't have to be afraid anymore.*

Dio stared up at the woman, feeling her hand cradle the back of his head.

"Mother…" he gasped.

"Shhh," Camilla soothed, stroking his hair with her other hand.

"I…failed," he mumbled. "I…"

"It's okay Dio," she reassured. "I forgive you."

"But…"

"Close your eyes," she said, stroking his cheek. She leaned in, kissing his forehead gently. He obeyed, feeling her warm fingers against his face.

"Mother…"

"It's okay Dio," she insisted. "I've got you now."

Chapter 32

Sukri crouched down on all fours on the wide tree branch she'd climbed up to, some eight meters above the forest floor. She perched there, eyeing a branch from a nearby tree. It was a good three meters away, and a meter lower than the one she was on.

You can do this.

She readied herself, then sprang forward, sailing through the air…and coming up a little short.

Uh oh.

Sukri stretched her arms forward, extending her claws, and managed to grab onto the branch, swinging forward and nearly losing her grip. Her claws saved her, and she waited until she stopped swinging, pulling herself up onto the branch and crouching there.

"Damn," she muttered.

Looking around, she spotted another branch nearby, the same distance away as the first.

Okay, she told herself. *You got this.*

She readied herself, then leapt, her powerful legs launching her upward and forward. This time she reached the branch easily, landing feet-first on it…and nearly stumbling off, her momentum carrying her forward. She dug her feet-claws into the bark, pinwheeling her arms, then catching herself.

"Now *that's* what I'm talking about," she murmured.

Sukri tried again, leaping to another branch, then another, each time managing to land a little more gracefully, until she was leaping from branch to branch fearlessly, barely pausing between jumps. Once she got the hang of it, it felt *good.* Like she was flying through the trees.

At length she stopped, perching on one of the tree branches, eyeing a piece of fruit hanging from a nearby tree…right above a wide tree branch.

"Oh I'm gonna smack the shit outta you," she promised, extending her claws.

Then she leapt at it, sailing over the forest floor and slashing at the fruit with one paw. She nailed it, sending it flying in a spray of juice…and overshot the branch, careening toward the ground far below.

"Shiiiit!" she yelled, spreading her arms and legs out wide, then flipping her tail sharply. This righted her, and she landed on her hands and feet with a grunt.

Completely unharmed.

Sukri got to her feet, glancing up. She'd fallen a good eight to nine meters…a height that would've killed her ass if she'd been human. Or completely human, anyway. She smiled, shaking her head.

"Oh I could get used to *this*," she said.

She crouched, then leapt up six meters, reaching the tree trunk and using her claws to climb up rapidly. Within moments she was on the tree branch she'd missed, perched on all fours. Searching for another fruit, she found one…but with no branch to land on underneath.

"Eh, what the hell," she told herself.

Sukri sprang forward at it, slashing it right from the tree, cutting it to shreds. And plummeted toward the ground, landing on all fours just like before.

Again, unharmed.

"Damn Sukri," she murmured. "You are *awesome*."

She heard leaves crunching behind her, and spun around to see Hunter walking toward her. He was dressed in a plain brown shirt and pants, his helmet – as always – on his head.

"You know you do that butt-wiggle thing before you jump," Hunter told her with a grin. "It's *adorable*."

"Hunter!" she cried, running up to him and leaping into his arms.

"Claws!" Hunter exclaimed, pulling away from her.

"Oops," Sukri replied, retracting her claws. "Sorry." She held him at arm's length, realizing she was grinning stupidly. "How'd it go?"

"Well, I didn't die," Hunter answered with a grin of his own.

"I noticed."

"We got to Tykus," Hunter said. He told her about what'd happened…and about Zagamar and the Svartálfar. Her eyes widened with each revelation.

"I can't believe there's more than one Tykus," she stated. "You're saying they're all over the place?"

"One's working with us now," he replied. "He's with Vi and Xerxes."

"And Zagamar's making a bunch of clones of himself like Tykus did."

"Right," Hunter confirmed.

"So we kill the clones and then kill Zagamar," she ventured.

"That's the idea."

She stood there, considering this. Then she looked down at her hands, extending her claws.

"Guess I got more training to do," she muttered.

"Vi's going to train you some more," Hunter reassured. "I need to fly Dominus to Camilla's place so they can coordinate with the Kingdom of the Deep."

"Wait, what?" Sukri blurted out. "You're actually gonna go back to that bitch?"

"Unfortunately yes."

"But…"

"Dominus says she won't try to hold me captive like before," Hunter reassured. Sukri gave him a sour look.

"You really gonna trust him?"

"Of course not," Hunter retorted. "But she won't go against me. If she does, I'll just let Zagamar out and kill her."

"God I hope she tries then."

"Kinda hoping that too," Hunter admitted.

"So what now?" she inquired. Hunter raised an eyebrow.

"I seem to remember you promising me something," he answered. "Something about how you'd let me give you my goo if…"

"I remember," Sukri interrupted.

"So…?"

"If we do this, I have to tell Kayla," Sukri warned. "I think she still has feelings for me."

"Ah," he replied. He paused for a moment. "Do you?"

Sukri sighed, lowering her gaze.

"A little," she confessed. "I mean, she was really kind to me. The first person that's been kind to me in a while. And…it was good," she added. Hunter gave a rueful smile.

"I know," he admitted. "I might of, ah, absorbed that memory too."

Sukri's eyebrows went up.

"Oh *really*," she replied.

"I understand it if you…" Hunter began, but Sukri stepped forward, putting a finger to his lips.

"Shut up," she ordered. He obeyed, his mouth snapping shut. "I like Kayla. Being with her would be…nice. But I've put a lot of thought into this, and I think I want to try us."

"You 'think?'"

"I haven't tried it yet," Sukri pointed out.

"Maybe you could have both?" Hunter offered, waggling his eyebrows. "We could all…"

"No."

"Worth a shot," he mumbled.

"Hunter, I've spent my whole adult life going from one relationship to the next," she admitted. "Kris was right about me, you know."

Hunter grimaced. Kris had been one of her best friends…and Sukri had argued with him right before he'd been killed by an Ironclad.

"He said I was controlling. That I pretended to be this cool chick, but inside I was so scared that I tried to control everything, and pushed everyone away."

"Sukri…"

"Do you know why?" she pressed. "Because I'm terrified that it won't work out if I'm myself. That being myself won't be enough."

Hunter put his hands on her shoulders, smiling down at her.

"Sukri, I know you," he replied. "I can know you better than anyone else."

"You know how terrifying that is?"

"My point is, I want you. Just you. Be yourself, and we'll try that out. If it works, great. If not…well, at least we tried."

Sukri nodded.

"All right Hunter."

She stepped in, and he wrapped his arms around her, spreading his wings and enclosing her within them. He leaned in, pressing his lips against hers.

The world faded away.

They kissed for what seemed like an eternity, until Sukri pulled away, staring up at him.

"What now?" she asked.

"I have a few ideas," he replied with a twinkle in his eye.

"Oh yeah?" she said, giving him a little smile. "Like what, dirty boy?"

"I could show you."

"Please do," she replied, standing up on her tip-toes and kissing him again. Then she grinned.

"What?" he asked.

"Just glad kissing you isn't like kissing my brother."

"You have a brother?" he pressed.

"No, but I've kissed a few guys and it felt like, I dunno, making out with my dad."

"You made out with your dad?" he shot back, a disgusted look on his face. She shoved him backward.

"You wanna get lucky or not?"

"Uh…really?" he replied. "Don't you want to get to know me better first?"

"Gotta know if you're any good," she retorted. "Unless you *don't* want to do it."

Yes ma'am," he replied.

"Then take off your pants," she ordered extending her claws. "Before I cut them off."

***

Hunter grunted, rolling off Sukri and laying on his back, staring up at the ceiling of the small shack they were in, trying to catch his breath. It was a cozy wooden shack built for him by the Ironclad, a single room with a bed of animal skins on one side. And after everything he and Sukri had done, it was oppressively hot.

"God damn," he gasped, sweat trickling across his temples. "Wow."

Sukri rolled onto her side, draping a warm, furry arm over his chest, tracing her fingers over his pecs.

"Right?" she replied with a grin.

"Uh huh."

"Tell me that was as good for you as it was for me," she said. He glanced at her, grinning stupidly.

"Fuck yeah it was."

"You just telling a girl what she wants to hear?" she inquired.

"Nope," he answered. "That was…wow." And it had been. Her smell, her taste, the way she moved…the way she seemed to relish every second of touching him and being with him. It'd been incredible. Better than just sex.

It'd been something bigger.

"Mmm," Sukri murmured, leaning in and smelling his arm, then kissing it. "You smell *good* Hunter."

"So do you."

"Sorry 'bout all the hair," she ventured, looking down at herself. She had short hair all over her body, even her face, and big golden eyes now. Even more golden than they'd been earlier in the day. She was changing before his very eyes.

"It's a little itchy now," he confessed. "But when it grows in it'll be softer."

"Did I chafe you?"

"Only a little," he said with another grin. "Totally worth it."

"So you don't mind the hair?" she pressed.

"First of all, it's not hair, it's fur," Hunter corrected, sliding a hand down her arm. "And no, I don't mind it." He smirked. "Glad your tongue didn't turn rough, by the way. I was worried about that."

"Told you I was soft on the inside," she replied. While her tongue was soft, she did have longer and sharper canines now. Apparently they'd used needles at the base of her gums to make that happen.

"*Yeah* you are," he agreed. "Got no complaints about your mouth."

"Bet you don't," she agreed with a smile. Then she leaned in, kissing him.

There was a *bang*, and the door to the shack burst open.

"What the..." Hunter blurted out, scrambling to cover them with a blanket. Vi stepped in through the doorway, standing before them and putting her hands on her hips.

"Alright," she declared, gesturing for them to get up. "Playtime's over kids."

"Could you freakin' knock next time?" Hunter yelled, glaring at her.

"Nah. Kinda wanted to see what you were up to." She wrinkled her nose. "Gawd, it *wreaks* of sex in here. Tell the Ironclad to put in a goddamn window or something."

"Get out!"

"Sure thing lovers," Vi replied with a wink, for once actually listening to Hunter and stepping out of the doorway. "But don't make me wait...we got work to do."

She shut the door, and Hunter got dressed, stepping outside with Sukri. He glared at Vi.

"You always know how to make an entrance," he grumbled.

"Come on love-bug," Vi urged. "Dominus is waiting by the front entrance to your Mom's house." She turned to Sukri. "And you and I have a date."

"Oh really?" Sukri replied.

"I need to up your training," Vi explained. "I take it Hunter told you everything?" Sukri nodded. "Then you know things are about to get real dicey around here. We need everyone to be able to handle themselves."

"I'm up for it."

"You better be," Vi warned. "I'm not gonna go easy on you."

"Good."

"That's the spirit Puss," Vi encouraged. "Now get outta here Hunter."

"Gimmee kiss," Hunter requested. Sukri smiled, leaning in and kissing Hunter, giving Vi quite a show. Until Vi couldn't take it anymore.

"All right all right," she grumbled. "Go, Hunter."

Hunter smiled, waving at Sukri, who waved back.

"Bye bye Crispy. Be a dear and kill Camilla for me."

"Only if she gives me another reason to," Hunter countered.

And then Hunter spread his wings, leaping into the air and flying away. Vi and Sukri watched him go, until he disappeared behind a hill in the distance.

"Wish I could do that," Sukri confessed.

"Not gonna lie, he sells it pretty well," Vi replied. She turned to Sukri then. "All right Puss, enough chatting. Kayla's waiting for us. Time to get to work."

CHAPTER 33

It was already sunset by the time Hunter reached the Lady's mansion, the sky an angry red-purple with the last of the sun's dying rays. Hunter aimed toward it, flying a good hundred feet above. Dominus was secured to his waist by a makeshift harness Vi had devised, a necessity given that Hunter wouldn't have been able to hold the man for the whole flight. And also because he almost certainly would've given in to the temptation to "accidently" drop the bastard. He glided down toward the gate at the fence surrounding the property, enjoying the descent. Landing was his favorite part of flying, the transition between utter freedom and being once again bound by the laws of man. It was a reminder of what he'd gained at the Kingdom of the Deep…a gift he was infinitely glad he'd been given.

He glided to the ground a few yards before the gate, making sure to land a bit harder than he normally would have. Dominus unlatched himself from the harness right before they struck the ground, landing with a grunt and stumbling forward awkwardly. Somehow the man managed to keep his balance, much to Hunter's disappointment. He landed ahead of Dominus, folding his wings and striding up to the gate. The guard beyond stared at him, then at Dominus approaching behind him.

"Open up," Hunter ordered.

The guard ignored him, eyeing Dominus.

"Do as he says," the former duke stated.

The guard unlocked the gate, opening it and gesturing for them to come through. They strode down the crushed stone path to the front entrance of the mansion, passing the field of crops on either side. Two more guards stood on either side of the double-doors leading into the mansion.

"We bring urgent news for the Lady," Dominus declared, stopping before them.

One of the guards nodded, opening the door and stepping through, closing it behind him. Moments later, the door re-opened, and the guard gestured for them to enter.

The Lady's mansion was just as Hunter remembered it, with cherry wood floors and ornate red wooden columns supporting the ceiling high above. They walked through the large foyer, passing through a doorway to the room beyond. A familiar staircase greeted him ahead, and an even more familiar woman was stepping down it. A woman in a blood-red dress, a tight corset studded with rubies glittering in the lantern-light. Long dark hair cascaded to her lower back, her corset plunging deeply in the front to reveal her impressive bust.

Hunter grimaced, resisting the urge to finger the hilt of his sword, and stopped a few yards before the stairs, watching as Lady Camilla made her way gracefully to the bottom. She arched an eyebrow at Hunter.

"Well well," she greeted, giving him a little smile. "What an unexpected surprise." She gazed at him for a moment. "My my," she added. "What marvelous wings."

"Go fuck yourself," Hunter retorted.

"Still upset I see," Camilla replied calmly. Hunter glared at her.

"Gee, wonder why?"

"Oh Hunter," she said, giving him an apologetic look. "All I ever wanted was to protect you."

"I think you wanted a little more than that," he retorted. She gave him that infuriating smile of hers, and shrugged.

"Perhaps so," she conceded. "But I was still acting in your best interest."

"Really?" he replied incredulously. "That's what you're going with?"

"It wasn't *all* bad, as I recall."

Hunter grimaced, remembering their…interactions.

"Don't fool yourself," he shot back.

"Oh please Hunter," she replied. "You struggled for a while, but we both know that, in the end, you were practically *begging* for it." Her smile broadened. "Go on," she added. "Deny it."

Hunter grimaced, clenching his fists at his sides. He *had* enjoyed it, at least at the last moments, when she'd brought him to the point of orgasm. He remembered giving in at last, going from hating her to desperately hoping she wouldn't stop. Remembered the ecstasy of that moment, of giving in to his baser desires. Of allowing the unthinkable.

"You needn't worry anymore," Lady Camilla continued. "I got what I wanted from you. Besides, current events being what they are, it appears we have far too much of Zagamar to go around."

"You mean the Svartálfar," Hunter stated.

"Correct," she replied. She turned to Dominus. "Hello Dominus," she greeted. "I assume you told Tykus?"

"I did," Dominus confirmed. He gave a short debriefing on what had happened, including the Ironclad attack on the Kingdom, and their conversation and proposed alliance with Tykus. Camilla listened intently without interruption until Dominus was done.

"I've already received word from the Kingdom of the Deep," she revealed. "They're mobilizing their…considerable resources to take out the Svartálfar. And Zagamar, of course."

"We should coordinate with the Kingdom's soldiers," Dominus stated. "They're marching south from Tykus to contain the Svartálfar. Hunter will help scout for the locations of the Svartálfar and, if possible, Zagamar."

"Unnecessary," Camilla retorted. "My scouts are already doing so, as are the Kingdom of the Deep's countless bird-people. We have more eyes in the sky than we need."

"We'll need to share that intel," Dominus noted. Camilla nodded.

"Of course," she agreed. Then she turned back to Hunter. "We do have to address the issue of *your*…involvement with Zagamar," she added.

"What's that supposed to mean?" Hunter demanded.

"You have Zagamar inside of you," she explained. "And he will slowly take over, until you are a second version of him. Likely a lesser Legend, but still with the power to create clones of him. We can't allow that."

"So what, you'd just kill me?"

"Well, I'd start by tying you down," Camilla replied with a little smirk. Hunter glared at her.

"Not necessary. I've already taken care of it."

"Oh really?" she inquired.

"I went to the Deep and locked him away."

"Ah," she replied, inclining her head. "A bold decision. I'm impressed that you survived the Deep," she added. "Well done, Hunter."

"You have no idea how much that means to me," Hunter grumbled.

"Come," she stated, turning and walking back up the stairs. "I'll fill you in on what we know."

* * *

The large library in the upper level of Camilla's suite was just as Hunter remembered it, with shelves on the walls holding countless priceless artifacts and a huge map of Varta on one wall. A large table sat near the middle of the room, another map draped over it. Hunter stood over it with Camilla and Dominus; it too was a map of Varta, focusing on Tykus to the north, bordering the sea, and the Kingdom of the Deep to the south. The Deep was further south, and far below were other kingdoms Hunter had never heard of.

The Lady had placed numerous small black tokens on the map, and it was to these that she directed their attention.

"According to my scouts, these are the locations of the Svartálfar," she explained. "Their range extends from this mountain range," she added, pointing to mountains to the east, which Hunter recognized as the general location of the Crypt of Zagamar, "…east to the River Ormr."

"They haven't crossed the river?" Dominus inquired.

"Not yet," Camilla confirmed. "They're moving south, but staying twenty or so kilometers north of the Kingdom of the Deep. Others have made it even farther north than here," she continued. "The bulk of the Svartálfar seem to be making their way toward the Fringe."

Dominus frowned.

"How far away are they from Castle Wexford?" he inquired. Camilla hesitated for a moment.

"I assume your former duchy will be destroyed shortly," the Lady stated apologetically. Dominus grimaced, but did not reply. "That puts the Svartálfar some seventy kilometers from Tykus," she continued. "And while their migration south has stalled, they're moving rapidly northward."

"Zagamar's aiming to take out Tykus first," Hunter guessed.

"It *is* the easier target," Camilla agreed.

"But is it?" Hunter pressed. "You've got big-ass wall surrounding the whole thing."

"And once that wall is breached, there are only humans defending it," Camilla pointed out. "The Kingdom of the Deep has defenses you can only imagine…and some you would not be able to. Like the Guardians."

"The Guardians?"

"Ancient beings that repelled the first incarnation of Zagamar," Camilla explained. "Two of the few known beings to survive the Greater Deep."

"The what?"

"The Deep, as you know, is a large pit. The Lesser Deep is the uppermost level of the pit, and the Greater Deep is much further down. The power of the Deep is greater the deeper one descends into it. And the deeper one goes, the less likely they will survive the process."

Hunter remembered the huge snake-like thing they'd fought just outside the deep, and the mass graveyard of creatures around the massive pit, and nodded.

"The Lesser Deep can merge living things," Lady Camilla lectured. "The Greater Deep, well…it can merge the living with the non-living." She gestured at the map. "In any case, we know the extent of the Svartálfars' current habitat. Zagamar will continue to create more, and they will not stay in one place for long."

"Why not?" Hunter asked.

"They're voracious eaters," Camilla answered. "Just like the dark elves of old. Some say their appetite is what destroyed them after Zagamar died thousands of years ago. They consumed everything around them, and had nothing left."

"So they starved to death," Hunter realized.

"Correct."

"Tykus confirms this," Dominus stated. "There were few left when he arrived through the Gate, and most were found dying of hunger or already dead."

"And that's how my scouts know where they've been," Camilla said. "Everywhere they go, the vegetation and animal life is decimated."

"Zagamar has an incredibly fast metabolism," Hunter admitted. "I can turn it on and off at will." He explained the sensation of becoming Zagamar, including the hunger, the fact that everything around him seemed slow…and Zagamar's formidable intelligence.

"That certainly explains their appetites," Camilla reasoned. She gazed at Hunter with newfound interest. "Perhaps your ability to conjure Zagamar could come in handy. We could use it to understand his motives and plans…and we could use that accelerated intelligence to find a way to stop him."

"Maybe," Hunter conceded. "But he knows some of what I know. He might refuse to go against himself, so to speak."

"Can you find a way to access his intelligence but control it?" she pressed.

"I can try."

"I would appreciate it," Camilla stated. He grimaced, feeling uncomfortable with her sudden civility.

"I wouldn't be doing it for you," he retorted.

"Allies don't need to be friends," she pointed out, smiling at him. "Isn't that right, Dominus?"

"It is," Dominus agreed.

"You said the Kingdom of the Deep was already mobilizing its army to take out Zagamar?" Hunter asked, changing the subject.

"That's right," she answered.

"Isn't he transforming everything around him *into* him?" Hunter pressed. "What if everyone we throw at him just turns into Svartálfar?"

"That takes time," she explained. "And Zagamar would have to let them get close to him to do such a thing. He won't risk it."

"So the Ironclad and Tykus should intercept the Svartálfar at the Fringe," Dominus interjected. "The Kingdom of the Deep can take them out from the south, and your scouts can track the movements of any remaining Svartálfar."

"And close in on Zagamar himself, restricting his movement and preventing him from creating more Svartálfar," Camilla concluded. "That's the plan."

"I don't know," Hunter grumbled. "That's a pretty simple plan. Zagamar's a lot smarter than you're giving him credit for."

"Plans can be simple," Camilla countered. "The key is in the execution."

Hunter looked down at the map, still unconvinced.

"Conjure Zagamar," Camilla urged, gesturing at Hunter. "Prove us wrong."

Hunter sighed, the nodded, closing his eyes. Luckily he hadn't eaten since the attack; hunger made it far easier to bring Zagamar out from the dark recesses of his mind.

He focused on the hunger, and the chanting of thousands of men called out to him, summoning their ancient master.

Seconds later, he opened his eyes, beads of sweat rising on his forehead, his breath coming in short gasps. He looked at Dominus, then at Lady Camilla.

"We," he declared, "…are in deep shit."

Chapter 34

Sukri stood with Vi at the entrance to a medium-sized underground room deep within the Ironclad lair, the sound of water flowing magnified by the room's stone walls. A small waterfall flowed down one wall, coming from a horizontal crack in the stone. It flowed down to a shallow trench that had been dug around the perimeter of the room and in a grid spanning the floor, forming a makeshift cipher room with numerous square platforms.

And on those platforms were countless artifacts and Ossae.

"Say hello to my collection," Vi said, gesturing at her stuff. "I had the Ironclad take most of my stash from my house in Canyon Falls to this place. You have *no* idea how much this stuff is worth."

"More than I'll ever make," Sukri guessed.

"Definitely," Vi agreed.

Sukri watched as Vi stepped carefully through the room, coming to one of the squares and picking something up, returning it to her. It was a necklace with numerous black claws on it.

"Put this on," she instructed.

"What is it?" Sukri asked, eyeing the necklace suspiciously.

"Don't worry, your personality is strong enough not to be changed by it," Vi reassured. "It's the claws of one of the better cat-people warriors who'd ever lived. Now put it on."

Sukri obeyed, pulling it over her head. Its claws rested on her upper chest.

"This'll jump-start your training," Vi informed her. "Now we gotta get you some armor. Our blacksmith made you something."

Sukri followed Vi out of the room and back into the maze of tunnels beyond. Vi led her through them, and after a few minutes, the rhythmic sound of metal banging on metal came to her ears. Her hearing was also quite a bit better than it'd been before, she'd noticed. Yet another perk of her transformation.

"Here we are," Vi said as they reached a large room ahead. It was a good fifteen meters squared, the ceiling four meters high. Its walls, unlike the cipher room and many of the tunnels, were made of brick. A large Ironclad stood on one end of the room, banging a red-hot piece of metal lying on an anvil with a large hammer. There were shelves and shelves – and more shelves – filled with pieces of armor and weapons. "Hey Amido," she greeted, waving at the Ironclad.

Amido nodded at her, stopping his banging.

"This is Hunter's girl," Vi introduced. Sukri smiled.

"Hi," she greeted.

Amido grunted, setting his hammer down and striding up to one of the shelves, pulling something from it. A few pieces of black and silver armor piled on top of each other. He handed this to Sukri, who grabbed it, half-expecting to drop right to the floor under its weight. But it was shockingly light, barely heavier than leather clothes would've been.

"Go on, try 'em out," Vi prompted. "Need to make sure they fit."

Sukri did so, pulling on her top first. It was a black padded shirt of sorts, with very thin fabric at her joints.

"Notice the layers," Vi instructed. "It's designed to absorb foreign wills and reduce their effect on you."

Sukri nodded, pulling on the next piece: a black and silver chain-mail top. It was tight-fitting, multilayered, and with sleeves that went down to her wrists.

"Chain-mail will let you move around more freely," Vi explained. "No point in putting you in full plate mail if your main strength is your agility."

"So don't get hit," Sukri translated. Vi smirked.

"Don't get hit too hard," she corrected.

There were padded leggings and chain-mail armor to match, and even gloves that protected everything but her palms and the last digits of each finger, allowing her to use her claws and grip with her palms for climbing. And a helmet as well…black and silver, like the rest of her armor.

"How do I look?" Sukri inquired, giving Vi a little turn.

"I'd hit it," Vi replied with a grin.

"Don't think Hunter would appreciate that," Sukri shot back. "Okay, now what?"

"Now for your weapon," Vi replied. "You said you liked Dio's staff, right?"

"No, but Dio thought I had some talent for it."

"Then staff it is," Vi decided. Amido grabbed a staff from one of the shelves, tossing it at Vi, who caught it, handing it to Sukri. It was wrought of black metal, and surprisingly light for its size. There were ridges in various places along its length for gripping, and sharp spikes at edge end, with blades along the sides near the end, kind of like a halberd.

"Wow," Sukri breathed, giving it a slow twirl. "Now that's sexy."

"Amido does good work," Vi said, nodding at the Ironclad, who grunted back…and immediately resumed working on whatever it was he was making. "All right," Vi added. "Go back to your cabin and get some sleep. Do it naked and wear that necklace so you can absorb some skills. Tomorrow I'll teach you how to not die."

***

The next morning, Vi took Sukri to a small clearing in the forest just outside Ironclad territory. Sukri stood there in her new armor, shifting her weight from one foot to the other, a long wooden staff in her hands. Vi had a wooden longsword, and faced Sukri, standing two meters away.

"Ready?" Vi inquired. Sukri wiped her sweaty hands on her armor, then nodded.

"Ready."

Vi lunged at her, thrusting at her chest. Sukri blocked it easily, Dio's painful drills having been, well, drilled into her. Vi followed up with another attack, which Sukri also blocked. Then another.

"Not bad," Vi admitted, taking a step back. "You're not nearly as useless as Hunter was when I started training him."

"He's not useless anymore," Sukri pointed out. Vi smirked.

"That's because I trained him."

Vi attacked again, each thrust and slash done with perfect form, each flowing smoothly into the next. Again Sukri blocked the attacks.

"All right," Vi stated, letting up. "Dio taught you *something*, I'll give him that."

"What's his story, anyway?" Sukri asked.

"Camilla took him in after his parents were murdered," Vi explained.

"Why would…?"

"He was strong-willed," Vi explained. "Born to weak-willed farmers. He absorbed skills very well, like I do. Kid like that can be extremely valuable."

"As a bodyguard?"

"As anything you want him to be," Vi replied.

"So she hired him?"

"More like adopted him," Vi corrected. "Dio's parents were murdered, and she took him in. Exposed him to all sorts of powerful artifacts and Ossae. She wanted to turn him into the perfect weapon."

Vi attacked again, this time speeding up with each attack, until they were coming so fast Sukri couldn't keep up. She took a thrust to her chest, and grunted, backpedaling quickly.

"You're too stiff," Vi scolded. "It slows you down."

Sukri nodded, trying to relax. Vi started in on her again, repeating the same process as last time, and got another thrust past her.

"Damn it," Sukri swore.

"You stiffen up whenever you get worried you're gonna get hit," Vi noted. "So then you get hit. Gotta break you of that habit Puss."

"Sorry."

"I'm not going to hurt you," Vi insisted. She pointed to her weapon, then at Sukri. "Wooden sword, full chain-mail armor."

"Okay."

"You can trust me," Vi insisted. "I'm not Dio."

Sukri smiled, then nodded, relaxing her shoulders. Vi came in, more slowly at first, attacking almost leisurely.

"Stop thinking so much," Vi instructed, continuing her gentle assault. "Thinking slows you down. In a real fight, you won't have much time to think. Trust your training, trust your body. Let it do its thing."

The continued like this for a while, and then Vi went a little faster. Sukri felt herself stiffening, and tried to relax.

"This isn't punishment," Vi lectured, thrusting at Sukri's chest. Sukri blocked it, and the slash to her neck following it. "This is play. Have fun with it."

"Tell that to Master Thorius and Dio," Sukri grumbled. "They're the ones who taught me."

"Please," Vi retorted. "Thorius just threw a medallion at you and had you spar a few times."

"True."

"And Dio didn't teach you, he just beat the crap outta you until you figured out a way to stop him."

"Also true."

Sukri realized Vi had sped up even more…and that, distracted by their conversation, Sukri had matched pace easily.

"You distracted me on purpose," she accused. Vi winked.

"Best way to get you out of your head."

"Who taught *you* how to fight?" Sukri inquired. Vi sped up a little more, her attacks coming one after the other now, with little pause in-between.

"I did," Vi answered. "Along with artifacts and the Ossae I collected. But I didn't just sleep next to them and hope I was learning something, like the Guild of Seekers does. I exposed myself to them, got into fights, and figured out what reflexes they'd given me. Then I tried to figure out why each reflex mattered, when to use it. That sort of thing."

"So you reverse-engineered their skills?"

"Right."

Vi had sped up even more, and to Sukri's utter amazement, she'd managed to keep up with her teacher. Her body *did* know what to do…and when she wasn't stressing out about sparring, it actually felt pretty good.

"Faster!" she cried.

Vi chuckled, picking up the pace. The *clack, clack* of their weapons echoed through the morning air, picking up pace every minute, until they were going so fast Sukri was amazed she could even keep up with Vi. Eventually they went *too* fast, and Sukri tensed up…and promptly got hit.

"Not bad Puss," Vi admitted, stepping back and nodding at her. "See what happens when you don't think?"

"Yeah."

"Now you know why Hunter got as good as he is," Vi stated with a devilish grin. "Now, there's one thing I noticed that you're doing wrong."

"What's that?"

"You never attack," Vi answered. Sukri gave a sour look.

"Yeah, Dio didn't get that far."

"That's because he's a mediocre teacher," Vi replied. "Luckily I'm not." She gestured for Sukri to come at her. "Go on," she prompted. "You attack, I defend."

"So just…attack?"

"Yep," Vi confirmed. "I'm not going to counterattack. You just try to hit me. If you can." She smirked. "You won't be able to."

"Oh yeah?" Sukri shot back. "You sure about that?"

"Give it your best shot Puss."

***

It was a few hours later by the time Vi and Sukri stopped for a break, the sun directly overhead now. Tykus had stopped by, sitting at the base of a tree trunk to watch them as they sparred. After letting Sukri gain confidence in attacking her, Vi had switched up to take turns attacking and defending. To Sukri's surprise, Vi had proven to be infinitely patient, identifying every one of Sukri's mistakes, correcting them gently, and encouraging her when she succeeded. It was unlike any training – or teaching, for that matter – that Sukri had ever experienced.

It felt…good.

Most importantly, Vi made Sukri feel safe. Safe to try new things, and safe to fail. In fact, Vi *encouraged* failure, using it to show Sukri a better way.

When they finished, Tykus stood up, nodding at them both.

"Well done Sukri," he congratulated. "You're an apt pupil."

"Thank you your Highness," Sukri replied. Tykus chuckled.

"No need for the honorific," he insisted. "I'm just a warrior, not a king. That was another life."

"Is that…weird?" Sukri asked. "Knowing that you're…"

"A copy?" Tykus inquired, raising an eyebrow. Sukri grimaced.

"Well…"

"It is at first," Tykus confessed. "My many predecessors have written about it, of course. Every Tykus is given a manual that guides us through our feelings, and reassures us that life will go on. And that our lives are worth living."

"Must be a hell of a mindfuck," Vi piped in, shaking her head.

"That's certainly one way to put it."

"So each one of...*you* takes a different role?" Vi inquired.

"Correct," Tykus confirmed. "Some serve as scouts, some as warriors. Some as Seekers, and some as explorers. Some are academics." He spread his arms out wide, smiling broadly at them. "I get to live many lives, and we all return to write about them, so that the king may know of our journeys...and our insights."

"Must have a whole library after all these years," Sukri said.

"Oh I do," Tykus agreed. "A Royal Library filled solely with books I've written, and many more libraries in secret places with copies of them."

"Secret places?" Sukri asked. Tykus glanced at Vi, then Sukri, then leaned in conspiratorially, his eyes twinkling.

"Do you think this is the only kingdom I rule?" he inquired.

Sukri stared at him, as did Vi. Both of their jaws were slack. Vi recovered first.

"But your Ossae," she protested.

"Only a fool puts all of his goats in one pen," Tykus declared. "The kingdom that bears my name takes great pride that they possess my original bones, embedded in a block of solid crystal. If only they knew that but a few of the bones are actually mine!"

"They're not?" Sukri blurted out.

"Of course not," Tykus replied. "My Ossae are scattered throughout the world in different kingdoms. A single bone is enough to recreate me...why would I put them all in one place, risking annihilation?"

"Damn," Vi breathed. "Wow."

Everyone was silent for a while. Then Vi shook her head.

"You're even smarter than I thought," she admitted. "And I assumed you were smart."

"And you are an excellent teacher," Tykus replied. He paused. "If I could be so bold, may I spar with you?"

"Sure," Vi replied. She tossed him a wooden sword, then grabbed another for herself from a pack on the ground. "Rules?"

"Be kind," he replied with a smile.

Vi lunged at him, chopping at a forty-five-degree angle at his neck, and he blocked it smoothly, kicking at Vi's knee at the same time. She stepped back to avoid his kick, countering with a slash to his sword-arm. He blocked it, thrusting at her chest...and missing as she dodged to the side, kicking him in the hip.

He in turned dodged this, slashing at her neck.

Vi blocked the attack, following with a string of attacks, moving at a fraction of the speed Sukri knew she was capable of. Tykus held his own, giving as good as he got. He moved quickly and smoothly, and even had a smile on his face as he fought, seeming to be thoroughly enjoying himself.

Vi stopped, taking a step back.

"All warmed up?" she inquired. He inclined his head.

"Quite," he agreed. "Shall we up the difficulty?"

"Be careful what you wish for," Vi shot back with a grin…and lunged at Tykus, moving twice as fast as before. Their swords struck again and again, and to his credit, Tykus managed to keep up with Vi. After a few minutes, they both stepped back.

"I suspect you're going easy on me," Tykus stated.

"I don't wanna kick your ass in front of Puss here," Vi replied.

"Aha!" Tykus declared, grinning at her. "Protecting an old man's honor in front of a fair maiden?"

"Sort of," Vi replied. "I mean, she's a cat."

"En guard!" Tykus cried…and lunged at Vi, thrusting viciously at her chest.

Vi blocked the attack, and then it got epic.

She attacked with a speed and ferocity Sukri had never seen, or even imagined, slashing, kicking, spinning, leaping…her sword a blur as she assailed Tykus. She snaked inside the man's defenses as he struggled to defend himself, striking his armor again and again, not giving him a second to recover. He stumbled backward, and Vi knocked his sword out of his hands, scoring more five hits on him before the weapon even struck the ground.

It was fucking *awesome.*

Vi stopped then, holding her sword at her side, giving Tykus a small courtesy. Tykus chuckled, shaking his head in wonderment, then retrieving his sword.

"I surrender," he declared, bowing before Vi.

"Do I get one of your kingdoms?" she inquired.

"You get my respect and admiration," he replied with a smile. "Will that suffice?"

"That'll do."

"I must admit, I've never seen your equal," he stated. "And I've seen a great deal in my lifetimes. I will write about you."

"Wait 'till you see me in battle," Vi replied with a wink. "You ain't seen nothing yet."

Tykus chuckled, shaking his head.

"I believe you."

"You're not bad at all," Vi admitted. "I threw some pretty tough stuff at you. Who taught you?"

"My father," Tykus answered, handing her the wooden sword. "He was a warrior himself, and a statesman and philosopher. My mentor and my idol."

"He did a good job."

"I believe he did," Tykus agreed. "He was a great man." He sighed. "None of my original children showed an interest in my pursuits," he admitted. "I often wonder if it was my failure as a father, or their failure as children. I suspect my not being able to be near them – for fear of changing them into me – had something to do with it."

Vi shook her head.

"Man, you lived a rough life," she murmured. "Probably enjoy being a copy more than a Legend."

"Without question," Tykus agreed. He inclined his head at her, then at Sukri. "I think I've taken up enough of your time," he stated. "Thank you for allowing me to watch…and for teaching me my weaknesses," he added. And with that, he left.

"Huh," Vi mumbled.

"What?" Sukri asked.

"I think I like him," Vi admitted. "Spent my whole life thinking he was just another piece of shit like his dukes, but I admit, I was wrong."

"Yeah."

"Speaking of liking people," Vi stated, "…I can't help but notice Kayla's not around anymore."

Sukri grimaced.

"She liked you, didn't she," Vi guessed.

"Yeah," Sukri admitted. "How'd you know?"

"I like women," Vi answered with a lopsided grin. "I notice these things."

"Ah."

"I'm glad you chose Hunter," Vi ventured. "He's a good guy, Sukri. And he deserves someone like you."

Sukri swallowed past a lump in her throat.

"You mean that?"

"You ever hear me say something I don't mean?" Vi retorted. "Just remember, Hunter's the kind of guy that will never give up on you. Ever. He's one of the best human beings I've ever met. But if you tell him that, I'll kill you."

Sukri smiled despite herself.

"Be good to him, alright?" Vi pressed.

"I will," she promised. "Thanks, Vi."

Vi leaned in, giving Sukri a hug, then pushed her away.

"All right, time for a break," she announced. "I'm getting hungry. Go fetch me some meat."

Sukri blinked.

"Huh?"

"Hunt something and kill it," Vi explained. "Then dress it, make a fire, cook it, and we'll eat it."

"I can't…I don't know how to."

"Here we go again," Vi grumbled, rolling her eyes theatrically. "Had to put up with the same shit with Hunter. Come on, I'll show you how to, you know, not die."

"I kinda gotta go to the bathroom first," Sukri admitted. Vi smirked. "Guess I'll have to show you how to wipe your ass too."

"I got that one down pat," Sukri assured her.

"Go on," Vi prompted, gesturing toward the woods. Sukri did so, walking out of the clearing and weaving through the trees. "Use leaves," Vi shouted after her. "No licking!"

"Ha ha," Sukri grumbled, continuing through the woods until she was far away from her teacher. Still, she found herself smiling, and for the first time in a very long time, she felt utterly at ease. No, she was having *fun.* This was exactly how she'd imagined training to become a Seeker would be when she was a kid. Having a mentor, learning to fight and hunt and be generally awesome. The Guild of Seekers had promised her that, but ended up being nothing more than a cult. She could only become a Seeker their way if she agreed to lose what made her *her.*

But with Vi, she didn't have to give up anything.

Vi was everything Sukri wanted to be. Strong, self-assured, a master of her body and mind. And all she asked in return was that Sukri try. That she try to be the best version of herself she could be.

Sukri found a spot to do her business, then cleaned up, walking back toward Vi. A shadow passed by overhead, and she looked up, spotting something flying past her over the trees. It landed in the clearing beyond, and Sukri broke out into a jog, making it back to the clearing. Her heart soared; there, standing next to Vi, was Hunter, Dominus beside him.

"Hunter!" Sukri cried, rushing up to him and giving him a hug. He hugged her back, then pushed her away gently.

"I need to get back to Mom," he stated, turning to Vi. "We have a problem."

Chapter 35

Zac opened his eyes, seeing the stars twinkling down from a velvety night sky.

He blinked, realizing that the terrible pain that had gripped his body, as if his bones were being crushed into dust, was gone. There was not a hint of discomfort anymore.

He sat up, finding himself perched on a small ledge a few hundred feet below the lip of the Deep. He looked down at himself, getting his bearings.

His breath caught in his throat.

For he was utterly nude…and that wasn't all. His skin was as black as night, his limbs longer than they'd been before. There was not a hint of fat on his body, his veins and muscles bulging under his skin. Long black claws extended from each fingertip.

It worked.

Zac smiled, turning his hands over, studying them. He closed them into fists, then opened them.

Then he stood.

The movement was surprisingly easy, so much so that Zac almost lost his balance. But he righted himself easily, turning to the thick rope he'd used to climb down here. It swayed ever-so-slowly in a slight breeze.

He grabbed it, hauling himself up the sheer wall of the Deep. Again, he moved with ease, lifting his own body weight without any struggle whatsoever. A far cry from his journey down.

It worked!

Zac was stronger now. Like a young man again. No, *better.*

He reached the top, standing at the edge and gazing at the magnificent pit of the Deep, giving it a silent thanks. Then he turned the way he'd come, starting the long journey back to the crypt. His army was still hard at work completing it…though it might now be all for naught.

He waded forward through the corpses of failed combinations of creatures, piled all the way up to his knees. The Deep was a blind tinkerer, without aim or purpose. Most of its experiments were doomed to failure. But Zac was not blind. He had not failed.

He looked down, gazing at the bones of the long-dead creatures stirred by his passage…and stopped dead in his tracks.

Something was wrong.

Zac slid his foot forward through the pile of corpses, watching as they were pushed away. Something was…*off* about the way they were moving.

He reached down, picking up one of the bones, studying it. Then he dropped it.

It fell slowly through the air.

One…two…three…

Downward it fell, rotating ever-so-slowly.

Seven…eight…nine…

It struck the ground at ten.

Zac stared at it for a long moment. Then he repeated the experiment with a different bone, with the same result.

What…?

He did it a third time, tossing a bone forward, watching as it sailed away from him. Then he strode forward, each step propelling him farther than he expected. He passed the bone he'd tossed, batting it aside as he went.

Mist swirled around him, agitated by his passage. Again with that agonizing slowness.

Then a shadow appeared through the mist ahead, a huge creature that vaguely resembled a panther. It was twice as big, with gray armored plates covering its body, its eyes faceted and colored iridescent purple. And even stranger, it had the wings of a dragonfly.

Zac paused, his body tensing. The creature's eyes narrowed, and it took a moment for Zac to realize it was lowering itself slowly to the ground.

Getting ready to pounce.

It launched forward at him, its front paws stretching forward, its claws extended.

Zac felt a burst of fear, his whole body tensing. But the panther sailed through the air toward him with the same slowness as the bones had. He frowned, sidestepping its attack easily, watching as its head tracked his movement in mid-air.

A while later, the panther landed, pivoting toward him. Then it lunged at him again.

This time Zac felt no fear. Only curiosity. He side-stepped again, this time extending his own claws. They sank into the beast's flank, as it passed by him, tearing through its armored flesh. Zac felt a tugging at his hand as the panther flew by, but again, the attack was almost effortless.

Blood sprayed from the wound a while later, droplets coalescing in mid-air and falling gracefully to the ground.

Zac watched this for a while, enjoying the odd spectacle.

And then the hunger struck.

It came suddenly, so powerful that it bent him over as if he'd been kicked in the abdomen. He gasped, clutching his belly.

The hunger was unlike any he'd ever experienced. Ravenous, demanding to be fed.

He grit his teeth against the sudden agony of it, his legs giving out underneath him. He fell slowly to his knees.

Everything else faded away. Nothing else mattered.

Zac spotted something in his peripheral vision, and turned to see the panther in mid-pounce, sailing toward him, its ears flat against its head. He felt a flash of irritation, and lashed out with one hand, shoving its paws to the side and slashing at its face.

The panther clipped him in the shoulder with its own, sending Zac flying backward...again with that terrible slowness. They both fell to the corpses below.

Son-of-a...

He got to his feet – far faster than the panther could – and kicked it in the flank as hard as he could. Its ribs crumpled with the force of the blow.

The hunger grew ever-stronger within Zac, gripping his guts and refusing to let go. It was torture, this hunger.

The panther had the audacity to bare its fangs at him, and started rising to its feet.

Zac leapt at the creature, tearing into it with his claws. Cutting deep gouges into its neck and face, rupturing its right eyeball. Before it could even understand what was happening. Before it had any chance to react.

He shredded the beast, raking at it with his hands and feet. Literally tearing it apart.

And when he was done, when the sudden rage began to subside, he stared at the bloody remains of the panther. The rage was gone, but the hunger remained. Demanding to be appeased.

Zac fell to his knees before it, and obeyed.

CHAPTER 36

Lady Camilla stepped into the large bedroom, moonlight casting the wide bed at the other end of the room in a silver hue. She expected her Dio to be in it, but he was by the side of the bed, doing pushups on the floor. A portly man with thick glasses stood to one side of him, clearly vexed.

"Dr. Phelbus," she greeted, nodding at the man. He turned to her and bowed.

"My Lady," he replied. "I've tried to get him to rest, but he refuses to listen to reason!"

"Go on Dio," she ordered. "It's late, and you need your rest."

Dio stopped immediately, standing up and getting into bed.

"How is he?" she inquired, gazing at Dio. It was strange to see him without his mask; something Dio rarely allowed. His eyes were narrow with slit-like pupils, fine silver scales surrounding them. The scales crossed the bridge of his nose, going down to his cheekbones, and then faded back to skin. There was a small pit in the scales below Dio's eyes, between his cheekbones and his nose. Heat sensors, she knew.

One of Dio's many…modifications.

"Recovering well," Dr. Phelbus answered. "I suspect his left lung had partially collapsed due to his impact with the river after his fall from the bridge," he theorized. "No ribs appear to be broken, but he has a sprained knee and several lacerations that I have repaired."

"Thank you doctor," Camilla stated. "You may leave us now."

Phelbus bowed, then left the room, closing the door behind him. Camilla sat on the edge of the bed next to Dio, smiling down at him. She leaned over, running a hand through his short blonde hair. He stared back at her with those strange, unblinking eyes.

"I failed you," he stated bluntly.

"Shhh."

"The girl escaped me," Dio continued. "I found the Original. He escaped as well."

"It doesn't matter now," Camilla replied. "What matters is that you're okay."

"It *does* matter," Dio insisted, his tone bitter. He turned his head away from her, staring up at the ceiling. His blanket only covered him from the stomach down, his chiseled chest bare. She gazed at it, not for the first time marveling at the thick muscle there. He was a singular specimen of a man, having grown up to be even more impressive than she – or anyone else – could have imagined.

Especially considering how…unimpressive his parents had been.

Camilla put a hand on his cheek, gently forcing him to turn back toward her.

"You needn't retrieve the Original or the Empath," she stated, smiling at him. "The Original just paid us a visit," she revealed. "We're allies for the moment."

Dio stared at her, clearly confused…but knowing that she would explain. A man of few words…a man of action. The two were often mutually exclusive.

"The creatures that attacked you were Svartálfar," she informed him. "Zeno reincarnated Zagamar and Zagamar is the source of the dark elves. We've allied with the Ironclad, Tykus, and the Kingdom of the Deep."

Dio just nodded once. No questions, no surprise.

"I need you more than ever," Camilla continued, stroking his cheek. "To protect me from our new enemy."

"Yes Mother."

She smiled, leaning in and kissing his forehead. Then the tip of his nose, and finally his lips. Gently, holding the kiss for a long moment. Then she disengaged, sitting up straight.

My Dio, she thought.

He'd been such a sweet boy, barely five years old when she'd discovered him. Five years old, yet able to play the piano as well as his father and knit like his mother. And butcher animals perfectly like his neighbor, the town butcher.

Able to do anything anyone else did.

It hadn't been long before people realized Dio's power. The ability to absorb skills so perfectly and quickly was rare indeed…and had made him a highly sought-after commodity. No shortage of patrons had visited Dio's parents, offering large sums of money to buy the child.

Including Camilla.

The parents had refused. They loved their son and would never part with him.

Camilla recalled the moment she'd rescued him from the men who'd tried to abduct him. Who'd murdered his parents. She recalled stepping carefully around the bodies lying motionlessly on the floor around Dio's room. His terrified eyes staring at those bodies, then at her. She'd reached out for him with blood-spattered arms, telling him that everything was going to be okay.

"Do you love me Dio?" she inquired.

"Only you," he answered.

She smiled, leaning in to kiss him again, then putting a hand on his chest. She slid it downward, feeling those thick slabs of muscle beneath her fingertips, followed by the peaks and valleys of his abs. She passed his bellybutton, pausing there for a moment. Waiting for his reaction.

She didn't have to wait long.

And then there was a loud *bang* from outside, following by an ear-splitting shriek.

Camilla froze, and Dio leapt out of bed, running to the window and peering out. Then he turned to face her.

"We're under attack," he warned.

Camilla ignored the chill running down her spine, joining him by the window and staring out of it. The front lawn of the mansion was three stories below, cast in silver from the three moons and countless stars above.

The gate at the fence surrounding the property was destroyed, dark shapes spilling through it. Hundreds of shadowy creatures swarming across the path and through the crops on either side of it toward the entrance to the mansion.

Her blood went cold.

Svartálfar!

She grabbed the whistle hanging from a chain around her neck and blew it.

The great horned serpent resting next to the path came alive, uncoiling rapidly. It reared its head, lunging for the nearest Svartálfar, snapping one up in its massive jaws and swallowing it whole.

More of them rushed at the serpent, hundreds of them crashing upon it like a black wave. They climbed atop it, hanging on as the serpent thrashed its long body, tossing some free and trampling others under its countless feet.

Still more came, engulfing her serpent, covering every inch of its silver body. More Svartálfar rushed at the mansion, slamming into the front double-doors while others started to climb up the walls themselves. Their black eyes stared back at her as they climbed, reaching the second story windows with frightening speed.

Glass shattered as they broke in, followed by muffled screams from the floor below.

"We need to run," Dio declared tersely. He was already pulling on his Seeker uniform, and got dressed in seconds. Grabbing his mask and his staff, he strode toward the bedroom door, pulling it open and gesturing for Camilla to follow.

They made their way into the wide hallway beyond, seeing guards and Seekers sprinting toward them.

"My Lady!" one of them cried. "We're under attack!"

"Set the front lawn on fire," Camilla ordered. "Guard the stairs. Don't let them up!"

"M'Lady…"

"Don't talk," she snapped. "Do!"

The guards broke off, rushing down the hall away from them, to the main staircase beyond. They shouted out orders, more guards congregating at the top of the stairs. The Seekers stayed with Camilla, and Dio led them past the guards. Camilla glanced down the stairs, seeing Svartálfar swarming up them, moving frighteningly fast.

"Protect the Lady!" a guard cried.

The guards held their shields tightly, the first of the Svartálfar smashing into them.

"To the roof!" one of the Seekers yelled. Dio led them and Camilla to stairs going up to the fourth floor, and they sprinted up. There was a sound of glass shattering from below, more Svartálfar breaking through the windows on the third floor.

She glanced back, seeing Svartálfar swarming over the guards below, tearing them limb-from-limb. More and more of the dark elves came, rushing up the stairs and leaping at the guards with abandon.

The guards' screams cut to her soul.

Camilla reached the top of the stairs, a narrow hallway ahead…and saw Svartálfar rushing across it toward her!

"Forward!" a Seeker cried. The Seekers rushed toward the Svartálfar, each unsheathing their dual scimitars. Dio stayed with Camilla, his staff still on his back.

The Svartálfar and Seekers met in the middle of the hallway, scimitars flashing as the Seekers fought the vile creatures back. Unlike the guards before, the Seekers did not fall so easily. Imbued with spirits of the Kingdom of the Deep, trained daily for battle, they were far superior.

One Seeker fell in a spray of blood, but not before taking out four Svartálfar.

"From behind!" Dio snapped.

Camilla glanced back, seeing Svartálfar rushing up the stairs toward her.

"Give me a weapon!" Camilla ordered. Dio obliged, retrieving a bloodied scimitar from the ground, dropped by one of the fallen Seekers. She gripped the hilt, facing the oncoming creatures.

And then Dio pushed past her, intercepting the beasts, pulling his staff from his back.

"Stay back!" he cried.

He burst into action, swinging his staff at the nearest Svartálfar, catching it across the temple. It flung to the side, slamming into the wall and ricocheting off…only to be hit again, the blades at the end of Dio's staff slicing through its throat.

Its head toppled from its body.

Dio's staff whirled, taking on the next Svartálfar, then the next, the hallway so narrow that only two could face him at a time. Camilla turned, watching as the Seekers fought back the Svartálfar. More Seekers had fallen…and the ones that remained were being pushed steadily backward, closing in on Camilla.

She was trapped.

A dark elf leapt over the Seekers, landing beyond them and lunging at her!

Camilla dodged to the side, reflexes she'd absorbed from her treasure-trove of artifacts kicking in. But the dark elf moved even quicker, extending an arm to clip her left shoulder with its claws as she ducked out of the way. This spun her off-balance, nearly throwing her to the ground. The creature lunged at her again…and was struck by a flash of silver.

Its head flew from its body, bouncing off the opposite wall and landing with a *thump* on the floor.

Camilla turned, seeing Dio standing beside her, his staff dripping with blood. He'd killed a dozen Svartálfar already, their bodies littering the stairs. But more were crawling over those bodies toward Dio and Camilla…and a third of her Seekers down the hall ahead were dead. The remaining Seekers were making headway, beating the Svartálfar back. There were stairs leading up to the fifth floor beyond, Camilla knew.

"You okay?" Dio asked, dodging out of the way of one of the dark elves' attacks, then chopping its arm off. Camilla glanced at her shoulder, seeing a small laceration there.

"I'll live."

Dio backpedaled, and Camilla did as well, advancing down the hallway toward the Seekers, who finished off the last of the Svartálfar ahead.

"Go, go!" one of them shouted.

Camilla followed behind them as they ran down the hallway, spotting stairs going up ahead. Dio followed behind her, staving off the Svartálfar as he went. One of them managed to slash his chest, ripping the leather there, and Dio made the creature pay for it with its life.

"To the library," Camilla ordered.

"Too dangerous," Dio shot back.

"I'm not leaving without the Epics," she argued. The most powerful of her collection of artifacts, she could not allow them to get in Zagamar's hands.

She went up the stairs, following her Seekers to the top, then turning right down a wider hallway. There were no Svartálfar ahead, only the ones behind. She spotted the door to the library at the end of the hallway, only ten meters away. Her Seekers led her to it, opening the door and ushering her through.

To her relief, the library was deserted.

"Hold them off," Camilla ordered Dio, running into the library and kneeling before a rug on the floor. She pulled it aside, revealing the wooden floor beneath. Lifting a false plank, she saw the knob of her safe below, and twisted it rapidly, entering the twelve-digit combination.

There was a *click*, and she pulled the safe door open, lurching back as she did so.

A poison dart shot straight up into the ceiling.

She waited, and a second dart shot upward. Then she leaned forward, reaching into the safe and pulling out a large obsidian chest. It was remarkably heavy.

"To the roof!" she commanded, running toward the library entrance. Dio was there at the other end of the long hallway, holding back a literal mob of Svartálfar. Her Seekers ran ahead of her, leading her to a side-hallway to the right. They hurried down it, skidding to a stop at one of the many doors on the left and throwing it open. There was a narrow staircase leading upward to the flat rooftop…and to the stable where her winged horses were kept.

"Dio!" she cried.

"Coming," he shouted. She saw him appear at the other end of the hallway, slashing at one of the dark elves. Then he turned and bolted toward her, more Svartálfar spilling down the hallway after him. Camilla ran up the stairs, following her Seekers through a doorway at the top.

The roof of the mansion spread out before her, bathed in the light of the three moons high above.

She saw the stables ahead, squat buildings with winged horses inside, and sprinted toward them, skidding to a halt before one of them. One of her Seekers opened the door, leading a winged stallion out, then lifting Camilla up into the saddle while another placed the obsidian chest in its saddle-bag. She reached for the harness to strap herself in.

"Hurry!" a voice shouted.

She glanced up, seeing Dio running like mad toward her, Svartálfar spilled out of the doorway she'd come through and onto the roof, chasing after him.

"Dio!" she cried. "Come on!"

"Go!" he shouted back. The Svartálfar were gaining on him, galloping like animals…and closing the distance between them rapidly. The Seekers were bringing more horses out from the stables, but stopped to face the oncoming horde, rushing in front of Camilla to protect her.

One of the guards stayed back, retrieving an unlit lantern from one of the stables. He lit it, then spilled its oil onto the roof. Fire spread across it, licking at the oil greedily.

"Set the mansion on fire!" he cried, rushing to another stable. "We burn or become beasts!"

The Svartálfar reached Dio, lunging at him…and Dio spun around, his staff moving so quickly it was impossible to follow. Beast after beast fell to his weapon, but for every one that fell, two more took their place. They formed a "U" around him, a few rushing past to attack the Seekers as they helped pour more oil on the roof. Black smoke rose from the flames, the fire spreading beyond the oil, consuming the roof itself.

"Dio!" Camilla cried.

And then a Svartálfar ran around Dio, leaping at her horse and ramming it in the side. The horse toppled over, tossing Camilla from the saddle, her sword flying from her hands.

She landed on the hard wooden roof, rolling to a stop on her back.

Camilla scrambled to her feet, and the Svartálfar leapt over her horse, crashing into her. The impact threw her backward into the wall of the stable behind her, and she ricocheted off, stumbling forward. The Svartálfar slashed at her with its wicked claws, raking at her corset. The thick leather repelled the attack, but the creature raked at her face with its other hand.

And flew to the side in a spray of blood right before it struck her.

She saw one of her Seekers standing before her, his scimitar dripping with blood.

"My…" he began…then was yanked backward, two more Svartálfar pulling him to the floor and raking at his face and chest. His uniform tore under the onslaught, claws ripping through his flesh, mutilating it.

His screams filled the air, and then were abruptly cut off as one of the monsters gripped his windpipe, tearing it from his neck.

Camilla spotted the doomed Seeker's scimitar on the floor, and grabbed it, turning left and breaking out into a run toward one of the other stables. But a wall of fire blocked her way…and a sea of Svartálfar were rushing toward her from directly ahead.

She spotted Dio backing away toward her, nearly surrounded by Svartálfar, barely holding them back with his whirling staff.

And then a dark shape burst through the wall of fire, leaping right at her!

Camilla backpedaled, then realized it was a flying horse, one of her Seekers sitting atop it. He dismounted, running up to her and picking her up bodily, lifting her into the saddle. He strapped her in tightly.

"Yah!" he shouted, then slapped the horse's hindquarter. The steed bolted forward, breaking out into an all-out gallop toward the edge of the roof ahead. Camilla grabbed the reins, pulling back on them as hard as she could, trying to stop the beast.

Dio!

But the horse wouldn't obey her. It went right for the edge of the roof, and leapt off, spreading its huge wings wide.

Camilla felt the horse lurch downward suddenly. Arms encircled her from behind, gripping her waist tightly.

Arms covered in black and red leather.

She twisted around, seeing Dio straddling the horse behind her, the roof of the mansion burning behind him as her winged steed flew away, gaining altitude as it went. Her body went limp, relief coursing through her.

"Oh thank god," she murmured, closing her eyes. "Thank god."

Then she opened her eyes, watching as her home burned, flames engulfing the roof and the Svartálfar atop it…and her Seekers. The poor men leapt from the rooftop, their bodies ablaze, falling five stories to the burning lawn below.

She turned away from the gruesome sight, focusing forward, at the vast expanse of wilderness ahead. Dio squeezed her waist from behind, saying nothing.

But from him, that one act said enough.

***

The smell of smoke lay thick in the air, the roaring of the fire engulfing the Lady's mansion only ten meters from where Jeb lay. Bodies surrounded him, his fellow guards torn to pieces by the black devils that had overrun the place. He'd feigned death, laying on his belly amongst his fallen comrades, spattered with their blood.

Jeb cracked one eye open, seeing the black creatures not twenty meters from where he lay. Swarming the Lady's great serpent, that invincible creature from the Kingdom of the Deep. It'd killed countless of the black beasts, yet still they came at it, climbing onto its back and covering its entire length. The huge serpent thrashed wildly, knocking some of them off…but more took their place.

The serpent was tiring.

Jeb grimaced at the heat radiating from the burning mansion, the exposed side of his face burning from it. He had the sudden urge to sneeze, and stifled it desperately, knowing that if he didn't, he would soon be dead.

Minutes passed, the serpent moving more and more slowly, until at last it lay still, panting, its long, forked tongue visible inside of its huge open maw.

Something came into Jeb's field of vision then. A tall, shadowy figure standing between Jeb and the serpent. It looked like one of the other creatures, but was taller, and almost completely human, save for its black skin and unusually long limbs.

It stared at the serpent, then strode up to one of the corpses of the guards, kneeling down and taking something from it.

A belt.

The figure wrapped the belt around its own left arm, cinching it tightly. One of the other beasts ran up to the figure, pulling its left arm taut…while another grabbed a longsword from the corpse, stepping up to the figure.

The beast raised the sword up high over its head, and brought it down right on the tall figure's forearm.

The tall figure grunted, blood oozing from the stump of its left arm. It signaled with its remaining hand, and the beast that was still holding its severed arm turned toward the serpent, clutching the limb to its chest and sprinting toward the huge snake…and leaping right into its mouth.

The beasts that had been holding its head down scattered.

The great serpent's head rose up, its jaws slamming shut. A muted shriek came from inside of it, followed by silence.

Jeb felt the urge to sneeze again, the air so thick with smoke now that it was almost impossible to breathe. He fought it desperately, but this time he could not stave it off.

He sneezed, the sound bursting from his nose.

The tall figure with the severed arm turned its head toward him, and Jeb closed his eyes, holding his breath and staying as still as possible.

Footsteps approached, coming right up to his head.

Jeb lay there, utterly still, waiting for the inevitable. For the sharp pain of steel sliding into his back. For claws to rake at his face, tearing out his eyes.

Make it quick.

His lungs began to burn, the urge to take a breath in becoming more and more urgent. He fought it, the raspy, quick breathing of the creature standing before him all the reminder he needed of the consequences of doing so.

He felt something hot and wet drip onto his cheek, and resisted the urge to flinch.

The sound of footsteps returned, but this time they were moving away from him. Jeb cracked one eye open, seeing the dark figure walking away, back toward the serpent. The hot fluid on his cheek dripped down the side of his face, to the corner of his mouth.

It tasted like blood.

His stomach growled loudly, and he grimaced, afraid that one of the beasts might hear it. But they paid him no mind, forming a circle around the tall figure instead. They began to chant, their voices rough and barely intelligible, some little more than garbled shouts. But these voices called out in unison, even as the beasts bowed down low, their foreheads touching the ground.

"Za-ga-mar, Za-ga-mar!"

His stomach growled again, hunger seizing him, the chanting continuing over and over. It grew louder, more insistent, filling the air. Filling his mind.

A vision of burnt-out buildings came to him, a town utterly demolished. Of men surrounding him, chanting just as these creatures were.

Za-ga-mar!

He licked his lips, tasting more of the blood. He swallowed it, suddenly eager for more. *Desperate* for more.

Za-ga-mar!

The voices from his visions melded with the chanting of the beasts, and he lay there, watching as the creatures stood, lifting their arms in the air. As their chanting got louder and faster.

And the lone figure stood there, in the center of it all, blood dripping from the stump of its left forearm. Stood there as these creatures – these abominations – called its name.

Chapter 37

Hunter stood before the pool that surrounded his mother's island, the ever-flowing water insulating the cavern from her indomitable will. Xerxes, Vi, Sukri, and Tykus were there, and Neesha herself stood in the middle of the pool, the blue tendrils of her hair and vein-like structures traveling down her limbs making the water around her glow brightly.

"We're all here," Vi stated. "What's this big problem, Hunter?"

"When I went to Lady Camilla's, she went over the locations of the Svartálfar," Hunter explained. "Camilla asked me to summon the Zagamar within me so we could try to anticipate what his next moves would be."

"A good idea," Vi admitted. "But wouldn't he avoid letting you know anything that could work against him?"

"He tried," Hunter agreed. "But he couldn't stop his thoughts when he looked at Camilla's map, any more than we can stop thinking about a pink elephant once we're told not to."

"Actually, that's not hard for us at all," Vi countered. "Considering we have no idea what an elephant is."

"A large creature with loose gray skin and an exceedingly long nose," Tykus answered. "I heard of them when I was growing up, but never saw one."

"So why would you ask us to think of a pink one?" Vi asked.

"That's not the point," Hunter grumbled. "The point is, he figured out what he'd do, and I know it now."

"Go on," Neesha encouraged.

"The details are still fuzzy for me, but from what I can tell, he was completely human once. Incredibly smart, smarter than anyone he'd ever met. He went to the Deep and fused with…something. Something that increased his metabolism, made him think faster, move faster."

"The Kingdom of the Deep's Elders confirm that he did," Tykus agreed.

"This gave him a lot more power," Hunter continued, "...but cursed him too. He was always hungry, having to eat constantly to feed his metabolism. And he aged more quickly than he'd expected to," Hunter added. "Anticipating his death, he created his crypt a few years before he died, and placed an amulet with part of his will outside of his tomb. All with one goal in mind."

"And that was?" Vi asked.

"He wanted to be reincarnated," Hunter stated, ignoring her. "But he knew that if he *was* reincarnated, he'd only live a short time before getting old and dying again. So he made sure that his medallion would impart his will enough that anyone exposed to it would be smart enough to wait until they'd solved that problem before resurrecting him."

"Xerxes' head," Tykus realized, nodding to himself. "It makes sense."

"Right," Hunter agreed. "Zagamar knew that if he had the ability to regenerate, he could live forever."

"And so far he's succeeded," Neesha noted.

"Oh it gets worse," Hunter warned. "Much worse. Zagamar can regenerate now, which means every time he does, the flesh he regenerates is Legendary."

They heard a sharp intake of breath, and glanced at Tykus, whose face had paled.

"Anyone who consumes his flesh will incorporate it into their bodies and gain a portion of his Legendary abilities," the man stated. "Which means..."

"That Zagamar can feed his flesh to his Svartálfar," Hunter concluded, "...and then they can go out and create more Svartálfar, just like he can."

"So you're saying there's more than *one* Zagamar out there?" Sukri blurted out.

"Not quite," Hunter corrected. "Zagamar wouldn't allow anyone else to become as powerful as him. He'd probably have a few generals drink his blood, getting a small portion of his Legendary power. Most of the Svartálfar are only partially changed into Zagamar for a reason...to prevent any of them from being able to challenge the one true Zagamar."

"So none of them can regenerate, think, or move like him?"

"Unlikely," Hunter agreed.

"Well that's somewhat reassuring," Vi stated. "And also terrifying. This means Zagamar can expand his army much more quickly."

"A stroke of genius, a Legend giving themselves the power to regenerate," Tykus opined. Neesha smirked.

"I agree," she quipped.

"Hey, why not just have Mom go and murder all the Svartálfar and Zagamar?" Hunter asked. "You're invincible!"

"True," Neesha admitted. "But I would start changing everything around me *into* me. One invincible Legend is enough."

"But Zagamar..."

"Only has a fraction of my ability," Neesha interjected. "Xerxes doesn't regenerate nearly as quickly as I do, and Zagamar can only have inherited a fraction of your brother's power."

"Ah."

"So we need to find these 'generals' and take them out," Sukri ventured. "How do we find them?"

"WE…JUST KILL," Xerxes piped in.

"I'm with Blue on this one," Vi agreed. "There's no way for us to tell the difference between regular dark elves and these generals. All we can do is kill as many Svartálfar as quickly as we can."

"We should mobilize the Ironclad army," Dominus stated. "March north to the Fringe just before the Deadlands." He turned to Tykus. "Can we rely on the Kingdom's armies to be there?"

"You can," Tykus confirmed. "Hunter, since you can fly, I will need you to notify another…me in Lowtown. He's the bartender of the Lucky Nuts."

"Catchy name," Neesha said.

"Been there," Sukri added. "That was you?" she asked incredulously, staring at Tykus. He nodded.

"I wear many hats," he explained. "No better place to keep a finger on the pulse of the people."

"I'll go tomorrow morning," Hunter promised.

"Xerxes will lead the Ironclad to the Fringe overnight," Neesha explained. "Hunter, you can fly out tomorrow morning. Notify bartender Tykus, then join Xerxes for the fight." She turned to Vi. "Vi, make sure Hunter doesn't die."

"Why do I always have to get the hardest job?" Vi quipped.

"I'm coming too," Sukri declared.

"Guess I have to make sure you don't die too," Vi decided. "Camilla should continue to coordinate with the Kingdom of the Deep. Let's hope she does her part."

"She will," Dominus assured.

"Wow, I feel so much better hearing that from you," Hunter shot back.

"I am no stranger to strategy when it comes to war," the former duke declared. "I suggest you grant me control over your Ironclad army so that you can take advantage of my experience."

"Done," Neesha replied immediately. Xerxes scowled at her, flashing a few angry-looking hand signals. "Don't argue," she snapped. "We must use everyone to the best of their abilities if we want any chance of winning."

Xerxes crossed both pairs of arms over his huge chest, glaring down at Dominus. But he said – and signed – nothing more.

"Xerxes, you take orders from Dominus now," Neesha declared. "That means you do too, Hunter and Vi." She glanced at Tykus, who gave Dominus a wry grin.

"It appears our roles have been reversed," Tykus stated.

"Your Highness, I…"

"I will serve as your advisor," Tykus interjected with a slight bow. "You are – as you have always been – the protector of our kingdom."

"Then it's decided," Neesha declared. "We march tonight. Good luck…and be careful."

* * *

The next morning, Hunter woke up to Sukri gazing at him, a small smile on her lips. Her irises were a deep golden color, and much larger than they'd been when she'd been human, her pupils narrow slits. Her face was completely covered in soft, short gray fur, save for her lips and nose, her ears pointed and small. She still had her hair, which was growing in gray at the roots, and her teeth were still mostly human, save for sharpened and elongated canines.

She was beautiful, in her own way. Different, yet the same.

He smiled back, leaning in and kissing her.

"Morning babe," Sukri murmured. "You sleep okay?"

"Oh yeah," Hunter replied. "Especially after that thing you did."

"You like?"

"I like."

She snuggled up to him, her body hot against his skin. She ran a few degrees hotter than him, like an electric blanket.

"What are you thinking?" he inquired.

"Who's the chick here?" she countered, grinning at him. Hunter smirked.

"I don't conform to gender stereotypes."

"So what you're saying is, you're my bitch," Sukri stated.

"Whatever makes you happy."

"*You* make me happy," she murmured, kissing him again. He felt a hot, furry hand on his groin, and it stirred immediately, joining them in the whole waking up process. Sukri smirked. "Dirty boy."

"Not getting an apology outta me," Hunter retorted.

"Nothing to apologize for," Sukri shot back, kissing him again. "Need some…relaxation before the big day?"

"I ain't saying no."

Sukri grinned, closing her fingers around his member, holding it gently. He felt it grow, pulsing in her grip, until it could grow no more.

"That was quick," she murmured, sliding her hand up and down slowly. "You never make me wait."

"That'd be downright rude."

"So thoughtful," Sukri mused, leaning in and kissing him again. She tightened her grip a little, moving faster.

"Just the kinda guy I am."

"Shut up," she ordered. He obliged, resting his head back and closing his eyes, feeling her work on him. Staying at that same pace, up and down, taking her time. No rushing, no hint of impatience. Then she switched things up, gripping him close to the top and rubbing her thumb in small circles near the head. He gasped at the unexpected change; it had its intended effect, bringing him quickly toward the inevitable conclusion.

Then she slowed, and stopped, holding him there.

"Vicious," he murmured.

"Thought I told you to shut up," she shot back, leaning in and biting his earlobe with one of her canines. She did it gently, just enough to hurt a little. Then she continued, circling with her thumb again. At the same time, she slid down, kissing his neck, then his chest, then his belly. His hips bucked involuntarily, and he bit back a moan, sweat beading up on his forehead. He was close now…very close. Hunter tensed up, holding back.

Then he felt warm wetness engulf him, and there was no holding back anymore.

He groaned, the end coming far more quickly than he'd expected, peaking within seconds. Hunter tried to warn her, but she ignored him, her pace unchanging. He cried out, wave after wave of pleasure overtaking him, until there was nothing left.

After a long moment, she released him, giving him a lopsided grin.

"Feeling relaxed?" she inquired.

He nodded mutely, wiping sweat from his eyes.

"All right baby," Sukri declared, standing up and turning away from him. "Time to go to work."

He watched as she got dressed, pulling on her armor. She turned to face him then, raising an eyebrow.

"You gonna get dressed?" she inquired.

"Uh, yeah," Hunter mumbled, getting up and doing just that. He retrieved his sword and bow, and the oversized quiver Amado had made for him after Hunter had complained about running out of arrows during the siege on Tykus. Then he followed Sukri out of the cabin, stepping out into the morning sun. The air was sweet with the fragrance of flowers, the sky utterly clear. "Good day for flying," he noted.

"Hey kids," a voice greeted. They turned, seeing Vi walking toward the cabin. Hunter frowned.

"What're you doing here?" he asked. "Aren't you supposed to be with the army?"

"I'll catch up," Vi answered.

"And how are you going to do that?" Hunter inquired. The Ironclad, being nocturnal, had most assuredly traveled all night long, and would be miles and miles ahead.

"I got lots of stamina, kiddo," Vi reminded him. "And after drinking your brother's goo, I can basically run nonstop. You guys ready?"

"Yep," Hunter and Sukri replied in unison.

"Good. Take care of yourself Hunter," Vi instructed, leaning in to give him a quick hug.

"You too Vi," Hunter replied. He smiled. "Love you."

"Love you too kiddo," Vi replied with a grin, tousling his hair. "Don't forget your helmet. We're all gonna need to wear one if we want to resist Zagamar's will."

"Don't *I* get a hug?" Sukri inquired. Vi obliged, embracing Sukri…and grabbing her butt with one hand. "Whoa," Sukri exclaimed. "Just gonna help yourself to my ass I see."

"Think I'm gonna miss that most of all," Vi replied with a wink. "All right, get outta here."

"See you soon," Hunter said. He went back to the cabin, retrieving his helmet, and the harness to hold Sukri while he flew. Attaching Sukri to himself, he wrapped his arms around her waist.

"Ready?" he asked.

"Ready."

He unfurled his wings, then leapt into the air, flying upward. He spotted Vi below; she waved at them.

"Fly fairy, fly!" she cried.

"Asshole," Hunter grumbled.

Within moments, they were soaring high above the forest, gaining altitude steadily, until they were several hundred feet in the air.

"Damn, but I will never get used to this!" Sukri exclaimed.

"Pretty cool huh?" Hunter asked.

"Turns out my boyfriend is pretty awesome," she agreed.

Hunter glanced at the sun, turning north. He relaxed into a glide then, feeling for favorable air currents. Warm, rising air filled his wings, and he used it, gaining more altitude as he went.

"You getting used to this yet?" Sukri shouted over the howling of the wind.

"Little bit."

Minutes passed, then hours, the landscape flying by. He gazed at the scenery, remembering how he'd taken days to journey from Vi's place to Lady Camilla's mansion in the past. A trip that he could accomplish in hours now, without fear of absorbing foreign wills. In the air, nothing could hurt him. He was safe.

Free.

Eventually he spotted dark shapes moving through the trees far below. At first he thought they were Svartálfar.

"There they are," Sukri declared, pointing downward. "Our boys!"

It *was* the Ironclad. A massive army advancing south. Sukri's eyesight was clearly better than his.

"Bringing us down," Hunter notified. He descended gradually, aiming toward a clearing a few miles ahead. A short while later, they landed, and Hunter unbuckled Sukri from the harness.

"All right Hunter," she stated. "I'll join up with your brother. You go find us something to kill."

"Yes ma'am," he replied. She leaned in to kiss him, then gazed at him for a long moment. "What?" he asked.

"Would it be too soon to say 'I love you?'" she inquired.

"Little bit," Hunter replied with a smirk. "Kinda makes you seem clingy."

"Well I might not get another chance," she retorted, putting her hands on her hips. Hunter grinned, pulling her in and kissing her again.

"I love you too," he murmured.

"Never said I loved you," she pointed out. "I just asked if it'd be too soon."

"Wow. You know, I'm starting to think you're a terrible person."

"And you love it," she retorted, her eyes twinkling.

"Kinda, yeah."

"Well I love you too, Hunter," she confessed, kissing him again. "Now love me and leave me."

"As you wish," he replied.

Chapter 38

Zac paced.

His tent, situated a few hundred yards away from his crypt at the base of the mountain, felt like a cage. A prison cell. He paced within it, waiting for General Roden to finish speaking. The words came out with agonizing slowness. He could practically make out each vibration in the man's vocal chords if he concentrated hard enough.

With effort, he could slow time even more than usual, but there was nothing he could do to speed it up. To make it normal again.

He grit his teeth, knowing everything Roden was going to say long before the man finished saying it. Whereas he'd once enjoyed the man's company, now he found it maddening. They were all maddening, the humans. Ponderously slow.

Zac realized that Roden was almost done speaking, and stopped pacing, putting a hand to his belly. The hunger was there, of course. It was always there. No matter how much he ate, it remained. Weaker at times, agonizing at others.

It was *irritating*.

"I don't care," Zac snapped, not even bothering to slow down his words for the man. "We march on Caeruleus in the morning!"

Caeruleus, the ancient kingdom to the north, by the sea. Home of those who'd called themselves Romans long ago. The most powerful kingdom in the known world, save for of course the Kingdom of the Deep.

"B…u…t…" Roden droned.

"I'll take them on myself if I have to," Zac interrupted, resuming his pacing. "The whole damn kingdom!"

He watched as Roden processed this, watched as the gears turned. The man would complain that their army was too small. The kingdom was too well-fortified. Blah blah blah. And it would take minutes for the moron to get it all out.

Roden had no *idea* what Zac was capable of now.

Zac suppressed his anger, grabbing a hunk of bread from the table and chewing on it. The hunger was making him irritable. Roden didn't deserve his scorn. The humans couldn't help being what they were.

Slow. Inferior.

I need to make them better, he realized.

Sure enough, Roden began arguing that their army was too small and that the kingdom was too well-fortified. Zac tolerated this, waiting as patiently as he could for the man to finish. Then he walked up to Roden, taking care to do so slowly, so as not to alarm the man. He put a hand on Roden's shoulder.

A spark of fear appeared in Roden's eyes, his throat bobbing as he swallowed nervously.

He's afraid of me, Zac realized. *Afraid of becoming what I've become.*

"I appreciate your concerns," he told his old friend, speaking slowly. "But you have to trust me, old friend."

Roden's shoulders sagged ever-so-slowly, and the man nodded.

The meeting ended, and Roden left the tent, taking what seemed like minutes to do so. Zac watched him leave, then waited a while, gorging himself on the food on the table. When he was as sated as he was capable of being, he stepped out of the tent and into the sunlight.

Soldiers and workers as far as the eye could see, all moving with that awful slowness. The whole world doing so.

He tried to remember when this had been wondrous for him. When he'd marveled at it.

Now Zac saw it for what it truly was. A gift and a curse, to sense time differently than his fellows. But he had a plan now. He would do as he had always done, offering humanity the chance to experience a sliver of his will. He would bring them into his perspective. *This* perspective. They would see the world as he did now, and he would be able to talk with them as he talked. Move with them as he moved. And then he wouldn't feel like he did now.

Alone.

Humanity, he knew now, was flawed. Weak and simple-minded. Slow and superstitious. Vain and petty. He would change that.

He would make them better.

* * *

The creature awoke, rolling onto all fours. It took only a moment for it to remember where it was, in a small burrow it'd dug in the forest floor. It emerged into the morning sunlight, shaking the dust off of it.

All around it, its fellow creatures did the same, stepping out of their own burrows. Disciples of the Dark One, thousands of them. Black brethren amidst the trees for as far as the eye could see.

No one had to tell them to march. No orders needed to be given. They all shared the mind of the Dark One. His plan was theirs.

And so the creature started northward with its fellow creatures, weaving through the trees. Marching as the Dark One had long ago, north toward the kingdom of Caeruleus. A kingdom now known as Tykus.

Millennia had passed, yet humanity had not changed. One kingdom had been replaced with another.

And just as Zagamar had laid siege to Caeruleus, deposing its king and anointing himself monarch, so too would they see to the fall of Tykus. Zagamar would rule, and with his wisdom, humanity would evolve. They would cast off the shackles of their humanity and become something more.

The Ascension had begun.

CHAPTER 39

The endless *thump, thump* of thousands of armored feet marching through the dense foliage of the Fringe reached Dominus's ears as he straddled his horse, his army of Ironclad having nearly reached their destination. A few more kilometers north and they'd reach the Deadlands. His new army had proven themselves incredibly resilient, marching without complaint or rest for hours on end. Long after a human army would've collapsed, they forged onward.

He glanced at Tykus, riding a horse beside him, then beyond at the sea of black-armored beasts at his command. Xerxes marched ahead of them, a full head and shoulders taller than any of them, his blue mane and tail making him impossible to miss.

A shadow passed by overhead.

At first glance it appeared to be a large bird, but then Dominus saw that it was a man with wings, carrying a woman.

"Everything going as planned," Tykus noted, watching as Hunter descended toward a clearing a half-kilometer ahead.

"So far," Dominus replied. Tykus chuckled.

"A Duke of Wexford is never satisfied," he mused.

"That's what makes me effective."

"But of course," Tykus agreed. "That's why I gave your progenitor the Duchy."

They rode for a while, and then Dominus glanced at the former king.

"What does it feel like, to not be king anymore?" he inquired.

"You mean to go from being a king to a lowly soldier?" Tykus asked. Dominus nodded. "Oh, it's an adjustment," he admitted. "A relief to discard the responsibilities of the throne, but difficult to come to terms with not mattering so much." He smiled. "And how do *you* feel?"

"Similar," Dominus confessed.

"The problem with *having* is that we feel like we've lost something when it's gone," Tykus stated. "Even if we never wanted it in the first place."

Dominus frowned.

"You never wanted to be king?" he asked. Tykus shrugged.

"Not really," he admitted. "If I'd had my way, I would've gladly spent my years exploring the land and writing books. Kingship was thrust upon me…and I just so happened to have a talent for it."

"That you did."

They reached the clearing, and found Hunter and Sukri there. Hunter waved at them, then flew off toward the Kingdom, leaving Sukri standing there in the long grass. Dominus gazed at her, both repelled and intrigued. A human who'd chosen – voluntarily! – to become a cat. To so visibly discard her humanity.

It was unthinkable.

"Hey boss," she greeted, waving at Dominus. "Hey king." Xerxes stomped up to her, dwarfing her by well over a meter.

"ON…BACK," he growled.

"I ain't saying no to a piggyback ride," she replied with a grin. She leapt up onto his back – a distance of nearly three meters – with ease. "Thank goodness your mane isn't too stiff," she stated, looking down between her legs. "Otherwise this would end up being a noisy ride."

Xerxes chuckled.

"NO…TELL…HUNTER."

"You got it big guy," Sukri agreed.

Dominus realized Tykus was watching him watch the two, and turned to the former king. Tykus's eyes were twinkling.

"Would you ever have imagined this?" he inquired, gesturing all around him. "Commander of the legions of Ironclad you once tried to destroy? The descendants of the very citizens who lived in the bustling city that is now the Deadlands?"

"Never," Dominus replied.

"Life is strange, isn't it?" Tykus mused. "I suppose that's why I never tire of it."

They rode in silence then, weaving through the trees, the King's Road visible ahead and to the right. After a few more kilometers, Dominus spotted a hint of yellow dirt in the distance…the telltale sign of the Deadlands.

"What's that?" he heard Sukri ask. She was looking up, pointing at another shadow flying in the sky. It took Dominus a moment to realize that it wasn't a bird…or Hunter. It was a winged horse, two riders on its back. It overshot them, then circled around, descending to land in the Deadlands ahead.

Dominus kicked his horse's flank, breaking into a gallop. There was a narrow dirt path through the trees, and he followed it, eventually arriving at the end of the tree line. The winged mount was ahead, a man and a woman dismounting from it. It was Lady Camilla, he realized, and her bodyguard. Dominus stopped before them, nodding at Camilla.

"Dominus," she greeted.

"Camilla," he replied. "Why are you here?"

"The Svartálfar destroyed my mansion," she answered. "Even my horned serpent was no match for them."

Dominus grimaced.

"Your artifacts?" he inquired. She – and her family – had undoubtedly collected a treasure-trove of powerful artifacts and Ossae.

"I saved the most valuable ones," she replied. "And I doubt they'll breach my underground stores. I also have a great deal kept in vaults in the Kingdom of the Deep."

Tykus rode up to them from behind, the Ironclad army close behind…and Xerxes and Sukri.

"Hey bitch," Sukri called out, glaring at Camilla. She turned her gaze to Dio. "Asshole." She leapt from Xerxes' back, striding toward them. "Not so tough now, huh Dio?"

"Sukri?" Camilla inquired, eyeing the girl. "You chose well."

"Go fuck yourself."

"Calm down," Dominus ordered. "Whatever your previous relationship, we're allies now."

"Speak for yourself," Sukri retorted. "Camilla's lapdog tried to kill Hunter and Xerxes." She smirked. "How'd it feel getting your ass beat, Dio?"

Dio did not answer.

"The Svartálfar have greater numbers than I suspected," Camilla told Dominus, ignoring the girl. "Zagamar must have anticipated our aerial surveillance. He may be hiding his true numbers underground."

"If so, they'll need a food supply chain," Dominus reasoned. "There isn't enough vegetation underground to feed a Svartálfar army. We should look for these supply chains."

"I'll tell the Kingdom of the Deep as soon as I get a chance," Camilla replied sarcastically.

"So we may be facing larger numbers here than we expected," Tykus interjected. "And they have the power to heal from terrible wounds."

"We need to use fire," Dominus said.

Footsteps approached, and Dominus saw a woman approaching them. A woman with that unforgettable brown leather uniform, the face of a skull embedded in her chest. She mock-saluted as she approached.

"Hey boss," she greeted. "Hey former boss," she added, nodding at Tykus. She passed by Sukri, making her way to Camilla and Dio. "Well well well," she proclaimed, putting her hands on her hips. "Look who the cat dragged in."

"It wasn't me," Sukri quipped.

"Noted Puss," Vi replied. "Hey Camilla. How's the raping little boys thing panning out for ya?"

"He was hardly little," Camilla retorted with a smirk.

"Don't want to know," Vi grumbled.

"Watch your tongue," Dio growled. Vi gave him a bemused look.

"You been practicing that in the mirror? You know, while taking your mom from behind?"

"All right," Dominus interjected. "Enough."

Vi winked at Sukri, then walked up to Dominus and Tykus. The former king inclined his head at her.

"Good morning Vi," he greeted. "I didn't expect you to get here so quickly."

"I ran," she explained. His eyebrows went up.

"All the way here?"

"Yep," she confirmed. "I got stamina like you wouldn't believe."

"I can confirm that," Camilla piped in.

Tykus considered this, then glanced at Dio and Vi.

"Seeing as we're just waiting on the Kingdom at this point, a little friendly sparring match wouldn't hurt, would it?" he suggested.

"We need to conserve our strength," Dominus pointed out.

"I know I'd enjoy seeing two fine warriors test their skills against each other," Tykus declared. "Perhaps it would serve to…ease the tension."

Dominus glanced at Tykus, then sighed.

"If you insist."

"IN…COMING," Xerxes warned.

Dominus followed Xerxes' gaze to the vast expanse of the Deadlands. A long line of soldiers was approaching far in the distance. The Kingdom's army. He frowned, turning to Tykus.

"That was awfully quick," he noted.

"If I were king, I would've had my army ready for deployment the instant a messenger gave the word," Tykus replied. He reached into his horse's pack, retrieving a helmet. The former king put it on, giving Dominus a wink. "Can't have them recognizing me," he explained.

Dominus nodded, turning to face the Kingdom's army again. He suddenly felt the weight of this moment, of the monumental task he'd been given. No, that he'd *asked* for.

Today would decide the fate of the Kingdom.

He was suddenly acutely aware of the sweet scent of grass and flowers coming from the Fringe, and the dusty, sterile smell of the Deadlands. The sound of leaves rustling, the slow beating of his heart in his chest.

He closed his eyes, an image of his hives coming to him. Crates stacked on wooden pallets, each crate filled with frames upon which his bees had constructed their perfect wax cells. For a lifetime he'd protected them. Nurtured them. Killed failing queens and supported strong ones.

I am the beekeeper.

The man outside of the hive, watching over it.

Dominus opened his eyes, struck with the magnitude of his role. The weight of six thousand years upon his shoulders, a legacy that had survived countless generations of Man.

If he failed today, that legacy would be destroyed. A single Legend would transform it all, and the Kingdom – the last bastion of humanity in this forsaken world – would be lost. Any Original coming through the Gate would find no shelter, no fellow man to greet them.

I cannot fail.

He felt a hand on his shoulder, and realized it was Tykus's.

"I believe in you," the former king murmured.

Dominus swallowed past a sudden lump in his throat, nodding mutely.

Eventually the first line of soldiers reached Dominus and Tykus, stopping a couple dozen meters away, eyeing the Ironclad army warily. Dominus rode forward, and a general rode out to meet him; a man in his late sixties with a long gray beard.

"Good morning general," Dominus greeted. It was Leo, one of the Kingdom's best. Leo's eyebrows went up in surprise.

"Duke Dominus?" he inquired. Dominus hesitated, then nodded. The general would of course assume that another Duke of Wexford had been generated by exposing a relative to Dominus's ancestral shrine. "Your excellency," Leo murmured, bowing his head."

"Wexford has been destroyed," Dominus declared. "Tykus and I have allied with the Ironclad and the Kingdom of the Deep to defeat the Svartálfar."

Leo gazed in disgust at the long line of Ironclad waiting at the edge of the Fringe, then turned back on Dominus.

"Allies with the monsters that just murdered thousands of our men, corrupting the streets of Tykus with their filth?" he spat.

"These are desperate times."

"Clearly," Leo muttered. "We have orders from the king himself to cooperate with these…*things*," he groused. "Fucks nearly crippled my oldest son, you know. Dislocated his shoulders and broke his ribs, without provocation. Damn lucky to be alive."

"I suspect every man here has a reason to hate them," Dominus conceded. "But King Tykus is wise."

"He's the only man I'd do this for," Leo grumbled. "But we do it on *our* terms. We fight separately," he declared. "I will not have my men risk any more corruption."

"Of course," Dominus agreed. "Even so, we'll all need Cleansing after this."

"We've ripped up half the streets in Tykus to Cleanse their corruption," Leo noted, glaring at the Ironclad. "We're installing metal plates below the wall to defend against future digging, and digging a moat around the wall. The big fucks'll sink if they try crossing it."

"I'd worry more about the Svartálfar," Dominus countered, seeing an opportunity to change the subject. It worked.

"What do we know about them?"

"They're fast, clever, and they regenerate rapidly," Dominus answered. "Killing them is not enough. You have to burn their bodies, or decapitate them."

"Do they use weapons?"

"Only those natural to them," Dominus replied. "They're mostly animal in origin, and have no armor or training. They attack with their claws."

"Should be easy enough then," Leo opined. Dominus shook his head.

"Don't underestimate them," he warned. "I've fought them personally. One is dangerous, but in numbers they're lethal."

Leo nodded.

"As you say, your Grace."

Dominus twisted around, gazing back at the tree line of the Fringe, then at the King's Road nearby.

"If my…beasts perform a pincer attack, your men can set the forest ablaze and burn them all. We'll pick them off with archers from above," he added, gesturing at the King's Road nearby, "…and your men can handle the rest."

"A good plan."

"You have oil and incendiary devices?" Dominus inquired. Leo smirked.

"Of course, your Grace," he confirmed. "We found them remarkably effective against the Ironclad. We'll pour oil in strategic places in the Fringe, then have our archers fire flaming arrows at them." Dominus heard the clopping of hooves approaching, and saw Tykus riding up to them.

"And who is this?" Leo inquired.

"My general," Dominus lied. "One of the few surviving soldiers from Wexford."

"I am Leif," Tykus greeted, saluting Leo.

"Leif?" Leo asked. "An unusual name."

"I was named after my father," Tykus explained. "Your men seem…tense," he noted, nodding at the soldiers, who were still eyeing the Ironclad with what could only be described as naked hatred. "We were just about to have a friendly sparring match between our two best fighters. Would they care to watch?"

Leo glanced at Dominus, who nodded, then looked back at his soldiers.

"Not a bad idea," he admitted.

"I promise it will be a good show," Tykus said with a smile. "Dio? Vi?" he called out, glancing back at the two. Dio and Vi approached, walking up to them. "These men want a show," Tykus declared. "Care to give them one?"

"Love to," Vi replied. Dio only nodded.

They both strode forward until they were directly between the line of soldiers and the Ironclad, then turned to face each other. Dio grabbed his staff, holding it before him, but Vi only stood there, her hands at her sides.

Dominus rode up to the line of soldiers, as did General Leo.

"I present to you Dominus, Duke of Wexford!" Leo declared. The soldiers saluted sharply.

"We stand here," Dominus stated, his voice carrying easily, "…enemies locked in battle only days ago. Man and beast, the pure and the corrupt."

There was grumbling amongst the ranks of the men.

"Many of you may know men that died yesterday," Dominus continued. "Or of families mourning the loss of a loved one. My own castle was attacked by this Ironclad," he proclaimed, pointing at Xerxes. "He killed nearly one hundred of my men. Good men. Loyal men. He tore them to pieces."

The soldiers muttered to themselves, glaring at Xerxes.

"Your anger is righteous!" Dominus declared, pumping a fist in the air.

The soldiers cheered.

"I despise this creature," he continued, still pointing at Xerxes. "I loathe him to my core. He is corrupt. A foul beast of the Deep Forest. He has no place in the kingdom of Tykus!"

More cheers from the soldiers.

He rode parallel to the line of soldiers, eyeing each of them as he passed.

"But there is a new threat to the Kingdom," Dominus declared. "A threat far greater than that of the Ironclad. Greater than that of the Civil War. Greater than anything the Kingdom has ever faced." He paused. "A threat that, if we do not succeed this day, will destroy us."

He stopped his horse, his mouth set in a grim line.

"The Svartálfar have returned," he announced. "The Legendary Zagamar has been resurrected. If we do not band together, Man and Ironclad, Tykus and the Kingdom of the Deep, the pure and the corrupt, we *will* be destroyed. The dark elves will swallow this land whole, corrupting everything in their path. Those of us unlucky enough to live will be transformed into mad beasts. Slaves of Zagamar. We will turn on our loved ones, killing them or transforming them into beasts. All of mankind will be destroyed."

There was utter silence.

"Cast aside your hatred," Dominus commanded. "Cast aside any thought of revenge. We come together today, or suffer a fate worse than death. Do it for your general," he continued. "Do it for your duke. Do it for your king."

Every soldier saluted, to a man.

Dominus gestured at Vi and Dio.

"Behold our greatest warriors," he declared. "Mortal enemies. If they had their way, they would kill each other without a second thought. Yet today, they have come together to fight as one. They have set aside their differences to defend you, the Kingdom, and all of Mankind."

He saw Tykus smile, nodding slightly.

"A demonstration of their skill," Dominus stated, inclining his head at Dio and Vi.

"Guess I'll have to go easy on you for a bit," Vi told Dio. "These boys'd be disappointed if it was over in a few seconds."

Dio just stood there, waiting.

"I'm sure your mom knows that disappointment well," Vi added with a grin.

And then Dio attacked.

His staff was a blur as it arced through the air at Vi's head, and somehow Vi's longsword was already in her hands, blocking the blow easily. She kicked at Dio's shins, and he blocked by lifting his foot, kicking at her belly…all the while slashing at her neck. She dodged the kick, blocking his staff and counterattacking with a thrust at his chest…which he blocked.

All in a span of seconds, so fast it was almost impossible to follow.

Vi grinned at Dio.

"You've gotten better," she noted approvingly. "*Much* better."

Dio stepped back, then lunged forward, his staff a blur as he attacked her, each hit coming so fast that Dominus couldn't follow. Yet somehow Vi blocked them all…and kicked him right in the chest.

Dio stumbled backward, but whipped his staff at her head at the same time. Vi pulled her head back, the deadly weapon missing her nose by mere centimeters.

"Tricky," she said, lowering her sword. "If I'd been as good as you, I'd be dead right now."

Dio circled around her slowly, but Vi stood right where she was. He lunged at her – a feint – but she didn't fall for it.

"You gonna dance or you gonna fight?" Vi inquired.

He answered with a lightning-fast thrust to her chest, followed by a flurry of slashes. Vi dodged, ducked, and parried, the *clanging* of their weapons echoing through the air in a rapid tempo. Dio ended with a leaping chop down on Vi's head, and Vi raised her sword to block it, dodging out of the way at the same time.

The blow knocked her sword right out of her hands, his staff missing her by a hair's breadth.

The crowd drew in a sharp breath.

Dio followed with a thrust to Vi's chest without pause, and Vi dodged again, grabbing his staff in the middle, and leaping up, kicking him in the chest with both feet. He flew backward, his staff pulled right out of his hands, and landed on his back in the dirt.

Vi smirked, watching as Dio transitioned smoothly into a backward somersault, leaping to his feet.

"Woulda died right there sweetheart," she stated. "But I'm not done playing with you yet." She tossed him his staff, one hand on her hips, the other gesturing for him to come at her. "Come get some."

Dio stared at her; she hadn't gone for her sword.

"Come on," she urged.

Dio hesitated, then strode toward her, twirling his staff slowly. He stopped two meters away, circling around her slowly. Feinting once, then again, he tried to get Vi to react. But she didn't.

Then he swung a third time, aiming right for her head…and pulled it back at the last moment, swinging the other end of his staff straight up under her chin!

Vi leaned backward, the blades at the end of his staff missing her by centimeters…then grabbed his staff on the upswing, leaping upward and forward with it. It swung over Dio's head in a half-circle, and Vi landed behind him, yanking on the other end of his staff and pulling him backward toward her.

And right into her jumping back-kick.

She pulled the kick at the last moment, striking below his butt. His legs shot forward underneath him, and he fell flat onto his back. A split second later, Vi stopped a vicious chop with Dio's staff a centimeter from his throat.

"Boom," she exclaimed.

The soldiers exploded into applause, cheering Vi, who grinned, reaching down with one hand to help Dio up. Dio hesitated, then grabbed her forearm, rising to his feet. She gave him his staff back, then put a hand on his shoulder.

"You're good," she told him. "Damn good. I'm proud of you, Dio."

Dio stared at her for a long moment, then inclined his head.

"Our winner," Dominus declared. "Vi!"

The soldiers cheered again, and Dominus allowed it, waiting for it to die down. Then he gazed across the sea of soldiers.

"Mortal enemies, yet we fight as one," he declared. "We are powerful separately, but together, we will be unstoppable!"

The soldiers cheered again, and Tykus nodded at Dominus, putting a hand on his shoulder.

"Well done," he stated.

"Thank you," Dominus replied. Tykus's eyes twinkled.

"I chose you for a reason Dominus," he said. "You, above all other men, are the one I trust to save everything I've built."

Dominus nodded, turning to look at the sea of men before him. Men trusting him to lead them to victory.

"I will not fail you," he promised, gripping his reins tightly.

"Not if you can help it," Tykus agreed.

Chapter 40

Hunter flew over the roofs of the ramshackle buildings of the Outskirts, passing the great wall surrounding the Kingdom into the barren rock and dirt of the Deadlands beyond. He gained altitude, following the King's Road as it led toward the Fringe miles ahead. It wasn't long before he spotted row after row of soldiers standing by the tree line in the distance, facing a sea of Ironclad amongst the trees…and archers standing on the King's road nearby. He glided toward them, enjoying the feeling of the wind in his wings and the sun beating down on his back.

He descended as he got closer, then changed his mind, flapping his wings instead to gain more altitude.

Might as well do a little scouting while I'm airborne.

Hunter passed beyond the tree line, scanning the terrain ahead. More Ironclad, and then empty forest. He spotted a narrow dirt path near the King's road, and realized it was the same one he'd taken with Sukri, Kris, and Gammon during their first Trial with the Guild of Seekers.

A couple months ago at most, but it seemed like a lifetime ago.

He continued onward, finding warm air currents and letting them fill his wings, maintaining his altitude. After a few minutes, he spotted something in the distance: more black between the trees, like the Ironclad before.

But as he got closer, he realized that these weren't Ironclad. They were too small, darting between the trees, rushing northward toward him. His blood went cold.

They were Svartálfar.

Shit.

He turned around sharply, flying back the way he'd come, flapping his wings to gain altitude as quickly as possible. Hoping that they hadn't seen him, or just thought he was a bird. But he knew better; if these things had even a sliver of Zagamar's intelligence, they'd have already figured out exactly what he was…and why he was there.

The forest flew by as he picked up speed, aiming for the start of the Deadlands ahead. Within minutes, he reached the end of the Fringe, descending rapidly toward the line of soldiers standing before it. He turned left then, flying parallel to the line, then touching down on the rocky terrain, slowing down right as he did so. He landed smoothly, running up to Dominus and Tykus, who were on horseback ahead.

"Hunter," Dominus greeted.

"We've got incoming," Hunter warned, stopping to catch his breath. "Svartálfar three miles south of here, and coming in fast."

"Did they spot you?" Dominus pressed.

"Probably."

Dominus turned to another man on horseback, dressed in the armor of the Kingdom's soldiers.

"Tell your men to get ready," Dominus warned. He turned to the Ironclad. "Form two lines, one on either side of the soldiers!" he shouted. Xerxes flashed a few hand signals, and the Ironclad obeyed, extending the line of soldiers on either side.

"The Svartálfar come, we stop them with our line, then the two lines of Ironclad on either side will circle around them to trap them," Dominus stated. "Your archers will set the forest ablaze with incendiary devices and fire arrows. Any questions General Leo?"

"None," Leo replied.

"If we fail, retreat to Tykus," Dominus instructed.

"The gatekeepers are already aware of that contingency," Leo informed them. "Pray we don't have to use it."

"You want me in the air or on the ground?" Hunter asked Dominus.

"In the air for as long as you can," Dominus answered. "When you run out of arrows, join the fight on the ground." Hunter nodded.

"Got it."

He strode up to Vi, Sukri, and Xerxes, who were standing just at the tree line. Xerxes smiled at him, and Sukri stepped up to give him a quick hug and a kiss.

"You guys ready?" he asked. Xerxes put a huge hand on his shoulder.

"Good luck," the big guy signed. "Stay safe."

"You too," Hunter signed back. Then he switched to speaking. "Take care of Sukri for me."

Xerxes grunted in the affirmative, and Vi smiled.

"No worries Hunter," she reassured. "We'll take care of her for you."

Hunter grabbed his bow, adjusting the straps to the large quiver on his back. Then he gave Sukri one last kiss.

"Guess this is it," he said. "Love you Puss."

"Yeah you do," Sukri replied, her eyes twinkling. She wrapped her hands around the back on his head, pulling him in again forcefully and kissing him…and not in a way that was acceptable in public. She shoved him back then. "Now go fly and kill some shit."

"Yes ma'am," he replied, saluting sharply.

He unfurled his wings, then leapt into the air, beating his wings rapidly, the ground pulling away from him. Soon everyone was far below, the forest extending to the horizon before him. He spotted black creatures swarming toward them, less than a mile away now…and closing the distance rapidly.

He took a deep breath in, steeling himself for what was to come.

Here goes, he thought.

* * *

Sukri watched as Hunter flew away, then reached for her metal staff, holding it before her. Vi unsheathed her longsword, and Dio readied his staff as well. Xerxes stood with them, hardly needing a weapon to ready. The huge guy *was* a weapon.

"Come back behind the front lines," a voice called out from behind. It was Tykus, riding atop his warhorse. "Our archers are preparing their first volley."

Sukri obeyed, following the others as they made their way to the back of row after row of soldiers. The men parted before them, none eager to be corrupted by Sukri or Xerxes. Or even Dio. They reached the back lines, where the archers were readying their bows. More archers stood atop the King's Road, aiming into the woods.

They waited.

The Fringe was eerily silent, the usual noises of birds and insects utterly absent. Which could only mean one thing: they sensed what was coming, and knew not to be there when it arrived.

Sukri glanced at Vi, who gave her a reassuring nod. She stared at the backs of the soldiers in front of them, the trees ahead visible over the men's' shoulders. The soldiers readied their weapons and shields, some carrying swords, others maces or warhammers. They glanced at each other nervously, some making jokes, others bouncing on the balls of their feet.

And then a hush went over them…and Sukri spotted movement in the forest.

Dark shapes bounding through the vegetation, black creatures running on all fours toward the line of soldiers and Ironclad. She heard the sound of bowstrings being pulled taught behind her, and saw the soldiers at the front of the line set wide stances, preparing for the onslaught.

"Archers ready!" Dominus commanded.

The Svartálfar rushed out of the Fringe, charging across the packed dirt of the Deadlands.

"Fire!" Dominus shouted.

Hundreds of arrows shot high overhead, arcing downward to the tree line in a rain of destruction. A few of the Svartálfar fell, and were quickly trampled by their brethren from behind. But most somehow managed to dodge the arrows.

"Fire at will!" Dominus shouted, and the archers nocked more arrows. The Svartálfar galloped toward the front line of soldiers, hundreds of the foul creatures, only thirty meters away now.

Twenty.

"Hold the line!" Dominus cried.

And then the Svartálfar struck.

They hurled themselves at the front line of soldiers, slamming into their shields. The impact sent the soldiers stumbling backward into the men behind them…just as a second volley of arrows flew overhead. The arrows fell into the middle of the swarm of Svartálfar, who dodged out of the way with frightening speed.

Few arrows struck.

The creatures tore at the soldiers, clawing and biting with no regard for their own lives. And for every beast that was cut down, another took its place.

"Ironclad, close ranks!" Dominus commanded.

The Ironclad on either side of the long line of soldiers rushed forward, corralling the Svartálfar in a huge circle three Ironclad deep, extending into the forest itself.

"Soldiers, push forward!" Dominus cried.

Another volley of arrows shot overhead, striking a scant few Svartálfar. The line of soldiers marched forward, one step at a time, forcing the Svartálfar back toward the tree line. The creatures attacked the Ironclad, but found them to be much more difficult opponents than the soldiers. Their claws were all but useless against the Ironclad's thick armor, and as quick as the Svartálfar were, with nowhere to run, the Ironclad grabbed them, tearing them limb-from-limb.

"Hey Blue," Vi called out. Xerxes glanced at her. "Go play. I'll protect Sukri."

Xerxes gave her an ugly grin, then strode forward, shoving the soldiers on either side away from him. He stomped up to the front of the line, reaching the Svartálfar. They turned on him, a half-dozen of the creatures leaping at him. Xerxes didn't even bother to block or dodge. He just stood there as the enemy clawed, kicked, bit, and bludgeoned him with their long limbs. As they crawled up onto his back and head. One Svartálfar on his back reached around to bury its claws into Xerxes' eye-sockets.

And Xerxes just let them do it.

"What is he *doing*?" Sukri demanded, turning to Vi.

"Watch," she replied.

Xerxes lashed out suddenly, punching a Svartálfar right in the chest. It flew backward, slamming into its brethren and knocking them down. He grabbed another by the throat with two hands, using his other two to twist its head around 180 degrees. He tossed it aside, reaching for a third Svartálfar and tearing its arms off, then beating at it – and any other Svartálfar that got close enough – with its own limbs.

"Forward!" Dominus commanded. "To the tree line!"

The soldiers nearest Xerxes pressed forward, emboldened by the huge Ironclad's rage. As more Svartálfar focused on Xerxes, the soldiers at the front of the line were able to gain ground, meter by meter.

Hunter flew by overhead, shooting arrows down into the army of Svartálfar in rapid succession. More of the beasts dropped or were injured, allowing the soldiers to cut them down. Xerxes continued his onslaught, tearing through the Svartálfar like the juggernaut he was. One of them grabbed a warhammer a soldier had dropped, swinging it at the back of Xerxes' legs.

Xerxes' knees buckled, and he fell onto his back on the dirt.

The Svartálfar swarmed on top of him, grabbing rocks and pummeling his face and body.

"We have to help him!" Sukri cried, rushing forward. But Vi held her back.

"He'll be alright," she countered. "And we've pushed them to the Fringe. Watch."

The soldiers and Ironclad *had* pushed the Svartálfar all the way back to the tree line; the creatures were amongst the trees now, the soldiers preventing them from moving forward and the Ironclad surrounding them on the sides and rear in the forest. Sukri glanced up at the King's Road to her right, spotting archers standing at the edge, lighting their arrows on fire.

"Ready!" Dominus shouted. "Fire!"

The arrows shot through the air toward the trees, and more flaming arrows flew overhead from the archers behind Sukri. The arrows fell into the forest, where the Kingdom's men had doused huge quantities of oil.

The forest burst into flames.

The fire spread rapidly, engulfing many of the Svartálfar, and even a few Ironclad. The Ironclad held the ring, trapping the Svartálfar within the rapidly expanding inferno.

The agonizing screams of the Svartálfar pierced the air, the fire greedily consuming them. Thick black smoke rose above the trees, bringing with it the stench of burning wood and flesh.

"Hold the circle!" Dominus commanded. "Don't let them through!"

The Svartálfar closest to the ring of soldiers and Ironclad tried to climb *over* them, and many were cut down in the process. But more Svartálfar crawled over their comrades' bodies, attempting to leap over or squeeze through the line. The line held, however, the soldiers and Ironclad cutting down the few Svartálfar that managed to break through.

Then the Svartálfar all moved as one, concentrating on the front of the line. Some of the beasts – still on fire – leapt into the soldiers, sacrificing themselves…but forcing the soldiers back from the flames. Other Svartálfar set themselves on fire deliberately, then rushed at the soldiers, doing the same.

The line of soldiers fell backward in the middle, and the Svartálfar started spilling through widening gaps between the soldiers…rushing right toward Sukri! Sukri swore, gripping her staff tightly.

And then Vi and Dio ran ahead of her, intercepting the black beasts.

One of the Svartálfar lunged at Dio, who dodged to the side, his silver staff a blur as it swung in a tight arc at the thing's neck…decapitating it. He took down another beast with a vicious downward chop, splitting its skull in two. The blade on his staff got caught in the creature's skull, and he yanked his staff – and the beast's corpse – toward himself, kicking it square in the chest and sending it flying backward into two other Svartálfar.

Dio leapt at the beasts as they dodged out of the way of their fallen comrade, smashing one in the temple and slicing another's throat in a spray of blood. All in a single, smooth chain of attacks.

But as impressive as he was, Vi was downright spectacular.

A Svartálfar leapt at her, slashing at her face with its claws. Her longsword moved so quickly it was impossible to follow, all while she dodged to the side.

The creature fell to the ground, its hand, forearm, and shoulder separated from each other, its head toppling from its shoulders.

Before it'd even struck the ground, Vi was already sprinting forward, right into the ever-growing swarm of Svartálfar rushing at her.

They attacked from all sides, and Vi spun in a circle, slicing off limbs and heads, her blade a blur amidst jets of crimson blood pumping into the air around her. She back-kicked one Svartálfar so hard it flew a good four meters, landing less than a meter from Sukri. Sukri backpedaled, staring at the thing, ready to attack it with her staff.

But it didn't have a head. Or a left arm. And there was a gaping wound at its groin.

She watched as Vi and Dio worked, twin gods of death amongst the Svartálfar. They were like night and day, Dio a ruthless, methodical killer, and Vi looking like she was having an absolute blast. Together, they were barely managing to hold the Svartálfar back, preventing them from getting to the archers and Sukri…and Dominus and General Leo.

But as more Svartálfar pushed through the line of soldiers ahead, it became impossible for Dio and Vi to hold all of them back, and the foul creatures began spilling around them on either side, rushing toward Sukri and the archers.

Shit!

She heard a *thump* behind her, and turned to see Tykus having dismounted. The former king rushed to her side, unsheathing his huge sword.

"Back-to-back!" he cried.

Sukri obeyed, pressing her back against his…just as the Svartálfar reached them.

One of them bound up to her like a dog, jumping at her and raking at her with its claws. She thrust the butt of her staff at its belly, but it batted her staff aside, clawing at her face. She jerked her head back, swinging her staff at its flank and shoving it to the side at the last moment.

It landed, immediately pivoting and lunging at her again…far too quickly for her to react to.

She felt Tykus turn, and saw a huge blade intercept the Svartálfar, slicing through its chest.

It fell to the dirt, dead.

Two more Svartálfar rushed at Sukri, attacking from either side. She slashed at one of them, but it grabbed her staff, yanking it right out of her hands. She stumbled forward, just as the other Svartálfar slammed into her back, throwing her toward the ground.

She rolled into a somersault, her cat-like reflexes kicking in, and got to her feet, extending her claws and slashing at the Svartálfar who'd grabbed her staff. Her claws raked its eyes, rupturing one of them and nearly taking its nose off.

It fell backward, and she retrieved her staff, spinning and striking the Svartálfar who'd rammed into her from behind. It ducked…and Tykus cut its head clean off its shoulders.

"Back-to-back!" Tykus repeated, and Sukri rushed to his side again. More Svartálfar came, forming a circle around them. Far too many for Sukri and Tykus to handle.

Thwap!

The sound of bowstrings firing came from behind, and a volley of arrows shot into the Svartálfar around them, dropping fully half of the creatures. The remaining beasts split in two groups, one rushing at the archers, the other attacking Sukri and Tykus.

Four of the deadly creatures rushed Sukri at once, leaping at her in unison. Sukri cried out, swinging her staff in an arc at them.

And then they all fell to the ground before her, their heads separated from their bodies.

Sukri stared at her staff in disbelief.

"Hey Puss," a voice greeted. She looked up, seeing Vi standing before her, longsword coated with blood. As was her leather uniform. And her face.

She was grinning from ear-to-ear.

"Vi!" Sukri cried in relief.

"Lose the staff," Vi instructed. "You don't need a weapon. You *are* a weapon."

Sukri nodded, throwing the staff to the ground. Another Svartálfar lunged at her, wrapping its hands around her throat.

She raked her claws across its face, then grabbed it, leaping a full four meters upward, then kicking the thing right in the chest. It flew backward, and she twisted in the air, landing on all fours.

A second dark elf attacked…and stumbled away a moment later, its intestines spilling from long gashes in its belly.

All right, she thought, dispatching yet another Svartálfar.

The line of soldiers re-formed, closing off the rest of the Svartálfar army within the circle. And in the distance, Sukri saw Xerxes in the forest, towering over the burning Svartálfar around him. One of his arms was on fire, a fact that didn't seem to bother him in the least.

They all watched as Xerxes tore Svartálfar after Svartálfar apart, even as flames engulfed the trees around them, the smoke so thick it was hard to see.

"Hot damn, but I do love watching Blue work," Vi mused.

* * *

Xerxes stood behind the line of soldiers, watching as the enemy poured out of the forest, thousands of little black animals rushing at the Kingdom's men. Volley after volley of arrows did little to stop the things; they moved too quickly, dodging out of the way. And despite their weapons and shields, the soldiers were too slow and fragile to withstand the onslaught.

He shifted his weight from foot to foot, glancing at Sukri. As much as he wanted to wade into the fight, he'd promised Hunter he'd protect Sukri.

"Ironclad, close ranks!" he heard Dominus shout. He suppressed his irritation at the man having the gall to lead *his* men. But Mom had spoken, and Xerxes would not disobey her.

The Ironclad circled around the little creatures, forming a ring around them.

"Soldiers, push forward!" Dominus commanded.

Row after row of soldiers obeyed, marching forward slowly, pushing the enemy closer to the trees ahead. Xerxes watched as the creatures killed soldier after soldier, and found himself clenching all four fists.

"Hey Blue," Vi called out. Xerxes glanced at her. "Go play. I'll stay with Puss."

Xerxes grinned at her, then strode forward eagerly, walking up to the rearmost soldiers and pushing his way through them. They parted before him, and he reached the front line…and the first of the little black beasts.

Their heads turned to face him, and a half-dozen of them rushed at him, leaping at him from the front and the sides. They slammed into him, their combined weight not even enough to force him back a step. They crawled up his body, clawing at his arms, his chest, his belly. He barely felt their little claws as they scratched harmlessly at his armor.

Xerxes smirked down at them, reaching down and petting one on the head, even as it tore at his chest.

"YOU…CUTE," he murmured.

The little thing snarled, jerking its head away and crawling around to his back. He felt it get on top of his shoulders, then felt its hands reach around to his face.

Its claws plunged into his eyes, a sharp pain lancing through his skull.

The world went black.

Xerxes clenched his fists, the sudden, excruciating pain a shock. He resisted the urge to tear the hands away from his face, feeling his bemusement turning quickly to anger. The creature raked its claws over his face, hooking one claw up his nostril and pulling. Hard.

He felt a sharp pain there, felt his flesh tearing, hot blood pouring down his lips.

Xerxes snapped.

He roared, punching out blindly with one fist, feeling it strike something. There was a loud shriek, and he reached out with another two hands, closing his fingers around something. A throat. He squeezed it so hard it crumpled under his palms, then reached out with his other two hands, grabbing the thing's head and twisting it all the way around with a loud *crunch.*

Xerxes tossed it aside, then reached out again, grabbing an arm and tearing it clean off. He swung the severed limb wildly, feeling it connect again and again.

All while the thing on his back was continuing to rake at his face.

He reached around at last, grabbing it by the head and plunging his thumbs into its eye-sockets, then tossing it aside. His vision returned quickly, blurry at first, then clear.

There were creatures all around him,

"Forward!" Dominus commanded. "To the tree line!"

The soldiers behind Xerxes pressed forward, and Xerxes waded forward with them, grabbing anything that got near him. They were fast, the little things, but with nowhere to run – and being pathetically weak – they couldn't evade his grasp for long. Their little arms tore from their shoulders easily, their scrawny necks snapping under his powerful grip.

He grabbed one by the throat, lifting it high into the air, then punching it in the face. He felt its facial bones cave in, and its limbs jerked uncontrollably as it seized, bloody spittle leaking from its mouth.

That made him smile.

Something heavy slammed into the back of his knees, and his legs gave out, sending him falling onto his back on the dirt with a *thump.* He grunted, the air blasting out of his lungs.

And then the creatures were upon him.

They swarmed on top of him, slashing at him with their claws. One of them had a warhammer, and sent it crashing down on his face. He felt his left cheekbone crumple, the sudden pain sending a jolt through him.

His vision blackened.

Xerxes roared, grabbing the warhammer and tearing it from the thing's hands. He used his other two hands to grab anything he could, crushing, yanking, and tearing. He kicked his legs, connecting with anything he could. Bit anything that got too close to his face. There was no thought. Only rage.

He let it take him, every enemy he killed feeding his bloodlust, every pain he endured making it grow. He wanted to kill everything. He *would* kill everything. Make them pay for threatening his family.

There was shouting from behind, and then a burst of heat. He heard screaming all around him…and the smell of burning flesh.

Xerxes' vision slowly returned, blackness replaced by light, then blurry colors. Black and orange and red. The heat intensified, and his vision sharpened.

The creatures and trees around him were on fire.

Enemies threw themselves on him even as they burned, trying to burn him along with them. He ignored the flames, rising to his feet and walking right into the fire, dragging the enemies around him into it. They screeched as they burned, their black fur smoking as the fire consumed them.

The flames licked at his armor, burning his flesh underneath. Xerxes ignored the pain, striding right through the flames, grabbing nearby beasts and tossing them into the inferno. Still the things swarmed around him, trying to drag him into the tallest flames.

He resisted, tearing off their limbs. Plunging his fingers into their eye-sockets and ripping out their eyeballs one-by-one. Reaching into their mouths and tearing out their teeth, their tongues. Destroying anything he could get his hands on.

Eventually the remaining creatures gave up, fleeing from him and running deeper into the forest, at the ring of Ironclad barring their way. Xerxes ran after them, watching as the little things swarmed his men, crawling over each other to leap past the circle entrapping them. They weren't even trying to fight anymore.

The Ironclad killed many of them, but some managed to escape, fleeing into the forest.

Within moments, every last one of the creatures had either escaped, been torn apart, or burned to death.

Xerxes surveyed the burning trees around him, thick smoke choking his lungs. He gazed at the bodies littering the ground, most of them the enemy, some of them soldiers and Ironclad. Then he strode back to the line of soldiers at the edge of the Fringe, watching as the parted before him, giving him wide berth. He strode through their ranks, ignoring their wide-eyed stares, reaching Sukri and Vi, who were standing next to the copy of the king.

“Feel better?” Vi inquired.

“BETTER,” Xerxes agreed. “HUNTER…OK?”

“Probably,” Vi answered. “He’s been flying around the whole time. Probably killed at least one of the Svartálfar,” she added.

There was a *thump* behind them, and Xerxes turned to see Hunter having landed a few yards away.

“Lot more than that,” Hunter retorted. “Hey bro, hey Sukri,” he added. “That wasn’t too bad.”

“Surprisingly no,” Vi agreed. “But we still haven’t seen Zagamar.”

“Probably didn’t have the guts to come at us himself,” Sukri guessed.

“Yeah, no,” Hunter countered. “Zaggie’s a megalomaniacal asshole. He won’t be scared of us. Vi’s right…we *should* be surprised that it was this easy.”

“The Svartálfar are very incomplete copies of Zagamar,” Tykus pointed out. “They were still predominantly animals.”

“Agreed,” Hunter said. “Which means these were pawns. Fodder.”

“They all will be,” Vi countered. “You yourself said Zagamar would never let any of them become too much like him.”

“We haven’t seen Zagamar yet,” Tykus warned, staring off into the woods. “This was a test.”

“A test we passed,” Sukri chimed in. “We should go after Zagamar before he has the time to make more of these things.”

“Agreed,” Hunter replied.

“We’ll take care of cleaning up here first,” Vi stated. “Otherwise a lot of these things are going to regenerate.”

Xerxes grunted, watching as the soldiers and his men attended to their wounded comrades. At least a quarter of the soldiers had been either killed or significantly wounded. The Ironclad had fared better, with a majority of them still standing. He heard the clopping of hooves from behind, and saw Dominus approaching. Even atop his horse, the man was still not as tall as Xerxes.

“Slit the throats of every last Svartálfar,” Dominus ordered his men. “Drag them to a pile in the woods and burn them.”

Xerxes signaled for his men to help, and the soldiers and Ironclad got to work, quickly forming a huge pile of black corpses in the charred forest. They poured oil on it, and shot a flaming arrow into the pile. Flames spread quickly over the mass of bodies, thick smoke billowing upward. The stench of burning flesh and hair reached Xerxes’ nostrils.

The smell of victory.

He stepped over to Hunter’s side, putting a hand on his brother’s small shoulder. Hunter glanced up at him and smiled.

“Good work bro,” he signed.

“You too,” Xerxes signed back.

The smoke from the burning Svartálfar filled the sky, mingling with the smoke from the burning trees around the huge funeral pyre and forming a thick haze in the forest, the intact trees beyond barely visible through it.

"Guys?" he heard Sukri blurt out. Xerxes glanced down at the little cat-girl.

"What?" Hunter asked. Sukri pointed at the wall of smoke far ahead.

"Thought I saw something."

Xerxes peered through the smoke, but saw only trees.

"NOT…SEE," he replied.

But then he *did* see something. A hint of movement beyond the flames and the wall of smoke rising from them.

He heard Sukri draw in a sharp breath.

"Guys!" she shouted.

Dark creatures burst out from behind the curtain of smoke, running toward them; a line of Svartálfar extending east and west as far as the eye could see. More and more of the beasts appeared, thousands of them rushing past the burning pyre. Hundreds of them crawled up the tall wooden columns supporting the King's Road, reaching the top and overwhelming the archers there, tearing them apart in seconds.

And then the Svartálfar stopped at the edge of the woods, an army easily ten times the size as the one they'd faced moments ago.

"Shit," Hunter swore.

"Circle up!" Dominus shouted. "Archers, prepare to fire!"

The soldiers and Ironclad obeyed, starting to form a huge circle around him. The Svartálfar horde stared at them, still standing at the tree line.

Then the ground rumbled.

Xerxes watched as the trees far in the distance – well beyond the creatures – shuddered, a loud *crack* piercing the air. One tree toppled over, then another, then another, like dominos. The line of Svartálfar directly ahead parted.

And something *huge* burst through the vegetation between them, knocking over the trees in its path. A giant serpent with legs like a centipede, silver scales covering much of its body. But the scales on its head were mostly black, as were its sunken eyes. A long, forked black tongue flicked out of its mouth, and it stopped at the tree line, rearing its head up until it was as high as the treetops on either side.

"Oh *shit*," Xerxes heard Sukri blurt out.

"What the hell is *that*?" Hunter demanded.

The serpent lowered its head, and Xerxes spotted something standing on its back. At first he thought it was just another of the Svartálfar. But it appeared to be a man. A man utterly nude, with skin as black as night, the muscles of his chest and abdomen rippling with every movement. His arms and legs seemed too long for his body, his face narrow with prominent cheekbones. His black, sunken eyes stared down at them.

He raised one fist in the air.

"Citizens!" he shouted, his deep voice carrying easily over the battlefield.

A hush went over the soldiers.

"Put away your weapons," he demanded. "Join me, and we will take back what is ours. We will crush the tyrants that seek to control us. To kill us for the crime of being ourselves!"

No one moved.

"I offer you the chance to stay yourselves," he continued. "Or if you wish it, to gain the gift of my will. I urge you to take it."

He gazed at the assembled soldiers. Not a single man moved.

"Go to hell," Dominus shouted. Zagamar turned to the former duke, then sighed.

"Very well," he stated. "Remember that I gave you a choice."

Then he brought his hand downward sharply, and the massive horde of Svartálfar attacked.

CHAPTER 41

Hunter burst backward as the massive horde of Svartálfar rushed out of the Fringe toward them, flowing around the still-burning funeral pyre and onto the packed dirt of the Deadlands.

"Back!" he shouted, grabbing Sukri and pulling her with him.

"Form a line!" Dominus shouted. "Archers, fire at will!"

The soldiers rushed to form a line in front of Hunter and the others, the archers falling back and readying their bows. A volley of arrows arced overhead, raining down on the Svartálfar right as their front line smashed into the line of soldiers. The soldiers raised their shields, stumbling backward but holding the line.

The Svartálfar leapt over each other, throwing themselves at the soldiers from above like people throwing themselves into a mosh pit. Wave after wave of the creatures crawled and jumped over each other, dogpiling the line of soldiers and forcing them to backpedal or get trampled under the sheer weight of the horde.

And one-by-one they did fall, the line of soldiers caving in, the Svartálfar tearing the Kingdom's men apart in a bloody massacre.

"Protect the archers!" Dominus cried. "Ironclad, hold the line!"

Another volley of arrows shot at the Svartálfar, dropping dozens of them…and not so much as slowing down the onslaught of the beasts. The Ironclad rushed in to help the soldiers, the huge, eight-foot-tall creatures forming a much more formidable barrier.

"Get on your horse!" Dio shouted at Camilla, dragging her winged steed by the reins toward her. He helped her mount it. "Fly!" he ordered, slapping the horse on the flank. It reared up on its hind legs, flapping its wings and leaping into the air. Dio rushed to the front lines with the Ironclad and the soldiers, his staff whirling as he took out Svartálfar after Svartálfar. Vi fought her way to his side, the two of them murdering the foul creatures in rapid succession…and barely managing to hold the line.

"Help them," Hunter told Xerxes. "I'll protect Sukri."

Still, Xerxes hesitated, staring at Hunter.

"I'll be fine," Hunter insisted. "If anything happens, I'll fly."

Xerxes nodded, then stomped up to the front lines, pushing soldiers and Ironclad out of his way. He joined Vi and Dio, grabbing any nearby Svartálfar and tearing them apart as if they were made of paper.

But there were far too many of the creatures for them to contain, and they spilled around the line of soldiers and Ironclad on either side, rushing inward toward Hunter and Sukri. And the archers, and Dominus, and Tykus.

"Circle up!" Dominus commanded. "Protect the archers!"

The line of soldiers and Ironclad fell backward at the edges, but the Svartálfar continued to rush past them on either side.

"Hunter!" Sukri cried, gripping his arm.

And then the creatures were upon them.

Hunter unsheathed his longsword as the nearest Svartálfar leapt at him, lopping off one of its arms, then decapitating it. Four more rushed at him in its place, and Hunter pushed Sukri back, focusing inward. His eyes were drawn to the tall man standing atop the serpent in the distance. A man with skin as black as night, a man instantly familiar, as if plucked out of his memories and brought to life.

He took a deep breath in.

Za-ga-mar!

He felt the Legend within him stir, and time slowed.

The four Svartálfar rushed at him in slow-motion, and his mind raced, planning the manner of their deaths in an instant. And in an instant, they died, their heads separated from their shoulders.

His mind calculated rapidly, studying the massive army before him. The man standing atop the horned serpent. The conclusion was instantaneous.

This was Zagamar reborn.

Hunter had a sudden urge to take his sword and thrust it into his own chest.

He resisted, knowing that the piece of Zagamar inside of him recognized that Zagamar had been reborn, and that Hunter – a mere fraction of the full Legend – was no longer useful. He wrestled control of his body, forcing Zaggie to work for him. Using him.

You're mine, he thought. *I'm in control now.*

Five more Svartálfar rushed at him, and he dispatched four of them rapidly. The fifth one leapt at Sukri, shoving her onto her back and clawing at her face. She raked at it with her foot-claws, tearing through its belly, its intestines spilling onto her. She slashed its face with her hands, rupturing its eyeballs with her sharp claws.

Hunter kicked it off of her, pulling her to her feet…just as dozens more of the beasts rushed at them from either side.

"Get behind me!" Hunter cried, gripping his longsword with both hands.

And then the giant serpent struck.

It lunged forward, swinging its long tail at the line of soldiers before it, sending Svartálfar and soldiers flying to the right. Only Vi and Dio managed to avoid the attack, leaping over the tail as it swept by. Everyone else was decimated…even Xerxes, who was tossed to the right, landing with a *thump* on the dirt. Svartálfar swarmed over him, piling on top of him.

The middle of the line of soldiers was gone, Svartálfar pouring through the gap toward Hunter and Sukri.

Hunter focused, time slowing even further as he gave in a little more to Zaggie. He set his feet wide apart, watching as hundreds of Svartálfar rushed toward him. He knew instantly that there were too many of them to take on single-handedly…even for him.

Vi turned and sprinted toward him, cutting down anything that dared to get in her way. Dio was right behind her, and Xerxes rushed toward them, Svartálfar hanging from his body as he waded through the swarming horde.

But there was no way they'd make it to Hunter – or the archers – before the Svartálfar did.

Another volley of arrows struck the beasts, felling dozens of them. But the Svartálfar behind merely trampled over their fallen comrades. Hunter gripped the hilt of his sword tightly, planting his feet wide. His heart raced in his chest, his breath coming in short gasps.

Can't maintain for long, he knew. *Body will give out.*

The slow-motion tsunami of Svartálfar reached him, an unstoppable juggernaut.

He felt the Legend within him calculating, taking in every detail, analyzing every possible strategy. Thoughts moving so fast they spilled over each other, impossible to follow. He didn't even bother, giving in to it. Trusting it.

And then he burst into action.

His blade moved in a slow-motion dance, faster than anything around him, a graceful harbinger of death. It cut into Svartálfar after Svartálfar, sprays of blood from their severed arteries heralding their deaths like crimson fountains all around him.

They attacked him, lunging at him, trying to overwhelm him. But he was not overwhelmed. He was incapable of being overwhelmed.

His deadly dance flowed effortlessly from one swing of his sword to the next, every attack planned long in advance. He saw Sukri behind him, watched as one Svartálfar tried to attack her. He lopped off one of its arms, even as Sukri raked her claws across its face, tearing the flesh from its bones.

She lifted her leg straight up in an axe-kick, sending it down, her foot-claws extended…and tearing the beast apart from the chest to the groin. Intestines spilled from its body, and it crumpled to the ground.

But even as Hunter destroyed the Svartálfar around him, more rushed past, reaching the archers and decimating them. The foul creatures lunged at Dominus and General Leo, attacking their horses.

General Leo fell from his steed, and was covered instantly in Svartálfar. They tore him apart, eating him alive.

Dominus fell from his horse, but somehow landed on his feet, drawing his sword instantly and moving with slow grace, killing the Svartálfar around him. Tykus joined him even as the Svartálfar felled the former king's steed, fighting back-to-back with Dominus as the beasts surrounded them.

Then the huge serpent rushed forward, the Svartálfar parting before it. It swung its tail in a wide arc, coming right for Hunter and Sukri.

Hunter grabbed Sukri, leaping into the air and beating his wings as hard as he could.

He lifted into the air just as the serpent's tail reached them, and it swung underneath their feet, obliterating the Svartálfar below. Vi and Dio managed to leap over the tail, but Xerxes wasn't so lucky; he flew to the side, sailing fifty feet to the right before landing amidst the sea of Svartálfar. The armor on his brother's right side had been crushed, blood spraying from cracks in the thick black plates.

Svartálfar pounced on Xerxes, clawing at his ruined armor, ripping hunks of it off and tearing at the exposed flesh beneath.

Xerxes threw the beasts off, rising to his feet and making his way toward the serpent. But the Svartálfar leapt on his back, while others pulled at his arms and legs, dragging him backward. The Svartálfar ahead of him clawed at his right side, ripping pieces of his flesh off and eating them.

He *howled.*

"Xerxes!" Hunter cried, flying above the fray.

"Drop me!" Sukri yelled. "Save him!"

He started to glide toward his brother, but Zagamar's voice inside him immediately rejected the idea.

Drop the girl and she dies.

Hunter hesitated, watching in horror as the Svartálfar pulled Xerxes down to his knees, ripping at his shattered shoulder and flank with their claws and their teeth. The huge Ironclad swung at them, smashing their faces and ripping off limbs, but for every Svartálfar he killed, another took its place.

The creatures dug into his blue mane, rupturing it and gorging themselves on the glowing gel within.

Shit.

Hunter felt a sudden pressure in his chest, and realized that his heart was beating far too quickly now. He shoved Zagamar back into the recesses of his mind, time speeding up instantly. He watched as the Svartálfar continued to consume his brother, eating through one of his right arms and tearing it clean off his body.

"Vi!" he cried. "Help Xerxes!"

Vi rushed toward Xerxes, cutting a swathe through the Svartálfar in her way. But the sea of enemies slowed her down, throwing themselves at her with abandon.

"Mother!" Dio shouted.

Hunter turned to see Lady Camilla riding atop her flying steed. She swooped down toward Dio, who used his staff to pole-vault up to the horse in mid-flight, landing to sit behind her. She flew right over Xerxes, and Dio leapt from the saddle, plummeting to the ground beside the Ironclad.

And then he went ape-shit.

Dio cut down the Svartálfar clinging to Xerxes, blood spraying from the wicked blades at each end of his staff as he hacked them apart. Xerxes recovered, rising to his feet and lashing out at the beasts around him with his three remaining arms.

Vi pushed through the masses, making her way to Dio and Xerxes' side.

"Go!" Dio shouted, fighting off the Svartálfar around them as Vi led Xerxes back toward Hunter…and a line of Ironclad and remaining soldiers that had formed between Hunter and the bulk of the Svartálfar army.

"Drop me," Sukri insisted. "Save your brother!"

"No, it's too dangerous," Hunter retorted. Dominus and Tykus were barely managing to hold back the Svartálfar directly below them; if he set her down, she'd get torn apart in seconds.

"I'll take her," he heard a woman say. He turned, seeing Camilla fly up to his side on her winged horse. Hunter flew up over the horse, lowering Sukri behind the Lady.

"Thanks," he said. Camilla nodded, then flew off. Hunter grabbed his bow, firing arrow after arrow, taking down as many of the black beasts as he could until Vi and Xerxes reached the line of Ironclad. The Ironclad surrounded Xerxes, protecting him from the Svartálfar, even as Vi returned to the fray, making her way back toward Dio.

The black-and-red uniformed Seeker was surrounded by Svartálfar…and the huge serpent was slithering toward him.

"Camilla!" Hunter warned, flying over the sea of enemies toward the serpent. He saw Camilla steer her winged horse toward Dio. But the serpent got to him first, rearing its huge head back, then lunging at the Seeker!

Hunter cursed, shooting an arrow at the serpent's eye. But it moved too quickly, the arrow missing its mark and bouncing off its scales…just as its gaping maw snapped at Dio.

But instead of running, Dio slammed the butt of his staff on the ground, pole-vaulting upward…and landing right on top of the serpent's head.

And sprinted down the thing's back without skipping a beat, charging right at Zagamar.

* * *

Dio ran down the back of the horned serpent's long back, his eyes on the tall man standing atop it ten meters ahead. If it was truly Zagamar – a Legend older than the Kingdom itself – Dio would know soon enough. The Legend's power would be overwhelming…and every second that he spent near Zagamar would mean losing a little more of who he was. Dio's mask would protect him somewhat, the multilayered wood helping to insulate him from the Legend's will. But not completely.

He would have to be quick.

Dio sprinted right up to Zagamar, whipping his staff in a lightning-fast arc at the Legend's long neck.

Zagamar stepped back, the attack missing him by a fraction of a centimeter.

Dio followed up instantly with another swing, then another, each attack following the last in rapid succession. But Zagamar dodged each with ease, contorting his tall, muscular body with inhuman speed…and then lashed out with a kick to Dio's belly, so fast it was a blur.

Dio stumbled backward, his breath bursting from his lungs.

"You're strong," Zagamar declared, eyeing him approvingly. "We could use a man like you."

Dio stared at the Legend, waiting for the pain in his abs to subside. He could *feel* the Legend's will, muted as it was by his mask.

His heart began to hammer in his chest, a sudden hunger gripping his gut.

Dio rushed forward, his staff whirling so quickly that it was a blur, attacking twice as quickly as before. Slashing, thrusting, and chopping with such fluid grace that each attack led into the next without pause, a deadly dance that no man – or woman, other than Vi – had ever survived.

But Zagamar did, moving faster than anyone or anything Dio had ever seen. Faster than the Svartálfar. Faster even than Vi.

The Legend dodged every attack each missing him by a hair's breadth. Dio pushed himself, moving even faster…but Zagamar kept his long arms at his sides, casually avoiding each blow.

Then he kicked Dio again, sending Dio stumbling backward a second time.

"Don't waste your life," Zagamar insisted. "I offer you a place at my side. A chance to save humanity from itself. To make it better."

Dio grimaced, taking another step back, staying as far away from the Legend's will as possible. He glanced down, seeing the silver scales of the serpent's back; the scales were completely black where Zagamar stood. The Legend was bending the serpent to his will.

Another chill ran through him, and he swallowed in a dry throat, feeling the hunger within him intensify. Speed was his strength, but Zagamar was faster.

He needed to fight smarter.

Dio lunged at Zagamar, striking at the Legend with three attacks in rapid succession. But the third attack was a feint; Dio pulled it at the last minute, switching direction and sending the other end of his staff up at Zagamar's chin in a vicious uppercut. Zagamar leaned backward, the staff barely missing him.

And Dio kicked the Legend right in the nuts.

But Zagamar twisted to the side at the last minute, grabbing Dio's leg and throwing it upward and backward, sending Dio into a backflip. Dio kicked out with his other foot, striking Zagamar under the chin.

Hard.

Dio finished his backflip, landing on his feet and rushing at the Legend, even as Zagamar stumbled backward. Dio leapt at him, thrusting his staff at the man's chest.

Zagamar was a blur as he dodged to the side, grabbing Dio's staff and tearing it from his hands.

Dio ducked, unsheathing a knife at his waist and thrusting it right under Zagamar's ribs, embedding it in the man's liver. Then he yanked it out, slashing at the Legend's neck.

Zagamar blocked the attack, slashing at Dio's face with one clawed hand. Dio's mask tore from his face, flying into the crowd of Svartálfar below.

The Legend grabbed Dio by the throat then, tossing his staff to the side and lifting Dio into the air.

Dio slashed at Zagamar's wrist with his dagger, cutting through the Legend's black flesh. Blood spurted from the wound in twin jets. But Zagamar ignored this, yanking the knife from Dio's hand, then pulling him closer, until their noses were nearly touching.

Dio felt the hunger within him intensify, voices calling out all around him. All of them chanting in unison.

Za-ga-mar!

"You feel me, don't you?" the Legend stated. "The gift of my perspective. It will teach you. It will help you understand."

Zagamar pressed his forehead against Dio's.

Za-ga-mar!

Dio cried out, kicking at Zagamar, but the Legend ignored the blows, letting them land without bothering to block them.

Then an arrow slammed into Zagamar's left shoulder, making the Legend stumble to the side.

Zagamar drew his head back from Dio, taking Dio's knife and jamming it into his shoulder. Dio howled, the pain shooting all the way down his arm, his fingers going numb. Zagamar tore the arrow from his own shoulder, tossing it aside.

Hunter flew by, shooting another arrow at the Legend, but Zagamar caught it in mid-air, throwing it at Hunter as he flew away. The arrow struck

Hunter in one wing, sending him into a barrel-roll above the sea of Svartálfar. Hunter only barely managed to level off, gaining altitude quickly.

Zagamar turned back to Dio, lowering his feet to the snake's back and gripping his cheeks with his other hand, forcing Dio's jaws open.

Then he kneed Dio in the belly. Hard.

Dio doubled over in pain, and Zagamar forced him to his knees, standing over him.

"You don't understand yet, but you will," the Legend promised. "Your mind is closed, but I will open it."

He forced Dio's jaw open further, placing his still-bleeding wrist over Dio's mouth.

No!

Blood spurted from the gash there, the warm, salty fluid gushing into Dio's mouth.

Za-ga-mar!

The voices were louder now, more insistent. Images of a burnt-out village came to Dio, thousands of men standing around him. Chanting that name.

Za-ga-mar!

Dio spat out the blood, but more pumped into his mouth, and he swallowed reflexively, feeling the hot fluid course down his esophagus.

"Hunter, help him!" he heard a woman's voice scream.

Zagamar dodged another arrow his eyes never leaving Dio's. The hunger was overwhelming now, the voices drowning out everything else.

Za-ga-MAR!

"Don't be afraid," the Legend soothed. "Soon you will be faster. Stronger." He smiled. "Better."

He let go of Dio's throat, and Dio stumbled backward, landing on his back on the serpent's spine.

Za-ga-MAR!

Dio gasped, struggling to his feet, the knife still protruding from his shoulder. He gripped the hilt, yanking it from his flesh…and saw Hunter flying toward him, Vi clutched in the boy's arms. They were a good thirty meters away, and closing in fast.

He turned to Zagamar, watching as the Legend stared at him, the bleeding at the man's wrist already having slowed to a trickle. Already healing.

"Dio!" a woman's voice called out. It was Camilla; she too was flying toward him. Dio stared at her, knowing that if she got too close to Zagamar, she would almost certainly die…or worse.

Za-ga-MAR!

Dio put a hand to his heart, bowing his head at his mother.

And gripped the hilt of his knife with both hands, plunging it into his own chest.

Chapter 42

Hunter flew toward Zagamar and Dio, watching as the dark Legend held Dio by the throat, pressing his forehead against the Seeker's. He shot an arrow, watching as it slammed into Zagamar's shoulder.

Yes!

He drew another arrow, firing it at Zagamar right as he flew past…and felt something hit his left wing. Pain shot through it, and he cried out, pulling it into him reflexively. The move sent him into a barrel-roll, and he extended his wing quickly, righting himself before plummeting into the sea of Svartálfar below. The dark creatures leapt up at him, trying to pull him out of the air; he flapped his wings quickly, rising far above them and circling back toward Dio.

Zagamar kneed the Seeker in the belly, bringing Dio to his knees on the serpent's back. Then the Legend brought his still-bleeding wrist to Dio's mouth, forcing the Seeker's mouth open. Blood pumped into Dio's throat.

No!

Hunter flew faster, nocking another arrow. He could only watch as Dio spat up Zagamar's blood. But even more spurted into the Seeker's throat, spraying his face and neck.

"Hunter, help him!" Hunter heard Vi shout from below.

He fired his arrow at Zagamar, but the Legend dodged it. He flew past, spotting Vi directly ahead, fighting the Svartálfar all around her. She waved him down, and he veered toward her, flying a few yards above the churning masses. She kneed a Svartálfar in the belly, then jumped on its back, leaping up at Hunter as he flew over her. Hunter caught her, pumping his wings and bringing them well above the Svartálfar.

"Get me to Dio!" she ordered.

Hunter complied, circling around and flying back toward the serpent. He saw Camilla approaching on her flying horse from the left, and saw Dio rising to his feet, a dagger in his hands. The Seeker turned to face Camilla, then put a hand over his chest, bowing at her.

And gripped his dagger in both hands, plunging it into his own chest.

"No!" Hunter cried.

Dio fell to his knees, then onto his belly, rolling off the serpent's back and falling into the horde of Svartálfar below.

"God *damn* it!" Hunter cursed. He pumped his wings, flying even faster, aiming right for Zagamar. The Legend turned to look at him.

Zagamar looked *pissed.*

"Hunter, watch out!" Vi cried.

And then the serpent's tail smashed into him in mid-flight.

The world spun around crazily, and Hunter felt Vi let go of him. He spread his wings out wide, and the spinning slowed, then stopped. The serpent's tail had shot him nearly a hundred feet to the right; he grimaced, clutching at his left flank. Every breath sent a stabbing pain through his ribs, shooting up to his left shoulder.

He focused, settling into a glide, then circling around, scanning the crowd of Svartálfar for Vi. She was a hundred feet from the serpent, surrounded by Svartálfar, fighting for her life.

As he watched, one of the foul creatures got past her defenses, raking its claws down her back.

Vi cried out, whipping around and decapitating the beast, then fending off the others. But for every one that she killed, two more replaced them. She killed three more…and a fourth slashed at her face, connecting in a spray of blood.

"Vi!" Hunter shouted, pumping his wings and zooming toward her. She recovered, thrusting her longsword into the Svartálfar's belly, then yanking it out. She leapt upward as Hunter flew by, grabbing him by the elbows. He flew upward as quickly as he could, feeling claws raking at his legs. He ignored the pain, turning back toward the line of Ironclad, which were barely holding the Svartálfar army at bay. Beyond, he spotted Sukri attacking a Svartálfar, Xerxes at her side. Dominus and Tykus were back-to-back a few yards away, Svartálfar surrounding them.

Hunter dropped Vi next to Sukri and Xerxes, landing and drawing his longsword.

In the distance, the serpent approached, annihilating the Svartálfar in its path.

"Retreat!" Dominus commanded, his voice booming over the din of battle. "To the Kingdom!"

The remaining soldiers obeyed, turning and running.

"Come on!" Vi shouted, pulling Sukri and Hunter away from the Svartálfar horde.

"We can't outrun them!" Hunter protested.

"Fly," Vi ordered. "Take Sukri and get out of here!"

"But…"

"No buts," Vi interrupted. "Dominus, flag down Camilla. Tykus, get on Xerxes' back!"

Everyone obeyed, and Hunter cursed, sheathing his sword and turning his back to Sukri.

"Get on!" he shouted.

She grabbed on to his waist, and he leapt upward, flying north toward the Kingdom. Vi ran alongside Xerxes, with Tykus on Xerxes' back. Somehow Vi managed to keep up with his brother, running even faster than the Svartálfar chasing after them.

And behind them, the Ironclad held the line, staying right where they were.

"Xerxes!" Hunter shouted. "The Ironclad!"

But Xerxes didn't respond. The remaining soldiers – less than a hundred of them – hesitated, glancing back at the Ironclad. The Svartálfar were piling on the armored warriors, taking them down one-by-one. There was no chance of winning, but still the Ironclad did not run.

They were sacrificing themselves.

"Go!" Dominus urged. "Don't let them die in vain!"

The soldiers retreated, and in the distance, the Ironclad fought on bravely, somehow managing to hold the line. The Svartálfar tried to leap up on top of each other to make it over the wall of Ironclad, but the Ironclad pulled them out of the air, tossing them back into their brethren.

Hunter flew above Xerxes, Vi, and Sukri, spotting the great wall of the Kingdom over a mile away.

"Camilla, warn the Kingdom!" Dominus shouted from below. "Make them open the gate!"

Camilla burst forward on her flying horse, sailing past Hunter toward the Kingdom. Hunter glanced back, seeing the huge serpent slithering toward the wall of Ironclad, the Svartálfar falling back all around it.

Shit.

The serpent reached the Ironclad, swinging its massive tail at them. It swept through their ranks, sending Svartálfar and Ironclad flying.

The line was decimated.

Svartálfar poured over the fallen Ironclad, tearing at them with their teeth and claws. But the Ironclad fought back, rising to their feet and fighting until their last breath, even as the Svartálfar ate them alive.

Within moments, the Ironclad were no more.

The army of Svartálfar rushed forward then, chasing after the fleeing soldiers.

"Go, go!" Dominus shouted, sprinting across the Deadlands with Tykus at his side. The Kingdom was only a mile away now, and the enemy was still a good quarter-mile away. Hunter glanced to his left, spotting the King's Road there…and Svartálfar running atop it, keeping pace with the soldiers.

"Guys!" he shouted. "Svartálfar on the King's Road!"

"Take them out!" Vi cried.

Hunter grabbed his bow, nocking arrow after arrow and firing them into the long column of Svartálfar rushing over the King's Road. He aimed for the front of the line, striking the beasts there. They fell, tripping some of the Svartálfar behind them, and a few toppled off the side of the road onto the ground twenty feet below.

He changed tactics, firing more arrows, this time at the Svartálfar in the front…but on the edges. These fell, causing more beasts to trip over them and fall off the King's Road. Still, it was like pissing in the ocean…there were hundreds more still coming. And he was running out of arrows.

We're not going to make it.

The Svartálfar on the King's Road reached the end, spilling out onto the Deadlands to block their path.

We're not going to make it!

"Keep going!" Dominus cried. "Fight through them!"

And then something came out of the open gate ahead at the great wall. A huge armored carriage like the ones Hunter had seen during the siege on the Kingdom days ago.

The ones that spit fire.

The carriage rolled toward the end of the King's Road, followed by another, then another. Soldiers flanked the carriages, holding large hoses and aiming them at the Svartálfar.

"Rain!" they cried.

Hot oil sprayed upward and outward, raining down on the black beasts. Some turned, sprinting at the carriages and the soldiers around them.

"Fire!" a soldier shouted.

Archers with flaming arrows appeared atop the wall, firing arrows down into the Svartálfar. The missiles struck, flames spreading through the beasts instantly.

"Push through!" Dominus cried. "Make a path!"

Xerxes dropped Sukri and rushed ahead, smashing into the burning line of Svartálfar blocking the way to the gate. He cleared a path through them, and Dominus, Tykus, Sukri, Vi, and the rest of the survivors ran through, emerging on the other side and making a mad dash toward the gate ahead.

And behind them, the main army of Svartálfar stampeded after them, less than a hundred feet away now.

"Go go go!" Dominus shouted, sprinting behind Xerxes as the huge Ironclad barreled toward the gate. Burning oil coated Xerxes' arms and chest, flames licking at his flesh. But the big guy ignored this, reaching the gate and rushing through. Sukri was right behind them, followed by Dominus and Tykus and the rest of the soldiers. Hunter dove downward, gliding right through the gate over them and landing to one side.

The army of Svartálfar trampled right over their burning colleagues, a tidal wave of bodies rushing after them.

"Close both gates!" Dominus cried, rushing through the second gate ahead. Hunter followed, as did everyone else, running out onto the long city street beyond. There were still soldiers pouring through the first gate.

The heavy gates began to close, but far too slowly. The black horde rushed at them, only sixty feet away from the outer gate now.

Forty.

"Form a line!" Dominus shouted, stopping and turning to face the inner gate. "Archers, fire at will!" he commanded. The archers standing on the walls on either side of the street beyond the gate nocked their arrows.

Svartálfar poured through the half-closed outer gate, rushing toward the inner gate.

"Brace!" Dominus cried.

The Svartálfar spilled out of the inner gate, hurtling toward them just as the outer gate closed.

Hunter unsheathed his longsword, standing beside Sukri and Xerxes. The first of the Svartálfar leapt at them, and Hunter thrust his sword at its chest, impaling it. Another Svartálfar leapt over the first one before Hunter could withdraw his sword, lunging at him with its claws bared.

And then the side of its face tore off in mid-air.

Hunter flapped his wings, bursting backward. The wounded Svartálfar fell to the street, missing him by a few inches. He yanked his sword free, chopping down at the back of its head, splitting its skull in two.

"You're welcome," Sukri stated. Hunter glanced at her, spotting half of a Svartálfar face hanging from her claws.

"Thanks love."

A rain of arrows shot down from the archers high atop the walls on either side of the street, impaling the Svartálfar ahead. They dropped like flies, the inner gate shutting behind them. Hunter slashed at another beast, then another…and then a second volley of arrows took the remaining Svartálfar out.

Hunter stood there, breathing rapidly, glancing around. The gates were closed, and there was nothing more to kill.

The men around them cheered, embracing each other and grinning from ear-to-ear. Tykus smiled at Dominus, putting a hand on the former duke's shoulder and gripping it tightly. Hunter turned to Sukri, giving her a hug, then glanced at Xerxes.

His brother looked awful.

"Jesus," Hunter breathed. One of Xerxes' right arms was gone, amputated at the shoulder. The other was half-eaten, and the armor at his chest was mostly missing. The flesh on his arms, chest, and belly was burnt to a crisp in large areas, and his legs were all chewed up. "You look like shit."

"GOOD…FIGHT," he declared.

"Yeah, well it's not over yet," Vi warned. "We got to burn these bodies…and we don't have much of an army left. There's a whole lot of them waiting at our door…and we didn't even get close to beating Zagamar."

She turned to the closed gate, shaking her head slowly.

"We," she muttered, "…are in deep shit."

Chapter 43

Dominus stood atop the great wall of Tykus, a cool breeze whipping through his hair as he gazed down at the sea of black creatures milling about on the Deadlands below. The Svartálfar had piled up against the wall on either side of the gate, many of them staring back up Dominus even as he looked down at them. In the distance, a good kilometer away, the great horned serpent slithered amongst the Svartálfar, Zagamar on its back.

Tykus stood at Dominus's side – the warrior Tykus – as did a large number of archers lined up against the wall, and a few generals.

"We can pour oil on them and have our archers set them on fire," one of the generals offered. Dominus sighed, shaking his head.

"That will only kill a fraction of them," he replied.

"Well we have to do *something*," the general insisted. Dominus ignored the man. Of course they had to do something. But what *could* they do?

"We don't have enough arrows to kill all of them," another general noted.

"And many will regenerate anyway," Dominus muttered.

"All the more reason to burn them," the first general pressed.

Dominus said nothing, glancing at Tykus. The former king was staring off into space; Dominus cleared his throat.

"What do you think?" he inquired. Tykus glanced at him, then sighed.

"I think the Svartálfar are the least of our worries," he answered. The first general glared at Tykus.

"That's insane," he shot back. "You're saying a whole damn army of…"

"Shut up," Dominus snapped, glaring at the man. The general flinched, his face going pale. Dominus held the general's gaze for a long moment, then turned back to Tykus. "What do you mean?"

Tykus glanced at the generals and the archers, then turned away from them, putting a hand on Dominus's back and leading him toward stairs that would bring them down to street level.

"Walk with me," he requested.

Dominus complied, and they made their way to the streets. The citizens of the Kingdom had been ordered to stay within their homes, leaving the streets vacant. Tykus gazed at the empty streets.

"This reminds me of the kingdom I arrived in when I came through the Gate," he mused. "Empty. Silent."

Dominus nodded, saying nothing.

"The Svartálfar now are identical to the Svartálfar then," Tykus stated. "You remember what I said happened to them?"

"They died off," Dominus recalled. "Starved to death."

"Precisely," Tykus agreed. "An army of that size won't last long without a truly massive amount of food. When it runs out, they'll start eating each other."

"But…"

"So they aren't the problem," Tykus interrupted, stopping and turning to face Dominus. Dominus stopped as well.

"Zagamar is," he muttered.

"Precisely," Tykus agreed. "He is the great mind that guides them. The power that creates them. Without him, they are merely vicious brutes, modified animals doomed to self-destruct."

"But how do we kill him?" Dominus inquired. "His army matters because it protects him."

"His army matters because you *let* it matter," Tykus retorted.

Dominus blinked.

"Your focus is on defending against the Svartálfar," Tykus explained. "On killing them. Yet you already know they will kill themselves, given enough time."

"So how do we kill Zagamar?" Dominus asked. Tykus smiled.

"That," he replied, "…is the right question."

"I was hoping for an answer," Dominus grumbled. Tykus chuckled.

"You have some of the finest men and women this kingdom has ever seen on your side, Dominus," he stated. "And even a piece of Zagamar himself." He smiled, putting a hand on Dominus's shoulder. "Ask *them*."

* * *

The large dining room of the Lucky Nuts, one of the most popular bars in Lowtown, was deserted, its usual customers having fled to their homes. Hunter, Vi, Sukri, Xerxes, and Dominus and Camilla – along with warrior Tykus – had pulled some tables together, forming a long table. They all sat in chairs around it, save for Xerxes, who didn't fit in any human-sized chair. The bartender – who just happened to be another iteration of Tykus – sat with them, opposite warrior Tykus.

Hunter found himself glancing back and forth between the two, fascinated by the differences. Warrior Tykus was muscular, grizzled, and tanned, while bartender Tykus was more than a little pudgy, in his fifties, with skin that was still baby-smooth.

"So the goal is to defeat Tykus," Dominus was saying. "The question is, how do we do it?"

Hunter turned to Vi, who was sitting opposite him. The deep gashes on her face from one of the Svartálfar's claws had already healed considerably, now reduced to angry red abrasions. She shrugged.

"I might be able to take him on myself," she stated. "If Hunter can get me close enough to him, and I don't have a damn serpent or an army of dark elves attacking me at the same time."

"So we need to separate Zagamar from his army," Sukri stated. Warrior Tykus nodded.

"It's the only way," he agreed. "The question is in the how."

There was a long silence then. Hunter glanced at Sukri, who shrugged, then at Xerxes, who seemed similarly stymied. The big guy's horrendous wounds had also healed considerably, on account of the enormous amount of food bartender Tykus had given him.

"Camilla can fly Tykus to Zagamar," Hunter reasoned. "If Vi and Tykus double up on him, and I distract him by shooting arrows at him…"

"Then the serpent is gonna smack you out of the air again," Vi concluded. "And the Svartálfar will swarm up onto the serpent and take us down."

"We need to kill him quickly then," Sukri piped in. "If Vi can go in, take him out before the Svartálfar and the serpent can react…"

"That's a big 'if,'" Vi countered. "I may need time to get a good read on Zagamar. Rushing in like Dio did might get me killed." She glanced at Camilla sitting next to her. "No offense," Vi added hastily, putting a hand on Camilla's. Camilla nodded mutely, her eyes downcast. She hadn't said much of anything since Dio's death.

"His speed is his main power," warrior Tykus observed. "And his ability to predict our next moves."

"He dodged most of my arrows," Hunter noted. "Unless he's distracted, I'm not gonna hit him."

"Unless you pit him against himself," Vi countered. All eyes turned to her. "You've got the same power he does," she pointed out. "If you invoke Zaggie, you should be able to predict *his* moves."

"Zaggie?" Dominus inquired.

"Nickname for the Zagamar inside my head," Hunter clarified.

"Helps prevent us from getting confused," Vi explained.

"It might work," Hunter agreed. "But I can only keep it up for so long before my body gives out."

"I'm so sorry Sukri," Vi quipped. Sukri rolled her eyes.

"What if Hunter flies over Zagamar and pours oil on him?" she asked. "Then he could set it on fire. That'd distract him."

"That's not a bad idea," Dominus admitted.

"He'd see it coming," Hunter retorted.

"Then set the serpent on fire," Camilla offered. All eyes turned to her. "My serpent is immune to most attacks," she reasoned. "But it isn't fireproof."

"If the serpent's on fire, it'll go crazy and set the Svartálfar around it on fire," Sukri admitted. "And Zagamar won't be able to ride it anymore."

"Thus separating Zagamar from the serpent," Dominus concluded.

"Gonna take a whole lot of oil to set that whole thing on fire," Hunter grumbled.

"Set the head on fire and it'll be plenty distracted," Vi reasoned.

"And then Zagamar will stand in the middle of his army and be unreachable," Tykus pointed out. Hunter grimaced; the guy had a point.

"Well, we still need to take out the serpent," he grumbled. "Got any better ideas?"

Xerxes perked up then.

"GUN," he grumbled.

"Pardon?" Vi asked.

"FAST…WEAPON," Xerxes explained. "HUNTER…HAD."

"That's true," Hunter admitted. He'd forgotten all about it…the revolver he'd taken through the Gate. The same one he'd blown Xerxes' face off with. It was no wonder that the big guy had remembered it. "But the Kingdom took it."

"We still have it," Dominus stated. "It would be in the lab where we study Original technology."

"No bullets though," Hunter pointed out. "I used the last one on you. Sorry bro."

"That's not…entirely true," Dominus countered. "We've recovered several of these weapons in the past. None exactly like yours, but a similar technology. I believe the Originals who had them called them 'rifles.'"

Everyone turned to the former duke.

"We've tried for decades to recreate the powder than drives the explosion," Dominus continued. "It appears to contain charcoal and sulfur, but there is another ingredient that we're having difficulty identifying. None of the Originals who had the weapons had exact knowledge of the composition of the powder."

"Do you have bullets?" Hunter asked.

"We do," Dominus answered. "For the rifles. But it's a limited amount."

"FLY," Xerxes grunted. "SHOOT."

"I'll blow Zagamar's face off this time," Hunter agreed. "He won't know anything about guns. We'll have the element of surprise…and then Vi can take him out quickly."

"How good are you at using the things?" Vi asked.

"I've shot rifles before," he replied. "So I'm better than anyone else. And Zaggie'll be even better."

"So shoot his face off, I finish him, and we wait for the Svartálfar to turn on themselves," Vi concluded.

"Works for me," Sukri stated.

"We still need to deal with the serpent," Camilla reminded them.

"Alright Hunter, that means you have to set its ugly puss on fire first," Vi decided.

"I can do that," Camilla countered. "My winged horse can fly with far more extra weight than Hunter can."

"Alright then, seems like we have a plan A," Vi stated. "Now we need a plan B and a plan C."

"Agreed," Dominus replied. "But let's not waste any time; we can talk on our way to the lab."

* * *

The lab was a large room within a nondescript building on the far western part of Hightown, more of an armory than anything else. It housed more than a dozen firearms, some appearing to be very old-fashioned muskets, while others were more modern-looking rifles. They looked like something that would've been used in the second world war. His revolver was among them, but the only one with a good cache of bullets was one rifle. It was resting on a long wooden table, an engraved metallic plate bolted to the table before it. "M1 Carbine," it read. The wood of the rifle appeared to have been replaced, as had some of the metal components, which made sense. For every one year that passed here, six passed on Earth. Which meant that if this rifle was some fifty to sixty years old on Earth, it was over three hundred years old here.

"The Original came with several of these," Dominus stated, gesturing at a couple of ammunition magazines nearby. "Some carry fifteen bullets, others twice that many. We've used up a few to analyze the powder."

"So we've got…" Hunter began, counting the magazines, "…sixty bullets? That should be more than enough."

"You sure?" Vi asked. "This *is* you we're talking about."

"Ha ha," Hunter grumbled. He grabbed the rifle, getting a feel for it, then checking it out carefully. There was a safety, a trigger, the magazine…pretty standard stuff. "I should fire a few practice rounds," he stated.

"Feel free," Dominus replied.

The rifle came with a shoulder strap, and Hunter slung it over his shoulder, grabbing the magazines and stuffing them in his pockets.

"Let's go," Vi prompted.

They made their way out of the building, descending the long stairway back to Lowtown.

"Hunter, if I might have a word with you," Tykus requested, putting a hand on Hunter's shoulder. Hunter hesitated, then nodded. "We'll meet up with you," Tykus promised Dominus.

"Very well," Dominus stated. Vi, Xerxes, and Sukri followed the former duke as he made his way back to the wall, and Tykus turned to face Hunter.

"Would you walk with me for a moment?" he asked.

"Yeah, sure."

The former king turned down a side-street, setting a leisurely pace. He clasped his hands behind his back, staring down at his feet thoughtfully for a bit. Then he turned to Hunter.

"You know Zagamar better than anyone," he stated.

"I do."

"What do you believe our chances are?" Tykus asked bluntly. Hunter hesitated.

"You really want to know?"

"Yes," Tykus replied. "Be honest."

Hunter turned to gaze to the wall in the distance, his jawline rippling.

"We're going to die."

Tykus sighed, but nodded, lowering his eyes to the street. Then he met Hunter's gaze.

"I always knew this day would come," he mused. "A day when a Legend like this would rise. It was inevitable I suppose."

Hunter said nothing.

"Our world – where you and I were born – isn't so different from this one," Tykus continued. "Though we didn't call them 'Legends' there. We called them 'leaders.'"

"I'd say there's a huge difference between a leader and someone who can turn you into themselves," Hunter retorted. Tykus raised an eyebrow.

"Oh really?" he replied. "I think they're the same. It's most people's nature to follow, you know. But do you know why?"

Hunter shrugged.

"Thinking is hard," Tykus mused. "Forming an opinion is hard. It takes experience, humility. Admitting you were wrong and changing over time. All traits that are portrayed as weaknesses by men who lead." He smiled. "It's far easier to adopt the opinions of others. Far more enticing to have your beliefs pre-formed for you by a higher authority. Leaders know this about people. They use it to control them. And most leaders aren't like me."

"What's that supposed to mean?" Hunter asked.

"I never wanted to be a leader," Tykus answered. "I had no desire to control or gain power or influence. I suppose my kingdom is lucky for that…and that I happened to have a talent for leadership. I have my father to thank for that."

"Your father?"

"You may know of him," Tykus stated. "Your mother did. A man named Leif Erickson."

Hunter's eyes widened, and Tykus chuckled.

"You *do* know of him," he said. "Over a thousand years have passed on our home world, and six thousand on this one, and yet people on both worlds still remember our family."

"Damn," Hunter murmured. "Just…damn."

"My father was a wise man, and a good leader," Tykus said. "As am I. But most men who want to lead are in it for themselves. They understand human nature and use it to their advantage. They tell their people what to believe, and the vast majority obey without ever realizing they're being used."

"You mean propaganda," Hunter guessed.

"Correct," Tykus agreed. "And the best propaganda is so subtle you'll never see it for what it is."

"Yeah, well sorry to burst your bubble, but I saw plenty of propaganda in the Kingdom," Hunter grumbled.

"Of course," Tykus agreed. "But I did not create it for my own benefit. And if you don't provide a belief system to men, they'll choose someone else's. Few will develop one on their own."

"And we're having this conversation now because…?"

"Because your mother is a Legend who was wise enough to protect others from herself. I am a Legend who similarly limited my influence. But Zagamar will not. And the danger he poses to Man is the same as a powerful leader in our home world: he will transform them into something like himself, thereby achieving utter control."

"And then…"

"The world we know…the haven I built for Originals like us who have the misfortune of coming through the Gate…will be gone. What is left of humanity will be gone. The Kingdom of the Deep and every other kingdom will fall. The great and varied cultures that span this world will crumble, homogenizing into one."

"Like the Kingdom," Hunter shot back.

Tykus smiled, his eyes twinkling.

"Exactly," he replied. "But I built a wall around the Kingdom."

"To keep us out."

"And to keep *us* in," Tykus added. "Legends threaten the very nature of this world. They steal the souls of everything around them. They are tyrants by their very nature…and if they don't stop themselves, then they must be stopped by others."

Hunter said nothing for a long moment, staring at Tykus. Then he turned to look at the Fringe again, picturing the vast army of Svartálfar that was coming for them.

"So what can we do about it?" he asked, turning back to Tykus.

"It is not the Svartálfar that threaten the world. It is not the horned serpent."

"It's Zagamar," Hunter realized.

"Correct," Tykus confirmed. "The army we face may overwhelm us. It is very likely that we will all die. But if we can take Zagamar with us, then we will have won. I will be reborn with the aid of my Ossae, and I will rebuild. And I will ensure, as has been my mission for six thousand years, that no Legend threatens the world like Zagamar."

Hunter stared at Tykus for a long moment.

"That's why you do this," he realized. "That's why you made the Kingdom." Tykus nodded.

"To preserve the great variety and cultures of the world," he agreed. "By creating a kingdom that walled themselves off from it."

Hunter said nothing. Didn't know what to say.

"And you, Hunter, have Zagamar within you. You have the gift of his power, but the wisdom and the inclination to use it for good. If the time comes – *when* the time comes – you must do everything you can to ensure that Zagamar falls. Do you understand?"

Hunter nodded.

"He must fall," Tykus stated earnestly.

"I understand."

"Perhaps," Tykus conceded. He sighed then. "Practice with the rifle. Then go back to your friends," Tykus advised. "Enjoy them while you can."

"Yes sir," Hunter replied. "And…thank you."

Tykus smiled, patting Hunter's shoulder.

"No Hunter," he corrected. "Thank *you*."

Boom!

The sound shot through the city like a thunderclap, echoing off the walls of the buildings around them. Hunter flinched, his head snapping forward. The sound had come from ahead.

Boom!

Far in the distance, something appeared just above the great wall. A dark shadow that blotted out the sun behind it.

Hunter's breath caught in his throat.

For there, rising above the wall, was the massive head of the horned serpent…and Zagamar standing atop it.

CHAPTER 44

Hunter burst forward, sprinting down the street toward the wall far ahead, Tykus running after him.

"Fly us to Dominus and the others!" Tykus ordered. Hunter skid to a halt, grabbing Tykus and leaping into the air. He beat his wings, rising above the buildings on either side and flying toward the wall. He spotted men standing on it, over a hundred feet from where the horned serpent's massive head was. It was Dominus and the others…and the archers he'd seen there earlier.

Hunter flew up to the wall, landing atop it. Dominus, Vi, Camilla, Xerxes, and Sukri were there, staring at the serpent in horror. Hunter followed its head down to its long body; it had formed a ramp from the Deadlands fifty feet below all the wall up to the wall.

And the army of Svartálfar was rushing up its spine.

"Oh *shit*," Sukri swore.

"Camilla, you're up!" Dominus ordered. "Archers, flaming arrows on my command! Hunter, get ready!"

Camilla gave a sharp whistle, and her flying steed appeared; she hopped onto the saddle in one graceful movement, strapping herself to the saddle and taking off. Several large bags had been hooked to the saddle on either side; the oil to set her serpent on fire. The archers set their arrows aflame, nocking them to their bows.

"Xerxes, Vi, Sukri…intercept those Svartálfar!" Dominus commanded.

The black creatures reached the serpent's head, leaping off to the wall below and rushing right at them. Soldiers formed a line with Xerxes, Vi, and Sukri, while Tykus stayed back with Dominus.

Hunter leapt into the air, grabbing his rifle and turning the safety off. The M1 Carbine was semi-automatic, with thirty rounds in the current magazine…and two more fifteen-round magazines in his pockets. He flew upward, hovering a good thirty feet above the wall and gliding toward Zagamar.

Camilla flew directly over the serpent's head, dumping one of the bags of oil. The black liquid rained down on the serpent's head, dousing it and many of the Svartálfar. But Zagamar knelt, the Svartálfar leaping atop him to form a shield; the oil splattered them, but left Zagamar untouched.

"Fire at will!" Dominus commanded.

Flaming arrows shot outward at the serpent.

The Svartálfar leapt to intercept the arrows, igniting instantly and falling to the wall in a flaming heap. More arrows flew outward at the serpent, but more Svartálfar leaped to intercept them with their own bodies. Not a single arrow managed to strike the serpent.

Vi ran back to one of the archers, grabbing their bow and nocking a flaming arrow.

"If you want something done right," she grumbled…and shot the arrow. It flew far left of the target…and then promptly curved rightward. A Svartálfar leapt to intercept the arrow…and the second arrow Vi fired followed directly behind it, slamming into the serpent's left eye.

Its head jerked back, flames engulfing its head in seconds. It roared, thrashing its head from side-to-side, then falling from the wall, plummeting to the Deadlands below and crushing the Svartálfar unlucky enough to be standing beneath it. It rolled madly, thrashing on the ground, trying desperately to snuff out the flames.

And through it all, Zagamar had calmly jumped from the serpent's head, landing on the wall behind the Svartálfar that were nearly upon Vi, Xerxes, and Sukri.

"Archers, fire at the Svartálfar!" Dominus shouted.

Arrows rained down on the Svartálfar, just as the foul beasts slammed into the line of soldiers.

Xerxes roared, battering the Svartálfar with his huge fists as Vi became a whirlwind of death, slicing through the creatures with lethal grace. One of the monsters slammed into Sukri, knocking her onto her back…and she promptly tore it to shreds, raking its belly with her feet. Many of the Svartálfar were struck by the archers' arrows and fell…but dozens more came, Zagamar following behind them.

"Fire on Zagamar!" Dominus shouted.

Arrows shot over the Svartálfar at the Legend…and Zagamar dodged them all effortlessly.

More Svartálfar piled on Xerxes and the others, and the huge Ironclad began tossing the beasts right off the wall, sending them hurtling to their deaths. Vi and Sukri managed to hold them off, but the soldiers weren't as lucky. One-by-one they fell, torn to shreds by the dark creatures' claws.

"Hold the line!" Dominus barked.

But the soldiers caved, and Svartálfar rushed to surround Vi, Xerxes, and Sukri. A few charged at Dominus and Tykus, who went back-to-back, cutting apart any that drew near. Sukri too was surrounded…but leapt backward nearly twenty feet into the air, landing on a Svartálfar next to Dominus and Tykus and taking it out.

Hunter readied his rifle, swooping toward the Legend. He peered through the scope at Zagamar, aiming for the head.

But Zagamar burst forward, charging at Vi and Xerxes!

Hunter cursed, flying past the Legend. He landed on the wall, skidding to a halt and turning around. Zagamar pushed through his Svartálfar, reaching Xerxes. The Svartálfar closed in behind the Legend, preventing Hunter from lining up his shot.

Damn.

He leapt into the air, flying upward and forward toward Zagamar…and watched as Xerxes swung his big fists at the Legend. Zagamar dodged each attack, punching Xerxes in the head five times for every swing Xerxes managed, his fists a blur as he attacked.

Xerxes stumbled backward, dazed…and then Vi stepped in.

"Hey asshole," she stated. "My turn."

She laid into Zagamar, her longsword a blur as she executed three rapid-fire attacks. But the last was a feint…and then she slashed with her sword and side-kicked him simultaneously. Zagamar dodged every attack…until she followed up with a spinning back-kick to his head and two more spinning slashes, at twice the speed of the first attacks.

The kick missed…but Zagamar dodged right into the last slash, blood spraying from his left shoulder. He jerked backward just in time to stop her from cutting off his arm completely, putting him on his heels.

And Vi kicked him in the knee, locking it, then spun, executing five quick slashes to his legs, abdomen, chest, neck, and head.

Somehow, Zagamar managed to dodge four of them, the fifth earning him a deep gouge across the cheek.

Hunter flew past them, still having no good shot. He pumped his wings, gaining a little altitude, then circling around. Vi continued her assault, moving faster than Hunter had ever seen. Zagamar struggled to get away from her…and backed up right into Xerxes, who tried to wrap his arms around the Legend.

Zagamar whirled out of Xerxes' grasp, somehow thrusting the Ironclad between him and Vi…and a few of Vi's attacks. Her sword bounced off the big guy's armor, and Zagamar kicked Xerxes square in the chest, shoving him into Vi.

They both stumbled backward.

Zagamar rushed around Xerxes so quickly Hunter could barely follow, slashing at Vi with his claws. Vi dodged, counterattacking with slashes of her own, but somehow the Legend managed to move even faster than her. He dodged her attacks, scoring a powerful kick to her belly, throwing her backward…right off the edge of the wall.

Vi!

Hunter veered toward her in mid-flight, letting his rifle hang by its shoulder strap and reaching out to grab her as she plummeted toward the army of Svartálfar – and the writhing serpent – below. He caught her, pumping his wings and flying back to the wall, dropping her next to Tykus and Dominus, some thirty feet from Zagamar.

"We need to work together!" Vi exclaimed. "Dominus, Tykus, help me out. Hunter, shoot that asshole!"

Vi, Dominus, and Tykus charged at Zagamar, slicing down any Svartálfar in their way. Ahead, Zagamar was still pummeling Xerxes…and tearing through Xerxes' mane with his claws, glowing blue gel leaking out. Zagamar consumed the gel greedily, licking it from his hands.

Shit.

Hunter leapt into the air, flying toward Zagamar and lining up a shot with his rifle. Vi reached the Legend, greeting him with a flurry of attacks…all of which Zagamar dodged. He seemed to be moving even faster than before, faster than anything Hunter had ever seen.

His body is stronger than mine, he realized. *He can push it harder.*

He slowed his forward flight, beating his wings and hovering in mid-air ten feet from the Legend, peering through the rifle's scope. Dominus and Tykus had reached Zagamar; with Xerxes, they had the man surrounded.

Which means Hunter couldn't hit Zagamar without hitting one of *them*…not with the Legend moving so quickly.

Unless…

He focused inward, concentrating. Feeling the hunger within him…not difficult, as he'd forgone any meals today. That hunger was the key, unlocking the memories of the Zagamar within him…and freeing the Legend's mind.

The world slowed to a crawl.

He pushed his body, feeling his heart pounding in his chest, his breathing rapid. Time slowed even more, each flap of his wings seeming to take minutes, the world all but standing still. He aimed down the scope at Zagamar, but Tykus was in the way, his back to Hunter. Zagamar struck the former king in the head with one clawed hand, Tykus's face splitting open in a spray of blood. The warrior lurched to the right…and gave Hunter his shot.

He pulled the trigger.

The butt of the rifle recoiled against his shoulder as the bullet shot outward, almost too quick to see.

It slammed right into Zagamar's back

Zagamar stumbled, the impact knocking him off-balance and throwing off his string of attacks. Vi took advantage of the Legend's confusion, thrusting her shortsword into his belly. He dodged at the last second, the blade piercing his right flank.

Zagamar kicked Vi in the crotch, shoving her – and her blade – back with his heel. Tykus, his face bloodied by Zagamar's claws, swung his huge sword at the Legend. But Zagamar stepped into the attack, grabbing Tykus's sword by the cross-guard and tearing it from the man's hands. He whirled in a rapid circle, slashing at everyone around him.

Vi leapt backward, dodging in the nick of time, but Dominus was slower. The blade tore through his belly, creating a gaping wound there…and then struck Tykus.

It went right through the warrior-king's torso, cutting him in half.

Tykus's upper body separated from his lower, blood spraying out of him in horrid jets. He fell, his eyes wide with shock.

"No!" Hunter shouted.

He aimed through the scope again, firing at Zagamar's heart. But Zagamar twisted away at the last minute, the bullet striking him in the right shoulder. The Legend grunted, then spun around, hurling Tykus's sword right at Hunter!

Hunter cursed, dodging out of the way as quickly as he could, but the sword clipped the tip of his right wing, severing it. The pain was instantaneous, and he cried out, retracting his injured wing reflexively…and plummeting downward. He caught himself, unfurling his wings again and beating them quickly. But each flap of his wings sent fresh waves of pain through him.

And below, Zagamar kept on fighting, his wounds barely seeming to affect him.

Dominus kept attacking the Legend, clearly slowed down by the gash on his belly, but enraged by Tykus's death. Vi continued her onslaught, keeping Zagamar on his toes. And Xerxes, the slowest of them all, kept swinging gamely…but hit nothing. *Nobody* hit Zagamar; he was just too fast. Dread gripped Hunter.

We're not going to beat him.

He glanced back, seeing Sukri fighting the remaining Svartálfar alongside the soldiers, the archers in the rear continuing to fire at the foul creatures. To his surprise, she was holding her own, dodging and slashing the beasts with her claws. She moved with fluid grace, far more effective fighting with her hands and feet than she'd ever been with a weapon.

Hunter focused, aiming down his scope at Zagamar once again. His heart was hammering rapidly, his body beginning to tire. Too much longer and it would collapse.

He aimed at the Legend's head…and fired.

Zagamar ducked a slash by Vi, and the bullet missed him by mere inches, ricocheting off the stone beyond. Hunter cursed, feeling suddenly lightheaded.

Enough.

He yanked control of his mind back from Zaggie, the world speeding up abruptly. He struggled with the sudden time-shift, flapping his wings desperately to maintain altitude. Dominus thrust his sword at Zagamar's back at the same time that Vi slashed at the Legend's throat…and Zagamar somehow managed to dodge both attacks, spinning around and tearing Dominus's sword from his hands. He brought the sword up in a tight arc…

…and Dominus's right arm separated at the elbow, falling to the ground.

Zagamar slashed again, this time at Dominus's throat…and his sword ricocheted off of Vi's blade.

"Get back!" she shouted, stepping between the two men and continuing her assault on Zagamar. Xerxes roared, lunging at Zagamar from behind. Zagamar spun around even as he evaded Vi's string of attacks, landing a brutal kick to Xerxes' midsection. The armor there absorbed the blow, of course, but the sheer power of the kick sent Xerxes stumbling backward…and right off the wall, luckily on the city-side.

"Vi!" Sukri cried, finishing off the last of the Svartálfar, then rushing toward Vi and Zagamar.

"Stay back!" Hunter shouted, lowering himself to the top of the wall.

BOOM!

The wall quaked, and Hunter snapped his gaze forward, his heart sinking. For there, clinging to the wall, was the horned serpent. Its head was still charred, but it was otherwise whole; a fresh wave of Svartálfar were rushing up its spine, making their way toward its head.

"God *damn* it!" Hunter swore.

The serpent roared, and Zagamar ducked under one of Vi's attacks turning and running back to the serpent. Vi sprinted after the Legend.

"Hunter!" she cried.

Hunter leapt into the air, flying after Zagamar. He aimed his rifle at the Legend, then lifted his scope to the horned serpent, seeing its black eye magnified there. He pulled the trigger.

Bam!

The serpent jerked its head back, Svartálfar falling from its spine. It roared again, lowering its head to the wall, clear fluid leaking from its ruined eye.

The long line of Svartálfar made it to the top of the huge creature's head, leaping down to the wall and rushing toward Zagamar and Vi. Hunter peered through the scope, aiming at the back of Zagamar's head, and fired.

The bullet veered off-center, taking Zagamar's right ear off in a spray of blood…right as the Svartálfar reached the Legend, rushing past him and blocking Hunter's line-of-sight.

Damn it!

He fired again and again, taking down a few Svartálfar. Then he pumped his wings, flying higher to get a clean shot on Zagamar. The Legend was less than a hundred feet from the horned serpent now. Vi was close behind him, cutting down the Svartálfar in her path without so much as slowing down. But as fast as she could run, Zagamar was faster.

Hunter pumped his wings again, then spread them out wide, gliding toward the serpent and lining up for one more shot.

And then something slammed into his right side, sending him flying to the left!

Hunter cursed, flapping his wings frantically and righting himself in mid-air. A bird burst past him, zooming through the air and gaining altitude quickly. A huge bird with black feathers and long talons…and a hideous black face.

A Svartálfar!

It *was* one of the foul creatures…but had clearly been a huge bird of prey originally. It circled around quickly, flying right back at Hunter, diving at him with its talons extended. There was no way he was going to outmaneuver the bird…it was far more agile than him.

He grabbed his rifle, aiming it at the bird and firing. Its head exploded, and it fell like a stone to the city below.

"*Boom* motherfucker," he quipped.

He turned in mid-air, searching the top of the wall for Zagamar. The Legend had made it all the way to the serpent's head, a steady stream of Svartálfar managing to stop Vi from catching up to him. They attacked her while others swarmed around her, rushing not toward Dominus and Sukri, but toward the stairs leading down into the city.

Hunter's blood went cold.

"The gates!" he shouted, flying back toward Dominus and Sukri and the remaining soldiers and archers. "Protect the gates!"

He dove toward the long street leading to the inner gate, spotting the Svartálfar rushing toward it. But something was standing before the gate; a black beast with three arms, nearly ten feet tall.

Xerxes!

The great Ironclad roared, tearing into the Svartálfar. But he was quickly overwhelmed, beasts leaping on him while others rushed past, grabbing the rotating lever that opened the gate. They turned it, and the inner gate began to open.

Hunter cursed, lifting his gaze to Zagamar, standing beside the head of the great serpent…and Vi, surrounded by a writhing wall of Svartálfar fifty feet away from the Legend. There was no way she was going to reach him…not in time. And the inner gate had opened enough for Svartálfar to duck through, and soon after came the screams of dying soldiers within the wall.

He resisted the urge to go to Xerxes' aid, remembering Tykus's words.

If the time comes – when *the time comes – you must do everything you can to ensure that Zagamar falls.*

There was a loud, inhuman cheer from outside the wall, and then Svartálfar poured through the open gates, charging into the city. They overwhelmed Xerxes, dogpiling on top of him and forcing him to his knees. Hunter stared as the Svartálfar clawed at his mane, his face, his three remaining arms. As they slowly took him apart.

Zagamar must fall!

He flew upward, leaving Xerxes behind and making his way toward Zagamar. His vision blurred, and he blinked away tears, his jaw rippling.

Sorry brother.

He gripped his rifle, aiming down its scope, centering the reticle on Zagamar's chest. Took a breath out, then held it.

And pulled the trigger.

Zagamar jerked backward, stumbling into the side of the serpent's head.

Yes!

But the bullet had missed his heart, leaving a hole in the right side of his chest.

Hunter cried out, pulling the trigger again and again. But the serpent lunged forward, blocking most of the bullets with its huge head. Hunter continued to fire, aiming for the serpent's other eye and shooting. The serpent's remaining eye ruptured, and it roared, jerking backward and falling off the wall once again.

And exposing Zagamar.

Hunter let go of the rifle, grabbing his longsword and unsheathing it as he dove downward at the wounded Legend. He focused inward even as he landed, summoning Zaggie, the world slowing as he swung his sword at Zagamar's neck.

Zagamar dodged with incredible speed, moving far faster even than Hunter…and whipping a clawed hand across Hunter's temple. Hunter's head snapped to the side, his helmet torn from his head. Even as it flew away, his mind raced, plotting every possible counterattack.

Enemy too fast. Need to match.

Hunter felt the world slow even further, watching as his helmet tumbled through the air with agonizing slowness. He saw Zagamar's leg rise up to kick him.

Aiming for hip. Will strike, forcing bend at waist.

He visualized the endgame instantly: his death.

That other mind within him ticked through dozens of possible counterattacks, anticipating Zagamar's responses. A long string of attacks and counterattacks, most leading to Hunter's death.

Zagamar's foot struck Hunter's hip, forcing him to bend at the waist. Instead of resisting, he went with it, using the momentum to chop down at Zagamar's head with his longsword. Zagamar dodged to the side, Hunter's blade missing by a fraction of an inch.

But also preventing Zagamar from executing a killing blow.

Hunter snapped his torso upward, bringing his sword straight upward to Zagamar's chin. Zagamar leaned backward, the tip missing him by a hair's breadth.

Not fast enough.

And Zagamar did a backflip even as he dodged Hunter's attack, kicking out with one black foot as he did so. It clipped Hunter's chin, snapping his head back and crushing his tongue between his teeth.

Hunter stumbled backward, blood filling his mouth.

Faster!

He concentrated, forcing time to slow even further…and his heart raced even faster, pushed to its very limit.

Zagamar landed, lunging at Hunter. Hunter thrust his sword at the Legend's chest, but Zagamar swiped the blade aside with one hand. Hunter used his sword's momentum to spin 360 degrees, slashing at Zagamar's neck. But Zagamar was *still* quicker, kicking Hunter in mid-spin, sending him tumbling to the ground.

Hunter rolled backward, rising smoothly to his feet…and barely managing to dodge a string of attacks from the Legend. He backpedaled rapidly…right into one of the Svartálfar behind him.

It grabbed his sword by the blade, trying to yank it out of his hands…just as Zagamar planted a kick square between his legs.

His legs buckled.

Hunter felt his sword pull free from his hands, saw Zagamar lean over him, grabbing him by the throat with one hand, then lifting him off the ground. Hunter's feet dangled from the top of the wall, his vision beginning to blacken as Zagamar squeezed his neck.

The Legend sighed, pulling Hunter forward until their noses were nearly touching.

"You're strong," Zagamar stated approvingly.

Hunter gasped, grabbing Zagamar's wrists, trying futilely to pry the man's hands from his neck. The Legend was impossibly strong, his grip like iron.

A hunger grew within Hunter, Zagamar's incredible will threatening to overwhelm him.

"You're strong, but you lack wisdom," Zagamar stated. "You fight what you don't understand. Your only sin is ignorance. Let me show you the truth."

Hunter croaked, struggling to breath.

"You've been fooled," Zagamar continued. "Your rulers control you. They force you to be like them, or be rejected. If you're weak, they control you. If you're strong, they destroy you. I offer a different path."

Images flashed through Hunter's mind, visions of an army of Svartálfar rushing toward the wall around Tykus. Of fighting a short-haired woman with impressive skill…and of fighting…

Him.

Of fighting *Hunter*.

The other within Hunter's mind processed this, understanding instantly what Hunter could not comprehend.

You're absorbing his memories!

Not just his memories of the distant past, but the memories of *now*. Every thought, every calculation. Hunter was reading his mind.

"You can't defeat me," Zagamar insisted. "But you can join me, and remain yourself."

Hunter gasped, trying to speak past Zagamar's iron grip. Zagamar humored Hunter, loosening his grip a little. Hunter gasped for air, letting go of Zagamar's hands.

"You're …right," he rasped. "I…can't defeat…you." Then he smirked. "But *you* can."

Hunter grabbed the mace at his hip, swinging it at Zagamar's flank. Without his helmet, he could *feel* Zagamar's thoughts. They were going far too fast for Hunter to follow, but the Zagamar within him had no trouble at all.

Zagamar dropped Hunter, dodging backward…just as Hunter knew he would.

Hunter stayed close, ignoring the rising hunger within him, and the chanting of voices long dead. He lunged at Zagamar, swinging his mace in a flurry of attacks…and knowing full well what the Legend's next moves were, five moves in advance. He pushed his body to the limit, ignoring the burning in his lungs as he gasped for air to feed his brain, his muscles. To feed the Legend within him.

Zagamar dodged and blocked each attack…until Hunter threw his mace at the Legend's head. Zagamar dodged to the side, just in time for Hunter to grab his rifle and aim it right where he knew the Legend's head would end up being.

He pulled the trigger, and the right half of Zagamar's face *exploded*.

Hunter aimed for Zagamar's heart as the Legend fell backward, pulling the trigger.

Click.

Hunter pulled the trigger again, but it didn't fire. He was out of ammunition.

Zagamar caught himself in mid-fall, putting a hand to his ruined face. There was a crater where his right cheek had been, his right eye drooping out of its socket. He glared at Hunter with his remaining eye.

"How?" he blurted out.

"Because I'm better than you, asshole," Hunter answered. He smirked, pulling the spent magazine from his rifle and reaching inside his pocket for another. "Time to die."

Zagamar lunged forward, and Hunter dodged to the side. But he was too slow; his body was starting to fail. Zagamar tore the rifle from Hunter's hands, slamming the butt of it into Hunter's belly.

The breath exploded from his lungs.

Hunter gasped, his vision blackening. He tried desperately to breathe, but no air would come. And without air, his body would fail completely.

His head swam sickeningly.

Zagamar grabbed Hunter by the throat with both hands, lifting him off the ground. His eyes narrowed.

"How did you anticipate my…"

And then there was a flash of silver, and Zagamar's left arm separated at the shoulder.

"Hey asshole," Vi greeted from behind…and slashed at Zagamar's neck.

Zagamar let go of Hunter, dodging Vi's attack and grabbing his own amputated arm as it fell, swinging it like a club and striking Vi across the temple.

Hard.

She fell, her eyes vacant as she struck the ground in slow-motion, her sword falling from her hands. Zagamar lunged for the blade, his fingers curling around the hilt.

Hunter's mind raced, noting his heart rate and breathing. His body would not hold up for much longer…and without Zaggie, there was no hope of winning. He ticked through the possibilities, but every action ended with the same conclusion.

His death…and Zagamar winning.

He lunged for Zagamar even as the Legend lifted Vi's sword from the ground, turning toward Hunter.

Zagamar must fall.

The Legend thrust Vi's sword at Hunter's belly, and Hunter felt the tip strike his abdomen, piercing through the leather armor and his skin. Felt it slide through his flesh even as he slammed into Zagamar, wrapping his arms around the Legend's torso.

The sudden pain was indescribable, searing through his belly, with a sudden, agonizing burst of pain in his back.

Hunter cried out, unfurling his wings and leaping into the air, flapping them as hard as he could. He rose into the air, pulling Zagamar upward with him.

"No!" Zagamar shouted, struggling to free himself from Hunter's grasp. But with one arm missing, he could not. Hunter pumped his wings, flying higher and higher, until they were a hundred feet above the city. Below, he saw Svartálfar swarming through the city streets, overwhelming the guards.

The kingdom is lost.

Hunter brought them ever-higher, feeling suddenly lightheaded, his heart jackhammering in his chest. There was a shout from below, and he saw Sukri and Dominus on the wall, gesturing wildly to the south. Hunter turned his head, his eyes widening.

For there, flying high in the sky over the Deadlands, were bird-men. *Thousands* of bird-men. Each armed with a bow.

They unloaded arrows at the Svartálfar army rushing toward the city, the sky blackening with the deadly rain. Onward they flew, passing over the wall, firing at the Svartálfar in the city streets.

"No!" Zagamar shouted, twisting around to stare at the carnage. "My people!"

"They're not your people," Hunter retorted. "You were just using them." Zagamar turned to face him.

"How can I use them?" he shot back. "They're all *me*."

"They didn't ask to be," Hunter gasped, his vision staring to fade. He let go of the Zagamar within him, time speeding up instantly. He flapped his wings one last time, then let go of Zagamar.

But Zagamar grabbed his arm, refusing to let go.

Hunter grabbed the hilt of Vi's sword, pulling it free from his own belly, screaming at the fresh wave of pain that brought.

"Don't do this," Zagamar pleaded. "You don't understand what you're doing!"

"Go to hell," Hunter spat.

"I can save you," Zagamar insisted. "I can make you better!"

Hunter smiled grimly at him.

"You already…have," he gasped.

And then he swung Vi's sword, slicing through Zagamar's neck.

Zagamar let go of Hunter's arm, plummeting toward the streets of Tykus hundreds of feet below. Toward the dying Svartálfar felled by the massive winged army of the Kingdom of the Deep.

Hunter watched the Legend fall, and then his vision faded completely, his sword slipping out of his hands.

He felt himself falling, the wind shrieking past his ears. But he didn't care anymore. It didn't matter. Nothing mattered anymore.

You did it.

Faster and faster he went, free-falling through space. Floating in darkness. The last moments of his life like the first, encased within his mother's womb.

Hunter smiled, knowing that this was the end. And of all the ends he remembered, the memories of the deaths of multitudes of men that he'd absorbed, this was the best.

He didn't even feel the impact when he struck the street of Lowtown, shattering the cobblestones beneath him.

CHAPTER 45

Hunter opened his eyes.

Harsh light greeted him, and he squeezed his eyes shut, his head pounding. He waited for the pain to pass, then squinted, his eyes slowly adjusting to the light. He was lying on his back on a firm mattress, he realized, a thin white sheet pulled up to his bellybutton.

And he was naked.

He blinked, looking around. A tiny room greeted him, smaller than a college dorm room. One with cheap wooden walls and a window that was really just a rectangular hole in the wall. Sunlight streamed through it, splaying over the bed and the floor. There was no furniture in the room save for his bed, and a wooden door to his right was the only way in or out.

Hunter groaned, rubbing his forehead.

What the hell…

There was a knock at the door.

Hunter froze, staring at the door. A few seconds passed, and the knocks came again, tentatively.

"Uh, come in," he called out.

The door swung open, and someone stepped into the room, closing the door behind them. It was a young woman, he realized. She was tall and slender, with long blond hair and striking blue eyes, her skin pale and unblemished. She wore a simple black dress, one that clung rather tightly to her body, outlining small, perky breasts and a pleasing hourglass figure…and stopping well above her knees. She was rather pretty, although not spectacularly so.

Hunter's breath caught in his throat.

"Hey Hunter," she greeted, walking up to the bed and sitting down on the edge. She smiled down at him, putting a hand on the sheet covering his lower belly. "How'd you sleep?"

"Uh..." he stammered, staring at her in disbelief. "Trixie?"

"Of course, silly," she replied, her blue eyes twinkling. She leaned down then, kissing him on the forehead. He was too shocked to stop her.

"What...what are you...?" Hunter asked, trying to make sense of what was happening. "How did I get here?" he added. For it was clear that he was back in his old apartment in the Outskirts, his home for the first few days of his new life in Varta. She gave him a confused look.

"We went back here after going out last night," she answered. She gave a little smile then. "I put you to sleep the way you like it."

Hunter frowned, trying to recall what'd happened last night. But his mind was hazy, his memories vague.

"Aww," she replied, running a hand through his short hair, then resting her warm palm on his cheek. "Did you have that bad dream again?"

"What?"

"The dream about that guy...what's his name," Trixie said. "It started with a 'Z.'"

Zagamar.

Hunter felt a chill run down his spine, and he stared at her mutely. She leaned in again, kissing him on the opposite cheek. The faint scent of flowers came to him, a scent that instantly brought back memories of the time they'd spent together. Long nights of making love, over and over again, until their bodies couldn't take it anymore.

He felt a stirring in his groin.

"You *did* have the dream again, didn't you," Trixie pressed. She pouted. "You're always like this after."

"How long have I been...back here?" Hunter asked.

"Since last night."

"I mean, since I started living here again," he clarified. Trixie frowned.

"You've been living here all along silly," she answered, leaning in and kissing his cheek again, just to the right of his lips. He smelled her scent, her soft lips warm against his skin. His groin stirred again, her touch awakening it.

She leaned back, glancing down at it, watching as it slowly uncurled.

"Looks like *someone* remembers last night," she quipped, sliding her hand down his belly over the sheet, and stopping just to the right of his member. That got it filling more rapidly, and it wasn't long before it lifted off his belly, straining against the sheet.

"We...did it?" Hunter asked.

"Mmm hmm," Trixie answered, leaning in and kissing him again, just to the side of his lips. "Need a little reminder to jog your memory?" she inquired, shifting a little, then pressing her lips fully against his.

An image of Sukri came to him.

Hunter pulled away quickly, clearing his throat.

"Uh, I…" he stammered, but Trixie put a finger to his lips, swinging a leg over the bed to straddle him. She sat down on his groin, and it was quite clear that the dress was all that she was wearing. Her groin pressed against his, the thin sheet the only thing between them.

Trixie lifted her arms up, tying her hair back into a ponytail…and arching her back as she did so, giving him a spectacular view. He stared at her, his heart pounding in his chest. She was just as he'd remembered, sweet and sexy, meek but utterly confident in bed. He'd never been able to resist her…not even after all of Vi's training. Of course, that'd been a long time ago…and he was a different man now. Unless…

He swallowed in a dry throat, watching as she finished tying her hair back. She leaned forward then, resting her belly atop his.

"Trixie…"

"Oh baby," she murmured, pressing her breasts against his bare chest, then leaning in and kissing him again. Her mouth opened, her tongue snaking into his mouth. His whole body tingled, her scent overpowering him. The combination of her taste and smell was downright intoxicating…and for a moment he got lost in it. He kissed her back, his tongue meeting hers, tasting her.

Oh god damn, he thought, a shudder going through him. *Oh god I missed this.*

It was incredible. Amazing. Far better than he'd remembered. How he could've forgotten this feeling was beyond him.

He felt Trixie lift her pelvis up from his, then rest her groin on his belly. She slid her pelvis down then, bringing the sheet down with it…and exposing his rock-hard member. He felt the heat of her naked groin atop it, felt her slide up his member, then down. All excruciatingly slowly, taking her time.

His body responded, his hips bucking, his member pulsing.

Fuck.

She pulled back from him, smiling down at him, then leaning in again, kissing him. More tongue, more of that unbelievable taste. It felt incredible.

It felt *right.*

He realized his hands were on her hips, and found himself sliding them down to her buttocks as she slid up and down him ever-so-slowly. Her buttocks tensed and relaxed under his fingertips as she massaged his groin with hers. It was slippery now, sliding freely…and the pressure within his groin was mounting, and suddenly he wanted nothing more than to let it do so. To give in to this woman, to let whatever was going to happen happen.

But Sukri!

He pushed the thought aside, knowing full well that it'd all been a dream. Zagamar, the Kingdom of the Deep, Camilla. Being with Sukri. All just a figment of his feverish imagination.

Trixie gasped, drawing back from him then, pulling her hair free from the hair tie. Long, golden strands fell across her shoulders, spilling onto Hunter's arms and tickling his skin. She laid down again, kissing him passionately, grinding her groin harder against his.

He moaned, his member rock-hard now, so much so that it was almost painful. He felt her body atop his, pressing him against the firm mattress, his wings crushed against it.

My wings!

He broke free from their kiss, turning his head to the side…and spotting a half-folded wing protruding from his back.

What the…!

He shoved Trixie off of him, and she stumbled, falling onto her butt at the foot of the bed.

"What the hell is going on?" he demanded, sitting up.

The door burst open.

Hunter scrambled backward in the bed, trying to pull the sheet over his groin. But Trixie was still on it, and it only covered him up to the knees. Someone stepped into the room, closing the door behind them. His heart leapt into his throat.

It was Sukri!

"Hey Hunt-" she began, then froze, staring at Trixie. Then at Hunter…and Hunter's still-hard erection.

"Sukri…" he began, but she cut him off.

"What the *hell* is going on here?" she demanded, putting her hands on her hips.

"It's not…" Hunter stammered. He drew his knees up to his chest, covering his groin with his hands, feeling his cheeks flush. "This isn't what it looks like!"

"The fuck it isn't!" Sukri retorted. She stormed up to the side of the bed, kicking him in the chest so his back slammed into the wall. "How *could* you?"

"I…"

"You said you *loved* me!" she yelled, turning to glare at Trixie. "And now you're right back to fucking…*this*?"

Hunter stared at her, at a loss for words. There was nothing to say. Nothing he *could* say.

And then Sukri burst out laughing.

"Oh shit," she said between guffaws, pointing at him. "Your face! Oh," she added. "I can't breathe." To Hunter's surprise, Trixie started laughing too, covering her mouth with one hand, her eyes twinkling.

"The hell is going on?" he demanded, utterly confused.

"You see the look on his face?" Sukri asked Trixie. Trixie nodded.

"Classic," she replied.

"What the hell is going on?" Hunter repeated, his frustration mounting.

"We were just playing a prank on you," Sukri explained, wiping tears from her eyes. Hunter stared at her blankly.

"A prank?"

"This isn't even Trixie," Sukri stated, gesturing at…Trixie.

"I'm Ella," the blonde woman introduced. She gave him an apologetic look. "We all look the same."

"Uh…nice to meet you?" Hunter replied.

"*Yeah* it was," Sukri agreed, looking down at Hunter's erection. She arched an eyebrow. "Damn hon, you were *ready* for her, weren't you."

"Wait, you guys did this on *purpose*?" Hunter blurted out. Sukri chuckled.

"I know. Dick move, right?" she replied. She turned to Ella. "Did he put up a fight?"

"Not really," Ella answered. "One kiss and he was ready and willing." That seemed to take Sukri aback.

"Damn Hunter, that's cold," she muttered. "You weren't supposed to *actually* cheat on me."

"Wait a second," Hunter stammered. "I didn't…"

"Bet you thought you could get away with it too," Sukri interrupted, crossing her arms over her chest and shaking her head. "Wow Hunter. Just…wow."

"You set me up!" Hunter complained.

"Yeah, but I thought you'd push her away, not let her ride your dick," Sukri shot back.

"She didn't…" he stammered.

"Oh I totally did," Ella countered.

"No, I never…!"

"I'd like to say I was glad I came before you did," Sukri grumbled, "…but I guess I can't."

"No, I didn't…I stopped her!"

Emma wiped a hand across her mouth, giving Sukri a look.

"I caught it all," she stated. "There was a *lot*."

"No!" Hunter nearly shouted. "She's lying!"

"Right Hunter," Sukri grumbled, crossing her arms over her chest. He stared at her, then at Emma, clenching and unclenching his fists.

Sukri burst out laughing again.

"Oh god," she gasped, pointing at Hunter. "You see his face?"

Emma chuckled.

"What…?" Hunter began. Sukri walked up to him, grabbing his hand and pulling him up off the bed.

"You hungry?" she asked.

Hunter just stared at her.

"Come on, get your clothes on," she urged. "Everyone just went to the tavern to grab some lunch."

"Uh…"

"I'll take that as a yes. You know, considering you haven't eaten in like three days." She put her hands on her hips. "Honestly, you look like a skeleton."

He stared at her mutely.

"Get *dressed*," she pressed, bending over and tossing a shirt and pants at him. They'd been folded nicely by his bed. "Thanks for everything," she told Ella. "You can help him get dressed, but no more sex, okay?" She turned back to Hunter. "I'll meet you outside."

And then she walked out of the apartment, closing the door behind her.

* * *

Hunter walked alongside Sukri as they made their way down the wooden ramp from the Outskirts to the streets of Lowtown, the sour smell of the lake below the makeshift neighborhood irritating his nostrils. They made their way up a flight of stairs, continuing onto the street beyond. Sukri hooked an arm around Hunter's, smiling up at him.

"Feels good to be back, doesn't it?" she asked.

Hunter looked down at her, not quite sure how to feel.

"Sukri, what the hell is going on?"

"You killed Zagamar," Sukri answered. "Saved the Kingdom, in fact. Hell, maybe even the whole world."

"Great," Hunter grumbled. "Somehow I'm not as excited about that as I thought I'd be."

Sukri laughed.

"Aww, poor Huntie," she murmured, tousling his hair. "So confused."

"Damn right I am."

"You fell from the sky after Zagamar splatted on the street," Sukri explained. "Camilla tried to catch you, but she couldn't get there in time. Your wings slowed your fall, but you still hit the street pretty hard."

"I must've, 'cause I don't remember any of this."

"Not surprised," Sukri replied. "You had a pretty good-sized dent in your skull from the impact. I honestly thought you were dead. You were for a while – you didn't have a pulse for about five minutes – but then you came back. Scared the shit outta me."

Hunter ran a hand through his short hair, half-expecting to find a dent in his skull, but there was none.

"Dominus brought you to the hospital in Hightown, but Vi said you'd be fine since you drank your brother's goo a couple of times. She was right of course. Xerxes gave you even more goo while you were asleep, just to be sure. Took you three days to recover, but you did."

"So how did I end up…"

"In your old apartment?" Sukri finished for him. "Vi and I came up with the idea while you were still out. Figured we'd play a prank on you and put you in your apartment so you'd wake up all confused."

"You succeeded," Hunter grumbled. Sukri cackled.

"Had to wait days for the payoff, but *damn* was it worth it," she agreed.

Hunter grew quiet, dreading what he knew had to come next. He took a deep breath in, then heaved a deep sigh.

"And Trixie?" he asked.

"You mean Ella?" Sukri corrected with a devilish grin. "That was all me, baby. Pretty funny, huh?"

"*Funny*?"

"Figured you'd get totally fucked in the head if we had her come in like none of this had happened. Like you'd dreamed everything, and woke up right where you'd been when you and Trixie were together."

He stared at her incredulously.

"You shoulda seen the look on your face when she came in the apartment," she said, cackling again. "Oh *god* it was perfect!"

"You were *watching?*" he blurted out.

"From the apartment next door," Sukri confirmed. "Figured you wouldn't notice, man that you are. You didn't even look out the window."

He stopped in his tracks, a chill running down his spine.

"Wait, you're saying you were watching the whole time?" he pressed. She practically giggled, nodding at him, her golden eyes twinkling.

"Mmm hmm."

"Oh *fuck,*" Hunter breathed. He thought back to what'd happened. To everything he'd done…everything he and Ella had done. To think that Sukri'd seen it all…

"I saw you push her off when you noticed your wings," Sukri offered. "Aww, my boyfriend. So loyal."

"Sukri!" he complained. "How could you just watch me…do that?"

"Please," she retorted. "You never were able to resist Trixie. I knew damn well you wouldn't stand a chance against an elite prostitute. That was the whole point."

"Huh?"

"Trixie was a higher-end whore, but Ella's elite," Sukri explained. "Her will is a lot stronger."

"I noticed."

"After we won, and the Kingdom of the Deep helped take out the rest of the Svartálfar, everyone was celebrating but me and Xerxes. Vi insisted you'd be fine, but watching you just lie there like that, with that horrible dent in your head…" She trailed off, shaking her head. "Anyway, I stayed with you day and night for two days. Didn't eat, barely drank. That is, until Vi got fed up with my moping and insisted on taking me out on the town last night. We got piss drunk, and we came up with this prank."

"Wow," Hunter muttered, taking a long moment to wrap his head around this. "Damn Sukri. That's fucked up."

"Never said I was normal," she replied sweetly.

"That's *really* fucked up," he opined. "Like, royally fucked up." She batted her eyes at him.

"Do you still love me?" she inquired.

"I mean, yeah."

"All in all, I have to say that was pretty damn entertaining," she mused, smiling at the memory.

"You're a twisted, conniving bitch," Hunter grumbled.

"Yup."

"So we're really okay?" he pressed.

"Of course babe," Sukri reassured, wrapping an arm around his waist and giving it a squeeze. He smiled, shaking his head.

"Shit babe, I still can't believe you did that."

"If you want, I can have Xerxes give you another head injury and make you forget all about it," she offered.

"Pretty tempting, actually."

"Gotta say, watching her with you made me jealous as fuck," Sukri admitted. "Gonna have to reclaim you tonight, if you know what I mean."

"That a promise?"

"*Oh* yeah," Sukri replied. She stared at him for a long moment, smiling to herself.

"What?"

"I'm glad you're back," she stated. "I missed you. And I love you. I mean that."

"Love you too Sukri."

"Good," Sukri replied. She turned then, pulling him down a side-street. "Come on," she urged. "Everyone's been waiting for you to wake up."

* * *

Xerxes, Vi, and the rest of the gang – including Camilla and Dominus – had congregated at the Lucky Nuts, bartender Tykus alive and well at the bar. They were all sitting around tables they'd pushed together, as before, with Xerxes sitting on the floor…and still managing to tower over them. They all stopped talking once Sukri and Hunter walked in, their heads turning to look at Hunter. They all raised mugs of beer to him, cheering loudly.

"There he is!" Tykus cried. "The hero himself!"

Xerxes stood, having to hunch over to prevent himself from scraping his head against the ceiling. The big guy stomped up to Hunter, giving him a big bear hug with all four arms…and crushing Hunter's wings against his back.

"Ow," he blurted out. Xerxes let him go, beaming down at him.

"WELCOME…BACK," he greeted.

"Thanks big guy," Hunter replied with a smile. "Good to be back."

"My turn," Vi called out, standing from her chair and walking up to Hunter, giving him a hug as well…and picking him clean up off the floor. Somehow she managed to squeeze him even harder than Xerxes had. She lowered him to the floor, grinning at Sukri. "How'd it go?"

"Exactly as we expected," Sukri answered with a wink.

"Hunter!" Vi admonished, feigning shock. "How *could* you?"

"Ha ha," Hunter grumbled. "Go fuck yourself, by the way."

"I told her not to do it, but she insisted," Vi confessed. "You guys good?"

"Yeah," Sukri answered.

"Told you he likes it non-consensual," Camilla piped in, giving Hunter a smirk, then taking a gulp from her mug. Everyone turned to give her a withering look.

"The only reason you're still alive is because you helped us," Hunter shot back. "Bitch."

"I second that," Vi piped in.

"Third," Sukri added.

Xerxes grunted, glaring down at Camilla.

"I appears I've overstayed my welcome," Camilla replied. "If it makes you feel better, I'll be leaving soon."

"It does," Hunter agreed.

"Have a seat," Dominus urged, patting an empty chair. Hunter took the former duke's offer, sitting down, with Sukri sitting on his other side. She put a hand on his thigh, and he put his hand on top of hers, flashing her a smile.

"How're things going?" Hunter asked.

"Very well, thanks to you," Dominus answered. He had bandages wrapped around his belly and on the stump of his right arm. "How much do you remember?"

"Not a lot," Hunter admitted. "I remember fighting Zagamar, but not much after that."

"I told him about his fall," Sukri offered.

"The Kingdom of the Deep helped kill the rest of the Svartálfar," Dominus explained. "We burned all the bodies once a favorable wind came."

"To blow the smoke into the Deadlands instead of corrupting the Kingdom," Vi added.

"We've been using giant horse-drawn rakes to drag the remains into the Fringe," Dominus continued. "We'll bury them deep beneath the ground there, and cover them with neutral soil."

"And Zagamar?" Hunter asked. "He may have died when he hit the ground, but he'll come back to life eventually…and anyone who goes near him is gonna get turned eventually."

"True," Vi admitted. "That's why we decapitated him, covered his body with cement, and dragged him out into the Deadlands. Your mother came by yesterday to pick him up."

"My mom?" Hunter blurted out. "Why?"

"She's a Legend," Dominus answered. "She cannot be transformed by him."

"Ah."

"She's bringing him to the Deep," Vi stated. "She'll drag his body by a rope, then throw him into the pit. No one will ever be able to resurrect him again."

"Thank god," Camilla muttered. Hunter scoffed.

"Technically this is all your fault," he pointed out. "If you hadn't sent me into the crypt, Zeno never would've been able to resurrect him."

"True," Camilla admitted. "But it was the Guild of Seeker's mission to resurrect him one day. If Zeno hadn't, one of his successors would have."

"And you were the only one who could beat Zagamar," Vi piped in, "…by pitting him against himself."

"True," Hunter admitted. He explained how he'd been able to read Zagamar's memories at the end, anticipating his every move in advance.

"I rest my case," Camilla concluded. "If I hadn't sent you to the Crypt of Zagamar, you never would've been able to defeat him. And even if he hadn't resurrected now, he would've eventually…and no one else would likely have been able to destroy him." She smiled. "It *had* to be you."

"How convenient," he grumbled.

"She is correct," Dominus piped in. Hunter gave him a look.

"Says the guy who tried to murder everyone at this table," Hunter shot back. "Except for Camilla," he added.

"Actually, I did try to have her killed, along with her family. After they fled Tykus during the civil war," Dominus confessed.

"So that *was* you," Camilla murmured. "Nice try."

"You do realize you're a supervillain," Hunter grumbled.

"To be fair, I've also tried to *save* everyone's life at this table," Dominus pointed out. "Having done both, I would much rather have you all as my allies than my enemies."

"Hear hear," Vi agreed. "But if you double-cross me again, I'll kill you. Definitively."

"I have no doubt you would," Dominus replied.

"Guess that settles that," Hunter decided. "Don't expect us to be best buddies though." Dominus gave a rueful smile.

"I've learned not to try to predict the future."

"Just to prepare for it," barkeeper Tykus piped in, refilling the beer mugs that needed it.

"Thank you your highness," Vi said, winking at the man. "Kinda miss warrior Tykus though."

"There's plenty more of me to go around," Tykus promised.

"You ever go real dark?" Vi inquired. "Like 'serial killer Tykus' or 'wife-beater Tykus?' Or like, 'drug-addict Tykus?'"

"I'm not certain," Tykus admitted. "King Tykus handles all the other Tykuses. But I suppose I've tried just about everything by now. We all go back to share our experiences at the end, to gain wisdom from them."

"Wisdom from being a drug addict?" Vi asked.

"There is wisdom to be gained from every experience," Tykus pointed out. "If you're open to receiving it. Living the lives my subjects do gives me compassion for them…and understanding of their difficulties."

Vi considered this, then started to take a swig from her mug. But Dominus stopped her.

"I propose a toast," the former duke declared, turning to Hunter. "To the hero who defeated one of the greatest Legends of all time," Dominus stated, raising his mug. Everyone else raised theirs. "An Original who defied a kingdom, a Lady, the Duke of Wexford, and King Tykus himself…and ended up saving them all."

"To Hunter!" everyone cheered, clinking their glasses and taking a gulp. Hunter did as well, setting his mug down and wiping the foam from his mouth.

"To my greatest pupil," Vi added, grinning at Hunter and taking another swig of her beer. "Hunter…destroyer of Legends!"

Chapter 46

The gardens outside of the Acropolis were just as Dominus remembered, untouched by the ravages of the Ironclad assault not long ago. Sunlight shone from the heavens, its warmth contrasting with the crisp coolness in the air. The coldest months of the year were here at last, the days short and evenings long.

Dominus smiled, feeling the grass beneath his bare feet as he walked, and glanced at King Tykus, who was walking at his side. The king had invited him for a stroll, and seemed a little quiet, even wistful.

"The world is quieter now," Tykus noted, as if reading Dominus's thoughts. "Everything is slowing down."

"We deserve a rest," Dominus replied. Tykus chuckled.

"Indeed we do."

They passed a long row of hydrangeas, their small purple-blue flowers having already begun to wilt. A few bees still buzzed around them, landing atop them and gathering their nectar. Dominus watched them, thinking back to his own hives in Wexford.

"The original Duke of Wexford was a beekeeper," Tykus informed him, following Dominus's gaze. "A bit obsessive about it, actually…like he was about everything else."

Dominus frowned; he hadn't realized his progenitor – the model duke, whose Ossae still lived within his ancestral shrine – had been a beekeeper as well. Most of their family history from that time had been lost. But of course Tykus would remember; his bones held those memories far more faithfully than any book.

"He told me once – during one of our walks, naturally – that he was trying to create the perfect bee," Tykus continued. "He became very upset when I laughed at him."

"Laughed?"

"Yes," Tykus confirmed. "He asked me why I was laughing. I'd never seen him so offended!"

"What did you tell him?"

"That his efforts were pointless."

Dominus stopped in his tracks, turning to face Tykus.

"Pointless?"

"Of course," Tykus replied. "You see, the bee was already perfect."

Dominus just stared at him.

"Your ancestor was never satisfied with the ways things were," Tykus continued. "Neither are you. Which is precisely why I hired you."

"What do you mean?"

"Perfection is a process, not a goal," Tykus explained. "You're obsessed with perfection…and have spent your entire life trying to perfect yourself, the kingdom…and your bees."

Dominus started to respond, then realized that Tykus was entirely correct…as usual.

"You and Nature have that in common, I suppose," Tykus continued. "Always pursuing perfection. But Nature does it effortlessly…it doesn't have to try. Because, like perfection, Nature is a process, not a thing."

"I don't understand," Dominus confessed. Tykus chuckled.

"Most don't," he agreed. "We live such short lives, seeing only what *is*. What exists. But I have lived across millennia. And what I have seen is a world in flux. To you, a river is a thing. To me, it is a process; water flowing down from the sky, taking the path of least resistance across the earth, then returning to the sea, where it will rise again to the sky. Leaving ever-deepening chasms in its wake, cleaving the land in two."

Dominus nodded; it was clearly true.

"Life is the same," Tykus continued. "It is ever-changing. Ever-improving; that which excels continues, that which does not, ends. Each generation of life comes from that which excels, and in turn the wheat will be separated from the chaff. Again and again, forever."

"Of course," Dominus agreed.

"These bees then," Tykus stated, gesturing at a few of them, "…have survived countless millennia. They are still here after a culling the scope of which we cannot fathom." He raised an eyebrow. "How could you argue that they are not already perfect?"

Dominus considered this.

"They are perfect for themselves," Dominus countered at last. "But not necessarily for humans."

"Aha!" Tykus cried, lifting both hands in the air. "And there we have it. Nothing is perfect to you unless it is perfect *for* you."

Dominus took this in, not saying anything. There was nothing to say…it was true. Tykus resumed their stroll, and Dominus followed at his king's side.

"I do recall some of your conversations with young Axio before he became me," Tykus revealed. "The day you first met him, you asked him who the king serves."

"I recall," Dominus stated.

"He didn't know the answer, so you gave him one. Do you remember what you said?"

Dominus thought it over.

"I believe I said that the king's duty was to preserve the identity of his people. Their customs, the noblest of their bloodlines, and their lands."

"That's precisely what you said," Tykus confirmed. "You have an excellent memory. But I have a better answer: the king's duty is to perfection. To see Nature's wisdom and emulate her. And to apply Nature's process – the process of perfection – to those he rules…and himself."

Dominus glanced down at the king's bare feet, and his own.

"That's why you connect with Nature," he realized. Tykus winked.

"Precisely," he agreed. "As you told Axio, you tended to your bees not for the honey, but for the perspective."

Dominus gave a rueful smile.

"I knew all along, without knowing," he realized.

"You applied your wisdom to the Kingdom instead of the world," Tykus stated. "Your myopia limited you."

They walked in silence for a while, until Tykus cleared his throat.

"Zagamar was the great Trial for humanity," he declared. "No different than the trials Nature brings to every generation of life. Simply greater in scope and degree. We have survived him, and so we live on."

He paused, as if searching for the right words.

"You told Axio that each caste plays a vital role in our government, from the lowliest peasant to the king himself…and that each is necessary to preserve the integrity of the kingdom, just as each type of bee is integral to the health of the hive."

"I did."

"But the hive is also dependent on Nature," Tykus pointed out. "Without plants that flower, the hive will die. My kingdom too will perish without the help of those outside of it."

"Such as me," Dominus realized.

"And others," Tykus stated. "Would we be having this conversation without Hunter? Or Vi? Or the Ironclad? Or Xerxes, without whom you would have succumbed to your illness long ago?"

Dominus shook his head.

"You told Axio that people were tribal…that they had loyalty first to their family, then their friends, then their nation and their people," Tykus reminded him.

"These constitute the 'us,'" Dominus replied.

"Quite right," Tykus agreed. "And you said that beyond these psychic borders are the 'them,' those that do not belong." He glanced sidelong at Dominus, raising an eyebrow. "What is the lesson here, Dominus?"

Dominus frowned, mulling it over.

"That the 'us' had to be larger," he answered at last. "More inclusive of others."

"I agree," Tykus replied. "And *that* is why I forged an alliance with Neesha long ago. And with the Kingdom of the Deep, promising never to attack them. Even as I set hard limits on my kingdom, I expanded my circle of 'us.'"

"While maintaining our culture," Dominus realized. Tykus nodded.

"A delicate balance," he admitted. "To protect one's way of life – a thing that has true value – one must avoid its corruption. And corruption can come from outside…or within. We must preserve it if we value it. But not to the exclusion of other cultures. For we can learn from others, and take what is good from their ways, just as they can do with ours."

Tykus stopped, turning to Dominus and putting a hand on his shoulder.

"Culture is subject to Nature, Dominus. An endless process of perfection. That which excels continues, and that which does not, ends." He gave Dominus a grave look. "We must excel, Dominus. We must prove ourselves worthy of the future."

Dominus nodded.

"With your wisdom, we have, and we will," he replied. Tykus sighed, taking his hand off Dominus's shoulder.

"And that is precisely the problem," he lamented. "Men will follow any man as long as he seems to possess confidence. It is human nature to equate confidence with competence, though the two are not often related."

"Rarely, in fact," Dominus agreed with a smirk.

"Most men are a hair's breadth from being won over by a tyrant," Tykus mused. "Tyrants are utterly confident. They don't ask for permission, nor forgiveness. They take whatever they can, however they can."

"Like Zagamar."

"Like Zagamar," Tykus agreed. "And wise men like me can only win by creating this," he added, gesturing all around them.

"I don't follow," Dominus admitted.

"Great fortresses!" Tykus exclaimed. "Great walls! A mythology of perfect men, of the natural separation of wills. Aristocracy." He gave a conspiratorial smile. "All of this," he added, spreading his fingers out wide and wiggling them in front of Dominus's eyes, "…is an illusion."

"An illusion?"

"Of power!" Tykus stated. "Tell me, what does the average citizen think of the great Tykus?"

Dominus stared at him.

"That he is powerful," Tykus declared. "Strong! Confident and sure!"

"But you are," Dominus protested.

"And yet I'm just a man," Tykus pointed out. "I eat. I piss and I shit. I pick my nose and I smell if I don't bathe frequently."

"And yet I would die for you," Dominus stated. "As would nearly any man in this kingdom."

"Yet not for the countless other Tykus's throughout this kingdom and beyond it," the king countered. "I daresay my iterations are all so similar our differences don't matter, yet none are revered as I am. In fact, some are treated quite poorly."

Dominus grimaced. The thought of this man enduring the scorn and mistreatment of common folk…of such a gem of a man being lost in the dung heap of the unwashed masses…

"I am revered because of my station," Tykus stated. "Isn't it grand? The crown, the scepter, my great Acropolis? It elevates this simple body. And it would elevate nearly any body as well as mine."

The thought of such a thing bothered Dominus greatly; Tykus had always been king. Six thousand years of his rule, uninterrupted, unending. He would *always* be king. A world without him was too terrible to imagine.

"Nature is too fickle to be trusted to produce wise rulers generation after generation," Tykus stated. "And Man is too easily fooled to be trusted to *choose* wise rulers."

"Which is why they need you."

"And why I need you, and Hunter, and Neesha. And Xerxes. And the Kingdom of the Deep," Tykus added.

"Neesha I understand," Dominus replied. "She is eternal. But the others…"

Tykus arched an eyebrow, a little smile playing at his lips. Dominus's eyes widened.

"I see," he murmured.

"They make far better allies than enemies," Tykus stated. "Do try to curtail your worst impulses, Dominus."

Dominus felt his cheeks flushing, a response only Tykus seemed to be able to trigger. Tykus chuckled.

"Who knows? One day you might even make some friends," he said. "Other than me."

Dominus blinked, taken aback.

"You would consider me your friend?" he asked. Tykus smiled, stepping in and embracing him. Dominus hesitated, then embraced the king back. Then Tykus pulled away.

"I would," he answered. "If you'd have me as one."

"I would be honored, my Liege," Dominus replied.

"Just Tykus, please," Tykus insisted.

"I would be honored, Tykus."

"A friendship that will span the ages," Tykus mused.

"One that only I will remember," Dominus lamented. Tykus frowned.

"And why is that?"

"You will grow old and die, then be reborn…and your memories of me will be lost forever," Dominus explained.

"Perhaps," Tykus replied.

Dominus gave him a questioning look.

"I'd better get back to my duties," Tykus stated. "Do visit again, Dominus. Perhaps in a month?"

"Of course."

Tykus smiled, then broke away, walking back toward the Acropolis. Dominus watched him go until the man had disappeared behind a tall row of shrubs, then lowered his gaze to his feet. Short blades of grass poked between his toes; grass with wills weaker than his own. When it inevitably began to transform from the influence of the humans walking over it, it would be replaced. A kingdom forever the same, generation after generation. If Dominus were transported a thousand years into the future, he would not be able to tell the difference.

Suddenly, it wasn't enough.

It was the corruption of his soul, he supposed. A shifting from the purity of his ancestors. A process that had begun long ago, with his son Conlan. He took a deep breath in, remembering some of his son's last words to him.

Take heart father. Even after I'm gone, you'll always have a part of me inside of you.

It'd been a cruel jab at the time, a bitter retort against a father who didn't understand. Who *wouldn't* understand. But now he did.

Dominus suddenly yearned for the grass of the forest, wild and free. Controlled not by the unending systems of the Kingdom, but by the powerful and infinitely more complex forces of Nature. The thought would have terrified him a few weeks ago…even a few days ago. But now it intrigued him. Here he had nothing to fear; this place held no danger for him. But it also held no mystery. Nature would inevitably change him, it was true…and in what way, he could not know. He might lose a part of himself, but in return he would gain something. Even as the world changed him, he would change it. And, fate willing, it would be for the better.

He closed his eyes, picturing Conlan's face. His grim smile as he stared his father down defiantly. Triumphant before his death. He wished he could speak to Conlan. Apologize to him. And thank him.

And as long as you're alive, you'll never be able to get rid of me, he'd said.

Dominus opened his eyes, smiling to himself.

"Good," he murmured.

CHAPTER 47

It was two days after Hunter awoke from his coma before Hunter, Vi, Sukri, and Xerxes decided to leave the kingdom of Tykus. They bade their farewells to Camilla, who'd convinced the Kingdom of the Deep to help finance the rebuilding of her mansion, and was preparing to fly back to the strange kingdom to live there until its construction. Dominus had decided to travel with Hunter and the gang, at least for a ways. They left the kingdom, passing through its two gates to the Deadlands, where armies of horse-drawn rakes were gathering the last of the Svartálfar corpses and dragging them – and any dirt they'd corrupted – toward the Fringe. Tykus had offered a luxurious horse-drawn carriage for their trip, but everyone had agreed they'd much rather walk.

So it was that Hunter found himself entering the Fringe, passing through the burnt-out section of forest they'd corralled the Svartálfar in during the first wave of attacks. They passed this, hiking through the woods. No one said very much, partially because it was still obscenely early, and because Dominus's presence made their usual irreverent banter seem a bit awkward. Vi, of course, didn't let that stop her.

"Kinda nice taking a stroll with my arch-enemy," she opined, eyeing Dominus. "Is there anyone you *haven't* tried to kill?"

"Myself," Dominus quipped. "And Tykus."

"Short list," Vi grumbled. "Little lonely being a sociopath, isn't it? Heard you killed your own son too."

Dominus's jawline rippled, but he said nothing.

"Now that's just cold," she continued. "What'd he do, forget to clean his room?"

"Enough," Dominus growled.

"Sorry if I hurt your feelings," Vi shot back. "Oh wait, no I'm not. 'Cause you're an asshole."

"I understand I hurt you," Dominus stated, somehow remaining calm despite Vi's baiting. "Believe me when I say I regret it."

"Because it's inconvenient now?"

"Partially," Dominus admitted. "But I also…everything I did was to protect the Kingdom."

"Bullshit," Vi retorted. "Everything you did was to protect yourself."

Dominus considered this, then nodded.

"It was," he conceded. "I wanted to be the one to continue to protect the Kingdom. I didn't trust anyone else to do it."

"And yet we did," she pointed out.

"I was wrong," he agreed. "And selfish. And…cold. I'm trying to do better now."

"Tykus give you a pep talk?"

"He did," Dominus answered, ignoring her snide tone. "But I didn't understand the Kingdom until I met Tykus. Until I talked with him. I thought I knew who the king was, but I didn't."

"I'll give you that," Hunter conceded. "I was imagining more of a Nazi racist dictator."

"A what?" Vi asked.

"A bad guy," Hunter clarified.

"I've done things I'm not proud of," Dominus confessed. "Things I may never forgive myself for. But if I don't try to move past them, they'll destroy me."

Hunter lowered his gaze, staring at his feet as he walked. He recalled the way he'd felt after thinking that Vi had died. How he'd hated himself for killing his mother and brother. As much as he hated to admit it, Dominus had a point…and if he was being sincere, the man deserved a second chance.

"You know, a few weeks ago I would have killed you on the spot," Hunter admitted. "I made it my life's work to get revenge on you and the Guild of Seekers."

"I don't blame you," Dominus replied.

Hunter hesitated, then stopped.

"Hold up," he stated.

Everyone else stopped as well, and Hunter gestured for Dominus to approach him. The former duke did so, eyeing him quizzically. Hunter removed his helmet.

"Take off your helmet," he ordered. "Press your forehead to mine."

"I don't…" Dominus began, then he stopped. After a moment's pause, he sighed. "Very well."

Dominus leaned in, pressing his forehead against Hunter's.

Images flashed in rapid sequence in Hunter's mind, a whirlwind of memories flooding his brain. He accepted them without reservation, allowing the transfer. At length, he backed away, letting go of a breath he hadn't realized he'd been holding.

"Damn," he muttered, staring at Dominus.

"What did you see?" Dominus inquired. It was clear that the man didn't appreciate having someone else in his head.

"Enough," Hunter answered. He hesitated, then inclined his head at Dominus. "I understand you now," he stated. "I don't agree with what you did – or why you did it – but I accept your apology."

Dominus smiled, extending a hand. Hunter shook it.

"Thank you," the former duke stated. And Hunter knew the man meant it.

"All right," Vi interjected. "I *have* to know what you saw."

"Dominus is…complicated," Hunter replied. "I'll let him tell you."

"Aww, come *on*," Vi complained. "Spoilsport." But she accepted this, much to Hunter's relief. They continued their trek, and Hunter took the ensuing long silence to process what he'd experienced.

There was one thing he knew for sure: it was next to impossible to truly hate someone when he understood their point of view…even if he disagreed with it.

"What're you going to do now?" Hunter asked Dominus.

"I'm not certain," he admitted. "I suspect I'll continue to work with Camilla after the mansion is rebuilt."

"Gonna shack up with her at the Kingdom of the Deep?" Vi inquired. "I'm sure she'll make it worth your while."

"I have no interest in that kind of experience," Dominus replied. Vi arched an eyebrow.

"What, Camilla or the Kingdom of the Deep?"

Dominus gave a wry smirk.

"The Kingdom of the Deep," he answered.

"Well now," Vi exclaimed. "Look who's ready to *get* some!" She elbowed Xerxes. "Guess your head brought Dominus's back to life."

Xerxes grunted.

"On that note, I should be leaving," Dominus declared, stopping in his tracks. Everyone else stopped with him.

"Where you going?" Hunter asked.

"South," Dominus answered. "I want to explore the lands beyond the Deep."

"Watch out for the Svartálfar," Vi warned. "There's bound to be a few of them running around."

"I'll be careful."

"Guess this is goodbye then," Vi said. She hesitated, then offered a hand. Dominus shook it, smiling at her.

"Goodbye Vi," he said. "You're the most impressive woman I've ever met."

"I know."

Dominus smirked, then turned to Hunter.

"Good luck," he stated, shaking Hunter's hand. "I, and the Kingdom, are in your debt."

"You're welcome," Hunter replied.

"If you ever need me, I will be there for you," Dominus vowed. Hunter nodded silently, and Dominus turned to Sukri, who put up both hands.

"Sorry, not ready to forgive you just yet," she stated. "You sent me and my friends to die."

"Understood," Dominus replied. He turned to Xerxes. "Thank you for giving me a second life," he stated. Xerxes grunted, but otherwise pointedly ignored him, crossing his four arms over his chest.

"Go on Dukie," Vi said, waving Dominus away. Dominus frowned.

"Dukie?"

"Best nickname I could come up with," Vi explained. "See, because you were a duke, and a piece of shit."

"Ah."

And with that, Dominus broke away from the group, walking off into the woods alone. They watched as he disappeared into the forest, then resumed their trek through the Fringe.

* * *

It was early afternoon by the time Hunter, Vi, Sukri, and Xerxes emerged from the woods into a small, familiar clearing, the bright sun contrasting with the crisp chill in the air. With the Kingdom and Dominus as allies – as well as Lady Camilla – there was no fear of anyone trying to attack her home down in the canyon. While she'd been given a home in Ironclad territory, Vi much preferred her own place, thank you very much.

And that is how Hunter found himself stopping at the edge of the cliff overlooking the huge canyon, gazing down at the large lake below with the twin islands in the center of it. It was just as he remembered, and he couldn't help but feel a little sentimental as he spotted Vi's house on the larger island.

"There it is," Vi declared, gesturing at the house. "Home sweet home."

"Uh," Sukri said, looking around. "So how do we get there?"

"We jump," Vi replied, winking at Hunter. She'd said the same thing to him the first time he'd been here.

"Ha ha," Sukri grumbled.

"Just seeing if you'd do it," Vi stated.

And with that, Xerxes leapt off the edge.

"Holy…!" Sukri blurted out, watching as the huge Ironclad fell like a rock toward the bottom of the canyon over three hundred feet below. A few seconds later, he smashed into the ground in a spray of blood and blue gel.

"Huh," Vi muttered.

"Now that looked like fun," Hunter stated, flashing her a grin. "I think I'll join him."

And with that, he leapt off the edge, plummeting toward the bottom of the canyon.

"Ha!" he heard Vi shout as he fell, accelerating rapidly. He felt the giddy terror of free-fall, enjoying the rush…and watching as the ground approached rapidly. He unfurled his wings then, feeling them fill with air instantly. His fall slowed quickly, and he settled into a gentle glide toward the larger island in the center of the lake, touching down a few yards from Vi's house. Then he turned around, waving at the tiny dots still standing at the edge of the cliff hundreds of feet up.

Hunter chuckled to himself, watching as Vi and Sukri made their way ever-so-slowly down the spiraling path to the bottom of the canyon. And as Xerxes started to stir, rising to his hands and knees. By the time Sukri and Vi reached the bottom, Xerxes had already mostly healed, and was striding across the long wooden bridge toward Hunter. The three reached him at last, and Xerxes grinned, punching Vi in the shoulder…or at least trying to. She dodged, slapping his arm away.

"JUMP…WORK," Xerxes grunted.

"Show-offs," Vi muttered. "Well played, by the way."

"Aww, is Vi Jealous?" Hunter inquired.

"I could get wings any time I wanted," Vi reminded him. "And if I wanted more of your brother's goo, he wouldn't be able to stop me."

Xerxes raised an eye-ridge at her.

"LIKE…CAMILLA?"

Hunter shot his brother a withering glare…and Sukri gave Hunter a look, her hands on her hips.

"That's the third time I've heard someone joke about that," she noted. "You're gonna tell me what that's all about."

"Uhhh…" Hunter stammered.

"So *anyway*," Vi interjected, "…I'm gonna stay here with Hunter and Sukri and try to teach them how to fight. You could use some lessons too, you know," she added, eyeing Xerxes.

"MAYBE…LATER."

"Suit yourself," she replied, turning to Sukri and handing her a bow and quiver full of arrows. "Go fetch me lunch, Puss."

Sukri stared at her, then glanced at Hunter.

"I'll show you," he reassured. "Don't worry…it doesn't get any better."

"That's for sure," Vi agreed. "Though I gotta say Hunter, you've sure come around since I first met you. Not gonna lie, I thought you were hopeless."

"So did I," Hunter admitted with a smile. He'd all but given up on himself and his future…long before he'd ever met Vi. Before he'd ever come to this world.

"Glad I didn't give up on you," she said.

"That's one thing she'll never do," Hunter told Sukri. "So don't bother trying to give up on yourself. Believe me, I've tried." He turned to his brother. "What're you gonna do bro?" Hunter inquired. Xerxes smiled.

"GO…HOME," he answered. "GET…REWARD."

"Reward?" Sukri asked.

"REWARD," Xerxes repeated. Vi smirked, putting her lips to Sukri's ear.

"He means he's gonna get laid," she explained.

"Ooo," Sukri replied. "Go *get* it Xerxes!"

"YOU…TOO."

Sukri arched an eyebrow, glancing at Hunter, who grinned sheepishly.

"I'm always up for it."

Xerxes gave a deep, rumbling chuckle, then leaned in, giving Hunter a four-armed hug…and lifting him right off the ground. Hunter hugged him back.

"Love you Xerxes," he said.

"LOVE…YOU," Xerxes replied, setting Hunter down and ruffling his hair affectionately.

"To family," Hunter declared, putting an arm around Sukri and Vi, then smiling up at Xerxes.

"FAMILY," Xerxes agreed.

* * *

After Xerxes left – making it quite clear that Hunter needed to visit soon and often – Vi went inside her house, leaving Sukri and Hunter outside on the larger island. Sukri turned to Hunter.

"Now what?" she asked.

"Come on," Hunter said, gesturing for her to walk back across the long wooden bridge toward the crescent-shaped shore beyond. There were trees there…including the same tree Vi had first taught him to fire a bow at. He brought Sukri there, stopping her a good twenty feet away. He could still see the holes in the rough bark where he'd managed to hit it. After a bit of practice, that was. And a whole lot of shit-talking from Vi.

He handed the bow and quiver to Sukri.

"Hit that from here," he ordered, gesturing at the tree.

Sukri grabbed an arrow, nocking it correctly on the bowstring…which meant she had *some* experience.

"Put your index finger and ring fingers above the shaft of the arrow, and your ring finger below," Hunter instructed. Sukri did so. "Draw it back."

Sukri drew the bowstring back, but her elbow dropped a little.

"Keep your elbow up. Legs planted," Hunter ordered. "Toes pointed perpendicular to the target. Good."

Sukri glanced at Hunter.

"Eyes on the target," he prompted. "Let go with your fingers only…don't move your arm."

Sukri did so, and the arrow shot forward, missing the trunk by a few inches and hitting the wall of the canyon beyond.

"Damn," she swore.

"Try again," he ordered. Sukri grabbed another arrow, nocking it. Then she glanced at him.

"This how Vi taught you?" she asked. Hunter smiled.

"Yep."

Sukri fired again, and the arrow struck the tree this time…but too low.

"Yes!" she exclaimed.

"Too low," Hunter stated. "Hit it at your chest level. Your straight arm is dropping…keep it pointing at your target."

"Got it."

"Then prove it," Hunter shot back. Sukri gave him a withering glare, but attempted to do just that, setting up, then firing another arrow. It struck the tree at chest level this time.

"Yeah!" Sukri exclaimed, flashing Hunter a grin. "Told you I had it!"

Hunter rolled his eyes, grabbing the bow from Sukri, along with three arrows. He turned about then, walking up to the long wooden bridge, then across it until he was standing at the other end. He turned around then, nocking an arrow, then firing. And again, and again.

Then he walked back to Sukri, who was staring at the tree trunk. All three arrows had struck…in a tight cluster around hers. He grimaced; Vi had done the same trick, but had been so good she'd split each arrow with the one after it. He still wasn't as good as she was…but Sukri was clearly impressed.

"Boom," he quipped, smirking at her.

"Damn," Sukri muttered.

"Come on buttercup," he stated, slapping her hard on the butt. "Impress me."

They practiced for the next hour or so, and then Hunter brought her up to the forest above the canyon to hunt. It was an abysmal failure, of course. Eventually Hunter had to take over, shooting down a few birds on his first try…much to Sukri's amazement, and chagrin. They went back down to the canyon then, returning to the larger island where Vi's house was. Hunter taught Sukri how to make a fire and dress the carcasses, then roasted the birds. The smell of cooking meat lured Vi out of her home, and they all sat by the campfire to enjoy a very late lunch.

"Mmm," Sukri murmured as she chowed down. "This is really good."

"Sure is," Vi agreed. She glanced up at Hunter, who – after three days of not eating – had a seemingly bottomless appetite. "God, this is so wrong," she stated. Hunter frowned.

"What?" he asked.

"You're eating your own kind," she pointed out. Hunter glanced down at the piece of meat in his hands, then shrugged, polishing it off.

"Guess I'm delicious," he replied.

"I can vouch for that," Sukri piped in.

"Gonna throw up now," Vi grumbled. But she did quite the opposite, eating more of Hunter's catch. They spent the rest of the meal in contented silence, eating until there was nothing left to eat. Then they all sat back, their bellies sated and their minds at ease.

"So," Hunter said, eyeing Vi. "What now?"

"What do you mean?"

"I mean...what now?" he repeated. "I found Mom, the Kingdom and the Ironclad are at peace, I've neutralized Zaggie, we've killed Zagamar. Everyone I wanted revenge on is either sorry or dead." He sighed. "I don't have anything left to do."

"That's a first," Vi agreed.

"I know," Sukri piped in. "For the first time in my life, I'm myself...and I'm around people that don't want me to be anyone else. It's...weird. Good, but weird."

"It's called being happy," Vi offered.

"Is that what this is?" Sukri asked.

"Feels weird, doesn't it?" Hunter replied.

"Well, I don't know about you, but I don't plan on resting on my laurels," Vi declared, throwing a stick into the fire. "I'm going right back to doing what I do best: being a Seeker."

"After you train me?" Sukri asked hopefully.

"After I *finish* training you," she corrected. "You did pretty well back there at the wall."

"Yeah," Sukri agreed, extending her claws. "These things are pretty badass."

"We'll train for a few weeks, then we're out of here," Vi decided. "If I'm gonna make halfway decent Seekers out of you, you'll need on-the-job training."

"I got some of that already," Hunter offered. "I got through the Crypt of Zagamar, after all."

"With my sword," she retorted. "Without it, you wouldn't have even gotten in."

"Granted."

"This time we'll find artifacts *without* getting possessed by a world-ending demonic bastard," Vi declared. "It's about time you started building up your stash."

"Stash?"

"Collection of artifacts," she clarified. "We collect artifacts, take what's useful from them into ourselves, and make ourselves better, bit-by-bit. That's what a Seeker does."

"I'm game," Sukri stated.

"Sounds good to me," Hunter agreed.

"Three weeks of training, then we're off," Vi decided. "I've got a few tips that need following up on. If I'm right – and I usually am – we're going to find some *really* good shit."

"Ooo, sounds like an adventure," Sukri said, rubbing her paws together eagerly. Vi grinned.

"Oh it will be," she confirmed. "Trust me." She got up then. "All right lovebirds, I'm headed to bed."

"What?" Sukri blurted out. "It's not even dark yet!"

"Sleep is good for the mind," Vi replied. "You should get some too. Gonna be long days ahead, Puss. Take care of your body and mind, and you might get through them."

With that, she waved goodbye, then went into her house, closing – and locking – the door behind her. Sukri stared at the door, then gave Hunter a quizzical look.

"So…where do we sleep?" she inquired.

"Over there," Hunter answered, gesturing across the long wooden bridge to the narrow crescent of rocky shore near the canyon wall. The animal skins that had served as his bed were still there, undoubtedly a little moldy now. Sukri gave them a dubious look, and Hunter got up, stretching his legs. He led her over the wooden bridge to the shore, and their bed. They aired out each animal skin, then laid them on the rocky ground. Hunter peeled off his armor, keeping his helmet on – as always – then lying down. Sukri did the same, removing every last bit of armor. Then – naked save for her fur – she laid down next to him.

"This isn't so bad," she murmured, snuggling up to him. Then she frowned. "What do we do if it rains?"

"Get wet," he answered.

"And Vi just…"

"Sleeps under a roof," Hunter finished for her. "Yep."

"Wow, what a bitch."

"I know, right?" Hunter replied. He frowned then. "You know what? I just realized she's forcing me to build my own house."

"Huh?"

"That's why she made me sleep out here. She built her house all by herself, and I bet you she was just *waiting* for me to ask her to teach me how." He slapped himself in the forehead. "Wow, I can't believe I missed that."

"Huh."

"I'll ask her in the morning," he muttered wearily. For, even though it *was* still somewhat light out, his full belly – and the day's exertions – had tired him out. An early sleep was just what he needed. He closed his eyes, laying on his back, Sukri on her side against him. She put a hand on his chest, then slid it down to his belly.

"You didn't say goodnight," she accused.

"Goodnight."

She fell silent, warm against him, her soft fur like a nice heated blanket. So much better than sleeping alone.

"Hunter," he heard her say.

"Hmm?"

"I can't sleep," she mumbled, sliding her hand down to his belly…and not stopping there. He felt her hand on his groin. "I need help," she added, stroking him through his pants. His groin responded.

"Want me to put you to sleep?" he asked, opening his eyes. He saw her big, golden eyes twinkle.

"Mmm hmm."

"Far be it from me to deny a lady," Hunter murmured, giving her a grin and rolling onto his side to face her. She arched one furry eyebrow.

"So you aren't in the habit of denying a Lady?" she inquired, with an all-too-obvious emphasis on the last word. Hunter grimaced, rolling back onto his back.

"And you just killed the mood," he grumbled. She laughed, climbing atop him and leaning in to give him a kiss.

"I'll bring it back to life," she promised.

"Can't we just cuddle?"

"After," she promised.

"So I don't have a choice in the matter?" he pressed. She smiled sweetly, planting another kiss on his lips.

"Nope."

"Story of my life," he grumbled.

They kissed again, and then Sukri laid her head on his chest, her body warm and soft against his.

"So this is it, huh?" she murmured. "Vi trains us to be Seekers, and we go out collecting artifacts and stuff."

"Guess so."

"Maybe have some babies along the way," she added. He frowned.

"Not anytime soon, I hope."

"Nah," Sukri replied. "Gotta make sure this whole thing works out first."

"Oh yeah?"

"Yeah. I give it a year or two before we hate each other."

"Works for me," he agreed.

"Wonder what they'd look like?" Sukri stated. "Our babies, I mean."

"Don't wanna think about that."

"Well, I guess they'll be like us," Sukri decided. "Misfits."

Hunter nodded, staring up at the sky. The sun was setting, the three moons of Varta glowing in the darkening sky. They were all misfits, he realized. Himself, Sukri…even Gammon and Kris had been, back in the Outskirts. Misfits searching for acceptance. Looking for a place – and a people – to belong to. The Guild of Seekers had been a cult, the Kingdom more of a religion. And Lady Camilla had been pure business, a relationship of convenience…where she always managed to profit at his – and everyone else's – expense.

But in Vi, he'd found something else. Someone who cared. Who accepted him for who he was and only wanted him to be a better version of himself, not to change into someone else. Who *demanded* that he be better. And Xerxes, well, the big guy loved Hunter for who he was, no matter what.

He'd failed to become part of something big, and instead had found meaning in becoming part of something small. A family of misfits. Misfits that had somehow managed to save the world.

Hunter smiled, stroking Sukri's back, running his fingers through her thick, short fur.

"Ever wonder if this is it?" Sukri asked. "Like, we've just experienced the most interesting moments of our life, and everything after this is gonna be boring in comparison?"

Hunter considered this.

"Nah," he answered. "Knowing Vi, she's going to get us into a whole lot of trouble soon enough."

"You really think so?"

"I know so," he confirmed.

And that was just fine by him.

Epilogue

A breeze whipped over the desolate landscape, a desert of rock and yellow dirt that extended in all directions for as far as the eye could see. The sun glared down from a cloudless sky, the air warmer now than it'd been in months. Spring was coming, but not a soul lived in this wasteland, plant or animal, the earth having been salted long ago.

And then *he* arrived.

A man appeared out of thin air a few feet from the ground, falling to the dirt with a *thump*. His eyes were open, but he saw nothing. His limbs jerked rhythmically, froth dripping from the side of his mouth.

A minute passed.

The jerking stopped, and the man lay still on the dirt, the front of his loose black pants wet with urine. He was middle-aged, with short salt-and-pepper hair and a goatee, his clothes covered in dust.

He lay there on his side, barely breathing, staring off into space.

And then he blinked.

More time passed, and the man came to his senses gradually, rolling onto his back and staring up at the sky. Then he sat up, rubbing his temples and looking around, squinting against the harsh sunlight.

His head was *pounding*.

The stench of urine reached his nostrils, and he grimaced, looking down at the wet stain on his groin.

The hell?

He tried to remember how he'd gotten here, and couldn't. His mind felt hazy, as if his memories were too far away to grasp.

Must've had another seizure.

He'd had at least two in the last few weeks, as best as he could remember. A devastating reminder of just how far he'd fallen over the years. And of how many years he'd lost himself in bottle after bottle, drowning his pain in alcohol. Trying desperately to fill the hole inside his heart.

Where am I?

He spun around in a slow circle, the movement making him a little nauseous. Desert all around him…and nothing else. He cleared his throat, realizing the sides of his tongue were throbbing…and that he could taste blood.

Shielding his eyes with one hand, he looked around again, seeing nothing but dirt and rocks. The landscape was mostly flat, save for a hill that sloped upward to his left.

He wracked his brain, trying to remember what'd happened before this. He'd been driving in his car, going somewhere. It'd been urgent. Something terribly important.

But the memory led nowhere.

The sky above was bright blue, not a cloud in it. There were no birds flying overhead; only the moon in the distance, barely visible in the daylight.

And another moon nearby…and a third moon.

The man stared at them in disbelief, rubbing his eyes, then looking again.

What in the holy hell?

He stood there for a long moment, then closed his eyes.

I'm dreaming.

Opening his eyes, he looked down at his left forearm, pinching it. There was immediate pain.

His heart began to pound in his chest, fear gripping his guts. He took a deep breath, then another, forcing himself to calm down.

Okay, he thought. *Think.*

He studied the dirt, looking for footprints, but there were none.

Get help.

The landscape stretched out in every direction as far as the eye could see, save for the hill. If he could get to the top of that hill, he'd have a better vantage point to study the terrain. He started up the gentle slope, his sneakers crunching on the dirt and small pebbles underfoot. After a few minutes of this, the terrain leveled off.

He froze in his tracks.

For there, perhaps a thousand feet ahead, stood a long row of large wooden pillars. They had to be at least twenty feet tall, and supported what appeared to be a stone bridge that extended to the left and right as far as the eye could see. He felt an immediate burst of hope.

If there were bridges, there were people.

An image of a black stone arch came to him then, bordering a wall of utter blackness. A memory of hesitating before it, his heart pounding in his chest.

Do it, he'd told himself. *You don't have anything to live for anymore.*

He'd stood there, staring into the blackness of oblivion.

Do it!

He blinked, snapping himself out of the memory. Remembering what he'd done. He'd touched the wall, his hand vanishing within.

I must've gone through, he realized, a smile curling his lips. He laughed out loud, relief coursing through him.

He'd gone through, and he hadn't died. Which meant…

Focus.

He studied the bridge carefully, then looked down. There were footprints in the dirt now. Lots of them. He squatted, peering at them carefully. They were all going in one direction: leftward, following the bridge.

He turned left, following the footprints for several minutes. The barren landscape sloped upward again, the bridge sloping upward with it; he climbed the slope, then frowned, studying the terrain ahead. There were long lines in the dirt, as if a rake had been run over it. A rake with thousands of tines stretching for a few hundred feet on either side of the bridge.

Huh.

He continued to hike up the slope, having to stop to catch his breath a few times. It surprised him how out of shape he was; he'd been incredibly fit a decade ago. Years of neglecting his body had worn him down, making him weak. A shadow of the man he'd been.

But he was *here* now. He'd crossed over.

Things were going to be different from now on. *He* was going to be different.

He continued forward, huffing and puffing until at long last he reached the top of the slope. Closing his eyes, he bent over, resting his hands on his knees and forcing himself to slow his breathing. Then he stood up straight, opening his eyes.

And drew in a sharp breath.

The landscape dipped downward ahead, forming a small, barren valley. Beyond this, there was a massive stone wall, easily fifty feet high, extending to the left and right for miles. The wall had been built at the foot of a huge hill, forming a massive rectangle around it that extended all the way to the sparkling waters of the ocean far beyond.

And within that great wall stood a huge, sprawling city.

He stared in disbelief, rubbing his eyes, then looking again.

Wooden buildings stood at the base of the hill beyond the wall, surrounding it. On the hill itself, tall white stone buildings rose, their golden roofs gleaming in the sunlight. And on the very top of the hill stood a building larger than anything he'd ever seen. A veritable fortress of white stone, with domed golden roofs rising far above any other building in the city. The massive building seemed to have been hewn from the stone of the hill itself, a great sculpture rising toward the heavens.

A city of gold and white standing against a great blue sea.

"Hey!" a voice shouted.

The man flinched, turning toward the voice. It'd come from the bridge to his right; he spotted a group of men clad in a thick brown leather uniforms standing atop it. Carrying…swords.

"Afternoon," one of them greeted, turning to the other men. "Drop the ladder," he ordered. The other men lifted a long wooden ladder from the top of the bridge. It had hooks on one end; the men lowered the ladder, which was just tall enough to reach the dirt. The hooks hooked the ladder to the edge of the bridge. "Come on up," the man prompted.

"Uh…"

"Come on," the man urged. "We're not going to hurt you. Trust me, we're the friendliest sight you'll see in this place."

He hesitated, then walked up to the ladder, climbing up with some difficulty. The man he'd been talking to lent a hand when he reached the top, pulling him onto the bridge. The guy was at least six-and-a-half feet tall, with arms as big as tree trunks. Scars crisscrossed his leathery face, and the sun shone off his bald, shiny head.

"My name's Alasar," he greeted. "And you are?"

"Uh, Taylor."

"Good to meet you Taylor," Alasar replied. He glanced down at Taylor's sneakers. "Came through the Gate, eh?"

"The what?"

"Stone arch with blackness that sucks you in," Alasar clarified. Taylor nodded.

"I think so."

"Another Original," Alasar mused. He eyed Taylor for a long moment. "You look familiar."

Taylor blinked.

"I do?"

"Yeah," Alasar replied. "Saw a kid come through the Gate a few months back. Never forgot his face," he added with a smirk. "He's the reason I got my shoulders yanked outta their sockets."

Taylor just stared at the man.

"Name was Hunter," Alasar continued. "You know him?"

Taylor's heart skipped a beat, a chill running down his spine.

"I do," he managed to reply.

"So does everyone else," Alasar said, putting a hand around Taylor's shoulders and guiding him toward the walled city in the distance. "Bit of a household name after the great war."

"Do you…know where he is?" Taylor asked.

"Nope," Alasar answered. "But I can find someone who does. Come on," he added, gesturing toward the city. Taylor walked alongside the man, making his way toward the city in the distance. The bridge eventually sloped downward to meet the ground a short distance before the great wall, and Alasar continued beyond the bridge, walking toward a huge stone gate in the distance. Two guards stood before the gate, and Alasar walked up to greet them.

"Got an Original," he stated, gesturing at Taylor. "Came through the Gate just now."

The guards stared at Taylor, looking him over. Then one of them turned to the wall, looking up and waving one arm.

The gate lifted upward slowly, revealing a large tunnel beyond. Alasar led Taylor into this tunnel, which was lined with more guards.

"Normally we'd have you meet with customs first," Alasar stated, bringing Taylor to a second stone gate at the other end of the tunnel. This too began to rise, just as the one behind them closed. "But we're a little short-staffed at the moment."

The second gate opened all the way, revealing a long street ahead, tall stone walls rising up on either side. Alasar stepped through the gate, as did Taylor. The burly man clapped Taylor on the back, grinning down at him, then spreading his arms out wide at the city before them.

"Welcome to the kingdom of Tykus," he declared. "And welcome home."

www.ingramcontent.com/pod-product-compliance
Lightning Source LLC
Chambersburg PA
CBHW030420310726
48979CB00009B/1548/J

* 9 7 8 1 9 4 8 4 9 7 0 3 9 *